200 HARLEY STREET:
THE SOLDIER PRINCE

BY
KATE HARDY

MILLS & BOON

Published in Great Britain 2014
by Mills & Boon, an imprint of Harlequin (UK) Limited,
Eton House, 18-24 Paradise Road, Richmond, Surrey, TW9 1SR

© 2014 Harlequin Books S.A.

Special thanks and acknowledgement are given to Kate Hardy
for her contribution to the *200 Harley Street* series

ISBN: 978 0 263 90769 8

Harlequin (UK) Limited's policy is to use papers that are natural,
renewable and recyclable products and made from wood grown in
sustainable forests. The logging and manufacturing processes conform
to the legal environmental regulations of the country of origin.

Printed and bound in Spain
by Blackprint CPI, Barcelona

200 HARLEY STREET

200 HARLEY STREET

*Glamour, intensity, desire—the lives and loves
of London's hottest team of surgeons!*

Continue your sensational eight-book journey with…

**200 HARLEY STREET: THE SOLDIER PRINCE
by Kate Hardy**

and

**200 HARLEY STREET: THE ENIGMATIC SURGEON
by Annie Claydon**

Kate Hardy lives in Norwich, in the east of England, with her husband, two young children, one bouncy spaniel and too many books to count! When she's not busy writing romance or researching local history, she helps out at her children's schools. She also loves cooking—spot the recipes sneaked into her books! (They're also on her website, along with extracts and stories behind the books.)

Writing for Mills & Boon® has been a dream come true for Kate—something she wanted to do ever since she was twelve. She's been writing Medical Romances™ for over ten years now. She says it's the best of both worlds, because she gets to learn lots of new things when she's researching the background to a book: add a touch of passion, drama and danger, a new gorgeous hero every time, and it's the perfect job!

Kate's always delighted to hear from readers, so do drop in to her website at www.katehardy.com

Cursed from an early age with a poor sense of direction and a propensity to read, **Annie Claydon** spent much of her childhood lost in books. After completing her degree in English Literature she indulged her love of romantic fiction and spent a long, hot summer writing a book of her own. It was duly rejected and life took over. A series of U-turns led in the unlikely direction of a career in computing and information technology, but the lure of the printed page proved too much to bear, and she now has the perfect outlet for the stories which have always run through her head: writing Medical Romance™ for Mills & Boon®. Living in London—a city where getting lost can be a joy—she has no regrets for having taken her time in working her way back to the place that she started from.

Dear Reader

I love writing continuity stories, as it's a great excuse to work with my fellow authors and bounce ideas around. When my editor suggested this one to me I leapt at the chance. Special thanks to Louisa George, Amy Andrews and Scarlet Wilson for letting me take liberties with their characters, and being so brilliantly accommodating. Thanks to my son, Chris Brooks, for answering questions about military stuff, and to Chris Craig for technical advice about the kind of workouts that Marco could do post-injury.

Becca Anderson and Prince Marco come from completely different worlds. And although there's a lot of attraction between them they also need to learn to trust each other before they can reignite their past love and get their happy ending. I love the way that Becca's managed to rise above such an awful past and a total lack of family support—and that she eventually finds the support and the family she deserves in Prince Marco. I also enjoyed giving Marco a tough time; for someone who's used to a life of action, having to wait and let things take their natural course is really, really difficult. And Becca most definitely teaches him patience...

I hope you'll enjoy Marco's fabulous house on the edge of Regent's Park. And the tango at the salsa club (we learned a couple of new steps in the tango at dance class while I was writing this, so it was great to do a bit of personal research!). But most of all I hope you'll enjoy seeing Becca and Marco fall in love all over again and this time learn to trust each other.

I'm always delighted to hear from readers, so do come and visit me at www.katehardy.com

With love

Kate Hardy

Dedication

For the *200 Harley Street* authors—I loved working with you!
Also, special thanks to Chris Brooks for technical help with
military stuff, and to Chris Craig for technical help with workout
programmes following injury—much appreciated, guys :)

PROLOGUE

THAT WAS THE last of the men.

Safe.

Or were they? The rescue had been slightly too easy for Marco's liking. The insurgents didn't usually give up that quickly. And this definitely felt like a false sense of security, he thought as he drove the Jeep back towards base.

'Pedro, I need you to keep a close eye out on the way back. Anything that makes you even slightly uneasy, you tell me immediately,' he said to his second-in-command.

'Sir. You're expecting an ambush?'

'Maybe.'

Pedro had worked with him long enough to follow his train of thought. 'You're right. It was a bit too easy. They're prob—'

The word was cut off by a loud boom.

Bomb, Marco thought, and was about to slam on the brakes when the blast wave smashed into the Jeep, cracking the screen. Marco put his left hand up automatically to shield his eyes; even as he did so, he was aware of splintering glass spiking into his skin.

But he didn't have time to worry about the pain. The blast wave had made the Jeep slew. He tried to steer out of the skid, but the blast wave was just too strong and the car rolled.

Everything went into slow motion, and Marco's senses

were working overtime. Everything felt magnified. The bang of the rest of the glass imploding, the scrape of metal, the salty, rusty smell of blood.

Finally, they came to a halt. Upside down.

Oh, great.

He knew they were a sitting target in the Jeep. They needed to get out—right now. It would take just one RPG fired into the fuel tank to blow them all sky-high…

Then again, Marco also knew that the insurgents preferred prisoners to dead men. Live prisoners would be much more useful to them. Especially if one of them was second in line to a throne—even if the throne in question was that of a relatively small south European country. Sirmontane still counted.

That was why it had been too easy. Because they'd known that Marco wouldn't leave his men, that of course he'd come to rescue them. That every single one of his team mattered to Marco; he wouldn't leave any of them behind to be tortured and hurt.

So, by coming to the rescue, by doing the predictable thing, Marco had put them all in danger. He cursed mentally. What an idiot. And he'd thought he'd been so clever, devising the rescue plan.

The first Jeep hadn't stood a chance. It had driven right over the bomb, setting it off. The pieces would be scattered everywhere, along with the remains of its occupants. There hadn't even been the usual warnings of large rocks or whatever blocking the narrow road; at least in those circumstances they knew that any possible alternative route was likely to be rigged and could check it out. The insurgents had been one step ahead, meaning that Marco's team had driven straight over a buried explosive device.

'Pedro? We need to get out. Now.'

'Uh…' came the response.

Concussion, probably. But Marco didn't have time to

be sympathetic. 'We have to take cover,' he said urgently. 'Look, I'll come and get you out.' He raised his voice. 'Everyone in the back, be prepared to evacuate and take cover.'

His hand hurt. It felt like a thousand needles burning into his skin. But he'd deal with that later. First of all, he needed to get his men to safety. What was left of them.

It took an effort to shoulder the door open, but he did it. He went round to the other side of the Jeep to pull the passenger door open and help Pedro out when he realised that something was wrong. He couldn't bend the fingers on his left hand.

Which meant it was useless; he couldn't even hold a gun, much less fire one, in this state.

Blood was oozing out of his hand, leaving a trail that just about anyone could follow. He swore, ripped a bit off his shirt and wrapped it round his hand to stanch the bleeding, and used his other hand to yank the door open.

Pedro was still groaning, but Marco was able to get him out of the Jeep, then move to the back and help the rest of his men out. Once he'd got them hidden in nearby vegetation, he used his elbows to propel himself to a better vantage position. Hopefully they'd been near enough to the camp for the blast to have been spotted on surveillance equipment, and help would arrive before things got really sticky.

He could see insurgents swarming all over the Jeep, and Marco prayed to the God he'd stopped believing in that something would happen before they searched the area and found his team.

Amazingly, his prayers were answered: screeching tyres and rapid bursts of fire drove the insurgents off.

'Thank you,' he whispered.

He could hear people calling. Knowing it was safe to do so, he yelled back. Got their attention. Help was on its way.

And finally the pain in his hand made him pass out.

CHAPTER ONE

MARCO CAME TO in unfamiliar surroundings, and tried to sit up. An arm held him down. 'Stay there, Capitán.'

'Where am I?' he asked.

'Back at base. In the hospital.'

Marco forced himself to focus. He recognised the medic from times when he'd treated some of Marco's team. 'Dr Herrera. How are my men?'

'We need to talk about you,' Dr Herrera said.

'We need to talk about my men,' Marco corrected. 'Were there any survivors from the first Jeep?'

'No, but all of those from your vehicle are safe. Some of them have impact trauma from the crash, but nothing too serious.'

Marco absorbed the information. 'OK. I need to talk to their families. The dead soldiers'. Tell them what happened. Apologise for not keeping them safe.'

'You need to listen to me,' Dr Herrera said, 'unless you want to lose the use of your hand permanently and be invalided out of the army.'

That got Marco's attention. Stop being a soldier? His mother would be ecstatic, he knew; but in his own view it was unthinkable. This was what he was born to do. 'Give me the bottom line,' he said.

'You have a flexor tendon injury.'

At Marco's blank look, Dr Herrera explained, 'The

flexor tendons connect the muscles of your forearm to the bones of your thumb and fingers. They let you bend your fingers, and the extensor tendons let you straighten them again.'

Remembering what had happened when he'd tried to open the door of the Jeep, Marco tried to bend his fingers. His index and middle finger wouldn't move, and his hand hurt like hell.

Dr Herrera rolled his eyes. 'Well, you can see that for yourself. I take it the window came in and you put your hand up to shield your eyes?'

'Yes.'

'Some glass shards must have severed the tendons. They won't heal themselves, because the tension in the tendons causes them to pull apart when they're broken—think of them working like a bicycle brake cable.'

'So I need surgery?'

'Microsurgery. And it needs to happen within twelve hours. Twenty-four at most. The longer it takes, the more likely it will be that scarring develops on the ends of the severed tendons.'

'Which means?' Marco prompted.

'Bottom line: you'll get less movement back in your hand.'

It was enough to convince Marco. 'OK. Do what you have to.'

Dr Herrera shook his head. 'I won't be the one operating. You're going to need specialist plastic surgery as well, once the tendons have been stitched and the wound has healed. We have a twelve-hour window from when it happened to getting you into theatre. Say two hours getting you back here from the site of the bomb, seven hours between here and London and an hour's transfer between the airport and hospital...' He grimaced. 'I need you on a plane to London now.'

Marco frowned. 'My men need me.'

'You wanted the bottom line, yes? Right now you're not much use to them, and you'll be even less use if you don't get your hand fixed,' Dr Herrera pointed out. 'I want you on a plane to London so they can operate.'

Marco's boss, Comandante Molina, came striding in and clearly overheard the last bit. 'You know the rules, Marco. Medical orders outrank military ones.'

Royal ones, too, Marco thought grimly.

'Get on that plane and get fixed up,' Comandante Molina ordered.

'What about my men?' Marco demanded.

'I'll sort out the medical side and fix them up again, good as new,' Dr Herrera promised.

'And I'll talk to the families,' Comandante Molina said.

'You seriously want me to go London?' Marco asked with a grimace.

'To the Hunter Clinic. Leo and Ethan Hunter. They have an excellent reputation for treating injured soldiers. One of them used to be an army doctor,' Comandante Molina said.

The Hunter Clinic. Marco had heard that name before. Marianna—his older brother Ferdinand's fiancée—had visited the clinic earlier this year for a blepharoplasty. And she'd had other work done there, too. 'I thought they just did cosmetic stuff.'

'They specialise in reconstructive surgery as well as cosmetic surgery. Burns, microsurgery.' Comandante Molina folded his arms. 'They have hand specialists. Which is what you need.'

Well, if his boss was insistent on it, it didn't look as if Marco was going to have much choice in the matter. Even so, for the sake of his men, he gave it a try. 'Why can't I be treated here? Surely it's better for everyone's morale if I'm treated here instead of being flown out to London as a special case. I don't want everyone thinking I get treated differently just because of who my parents are.'

'It's nothing to do with that. We can't guarantee to hold the media off. Not now you've been injured,' Comandante Molina said. 'Though I admit that, yes, your mother has views on the subject.'

His mother hated him being a soldier on active duty, worrying constantly that he was in danger and would get hurt. Marco had had enough conversations with her on the subject. And the injury to his hand would make her worries increase exponentially. Giving a little ground now might make it a bit easier on his mother.

'She wants me out of here, doesn't she?'

Comandante Molina said nothing but gave him a sympathetic look.

'OK,' Marco said, resigned. 'I'll go to London. But only for as long as it takes to get me fixed. I intend to be back on duty as soon as possible.'

'Marco, your dedication has never been in doubt,' Comandante Molina said softly. 'And your men know you don't think of yourself as any different to them. If this was Pedro sitting here, not you, wouldn't you be demanding that he gets the right medical treatment in the right place?'

'You have a point,' Marco acknowledged.

'So listen to Herrera, here, and do what he tells you.'

Marco said nothing.

'While you were out cold I flushed your hand with saline to get the grit out and avoid infection setting in. I need to give you a tetanus shot now,' Dr Herrera said. 'Antibiotics are controversial but, given that you're travelling for hours to another country for surgery, I'd rather you had them now to avoid the risk of infection.'

'Fine. Do whatever you need to,' Marco said.

'Thank you.' Dr Herrera smiled at him. 'I've spoken to the surgeon in London. He doesn't want me to suture your skin as your palm is a mess. I'm just going to dress your wound so it holds until you get to London.'

He talked Marco through what he was doing: a petroleum-impregnated gauze for the first layer of the dressing, to stop the wound sticking to it. Then another layer of gauze, this time soaked in saline but with the excess fluid wrung out, to let any blood escape and avoid a haematoma forming. The third layer was gauze fluff for padding, topped by a loose wrap, and finally there was cast padding with a fibreglass splint to protect the wound from further injury.

'There's a helicopter on standby to take you from the airport to the clinic,' Comandante Molina said. 'We'll talk later.'

'Right,' Marco said wryly to his boss's retreating back.

He was pretty sure his mother would put pressure on his father now to make sure his tour of duty was over, and the injury—even though it wasn't life-threatening—would probably make his father agree and put pressure on Comandante Molina to give Marco an honourable discharge. And there was only one circumstance in which Marco would accept that.

'When the tendons are repaired and the wound's healed,' he said to Dr Herrera, 'is the injury going to affect the use of my hand at all? Can I still do my job?' And he knew the doctor would understand what he wasn't asking: would he be able to work alongside his men without putting them in danger because his hand would be too weak for the job?

'I'm not going to lie to you,' the doctor said. 'There may be some loss of movement in your hand. It's your flexor tendon that was severed, which means it's likely to affect the strength of your grip.'

Loss of movement. Loss of grip. His left hand. The hand Marco needed to steady a rifle or change a magazine in a machine gun.

And it also could affect him playing his guitar again; with a classical guitar, you needed a strong grip to press the strings against the neck. Playing the guitar was what always calmed Marco down and swept away the stress.

If he couldn't do the job he loved…well, then he could still do his duty to his family and his country. Marco had always known that one day he'd have to leave his military career behind and go back to his royal duties. But he hated the pressure of that world. And if he was going to lose the one thing that could always soothe his soul, what would his life become?

Eight hours later, Marco was in London, sitting in a waiting room at 200 Harley Street. Everything about the place was discreetly luxurious: polished marble floors, white leather sofas, chandeliers, soft lighting. It felt more like a luxury hotel than a clinic. Though, for all Marco cared, the clinic could have been a shack thrown up out of corrugated iron and bits of reused timber.

He just wanted his hand fixed.

And for life to be back as normal.

Preferably yesterday.

OK, so the surgeon who was meant to be sorting him out had been called to see a patient urgently. Marco could understand that. He knew he wasn't the only patient at the clinic. He probably wasn't from the richest family or the most titled family there, either; the little time he'd had to glean information from the internet had told him just how exclusive this place was.

But the longer he waited, the more use of his hand he'd lose. And he really wasn't prepared to accept that.

'But, Ethan, you're Leo's brother. Surely you should be the one to head the Hunter Clinic in Leo's absence,' Declan said.

Ethan shrugged. 'You're Leo's second in command.'

'But *you* have the Hunter name.'

Yeah. And didn't he know it. The albatross round his neck. 'Declan, you've worked for it. I don't have a problem with you being in charge.'

Ethan was aware that the other surgeon was eyeing him curiously. Probably wondering if he and Leo had had yet another row and this was Ethan's way of getting his own back. It probably had something to do with it. But Ethan knew that Declan would never ask. The Irish doctor was charming, yet he kept people at arm's length and he knew to keep out of other people's sore spots.

'And you're better at PR than I am,' he added.

'That's the Blarney Stone for you,' Declan said lightly. 'Ethan, are you quite sure about this?'

'It's the right decision for the clinic. And the clinic's what matters, right?'

Declan nodded. 'Then, thanks. I'm happy to do the job.'

'Good.' One problem down. At least for a little while. 'I have a patient to see. Catch you later?' Ethan asked.

'Laters,' Declan said with a smile.

Just as Marco was about to go and find someone and ask— very politely, and through gritted teeth—if they could give him any idea how much longer he'd have to wait, a man walked into the room.

Well, *limped*.

He was about six foot two—Marco's own height—with dark brown short hair, dark brown eyes, and stubble that Marco thought privately was just on the wrong side of what women found sexy. If this was the doctor and he didn't give a damn about his appearance, did it follow that he also didn't give a damn about his job? Or was this guy some kind of porter?

'Ethan Hunter,' the man drawled.

One of the Hunter brothers, then. Surgeon. The one who was going to treat him?

He didn't try to shake Marco's hand. 'Sorry to keep you waiting.'

Marco had the distinct impression that the other man wasn't sorry at all. There was an edge to his tone, though right at that second Marco couldn't work out why.

'And I'm sorry it's me you're seeing rather than my brother—he usually does the royals and celebs, but rather inconveniently he's gone on honeymoon.'

Royals and celebs, hmm? Suddenly it was clear: Ethan Hunter had an issue about that kind of lifestyle. He'd automatically assumed that just because Marco was the younger prince of Sirmontane he was an over-privileged, thoughtless and selfish socialite. And Marco was in just enough pain now not to be able to rise above it. If Hunter wanted attitude, then he'd get it. Every damn step of the way.

'So how did you do it?' Ethan asked.

'How do you think? Skiing, drinking with my celeb friends and guffawing so hard at the peasants I didn't look where I was going, fell over and severed my tendons,' Marco drawled.

Ethan gave him a level stare. 'How about the truth?'

Common sense kicked back in. Hunter needed to know what had happened because it might affect the way he fixed the damage. Dr Herrera should have briefed him fully, but then again maybe Hunter was the thorough type and didn't just take other people's words for granted. Marco himself never accepted a brief without asking questions to make sure that nothing had been missed. Maybe Hunter was the same.

'I was in a convoy of Jeeps. The one in front of me drove over a bomb. My windscreen imploded and I put my hand up to protect my eyes.' Judging by the mess of his hand, that was just as well—or he'd be blind as well as having a potentially useless hand.

'Bomb.' Ethan stiffened. 'I see.'

Interesting, Marco thought. Was this the brother who'd been an army doctor? Marco shrugged with the shoulder that wasn't strapped up. 'I was in Afghanistan.'

'You were a soldier.'

'*Am* a soldier,' Marco corrected. 'And I hate being cooped up instead of being where I belong, leading my men and sorting out that whole mess out there. Making a difference. Making things better. But...' He blew out a breath. 'I guess it's still no excuse for being rude to you just now.' He'd been unprofessional and let the pain get to him when he should have known better—both from growing up as a prince in the glare of the public eye, and then from his military training. Time to defuse the situation. 'I apologise.'

'I apologise, too,' Ethan said, surprising him. 'Just because you're rich and royal, it doesn't mean that you're...' He grimaced.

Marco knew exactly what he meant. It was something that he hated himself, particularly in some of the people who liked hanging around his brother. He gave a mock braying laugh, and grimaced back. 'Pampered.'

Ethan seemed to relax at last. 'Yeah.'

'You were out there, too?'

Ethan shrugged. 'That's not important.'

'When did you get hit?'

Ethan's eyes narrowed. 'What makes you think I was hit?'

Marco nodded at his own arm and Ethan's leg. 'Different limb, same kind of pain.'

They shared a glance, and Marco knew that Ethan Hunter understood the rest of it. The frustration of being stuck here when your heart was back there.

'What have they done so far?' Ethan asked.

'Flushed my hand to clean it, put on a dressing. I take it you were the one who said not to suture my palm?'

'Yes. Can you feel anything in it still?'

'I'm not sure,' Marco admitted. 'The pain's gone into a blur.'

'Was it just glass, or is there anything else I need to know about?'

'Glass, mainly. Maybe a bit of dirt. But Herrera cleaned me up.'

Ethan nodded. 'Glass isn't going to show up brilliantly in radiography. I need to give you a CT scan to make sure all the glass is out and nothing else is lurking in there, and then I'll do the op.'

The scan seemed to take for ever. But finally Ethan Hunter was satisfied.

'No more glass. Good. OK, what I'm going to do is open up the wound so I can find the cut ends of your tendon, and then I'm going to stitch them back together. I'll put a splint on to protect the repair. Your skin's a mess, so you might need plastics—we'll see what it looks like when your hand's healed. And you'll need physio to get that hand working properly again.'

'Right. So how long will I be in the clinic?'

Ethan looked thoughtful. 'This happened nearly twelve hours ago and you've flown a long way. I want you in here for the next twenty-four hours so I can keep an eye on the repair. Theoretically, then you could go home. But, given who you are and the fact that you'll have the press hounding you all the way between your place and here when you come in for treatment...' He rolled his eyes. 'And we can certainly do without them hanging round outside and getting in the way while they wait for a glimpse of you.'

Marco could do without that, too. 'I don't want the press knowing I'm in England. If the story blows, then I might not be able to resume my tour of duty. It'll put my men at risk.' The ones that were left. The ones that hadn't been killed, thanks to his wrong judgement call.

Ethan nodded. 'Then you're better off staying here for a while. You'll need to see the hand therapist in any case.'

Marco frowned. 'But if I do go home after a few days, can't the hand therapist come to me?'

Ethan gave him a look that said very clearly, *Stop being a spoiled rich prince.* 'You're not her only patient.'

'Of course. Sorry. Patience isn't one of my…um…virtues.'

That earned him half a grin.

'Thank you. For sorting this out.'

Ethan shrugged. 'You don't need to thank me.'

Marco knew why he'd said it. 'Because it's your job,' he said quietly. 'That's what you did out there, too.'

Ethan turned away so Marco couldn't read the expression in his eyes—which in itself told Marco a lot. He'd seen that a few times before, in other people. So he was pretty sure that something had happened out there and Ethan Hunter didn't want to think about it.

'I need to get you in the operating theatre,' Ethan said. 'I'll do the repair under a general anaesthetic because it's fairly complex. It should take about an hour; though it might be longer if I find more damage once I open up your hand.'

'I'd rather not be out cold.'

Ethan rolled his eyes. 'OK, Zorro, if you want to be a hero.'

'Zorro?' Marco narrowed his eyes at him.

Ethan didn't look away or flinch; he clearly wasn't fazed by who Marco was.

'OK,' Marco said, 'I admit I learned to fence at school, and I did some training with the Sirmontane international fencing team.' Not that he was going to boast about the gold medal he'd won. He didn't need to score points with Hunter.

Ethan shrugged. 'I picked the right name for you, then. Probably that's what your men call you when they don't think you can hear them.'

For the first time in what felt like half a lifetime, Marco heard himself laugh. 'Yeah, probably. OK. If you need me out totally, then fine. Do what you have to. But make it quick.'

'Is this your sword arm?' Ethan asked.

'No. It's my fret hand.'

'You play guitar, too?' Ethan feigned a yawn. 'You're such a cliché, Zorro. Do you dance flamenco as well?'

'Flamenco's dull. I prefer tango.' Marco waited a beat. 'You get better sex after a tango.'

Ethan grinned. 'Probably just as well you won't be playing guitar for a while.' Then he sobered. 'Don't flirt with my female staff, Zorro. Any of them.'

'As if I would,' Marco said, enjoying himself now. He had a feeling that he and Ethan Hunter could be friends. Scratchy friends, maybe. But still friends. Because they each understood where the other was coming from.

Another busy day ahead, Becca thought as she walked up the steps to 200 Harley Street. And that was just how she liked it.

Or maybe not, she thought, as she walked into the reception area to find the clinic's Head of PR in a smooch with her new husband.

'Put the surgeon down, Lexi,' she said with a smile.

'Very funny.' Lexi gave Iain a last kiss and waved him off to his consulting room. 'Actually, Becca, you're just the woman I wanted to see.'

'Oh, yes?' Becca asked carefully. Usually this meant that Lexi was planning a PR campaign and wanted to talk the staff into doing something crazy. If Lexi had been anyone else, Becca would have made a polite murmur and avoided her, but Lexi was one of the few people she'd grown close to. Not quite close enough to confide in her about the past, but she was the nearest Becca had to a friend.

'I wanted to give you the heads-up on our new patient. Well, he's going to be yours. He's in Theatre with Ethan right now.' Lexi shepherded Becca towards her office. 'He's a bit high-profile—'

'So we need to keep everything under wraps.' Becca rolled her eyes. She was familiar with the drill. 'Got it.'

'I know you're the soul of discretion—but I wouldn't be doing my job properly if I didn't dot all the *I*s and cross all the *T*s,' Lexi pointed out gently.

'I know.' Becca smiled at her. 'Sorry. I guess I got out of the wrong side of bed this morning. So tell me about my patient.'

'A prince, no less.'

Becca wasn't that impressed, knowing that the clinic had an A-list clientele. 'What's he in for?'

'Flexor tendon. He was injured on a tour of duty, so that's another reason we want it kept under the media's radar.'

'A soldier prince?' Despite herself, Becca was intrigued.

'Young, tall, dark and handsome,' Lexi intoned. 'Prince Charming.'

A heartbreaker, then. Becca had met the type before. And been stupid enough to get her own heart broken by one, at a time when she'd still been dragging her life back out of the gutter.

Most of the women at the children's aid camp in South Africa had fallen under Seb's spell; but, knowing that men couldn't be trusted not to hurt you, Becca had avoided Seb like the plague. She'd been so determined to stay in the safety of her shell. But Seb had been patient. He'd made her feel special, had spent time talking to her about everything under the sun. And finally she'd relaxed with him and let him bring her out of herself. In the process, she'd fallen deeply in love with him. Enough to give herself to him. She'd even let herself dream of a future with him...

And then he'd left. Without even saying goodbye. He'd abandoned her. And the lesson had been branded on her heart: the only person she could ever really rely on was herself. Which was why she'd kept people at arm's length and dedicated herself to her career ever since.

Lexi frowned. 'Are you all right, Becca?'

Wild horses wouldn't drag the truth from her. 'Sure.' She faked a smile.

Luckily it was convincing enough, because Lexi continued, 'Even covered in mud, and looking as if he hasn't slept for days, our prince is sex on a stick.'

Becca groaned. 'And here's you married for about five seconds. Shouldn't you still be in the disgustingly loved-up stage, too busy to notice other men?'

'I'm married, not blind.' Lexi grinned. 'And don't tell Iain I said that.'

Becca just laughed. 'Right. I have patients to see. Catch you later.'

After the operation, Marco woke in the recovery room. It was warm and comfortable and he wanted to go back to sleep.

Except then he threw up. Violently.

'OK. We've got you.' Gentle hands wiped his face clean and helped him sit up.

'I'm sorry,' he said to the nurse.

'Don't worry. It happens all the time.'

Right at that moment, Marco was really grateful for her kindness.

'You're round, then?' Ethan asked, coming over to him.

'Uh-huh.' And his mouth felt disgusting. 'Did it work?'

'We'll see.'

'My arm feels numb and floppy.' Which was enough in itself to make him panic. And it was at that point that he noticed it was propped up on pillows. 'Does this mean I can't use it?'

'It's completely normal for your arm to feel numb and floppy after an op. And the pillows are there to support your arm and keep it elevated—that controls any potential swelling. I want your arm up at shoulder level and your hand above your heart, and you need to use pillows to support your hand when you sleep,' Ethan said.

'Got it.' Marco still felt groggy. 'Though you might have to remind me again tomorrow. I'm not sure how much of what you're saying now is going to stay in my head.'

'Sure.' Ethan paused. 'When the anaesthetic wears off, it will be painful. So don't be a martyr, Zorro. Take the painkillers my team offers you.'

Marco had the distinct feeling that Ethan was talking from experience. What had happened to him in Afghanistan? Had he lost someone—a member of his team, or someone he loved? Did he blame himself for it, the way Marco blamed himself for losing some good men? Had he not taken painkillers as a way of punishing himself?

'So when can I use my arm?' Marco asked.

'The short answer is, you can't. If you try to use that hand before your tendons have healed fully, the tendons will split apart. And, apart from the fact that I don't like having to repeat work, a second repair won't be as effective as the first.'

Marco absorbed this. 'How long do the tendons take to heal?'

'A couple of months.'

Marco stared at him in disbelief. 'No way. You're kidding.'

'And that's only for using your hand for *light* activities. You drive a motorbike?'

'Car,' Marco said.

'Good. That'll probably be OK in a couple of months. A motorbike would take a bit longer.'

'Mountain bike?'

Ethan shook his head. 'Sports you can do a month after that. And then maybe you can start to do heavy activities, as long as you haven't had any problems with scar tissue.'

Marco stared at him, horrified. He couldn't possibly be serious? But Ethan wasn't smiling. 'So basically you're saying I take at least three months off and be a pen-pusher?' Do a safe job while his men faced all the danger. Be a spoiled prince, leading safely from well behind the lines. That *so* wasn't who he was. He sighed. 'That really doesn't sit well with me.'

'Tough. It takes as long as it takes.' Ethan shrugged. 'Don't get that splint wet. You'll need to bag it completely and tape the bag to your arm if you want a shower or bath. Swimming's definitely out—and you don't take that splint off until I tell you or your physiotherapist tells you. Which is probably a month from now, minimum.'

The more Marco heard, the less he liked. 'No exercise. That's not good. I'm going to lose muscle mass.' And fitness. Which would delay his return to the army even longer.

'No push-ups, no pull-ups, no burpees, no weight training,' Ethan said.

Oh, great. That was pretty much his workout routine out of the window. And it definitely confirmed that Ethan Hunter had trained in the army.

'Running? Any form of cardio?' he asked, trying not to let the desperation show in his voice.

Ethan shook his head. 'You need to use your arm muscles to hold your arm across your chest with your hand to the opposite shoulder. So you'll be off balance for running or using an elliptical.' He shrugged. 'No fencing, either, Zorro.'

Because with one arm strapped up he wouldn't be able to balance himself properly. 'So that's a no.' Marco rolled his eyes. 'I'm going to go insane.'

'Very probably, Zorro,' Ethan agreed. 'No horse-riding, no guitar-playing, no…'

'No sex?'

Ethan grinned. 'Not if you insist on being on top, no.'

'I think I hate you,' Marco said.

'No, you don't. I fixed your hand. And I'm good at my job.'

'You'd better be, Clavo,' Marco said through gritted teeth.

Ethan raised an eyebrow. 'Clavo?'

'It's Spanish for Spike.' Marco gestured with his free hand. 'Face. Attitude. The thing you use to cut people open.'

'Technically, that would be a lancet.'

Marco shrugged. 'Clavo will do. You're sure my hand's fixed?'

'Yes. Unless you do something stupid, like try to use your hand too early.'

Marco groaned. 'You're telling me that I'm going to be stuck here for a whole *month*?'

'I didn't say that. I said you'll wear the splint for a month. You'll have physio every single day. Several sessions. I want to make sure there aren't any contractures to your palm, so you need to do stretches and gentle work. You do what the hand therapist says, when she says it, and nothing else. Got it?'

'Because, if I don't, then my hand's gone for good.'

'That's about it.'

So he had no choice. 'OK. I'll do what you say. And the hand therapist,' he added with a grimace.

'Good. Think yourself lucky it wasn't a severed thumb, Zorro. I would've had to replace it maybe with your big toe, and stick leeches all over you.'

Marco gave Ethan a reluctant smile. 'Remind me, which century is this again?'

Ethan laughed. 'I'll have you know leech saliva is the best anticoagulant ever—it's a hundred times more effective than heparin.'

'So I've got nothing to do except pace this room?' And, for the umpteenth time, wish to hell he'd out-thought the enemy. Wish his men hadn't died. Wish he'd managed to get them *all* to safety.

'Like a caged tiger,' Ethan agreed. He paused. 'There's a gym in the basement. It's really for the staff, but patients can use it.'

'I thought you just said I couldn't run or do weights?'

'You can't. The treadmill and elliptical are both out of bounds, ditto all the free weights and the machines.'

'Right.' Everything he was most likely to use. 'Which leaves me what, precisely?'

'The static bike,' Ethan said. 'And *don't* use your arms.'

That was Marco's idea of tedious. A proper bike in the mountains, yes, with steep inclines and rough terrain to challenge him; a static bike, even if it had programmes to change the resistance, wouldn't challenge him at all. 'Great,' he said, curling his lip.

'You can do walking lunges,' Ethan said. 'But that's bodyweight only. Just to be clear, that means not having a bar across your traps, and no using dumb bells, even with your good hand. Got it?'

'Got it.' Marco rolled his eyes again. 'Marvellous.'

'And you can do squats—again, bodyweight only, with a stability ball against your back.'

'What? Like a total novice?' Marco asked in disgust.

'No, like someone who's going to have one arm strapped up so his balance is going to be out and he's not going to be stupid enough to risk damaging his tendons again before they heal. You cross your other arm across your chest like this—' Ethan demonstrated '—and at least this way you can keep your core strong.'

Which was something, Marco supposed. Bodyweight exercises. 'Floorwork?' he asked.

'No. But you can do sit-ups on the stability ball.'

Marco couldn't bring himself to say anything.

'It's better than nothing at all,' Ethan said, and there was a brief flare of sympathy in his eyes.

'I guess.' But Marco was pretty sure that this next month was going to be the longest of his life.

Becca pulled herself out of the pool and squeezed the water from her shoulder-length hair before padding through to the showers. One of the things she loved about working at the Hunter Clinic was the pool in the basement; a swim after work always got the knots out of her muscles and her head in the right place before she headed for her stint at the rehab clinic.

On her way out of the building, she glanced through the glass doors of the gym. There was a man doing lunge walks down the length of the gym; his back was to her, but given the evidence she could see of a strapped-up arm he was clearly one of the patients.

Dark hair, tall, just like Seb...

Her heart skipped a beat.

Stupid.

It had been years since she'd last seen Seb. *Years.* It was about time she put him out of her head and stopped thinking about him every time she saw a tall, dark-haired man. Particularly as he'd made it very clear that he hadn't returned her feelings. He'd left the children's aid camp in South Africa without so much as a word to her. *Dump and run.*

'Get over it, Becca,' she told herself sharply. 'You've got a new life now. And you don't need a man to make it complete.' Besides, she had work to do. Somewhere she was needed.

Shaking herself, she walked up the stairs to the reception area and out into Harley Street.

Over the next couple of days, Marco was thoroughly bored. He tried to be charming to the nurses who came to check on him, but he hated all of this. Being fussed over. Smothered. Suffocated.

Even the gym wasn't a respite. Yes, it meant he could still work out. Of sorts. But he would have been much happier using the top-of-the-range free weights available, lifting until he'd reached his maximum one rep and then pushing himself just that little bit more. Doing a novice type programme just wasn't satisfying. The only reason he'd been able to keep himself in check was the fear of rupturing the repair work on his tendons and being permanently without the use of his left hand. Three months would be tough enough. For the rest of his life would be unbearable.

'You hate this, don't you, Zorro?' Ethan asked when he dropped in to see Marco at the end of the day.

'Sitting here, being useless, when I know I'm needed elsewhere?' Marco scowled. 'Wouldn't you?'

'It's not the easiest thing to deal with,' Ethan agreed. 'You just have to learn to be patient.'

'Is that what you did, Clavo?' Marco asked.

'Just do as I say,' was the level response.

'So you didn't.'

Ethan shrugged. 'This isn't about me; it's about you.'

'I hate this,' Marco admitted. 'I'm used to doing things. Not just sitting here. And your gym is pure torture. All the things I want to use and can't.'

'Patience,' Ethan counselled.

Marco just scowled at him.

'Let's have a look at your hand.' Ethan inspected it, then smiled. 'Good news, Zorro. You get to meet your physio tomorrow morning.'

'So I can start exercising my hand?'

'You do,' Ethan said, 'everything she tells you. And no more than that.'

'Or I'm risking permanent damage. Yeah, yeah. You've already told me.' Marco took a deep breath. Damn. He was being rude again, and the doctor meant well. 'Sorry.'

'Frustration. It gets all of us at some point. Don't worry about it. See you tomorrow, Zorro.'

'*Hasta luego*, Clavo.' Marco sketched a salute with his right hand, and both men laughed wryly.

Becca was still thinking about what Lexi had told her about her new patient. Prince Charming. *Ha*. She'd met men like him before. The last time she'd made the mistake of falling for charm she'd learned the lesson well. In a way, she supposed that Seb had done her a favour. He'd left her at a crossroads. One way had led back to addiction, trying to wash away the pain with vodka—making her mother's mistakes all over again. The other way led to working hard and making the best future she could—for herself, because Becca knew that she was the only one she could really rely on.

She'd made the right choice, and she wasn't going back.

Ethan had said that the Prince was bored. So no doubt he'd be super-charming to her, wanting a distraction from his situation. Fine. He could be as charming as he liked. She'd be sweet and charming back, for the sake of the clinic. But she'd also make very sure that there was a professional distance between them, because she had no intention of being the Prince's personal distraction.

The next morning couldn't come fast enough for Marco's liking. Even though he knew that 'morning' could mean technically anything from one second after midnight until one second to noon.

At last Ethan strolled in to Marco's room followed by a woman in a white coat.

'Zorro, I've got someone you're dying to meet.' He smiled. 'Becca, I'd like you to meet—'

The woman in the white coat stepped to the side and stared at Marco. 'Seb,' she cut in, her voice a hoarse whisper, and all the colour drained from her face.

CHAPTER TWO

'No, this is Marco—Prince Marco of Sirmontane,' Ethan said.

Prince? What? The man definitely hadn't been a prince when Becca had known him in South Africa at the children's aid camp. He'd called himself Seb. Nothing more. No surname, no nothing. And she hadn't asked for any more details because she'd had her own secrets to hide and hadn't wanted to trade them.

At least he looked as shocked as she felt. That was one thing.

'Becca. I didn't know you were a hand therapist,' he said.

'I didn't know you were a prince,' she said, a little more tartly than she'd intended. Bad move. She didn't want him to know that it bothered her.

'You know each other?' Ethan asked, looking surprised.

Oh, yes. In the Biblical sense, too. 'You could say that.' Though it turned out she hadn't really known Seb—Marco—at all.

No wonder he'd left without a word. He was a prince, not an ordinary guy, and obviously he'd just been slumming it at the aid camp—something to do between finishing university and starting whatever it was that princes were supposed to do. Which made her relationship with him worth even less than she'd thought.

And how the press would dine out on that if they knew. A girl from the wrong side of the tracks, a girl who'd been hooked on vodka and E, a girl who'd almost ended up in the gutter…and she'd had a fling with a prince.

'Becca—a quick word?' Ethan said, gesturing to the door of Prince Marco's—she couldn't think of him as just Seb any more—room.

She went outside into the corridor with her boss.

'Clearly there's history here. Would you prefer someone else to treat Prince Marco?' Ethan asked gently.

Yes, she would. She didn't want to treat the boy she'd fallen in love with one dreamy summer. The boy who'd played guitar to her under the stars and sung songs of love in a language she didn't know. But she'd seen the emotion in his face and known exactly what the words meant. The boy who'd made her feel so special—and then left without a single word, letting her dreams crash down round her.

But that was an emotional response. And Becca didn't do emotional any more. She'd promised never to let herself get in a vulnerable state again. Yet, two seconds after seeing Seb for the first time in seven years, she was a mess. In shock that the past had come back to haunt her. Trying to process just how many lies she'd fallen for. Trying to get her head round the fact that Seb—the man she'd thought had been an ordinary boy—had actually been a prince in disguise.

With an effort, she pulled herself back into professional mode. 'I'm the hand specialist. It's my job to treat him.'

'Not if it's going to be a problem for you.'

She liked the fact that her boss was standing up for her. Having someone in her corner felt good; it was something she'd never known, growing up. But it also wasn't fair to lean on Ethan and let him make excuses for her. Seb—Marco—whatever he wanted to call himself—was a patient here. Given that he was royalty, no doubt he was only here because of the reputation of the Hunter Clinic. And Becca wasn't going to let any unprofessional behaviour on her part do anything to tarnish that reputation.

'It's not a problem, Ethan,' she fibbed. 'But thank you.'

'Sure?' he checked.

'Sure.'

'So just how *do* you know each other?' Ethan asked.

'We both worked at a children's aid camp. Years ago. I was still a student. He'd just finished university.' If that was true. For all she knew, that could have been another lie. She flapped a dismissive hand. 'It's not important.'

Ethan's eyes narrowed slightly. 'OK. But if treating him does turn out to be a problem just talk to me and I'll get someone else in to cover his case.'

'Thank you. But it'll be fine,' Becca said. Prince Marco wasn't going to break her heart again.

How could you break something that was already broken?

'I guess I owe you an apology,' Marco said when Becca walked back into the room.

'Why?' Becca asked. For being yet another man who'd used her and broken her heart? As if a European prince could give a damn about how an unimportant girl from an obscure family felt.

He grimaced. 'You know why.'

And of course now she was expected to make it easy for him. Be gracious about it. Or maybe she'd just act cool and casual, as if their summer fling had been just as unimportant to her as it had obviously been to him. 'There's nothing to apologise for,' she said, hoping that she sounded a lot more dismissive than she felt.

'I didn't tell you who I was, back then.'

'No.' She knew it would be hypocritical of her to be mad at him for that. She'd kept her own past a total secret—from everyone else at the camp as well as him. And nobody here at the Hunter Clinic knew about that part of her life, either.

'But I didn't lie to you completely. My name's Marco Sebastian Enrique Guillermo García.'

'Uh-huh.' Becca tried to maintain a semblance of cool. Though right at that moment she was remembering her first introduction to Seb, the guy who was to lead her team at the aid camp. She'd been nineteen and he'd been twenty-one, just graduated from university—well, unless he'd lied about his age as well. And Seb had been the most gorgeous man she'd ever laid eyes on. Tall, dark and handsome, with soulful eyes and a voice like melted chocolate, just a hint of a Southern Mediterranean accent. All the girls at the camp had been in love with him, and when he'd smiled at Becca she simply hadn't stood a chance. She'd fallen for him almost the second she'd met him.

She'd fought the attraction at first, knowing that men couldn't be trusted to do anything else but hurt you; but Seb had been patient with her. Gentle. He'd talked to her, skilfully drawn her out of her shell. It had amazed her that, despite the fact he could've had his pick of all the girls at the camp, he'd actually chosen *her*.

Fast forward seven years to now. There were shadows beneath those beautiful eyes—a combination of exhaustion and pain over the last few days, she'd guess—but Prince Marco was still the most gorgeous man she'd ever seen. And now he was a man, not a boy. The youthfulness had gone from his face, and he'd filled out from being a tall and slightly skinny youth to having hard, perfect musculature.

And his mouth… It still promised sin. The ultimate temptation. A mouth she could remember giving her almost unbearable pleasure. It would be oh, so easy to let herself act on the old attraction.

Well, she was just going to have to resist that urge, because the likes of him were definitely not for the likes of her. And she wasn't stupid enough to jeopardise her career for one of the few sweet memories of her past. She'd worked way too hard for that.

'My grandfather's called Sebastian,' he continued. 'I was named partly after him. So it made sense to use his name—one of my middle names.'

'What was wrong with calling yourself Marco?'

'It would've made it too easy for the press to make the link,' he said. 'And I didn't want everyone thinking that I was just some bored aristocrat slumming it.'

'Weren't you?' she asked, before she could stop herself.

'No,' he said softly. 'I wanted to make a difference.'

She could almost believe him.

Except... 'You left without a word.'

He sighed. 'I was called back to the Palace. My grandfather was ill. It would've been too complicated to explain.'

'And you couldn't have told me that you'd been called home because of a sick family member? You were *that* paranoid about the connections being made?'

'I didn't say that all my decisions have been the best ones—or the right ones,' he said, and looked wryly at his strapped-up hand. 'Or I wouldn't have this.'

'What happened?' she asked.

'Shrapnel. Well, glass,' he said. 'It severed a tendon.'

Which was pretty much as she'd been briefed. Patient: male, late twenties, royal, soldier, severed flexor tendon, needs physio work to regain mobility and movement in his hand.

The last thing she'd expected was for it to be the man who'd broken her heart to the point that she'd sworn off relationships for good and focused on nothing but her career.

Which was what she should be doing right now. Professional was good: it would put some much-needed distance between them. 'Ethan said the repair was a success. So now it's my job to get your hand mobile and working properly again.'

'Is it going to be a problem, Becca?' he asked. 'Working with me?'

She shrugged. 'You're a patient, Your Royal Highness. This is my job.'

Was it her imagination, or had she seen a flicker of hurt in his eyes just then?

Well, tough. He'd hurt her. Badly. And, besides, she was pretty sure it was his ego that was hurt and nothing else. He might think of himself as Prince Charming, but she had absolutely no intention of playing Cinderella. Or fawning adoringly over him. She'd be cool and calm and professional, and treat him just as she would any other patient. With care and kindness, and just a little bit of necessary detachment.

'You can drop the "Royal Highness" bit,' he said.

'What would you like to be called today?' The snippy question was out before she could stop it.

He sighed. 'I guess I deserve that. Call me Marco. And I hope I can still call you Becca.'

Oh, help. The way he said her name. That slight trace of a Spanish accent, so incredibly sexy. It made her knees buckle.

Resist, she reminded herself. This was a job. He was a patient, and she had to treat him with the utmost professionalism. And he was also a prince. They had no possible chance of a future together, and she wasn't going to wreck her career for just a fling.

'I guess. May I have a look at your hand?' she asked.

He indicated his strapped-up arm with his free hand. 'Help yourself.'

Gently, she removed the strapping and took the hand strap off the splint.

* * *

Seven years.

She'd changed. Back then Becca had still been a girl. Nineteen years old, a little shy. Beautiful.

Now she was all woman.

Even with her soft curves hidden beneath a sexless starched white coat, with that glorious auburn hair tamed back in a ponytail and those beautiful green eyes hidden behind wire-rimmed glasses, Becca Anderson was gorgeous.

Worse still, Marco knew what it felt like to kiss her. How her body responded to his when they made love. How her breathing changed just before she climaxed.

Ah, hell.

This was so inappropriate it was untrue.

Becca Anderson was his hand therapist, and Ethan Hunter had told him not to flirt with any of the female staff at the clinic.

Ha.

Flirting wasn't the half of it.

What would Ethan Hunter say if he knew just how far things had gone between Marco and Becca all those years ago?

Marco had to get a grip.

Which was half the problem; right now his left hand didn't have a grip. That was what Becca was going to fix.

And he needed to think of her as a medic. Not as a woman.

In fact, he needed not to think of her at all. Since he'd left her behind in South Africa he hadn't let himself think about her. Well, apart from the day after the doctor had confirmed that his grandfather had come through the heart bypass operation safely and would be just fine. Marco had gone back to the children's aid camp, then. For her.

Except she'd left, two days previously, with no forwarding address.

The one girl who'd seen him for himself instead of as a prince. Who'd made his summer feel full of magic. Who'd made him fall in love with her shy, gentle sweetness.

He'd lost her. And he hadn't been able to track her down, even with the help of a private detective; somehow she'd managed to vanish completely.

And all sorts of things could have happened in the last seven years. He glanced swiftly at her left hand. There was no wedding ring, but that didn't mean that she wasn't committed. She might not wear rings to work, given that she was a hand therapist. She could have a family, now. A child.

Besides, she'd made it very clear how she regarded him now. *'You're a patient, Your Royal Highness. This is my job.'*

So he needed to stop thinking about her, right now, and do what he'd done for the last seven years: keep himself busy at work, and then play just as hard with a string of totally unsuitable women. Not let himself think about the girl he'd left behind.

'You've made a real mess of this,' she said, examining his palm. 'How did it happen?'

'Hunter didn't tell you?'

'Soldier, severed tendon.' She shrugged. 'So I'd guess it happened in action?'

'My windscreen was blown out. I put up my hand to protect my eyes.'

'No wonder you severed a tendon. You're lucky it didn't sever an artery and you bled out on the field. Or it could've severed your whole hand.'

'I know.'

Not that it made him feel any better. He'd been over and over what had happened the last two days and nights.

Thinking about what he could have done differently. What he *should* have done differently. But it didn't change what had happened. Or do anything to lessen the guilt. He'd phoned every single wife, every single mother, and apologised for not taking better care of their loved ones while they were under his leadership. They'd all been grateful that he'd phoned, amazed that a prince would bother to share his memories of their husbands and sons. They'd cried. They'd even thanked him.

And it hadn't made a scrap of difference. He still hated himself for making those mistakes. For not bringing all his men safely home.

'Others weren't so lucky.' He sighed. 'Those who were injured have the best possible care. Those who…' There was a lump in his throat and he couldn't say the rest of it.

'Marco, you were in a war zone. People get injured. They die. You can't blame yourself for that.'

'They were acting under my orders.'

She shrugged. 'I take it other people were injured, or killed, following the orders of someone else?'

'Well—yes,' he admitted.

'And do you blame the officers for those deaths?'

He sighed. 'I guess not.'

'Then don't blame yourself. If it hadn't been your orders, it would've been someone else's. I think you're suffering enough without adding guilt to it. You just did your job, Marco.'

How had she become so wise? he wondered.

To his relief, she changed the subject back to his injury. 'The first few days of physio, you're just going to do some gentle exercises. These will help to prevent your tendons becoming stuck in your scar tissue.'

'Stuck?'

'Then Ethan would have to operate again. And the outcome might not be so good second time round.'

'Right.' He paused. 'I'm under orders to do what you tell me.'

She raised an eyebrow. 'And a prince takes orders from ordinary people?'

Score one to her. 'The rule is, medical orders outrank military orders.'

'What about royal orders?'

He shrugged. 'As far as I know, royal orders from Sirmontane only work inside my country. And right now I'm in your country, not mine.'

'Touché.' She sighed. 'Sorry. I don't mean to snipe at you.'

'But I lied to you about who I was. I can understand you being angry about that.'

'It's not so much that you didn't tell me who you were, it's the fact that you left without a word.'

'So did you,' he pointed out.

She blinked. 'I did not. You were the one who left, not me.'

'But you left the camp without a forwarding address.'

She frowned. 'How do you know that?'

'Because I came back for you when my grandfather pulled through his operation,' he said.

Her cheeks went pink. 'I didn't know that. And, anyway, what happened between us was obviously just the equivalent of a holiday fling. It was over *years* ago, and we're both very different people now.'

He caught her gaze and held it. Was it over? The attraction was still there, for him. And the way her pupils grew slightly larger when she looked at him made him think that maybe, just maybe, it was the same for her. 'Are we?' he asked softly.

'Yes.' She looked away. 'I worked hard to get this job. I'm not going to let anything put that in jeopardy. You're in London for a few days—maybe a few weeks, until your tendon is healed enough—and then you'll be back to doing whatever it is princes do.'

He raised an eyebrow. 'Which is?'

'How should I know?'

She sounded ever so slightly flustered.

Interesting.

Was it seeing him again? Had it brought back memories? Did she remember what it felt like to kiss him? Was she, like him, tempted to find out if it was still the same between them?

'And it's none of my business what you do,' she said.

'I was in Afghanistan,' he said softly. 'There's a media blanket in place to keep my regiment safe. They don't report anything about me, so my team isn't targeted. Nobody knows I was hurt out there, and nobody knows I'm here. Well, apart from my team back at the base, my family, and the clinic staff here.'

'And you want to keep it that way.'

He nodded. 'To keep my team safe. I guess the media will find out eventually that I'm here.'

'Not from me or anyone else at the clinic, if that's what you're asking. There is such a thing as patient confidentiality. And we're very strict about that, I can assure you,' she said crisply.

'Thank you.' He took her hand with his good hand, and squeezed it lightly before letting her go again.

Mistake.

Because his body remembered the feel of her skin against his. Intimately. And it reacted instantly.

Oh, hell.

Just as well she wasn't looking at anything other than his busted hand. He took a deep breath, willing his body to calm down. This wasn't what was supposed to happen. He was supposed to be following her instructions, not lusting after her.

'Now, you need to do these exercises every hour,' she said.

All businesslike and bossy. And Marco rather liked this new side of Becca. She was professionally confident, rather than the shy teenager she'd been.

'You need to keep the splint on, but you can take the hand strap off while you're doing the exercises. You start with three reps of this one.'

'Three reps?' He smiled. 'You sound like a gym instructor.'

She frowned. 'Stay out of the gym. Any pressure on this hand while it's healing and you'll be looking at permanent disability.'

'I've already had that talk from Ethan. Though he says I'm allowed in the gym to do sit-ups and squats with a stability ball, provided I keep my body balanced and don't use my left hand.'

'That figures,' she said. 'Bodyweight exercises only.'

'And walking lunges.'

She went pink again. 'So was that you in the gym, the other day?'

She'd recognised him without seeing his face clearly? That was even more interesting. 'I didn't see you there.'

'I wasn't there. Just passing the glass door on my way out of the pool. And I assume Ethan told you to stay out of the pool?'

'And put a bag over my arm when I have a bath or shower so I don't get the splint wet. Yup.' He looked at her. 'But I could spectate at the pool. Do you swim a lot?'

'It's in my schedule.'

So she wasn't going to let him push her into telling him anything about herself. Interesting.

'It's a cliché, you know,' he said, enjoying himself.

'What is?'

'Having a temper to go with your hair colour.'

'I don't have a temper.'

'Don't you, Becca?' he asked softly. 'Or are you just gentle with your husband and children?'

'My marital status is *my* business,' she said coolly.

Maybe, but at least now he knew what it was. If she'd actually been married she would've told him, to put him in his place. Or she would've turned into a proud *mamá* like his sister Arabella, ready to show off photographs of her children at the least excuse.

'Your first exercise, Your Royal Highness,' she said crisply. 'Use your right hand to curl each finger of your left hand down to the top of your palm.' She demonstrated with her own hand.

He couldn't help flinching as pain lanced through his hand.

'Did that hurt?' She didn't sound like a vengeful harpy. She sounded concerned. Caring. But in a professional capacity.

'A bit,' he admitted.

'Did you feel anything pull?'

'I don't think so.'

'Maybe,' she said, 'I need to massage your hand first, to warm up the muscles.' She frowned. 'I'd better warn you now that it might hurt a bit.'

'If it gets my hand working again and it means I can go back to work, then I don't care if it hurts,' he said. 'Do whatever you need to. I'm in your hands.'

She went very, very pink.

Yeah.

He could feel the heat rising in his body, too.

'Lie back with your palm upwards.' She sounded slightly flustered and she was clearly making an effort to be professional.

OK. He'd behave. Even though what he really wanted to do right now was slide his good hand round the nape of her neck, draw her to him, and spend a very long time kissing her.

She pulled a chair round to the side of the bed. 'Tell me if anything hurts.'

Wild horses wouldn't drag that particular admission from him.

He closed his eyes as she massaged his hand. Yes, it did hurt; but at the same time it made his hand feel better. And he liked the feel of her skin against his. Warm. Gentle, yet firm at the same time. Soft. She was near enough for him to smell the light floral scent she wore. She'd always smelled of flowers in South Africa, he remembered. Roses.

With his eyes closed, and mercifully silent, Marco was a lot easier to deal with.

Maybe she ought to tell Ethan that she couldn't cope with her new patient. But then her boss might think less of her—and she'd worked damn hard for her job here. After South Africa she'd thrown all her energies into her studies, graduating with top marks and quickly gaining promotion at the hospital where she'd worked. She hadn't let any relationship get in her way.

Hadn't had another relationship since Marco, full stop.

Until today, that hadn't mattered. Work here and volunteering at the rehab clinic had been her life, and it was good. But seeing Marco again…it had brought everything back. The sheer passion he'd made her feel. The confidence his love had given her.

And then the bone-deep devastation when he'd abandoned her and she'd realised that he was yet another man who'd let her down.

OK. She could understand it a bit more, now she knew who he really was. Being in the public eye all the time must be draining and it would be hard to know who to trust, who would sell you out to the press.

But she would have kept his secrets.

Just as she'd kept her own. Nobody at the camp had known that she'd spent time in rehab at the age of sixteen. Nobody here knew about those things, either. The past was the past. OK, so she hadn't learned from her mother's mistakes, either with the drink or with the men she'd chosen. But she'd learned from her own mistakes. Really learned. She had no intention of repeating those mistakes ever again. No drink, no drugs, no men—and definitely no heartbreak.

'Better?' she asked when she'd finished massaging his hand.

'Better,' he agreed.

She took him through the first exercise again. 'Good. Now repeat.'

He was a fast learner; she didn't even have to talk him through it, the last time.

'Is that it?' he asked.

'Three reps,' she said. 'And now you do it again, but this time keep your fingers flexed. Use your muscles as you let go with your other hand.'

Again, he did exactly as she asked, and she didn't need to repeat the instructions.

'Good. Last time now,' she said. 'Touch your palm, just using the muscles of your left hand, and extend your fingers back so your fingernails touch the splint.'

He did as she'd asked him to do.

'OK. Now, is your wrist feeling stiff and awkward to move?' she asked.

'A bit,' he admitted.

'OK. Lift your hand up—' she demonstrated the movement '—and let it gently fall forward. Keep your fingers relaxed. Good.' She gave him an encouraging and strictly professional smile. 'Now, back the other way, still with your fingers relaxed, so the back of your hand moves back towards the splint. Better?'

'Better,' he said.

'Good. Last two—your shoulder and your elbow. Stretch your arm above your head. Down. And again.' She talked him through the shoulder stretch. 'Now, bend and straighten your elbow. And again.'

When he'd done the last repetition of ten, she said, 'And that's it for this session.'

'How often do I need to do this?' he asked.

Too often for her peace of mind, given that she was going to be working with him. 'Hourly,' she said. 'So I'll see you later.' Hopefully her common sense would be back in charge before their next session.

'OK. And, Becca?'

'Yes?' She turned to face him. Mistake. Because he still had that make-you-weak-at-the-knees smile.

'Thanks.'

'You're welcome,' she said, and fled.

When she got home from her session at the rehab centre that night, Becca switched on her laptop and looked up Prince Marco of Sirmontane on the internet.

There were lots of pictures of him with beautiful, eligible woman—glittering socialites and A-list celebs. Models, actresses and singers. On a yacht at Monaco. At the film festival in Cannes. Skiing in Sirmontane. He was photographed with a different woman every time—and Marco didn't even seem to have a particular type. Tall, petite, slender, curvy, blonde, brunette, auburn...

The only requirement Marco seemed to have in his girlfriends was that they had two X chromosomes, she thought wryly.

All the gossip columns referred to him as the 'Playboy Prince' and speculated about who would be the woman

to tame him. Unlike his much more serious older brother
Ferdinand, who was first in line to the throne; Ferdinand
was settled, engaged to Princess Marianna. The gossip
columns described the older prince of Sirmontane as the
perfect king-to-be.

Was that why Marco had thrown himself into his social
life? Because he was only second in line always destined
to live in his brother's shadow?

No, she didn't think so. Marco wasn't a spoiled brat or
he wouldn't be a serving soldier. Besides, she knew that
Ethan Hunter had little time for their A-list celeb clients,
and yet she also knew that he dropped in to see Marco
several times a day for a chat. Maybe they'd bonded over
the fact that they both had a military career. But Ethan
definitely wouldn't have bothered spending time with the
Prince if Marco was shallow and vain and spoiled.

Prince Marco of Sirmontane was a puzzle.

And one that Becca needed to stay away from. For the
sake of her own sanity.

CHAPTER THREE

ETHAN CAME IN to chat to Marco that evening and to check up on his hand. 'It's looking good, so far.' He paused. 'So how are you getting on with Becca, Zorro?'

'She's very good.' Marco raised an eyebrow. 'And bossy.'

Ethan smiled. 'Right, on both counts. That's why we hired her.' His smile faded. 'So how do you know her?'

'I worked at a children's aid camp in South Africa for a couple of months when I finished university, before I joined the army. She was there during the university summer holidays.'

Ethan gave him a narrow look. 'That's what she said.'

Marco shrugged. 'So you could say that we're old friends.'

'Such good friends, Zorro, that you didn't even tell her your real name?'

Marco sighed. 'Trust me, being a prince has its downsides. Half the time people don't see me; they see the money and the trappings that go with who I am. So I'm never sure whether people want to be friends with me for myself, or for what they think I might be able to do for them.'

Ethan nodded. 'That's the thing about being rich. Having socialites for parents.'

'You, too?' Marco asked.

Ethan gave him a rueful grimace.

'But you have a brother, right, Clavo? The one who's on honeymoon?'

'Yes.' Ethan sounded cagey.

Marco frowned. 'So you're not close.'

For a moment, he thought that he'd pried too hard and the surgeon was going to walk out. But then Ethan sighed. 'We have…issues.'

'That's tough,' Marco said. 'I'd be lost without Ferdy.'

'Your brother?'

Marco nodded. 'A lot of people think I should be jealous because he's first in line to the throne, but being the second son—the baby of the family, I guess, as our sister Bella's in the middle—means I get away with an awful lot more than he ever can. I can choose my own job, within reason. Ferdy's life is mapped out for him and he has no choice at all. He's the one with all the responsibility and the weight on his shoulders.' He lifted his chin. 'But I always have his back. *Always*. I would move the mountains of Sirmontane for him if he asked me. Even if my hand was still strapped up and I could only use one arm.'

'So you don't resent him being the eldest and the one everyone thinks is so wonderful?' Ethan asked, sounding curious.

Marco laughed. 'No. I guess I'm kind of glad it's not me. I wouldn't enjoy being king. It'd be like being boxed in. Obviously I'd do it if I had to, because it'd be my duty and I'd never let my family or my country down, but I'd hate it.' He shrugged. 'And, anyway, Ferdy *is* wonderful. He's one of the good guys, and I know if I was ever in trouble he'd be the first person I'd call.' He smiled. 'Ferdy understood why I needed to be on active service for our country, and he talked our mother round. If she had her way I'd be wrapped in cotton wool and not allowed out of the palace grounds. And Ferdy's the reason she's not here right now, smothering me to keep me safe and driving me nuts.'

'You're safe here,' Ethan pointed out. 'I know you have your bodyguard outside the door, but he also checked out our security system and he's happy with it. And nobody here will talk to the press.'

'I know, and it's appreciated.'

'OK. I'll let you get some rest. Oh, and Zorro…?'

Marco rolled his eyes. 'What?'

'Remember what I said. No flirting with my staff.'

Marco knew he was being warned off Becca.

The problem was the warning was too little, and way too late.

Breezy and light. That was how she had to be with Marco, Becca told herself as she walked to the clinic, the next morning. Brisk and breezy and light. Professional. Nothing in the slightest bit personal.

But it was so much easier said than done.

She'd spent seven years suppressing her feelings for him, seven years burying herself in study and hard work.

Yet that first time she'd seen him again it had been as if nothing had changed. As if she was still that young, naive girl in South Africa who'd fallen in love with a boy whose smile was full of sunshine.

But that wasn't who she was any more and he needed to realise that, too.

She nodded to the bodyguard outside Marco's room who, as usual, simply nodded back, and walked in, ready for the first physio session of the day. *Professional*, she reminded herself.

'Good morning. Did you have a comfortable night?'

'Yes, thank you.'

Marco was equally polite with her. Obviously he'd had

time to think about it and be sensible, too. Good. That would make it easier.

'How's your hand this morning?' she asked.

'A little sore,' he admitted.

Which might not be good. The last thing he needed now was an infection in the wound. 'Let me take a look.'

She sat down next to him and willed herself not to be affected by his nearness, to ignore that tangy sandalwood scent he wore, as she took his hand and released the strap on his splint so she could take a look at the wound.

But she then glanced at him and was lost. He was staring at her face almost as if he were trying to memorise it.

'Marco,' she said softly. 'Your *hand.*'

'Yes.' But now he was looking at her mouth. As if he remembered what it felt like against his. As if he wanted to kiss her again.

Oh, help.

Because now she wanted to trace the curve of his lower lip with the pad of her thumb. Feel how soft it was, how warm.

She never, ever behaved this unprofessionally with a patient. No matter how good-looking he was.

Then again, nobody had been as close to her as Marco. He was unlike anyone she'd ever met. There had been a time when she'd thought he could see into her soul.

And how stupid she'd been. How naive and pathetic.

With an effort, she pulled herself together. 'It's a little bit red. We need to keep an eye on that. I'll tell Ethan and see if he wants you to have antibiotics.' Gently, she put some aqueous cream on his palm and massaged his hand. 'Is that OK? Sore? Stinging?'

'It's fine. Better now,' he said softly, his voice a husky whisper.

This really wasn't fair. That accent, combined with that sexy, husky voice. It just blew her common sense away.

'I have another patient in fifteen minutes,' she said. 'We need to go through your exercises.'

'So you're not exclusively mine?'

She knew he was talking about the situation from a work point of view. Not personal. She dragged in a breath. 'No.'

'Uh-huh.'

He held her gaze for a moment, and she was pretty sure he knew what kind of effect he had on her. What kind of effect he had on most women, according to the gossip columns.

'You never said you were going to be a physiotherapist, Becca.'

'You never said you were a prince,' she pointed out.

'It was complicated.'

'How?'

He sighed. 'I wanted to be seen for *me* in South Africa. Not for my role. Using another name was the only way I could do that.'

It hadn't occurred to her before but, yes, people *would* see him firstly as a prince and secondly as a man. She could understand that.

Though he'd still hurt her. He'd been careless of her feelings. And that she couldn't forgive quite so easily.

He went through the first of the exercises she'd taught him and she watched the range of movement carefully, checking that the tendons were still working and hadn't stuck in the scar tissue.

'So what kinds of things do you treat?' he asked.

'Apart from people with tendon injuries like yours? All kinds of hand problems.' Talking to him about work made this easier. Gave her space. Stopped her doing something really stupid—like taking his hand and pressing a kiss into his poor, damaged palm. 'The Hunter Clinic does a lot of work with burns; as well as damaging skin, burns can damage nerves and I need to help with that and any post-op rehabilitation. I work with people who have carpal tunnel problems and RSI; not just on the physio side. Sometimes I do a site visit and I can recommend changes to the way a workstation is laid out, or alternative work methods.'

'So you prevent the problem happening in the first place?'

'Where I can, yes. Sometimes it's helping with sports injuries—I treat things such as ligament damage and skiers' thumb. Or maybe my patient has a progressive disease such as arthritis, which means their hands are painful and stiff. I can help them regain some mobility and movement in their hands, and work on pain management. I was thinking about doing an acupuncture course as well, so I can offer more than just a TENS machine or drugs for pain management.'

'Adding to your skills? Good idea.' He paused. 'What made you specialise in hands?'

She shrugged. 'The importance of touch, I guess.'

Wrong phrase—because now she was remembering touching him. Remembering the way he'd touched her, his hands caressing her; his touch had set her on fire.

'Making a difference,' he said.

Becca was hugely relieved that he wasn't able to read her mind. And now he'd given her another safe topic: *his* work. 'Like you—at least, I assume that's why you became a soldier.'

He nodded. 'I don't have the patience to be a medic and make a difference that way, but I'm good with systems—I learned that in South Africa. I can see ways to change infrastructures and make them work better for the people they're meant to help.'

'You were good at teaching, too,' Becca said, remembering. 'You were good with the kids.'

'I like children,' he said simply. 'They're straightforward. No hidden agendas. You know where you are with them.'

That sounded heartfelt. She wouldn't have a clue what kind of pressure a prince would face, apart from having to live in the public eye so every single mistake would be picked up and magnified. But it sounded as if Marco was really weary of having to watch every single move and not knowing who was a friend and who was waiting for him to fail.

'You picked up their languages quickly,' she added, hoping to shift the conversation to something a little less painful for him.

'My parents always got me to learn a few basic phrases in the language of any visitors we had, so I could help make them feel at home,' he said. 'Not that I'm trying to boast, but it means I can greet people, say please and thank you and wish them a nice day in twenty different languages. And, actually, it's good to make that effort. I like seeing people relax and be themselves instead of trying to be something they think is expected of them.'

'Your English is perfect,' she said. 'I know nothing about Sirmontane—is English the official language of your country?'

'No—that's Spanish,' he said. 'Though I was educated in England.'

At one of the top public schools, she'd guess. Eton or Harrow or Marlborough. And then Oxford or Cambridge; the other thing she remembered from South Africa was that Marco was very, very bright. 'So tell me about Sirmontane.'

'It's on the Spanish border,' he said. 'It's a mountainous country—we don't have a coastline.'

'So it's cold?'

'In winter, it can be.' He smiled. 'Tourists come for the skiing in the winter and for the lakes and the walking in the summer. We also have a thriving wine industry—it's hundreds of years old, from the days when monks used to let the wine mature in cisterns they'd hollowed out in the stone. And our dairy products are renowned. We have lots of cattle on mountainous pasture.' He grinned. 'I think our chocolate is better than Switzerland's, but then I guess I would say that.'

'Lizzie Hunter, our head nurse, is a total chocolate addict,' she said. 'Maybe you should get her to do a taste test. She'd give you an impartial opinion.'

'Don't *you* like chocolate?' he asked.

Oh, she did. But the idea of eating chocolate with Marco, being fed one morsel at a time—especially if he teased her, made her reach up to take the piece of chocolate between her lips...

She pulled herself together. 'I'm about to be late for my next patient. You're doing well. I'll see you in an hour to go through the whole lot again.' Swiftly and surely, she refastened the hand strap of his splint. 'See you later.'

Even as she left she knew how much she wanted to linger. It was probably just as well that she had an appointment with Mrs van der Zee to take her mind off Marco.

'Good morning. How are you today?' she asked as she ushered Mrs van der Zee into the treatment room.

'A little sore. But I know my Becca's going to make me feel better because you always do,' Mrs van der Zee said, patting her hand.

Gently, Becca removed the splint and examined the old lady's hand, mentally noting the changes since her last appointment. 'The swelling's definitely gone down, so I think that flare-up's over. Did you find wearing the splint at night helped you to cope better with the pain?'

The old lady nodded. 'Much better. And alternating the heat pack and ice pack helped, too.'

Ice for swelling and heat for comfort. 'I'm glad. Are

you happy that we work on making your hands a little more mobile today?'

'Yes, that's fine.'

Becca massaged the old lady's sore hands, warming the muscles. She knew that you weren't supposed to have favourites, and she always gave her patients her best regardless of who they were, but Mrs van der Zee was special. Like the grandmother Becca had never had and always wanted: full of smiles and stories of the past.

'Let's start with your fingers,' she said. She talked the old lady through the exercise, showing her how to hold her hand so the fingers were straight and close together. 'Then I'd like you to bend the top and middle joints, keeping your knuckles straight. That's perfect. Now, slowly unroll them again, and we'll repeat it with the other hand.'

From there, she guided the old lady into making a loose fist while resting her hand, wrist and forearm on the tabletop.

'And now we'll work on your thumb,' she said. 'This first one will help you make the joint more stable.' She showed the old lady how to make her hand into a C-shape, as if she was holding a glass or a hand. 'And now we'll stretch it out.' She guided the old lady's hand into a neutral position. 'Try and touch the base of your little finger with the tip of your thumb.'

Mrs van der Zee tried several times and shook her head. 'It won't go that far, Becca.'

'With practice and time, it will,' Becca said. 'And you've done really well, so don't think you've failed. We know how far you can move your thumb now, and that's a really good baseline. We'll work to increase that range a little bit more every time.' She smiled at Mrs van der Zee. 'Last bit, now—we'll stretch your fingers.' Under Becca's guidance, Mrs van der Zee put her hand back in the starting position. 'Now make your first finger and thumb into an O shape.'

'I can do that,' Mrs van der Zee said with satisfaction.

'And now your middle finger.' Gently, Becca talked her through making the same movement with each finger. 'That's great. You're doing really well.'

'Is that it for today?'

'Nearly. Just the finger walking to go, and we're done. Put your hand flat on the table, palm down. That's perfect. Now, move your thumb away from your hand, keeping it in contact with the table. And now move your first finger towards it.'

Once the old lady had stretched each finger in turn and repeated the moves several times with both hands, Becca was satisfied.

'Lovely. You've worked really hard on that today, Mrs van der Zee. And if you try to go through that routine every morning, after you've massaged your hand, it'll make moving a lot more comfortable for you.'

'Thank you, dear.'

When Mrs van der Zee had left, Becca wrote up her notes, then glanced at her watch. Time to go back to Marco.

'How was your patient?' he asked as she walked into his room.

'That's confidential, I'm afraid,' she said with a smile.

'Of course.' He smiled back at her, then went through the arm and shoulder exercises she'd taught him.

She noticed this time that he winced when he lifted his arm above his head. 'Where does it hurt?' she asked.

'It doesn't hurt, exactly—my shoulder's a little stiff.' He looked resigned. 'I guess it's only to be expected with having a sling and my arm being held up like this.'

'Let me take a look,' Becca said, and gently took his arm out of the sling so she could remove his pyjama top.

The worst thing was it meant she was going to be skin

to skin with him. Her fingers tingled where they touched him, and she felt her breathing going shallow.

Stop this, she told herself. *Think of him as just another patient. Be professional.*

But that tingle of desire wouldn't go away.

It was years since she'd last seen his naked, muscular back. Sculptors would fall over themselves to use him as a model.

And he was her patient.

Focus, Becca, she told herself sharply. *This is work.*

'Yes, your muscles do feel a bit tight. I'll loosen that up for you.'

Aqueous cream was the most unsexy stuff in the world. Plain, unscented, and easily absorbed by the skin. Not like oils, which would leave a sheen on the skin and then release a scent as it was warmed by body heat.

This was supposed to be a medical treatment.

She shouldn't be enjoying this anywhere near as much as she was.

And Marco was enjoying it, too. His breathing had changed; it was shallow, almost rasping. It had nothing to do with any kind of medical condition and everything to do with the connection between them, the burning need that sizzled as their skin touched.

He turned round and they looked at each other. His pupils were huge, and she was pretty sure that hers were the same. And that slash of colour across his cheekbones was echoed on hers.

Her mouth went dry, and she really couldn't help sliding the tip of her tongue between her lips to moisten them.

Marco leaned forward, slid his right hand to cup the nape of her neck, and brushed his mouth against hers. The kiss was light, gentle, dreamy—as if they were thousands of miles away from London, under a wide starry sky. Just as it had always been between them. And it felt as if fireworks were going off in her head.

'Becca,' he whispered when he broke the kiss.

She pulled away. 'Marco, we can't do this. You're my patient.'

He shrugged. 'I don't care.'

'I do,' she protested. 'I could get struck off for unprofessional conduct!'

'I'm not going to let that happen.'

Her lip curled. 'Right, and just because you're a prince you can order a professional body to believe that I haven't done anything against the rules? I don't think so.'

'We have unfinished business, Becca, and you know it.'

'I'm your hand therapist. You're my patient. You're in pain and you're vulnerable.'

'Yes, to the first, second and third. Absolutely not to the last,' he said crisply. 'My left hand might not be working right now, but the rest of me is in full working order, I can assure you. I know what I'm doing, Becca. And I want you. I want to kiss you. Touch you. Make you feel the way I'm feeling right now.'

She dragged in a breath. *Oh, help.* She wanted him, too. Just as much.

But.

It was mad. A quick path to getting hurt again. How stupid of her to think that he wouldn't be able to break her heart a second time. Of course he could.

And would, if she didn't stop this right now. They didn't have a future. Couldn't have a future. He was a prince, and someone with her kind of past was totally unsuitable for him. The only thing he could offer her was a fling. Was that enough? Right now, she didn't think so.

She lifted her chin. 'I'm not going to be like the women you spend your time with.'

He frowned. 'What women?'

'I looked you up in the gossip columns,' she said.

He rolled his eyes. 'They're called gossip columns for a reason—the hacks write what they think their readers want to hear, and that can be a million miles away from the truth.'

'There were plenty of pictures of you escorting different women,' she pointed out.

'Which doesn't mean I slept with them or even kissed them.'

'Who you sleep with,' she said coolly, 'is absolutely none of my business.'

'Becca.' He drew her hand up to his lips and pressed a kiss into her palm, his mouth warm and soft and so sweet that it made her want to cry.

'We can't do this,' she said. 'This is a seriously bad idea.'

'It's the best one I've had in a long time. I haven't been able to get you out of my head since I saw you again.' He held her gaze. 'And it took me a long time to get you out of my head after South Africa.'

He'd thought of her after South Africa? He'd missed her?

Really?

The thought made her head spin. And it would be oh, so easy to give in to the demands yammering through her body.

Marco had been her first lover. And her last.

And she still wanted him.

But if she gave in to the hot tide of desire—what then?

Marco had nothing to lose. He was a prince. Sure, the press might write a few stories about him, but at the end of the day he could do whatever he wanted.

Whereas Becca had everything to lose. Her career. The life she'd built so carefully for herself. Without those what did she have? With nothing left, would she fall back into her old ways? Would the oblivion that a bottle of vodka could bring—and had brought in the past—be all she had in the future?

She couldn't afford to take that risk.

'No,' she said, loosening her hand from his and taking a step backwards in the hope that putting physical distance between them would bring her common sense back. 'You're a prince, I'm a physiotherapist at the best private clinic in London, and our lives are on totally different paths.' She lifted her chin. 'And if that's not enough for you, I might point out that you've already dumped me once. I don't repeat my mistakes.'

'I'm sorry I hurt you.'

He sounded sincere enough, but she didn't fully trust his words.

'I'm older now. Wiser.'

'But you still can't offer me a future.'

'Is that what you want?' he asked.

It was something she hadn't allowed herself to think about; instead she'd concentrated on her career, working her way upwards and filling her life with work. 'I don't know,' she said. 'Maybe.'

'One thing I learned as a soldier,' he said softly, 'was to take happiness with both hands. Live in the present, don't worry about the future or the past. Enjoy the warmth of the sunshine, the coolness of the rain. Just *be*.'

Where was he going with this?

'Maybe that's what we need to do right now,' he said. 'Forget the past. Don't worry about the future. Just enjoy the here and now.'

If this was the way he talked women into bed, no wonder the gossip columns were full of pictures of him dating.

'Excuse me. I have another appointment now,' she said, and fled to the safety of her office.

CHAPTER FOUR

BECCA WENT OUT at lunchtime, hoping that a walk would clear her head. It was actually sunny for once, and it might turn out to be the only nice day London had for the whole of June, so she wanted to make the most of it. Only she couldn't just enjoy her favourite summer lunchtime treat of heading over to Regent's Park and walking among the roses. All she could think of was Marco.

She had to face it: she was still attracted to him. He'd made it clear that he was still attracted to her. But it was pointless starting something that could never have a future. Why set herself up for the misery of having to give him up to his royal duty, once his treatment was over?

Besides, if he knew the truth about her, he'd run a mile. Her past could blow up in their faces and cause untold amounts of damage to both of them. The press would have a field day—and she hated to think what kind of headlines they'd think up.

The Prince and the Addict.

Prince Charming and Vodka-Ella—and maybe they'd put the E in a different colour, just to make the point.

It would embarrass his family, it would embarrass the clinic, and...just *no*.

Yet Marco's words stuck in her head.

Take happiness with both hands. Live in the present—

*don't worry about the future or the past. Enjoy the warmth
of the sunshine, the coolness of the rain. Just* be.

Could it really be that easy?

Could they have a fling and walk away intact at the
end? If they went into it knowing that it would have a
definite end would it mean that neither of them would get
hurt this time around?

The thoughts spun through her head, making her dizzy.
She had no answers. No idea at all about what to do.

Part of her was tempted to discuss it with Lexi.

Then again, that would mean telling Lexi about all of
her past. Not just the fact that she'd fallen in love with
Marco before and he'd abandoned her, but the really hard
stuff. The way she'd been brought up. The way she'd
longed for love but had it taken from her time and time
and time again. The way she'd fallen into that vicious circle of needing more and more vodka—and almost been
dragged under by Barney.

She couldn't do it.

So it was better to try to keep her distance from Marco.

Marco didn't raise the subject when she called in to
run through his physio exercises with him. Part of Becca
was relieved; part was worried. Was she just a whim—
something to amuse a bored, spoiled prince? Or was she
being unfair to him?

She couldn't think straight when he was around, and
it made her tetchy. She wasn't used to her world being
turned upside down like this. She'd worked hard to keep
everything on an even keel, and now everything seemed
in jeopardy. The life she'd made for herself, her peace of
mind and the walls she'd built round the ruins of her heart.

But on her last visit of the day he took her hand. 'Becca.
When are you off duty?'

'You're my last patient,' she said. 'I just need to update
my notes.'

'Uh-huh.' His eyes were unreadable. 'What are you doing this evening?'

Well, that was progress. He finally seemed to realise that she did have a life outside the clinic and that she might actually have plans that didn't involve him. Even if it wasn't really that much of a life, if the truth be told: her usual routine was work, a swim, and her voluntary work at the rehab centre, with the occasional team night out to make a change.

For the last year or so it had been enough for her.

Until Marco had walked back into her life.

And now she realised that she'd just been existing, not living.

'I have to be somewhere this evening—it's an arrangement I can't break,' she said.

'Boyfriend?'

She glowered at him. 'Do you honestly think I would've let you kiss me this morning if I'd been involved with someone else? Thank you very much. Why don't you just call me a faithless cheat and be done with it?'

Marco fanned himself. 'Wow. You are woman, hear you roar. I think you're more effective than a flame-thrower.'

Flame? Was this a veiled remark about her hair being red? She scowled. 'Don't make stupid clichéd comments about my hair, either.'

It upset her that she was letting him get to her like this. So much for keeping her cool. If she carried on like this, Marco would guess in seconds that she still had feelings for him. Feelings that she'd thought she'd buried but had still been smouldering without her permission. And now he was fanning the fires again just by being here.

'I'm sorry.'

His apology took the wind out of her sails. 'I'm sorry, too. I didn't mean to snap at you. It's just that I don't do this sort of thing.'

'Just so you know,' he said, 'neither do I. The press is very good at twisting circumstances.' He paused. 'I appreciate that you have other commitments, and I don't expect you to rearrange your life just to suit me, but do you have time to have dinner with me this evening?'

Even if she skipped her swim, she really didn't have time tonight. 'Sorry. Another evening, maybe?' When she could work out how to carve out some time in the evenings without breaking promises to the girl she'd been supporting at the rehab centre. Short of cloning herself.

'How about a cup of coffee, then?' he asked.

'I'm not playing hard to get, Marco,' she said softly.

'But you have a life outside here.' He sighed. 'And I'm being selfish. I should be grateful I still have one working hand and the use of both my legs. Other people haven't been so lucky.' His face twisted. 'Thanks to me, some of my team won't see their kids grow up.'

'You can't change the past,' she said, 'so why beat yourself up about it?' Though at the same time she was wryly aware of what a hypocrite she was; she was just as hard on herself for making mistakes.

'If I didn't care,' he said, 'I'd be less of a soldier. I'd be a monster.'

'There's a difference between caring and wallowing,' she said, 'and you're in danger of wallowing.'

He winced. 'You don't pull your punches, do you?'

She shrugged. 'You need something to occupy your head and stop you brooding about the might-have-beens.'

'A distraction.' He looked straight at her. 'You could distract me.'

She knew that. Just as he could distract her. 'I'm not offering.' Though she could feel her cheeks turning pink. It would be so easy to offer him comfort. And then, once he'd gone, he'd leave her bereft. She wasn't up for that.

'So what do you suggest?'

'I know it's difficult for you, not being able to do things the way you normally do.'

'It's making me a bit twitchy,' he said, and grimaced. 'When I'm stressed, I usually play my guitar. It's got me through any difficult times for years.'

She remembered him playing guitar at the children's aid camp. Songs that everyone knew and could sing along with, so he'd managed to take everyone's minds off things for a while. Pretty classical pieces that had taken her breath away. And then there had been the songs he'd sung privately to her.

'And right now I can't play. I can't use my left hand at all for at least the next month. I *hate* not being able to play. Or being able to do a proper workout in the gym. Or being able to do practically anything else I normally do to relax. As for not being able to do my job… Don't even go there.' He scowled. 'I really hate being so *useless*. Right now I feel like a waste of space.'

'I would offer you a massage to take the knots of tension out of your muscles,' she said, 'but, given what happened this morning, that might not be such a good idea.'

'Yes.' He dragged in a breath. 'I might have to kiss you again.'

The worst thing was, she knew she'd respond if he did. Slide her fingers along the back of his neck. Stroke his face. Tease his lower lip with her teeth, her tongue…

She shook herself.

'Look, I know it's tough—but you have to give yourself time to heal. It'll happen.' She paused. 'Just not as quickly as you'd want it to. And unfortunately you can't change biology. Nothing and nobody can make you heal any faster.'

'I know. I have to learn to be patient.' He rolled his eyes. 'Sadly, patience isn't one of my virtues.'

She wasn't so sure. He'd been patient with the children

in South Africa. And with her. Maybe it was just himself he couldn't be patient with.

'I'll see you tomorrow,' she said. And she'd have a quiet word with Ethan on the way out. Maybe he could think of something to help their patient.

Their patient. Marco had a professional relationship with her now, not a personal one. And she needed to keep that uppermost in her mind, rather than letting herself think of him as a man.

By the time Becca walked back into his room for his first physio session the next morning, Marco was a mass of seething frustration. He'd had a whole night to think about it. A whole night to remember what it had felt like, losing himself in Becca. A whole night to wonder what it would be like between them now they were older and had more life experience. He'd never found that particular sweetness when making love with anyone else. Now they were older, would it have changed? Would it still be as sweet? Or was he chasing some distant dream that could never be recovered?

He'd driven himself half crazy with wondering.

Even verbal fencing with Ethan at the end of the evening hadn't taken the edge off Marco's need for Becca. And he'd only just managed to convince the surgeon that it was the frustration of not being able to use his hand that was making him so edgy, not sexual frustration. The last thing Marco needed was for Ethan Hunter to pull rank and decree that someone else would have to treat the prince.

Marco wanted Becca.

In every single way.

And he wanted her *right now.*

'Good morning,' she said chirpily.

'Yeah.' He knew how grumpy and out of sorts he sounded, but he couldn't help it.

She raised an eyebrow. 'What's the matter, Zorro?'

'Don't *you* start with that ridiculous nickname. I get enough of that from Hunter.' He scowled at her.

'Oh, come on. The Spanish nobleman who's a freedom fighter and a dab hand with a sword?' she teased. 'Ethan's right. It's you to a T. You know, I was thinking about getting you a domino mask. I think you'd look cute in it.'

'Yeah, yeah.' He flapped his right hand dismissively.

She sat on the edge of his bed, next to the comfortable armchair he was occupying. 'OK. Tell me now. What hurts?'

His heart.

Which was even more shocking, because he'd never actually let someone get that close to him before. 'Nothing.'

She unhooked the hand strap and examined his palm. 'It's not so red today. That's good. OK. Now lift your arm up.'

'Why?'

'So I can see if there's any stiffness in your shoulder.' She gave him a concerned look. 'You're in a hell of a mood, Marco. Has something happened? Something with your team? You've had some kind of bad news from home?'

He hadn't even thought of Sirmontane for the last day. And that made him feel guilty. He'd been totally self-indulgent and selfish. Spoiled. Brattish. 'No.'

She sighed. 'I know you hate being hemmed in and unable to do much. But, as I said to you yesterday, it takes time for your tendons to heal and it's beyond the laws of physics to speed that up. You'll just have to find something else to keep you occupied.'

'Like what? Playing endless games of patience with a pack of cards?'

'Sure. Or maybe a jigsaw puzzle.'

He closed his eyes. 'I know you're trying to be helpful, but really—can you see me doing a jigsaw puzzle?'

'I guess not,' she admitted. 'So what do you suggest?'

He opened his eyes again and looked at her. 'You could kiss me better.'

There was a long, long pause. And then she sighed. 'I've already told you I can't do that. You're my patient. Anything else is against the rules.'

'Rules can be broken,' he pointed out.

'Not these ones.' She bit her lip. 'Please don't make this any harder for me.'

So she found it tough, too? Oddly, that actually made him feel a bit better. A bit less alone in this. And even though it frustrated him that she clearly felt the same attraction as he did but refused to act on it, he could respect that she wanted to keep her professionalism. 'OK. I'm sorry. I'll back off.'

'Thank you.'

She took him through the set of exercises, barely saying a word except to guide him a little more on the physio. Cool and calm and completely impersonal.

She hadn't always been like that. When he'd first met Becca she'd been sweet and shy. For him, she'd been like a breath of fresh air—she'd made him feel as if he could have anything he dreamed about. And he was sure he'd helped her, too; he'd brought her out of her shell.

Oh, hell. He'd thought he could do this. That he could back off and let her be professional and detached. But, actually, he couldn't. He wanted that breath-of-fresh-air feeling back. The warmth. The sweetness.

This was crazy. It had been tough enough to get over her last time. And he knew that all he could offer her was a fling, and that wasn't fair to her. He couldn't offer her anything more because he had a duty to his country and his family, and he knew he'd have to marry the same kind of woman as his brother was marrying. So for now he'd have to keep his dreams and his libido tightly under control.

Having Becca's hands on his skin really wasn't helping. He needed a distraction.

Like *now*.

'Becca. Talk to me,' he said.

'What about?'

Anything. Everything. He picked the first question that came into his head. 'Is being a physio what you dreamed about doing when you were a child?'

'No.'

'So what did you want to do?'

'I can't remember,' she said with a shrug. 'It was a long time ago. How about you?'

He raised his eyebrows. 'My job was already pretty much decided for me the day I was born. Until Ferdy and Marianna have kids, I'm second in line to the throne of Sirmontane. There wasn't really another option.'

'I guess not.' She looked curious. 'So what was it like, being a prince and growing up in a castle?'

'Honest truth?' he asked.

'Honest truth.' She paused. 'And it counts as medically confidential, just in case you're worrying about that.'

So she'd worked that one out, at least. Marco was shocked by how relieved it made him feel. 'I loved the castle. The suits of armour, the paintings of knights, the pageantry of the guards marching up and down outside.' He sighed. 'I liked sitting on my *abuelo's*—my grandfather's—lap,' he said, 'and hearing about all the tales of old. The warrior kings, the old legends. I pretty much drank them in. I used to spend hours making cardboard shields and swords.'

She looked surprised. 'Wouldn't your parents buy you a toy shield and sword?'

He laughed. 'Of course they would've done, if I'd asked. But a true warrior forges his own sword. And I guess it kept me occupied for a while. They knew if I was colouring in some intricate design on a shield, it would keep me out of mischief.'

'And being a soldier when you grew up was the closest you could get to being a knight or a warrior?'

'While still doing my royal duties. Pretty much,' he said with a smile. 'I've just never been one for sitting still. Ferdy was always fine, curled up with his nose in a book or drawing. He's fantastic at art. Visiting dignitaries were always pleased with him—a child who was seen and not heard.'

She raised an eyebrow. 'I take it you were the opposite?'

'My mother had to spend a lot of time apologising for me,' Marco admitted. 'I was a bit of a nightmare child, always doing things that I shouldn't—climbing trees, sliding down the banisters at the castle, that sort of thing. I was lucky that we had a fabulous nanny who adored us—and who still works for us, though obviously not as a nanny now.' He grimaced. 'But we also had a very stuffy butler, who didn't approve of me at all and was forever telling tales to my father.'

She smiled. 'And then you batted those incredibly long lashes, and looked up with those big brown eyes, and everyone forgave you.'

'I'm not *that* manipulative,' he said dryly.

'I didn't mean that. Just that you—well, you're charming. I'd guess that you were a hit with all the princesses.'

'The ones of my parents' generation, yes. The ones my age, no—up until the age of about ten they were only interested in boring girly things and they didn't appreciate being introduced to my pet frog. They actually called him slimy,' he said in disgust.

Becca laughed. 'And after the age of ten?'

'They wanted to talk about clothes,' he said. 'Tiaras. Shoes. Lipstick. Dull stuff like that. The ones who liked horses weren't so bad, because they didn't mind getting a bit grubby or pretending to chase dragons. But the ones who were introduced to Ferdy as a potential future queen...' He shook his head. 'That's when I was *really* glad to be the second son. Because I'd hate to have to marry someone I couldn't talk to.'

Becca frowned. 'I've met Princess Marianna. She seemed very sweet.'

'She is—she loves Ferdy to bits and she suits him down to the ground. But she's not the type of woman I could be happy with.'

Becca couldn't resist asking, 'So what type of woman *would* you be happy with?'

'Someone I can talk to. Share ideas with. Share my dreams with. Someone who can think outside the box.' He looked almost dreamy as he added, 'Someone who's a breath of fresh air.'

Becca knew it was a dangerous question—one she shouldn't ask because she was pretty sure she already knew the answer—but she couldn't help herself. 'So, as the second son, can you actually choose your own bride?'

'As the second son,' he said, 'I don't have quite as much pressure to get married and produce an heir.' He grimaced. 'Though I guess I'm still expected to marry the right sort of woman.'

Any last little wisps of the dreams Becca might have secretly had—that *she* was the kind of woman he could talk to and share his dreams with, and that she and Marco could possibly recapture what they'd had in South Africa—vanished completely at his words.

Of course Marco would be expected to marry the right sort of woman.

Which meant royalty. Or, even if he did choose to marry a commoner, someone from an impeccable background who'd been to the right sort of school. Not someone whose mother had forever sought her own Prince Charming and spiralled into drink and despair when he didn't turn up.

And definitely not someone who'd repeated her mother's mistakes in thinking that the answer lay at the bottom of a bottle.

'What about you?' he asked.

'What *about* me?'

'You never really told me much about yourself in South Africa. I mean, helping at a children's aid camp—your parents must've been proud of you for doing something that would make a difference. Especially as it meant travelling so far from home in England.'

Her parents had both died by then. There hadn't been anyone to care, or to be proud of her. 'I guess…' she said neutrally, not wanting to tell him about that or see the pity in his face.

'So you're an only child?'

'Mmm,' she said. It was true enough; she was the only child of *her* parents. She had half-siblings she'd loved dearly as babies, but their fathers had always taken them away after the inevitable break-up of their relationship with her mother and cut all ties with both Becca *and* her mother.

And she really didn't want to tell Marco about all of that. She wanted to keep the past where it belonged. Buried. For good. 'I'm sorry. I have another appointment.'

'And it isn't fair of me to make you late.'

'I'll see you later,' she said, and disappeared.

What was she hiding? Marco wondered. He'd noticed that whenever he brought up the subject of her childhood she either changed the subject or vanished. It was clear that she came from a much more modest background than his own. But did she really think he was so much of a snob that he'd hold that against her?

He mixed with people from all sorts of backgrounds as part of his job, and it had never bothered him whether someone had been to the 'right' sort of school or if they spoke with a regional accent instead of being 'posh'. It was how you treated others that counted with Marco, not where you came from.

Maybe he could get her to open up to him tomorrow.

Maybe.

CHAPTER FIVE

O<small>N THE</small> T<small>UESDAY</small> morning Ethan walked into Marco's room with Declan Underwood, the acting head of the clinic, looking grim. 'Well, Zorro, it looks as if someone's ratted you out,' he said. 'The paps are three deep outside, waiting for a glimpse of you. And we can hardly give our clients the discreet service they expect from us when there are hundreds of cameras out there.' He tossed a tabloid newspaper onto Marco's bed.

Marco glanced at the front page. There was a picture of him in uniform, taking up half the page, with the headline: *Wounded hero returns to London.*

He scanned the text swiftly. Just as he'd feared, they'd run a story about him rescuing his men in Afghanistan and how he'd got everyone out of his Jeep even though he couldn't use one hand.

He shook his head. 'I'm not a hero. I just did my job—I did what anyone else in my position would have done.'

Ethan looked sympathetic, almost as if he'd been there.

'And you know as well as I do it turned out not to be the right thing in any case. They'd rigged the road and men *died* because of me.' Marco scowled at the newspaper.

'Nobody from here broke the story,' Ethan said.

'Of course not. Apart from anything else, there are details here that only someone from the camp would know. Or their families, maybe.' Marco sighed. 'I'm so sorry you've been dragged into this. I imagine this is going to cause you a few problems.'

'It's going to be a bit tricky for some of our clients,' Ethan agreed.

'So how do we get rid of the press?' Marco asked.

'You need to work with them,' Declan said. 'Give them enough to keep them on side without breaching any confidentiality issues.'

Ethan curled his lip. 'They make up what they want. And they'll dig until they find what they want to see.'

That sounded personal, Marco thought. Had the press trashed him in the past? Or maybe someone close to him? 'They do exaggerate,' he agreed.

'But if you work with them it'll lessen the damage. We need to build a relationship with the press,' Declan repeated.

'That's why I brought him here,' Ethan said. 'Declan's a lot better with them than I am. He's good with the blarney. Not to mention the fact that he sweetened them up last time we were papped by sending them tea and biscuits because it was cold.'

'I just want to do my job,' Declan said, 'and getting the press on our side means fewer delays.'

'You could give them a photo opportunity, Zorro,' Ethan said. 'Perhaps a royal wave from the balcony with your good hand—but do make sure they see the strapping for your war wound so they can see the work we've done on you.'

'Not funny, Clavo,' Marco said, narrowing his eyes. 'I don't give a damn what they say about me—but now the press blanket's been breached it means my regiment is in danger.'

'But everyone knows you're in London. There's no point in anyone targeting your regiment as they know they're definitely not going to capture *you*,' Declan said.

'They can capture others and demand me in exchange,' Marco pointed out.

'As *if* your family would ever agree to that,' Ethan said, rolling his eyes. 'Get real, Zorro.'

'I need to go out there and calm the mob down,' Declan said, 'so our staff can actually get into the building. I think we need to tell them that, yes, you are here, Marco, and, yes, you've had an injury to your hand, but that I can't go into further details because of patient confidentiality; you're making a good recovery and we'll update them as and when we can; and you'd like them to continue their good work in being careful about what they report so they don't put your team's safety at risk.'

'That works for me,' Marco said. 'I'll call my father and tell him how we're handling it. You have a PR team here?'

'Lexi's the head of our in-house team,' Declan confirmed.

'My father's PR team will probably want to liaise with her. Oh, and it's warm outside, right?'

'Right,' Ethan said, looking mystified. 'Why?'

'Because it's not the right weather for tea and biscuits. Send the paps ice creams and cold drinks, and I'll pick up the bill.'

'Now, that,' Declan said with a smile, 'is a great idea.'

'I don't think anyone could miss the press pack outside the front door,' Declan said at the emergency staff meeting that morning. 'I've told them, with Marco's permission, that he's here, we've treated him for a hand injury, he's comfortable and he's making a good recovery. I've also told them that I can't give them any more information, because of patient confidentiality. So if any of them ask you for more, just smile and say he's comfortable, and you're sorry but you can't break patient confidentiality, and I'll update them as soon as I can.'

'Got it,' Becca said. But her stomach knotted in panic. If the press couldn't find a story about Marco, would they start digging elsewhere? Supposing they started researching the pasts of the staff at the Hunter Clinic? They'd broken the story about Ethan and Leo's father, years before. And there had been another story, about the rescue Ethan had been involved with in Afghanistan; Becca could still remember Leo's reaction to that. The shock. The hurt.

With a bit of digging, the press could find out about the sordid mess of her past—and that would cause shockwaves through the clinic. It would mean she'd have to resign. What kind of patient would agree to be treated by a former addict, even though she hadn't had a drink or touched any tablet stronger than paracetamol for more than seven years now?

And, worse, if they found Barney and he told them what he knew... Of course he'd leave his own part out of it, and the press wouldn't care what he'd done to her because they'd have their story. She'd have to leave the job she loved so much. She might even be struck off the professional register for something that had happened when she was still little more than a child. OK, so technically she'd been over the age of consent, but...

This wasn't *fair*.

Worry made her short-tempered. She was short with Marco when she went in to do his physio—even though she knew she was being grossly unfair, because it wasn't his fault that the press was doorstepping him. Though she noticed that he was equally short with her.

The last few days had been a sweet, romantic dream. They'd been cocooned in a bubble, where perhaps they could start to fall in love with each other again and everything would be perfect.

But now it was time to wake up, face reality, and know that it was over.

* * *

'I've spoken to my father,' Marco said to Ethan. 'And his media team has come up with a fix. Tell the press you've done such a great job of mending my hand that I can be discharged from the clinic and move out to my family's London apartment. So there'll be no point in the press camping out here any more, because they're not going to get a glimpse of me—I won't be here.'

'Thank you,' Ethan said. 'But we *haven't* actually finished treating you, have we? There's the small matter of physiotherapy. And if you don't keep up with the exercises, then you'll risk losing movement in your hand. As it is, I'm concerned about your grip. I'd advise very strongly that you continue your therapy.'

'So what do you suggest? If I come back here for treatment, you'll still have the press doorstepping you.' Marco paused. 'Unless your staff could visit me? Although, as you've already pointed out to me, I'm not Becca's only patient. I know my family's place isn't that far from here, but she still wouldn't have enough time to come to me, treat me, come back here in time for her next appointment, treat her patient, and then be back with me for my next physio. Not to mention doing all her paperwork. It wouldn't be fair to her.'

'That kind of routine's not doable,' Ethan agreed. 'But I'll talk to her. If she's happy to work with you on a one-to-one basis, and for you to be her only patient for the time being, then I can arrange a stand-in physio for the rest of her caseload.'

And maybe, Marco thought, once they were outside the clinic Becca's professional distance might dissolve. In the times when she wasn't treating him they could grow closer. Be friends instead of patient and therapist. Maybe they could even become lovers again? He'd get the chance to discover who Becca had become—and maybe they'd sort out this thing between them and find out what the future held.

He damped down the surge of optimism. 'And if she's not happy to do that?'

'Then you get the stand-in,' Ethan said. 'And may I remind you—?'

'No flirting with your staff,' Marco cut in, rolling his eyes. 'I remember.' Strictly speaking, he wasn't flirting with any of the staff at the Hunter Clinic. But at his home... things might be different. Because then different rules would apply.

'Becca—a word?' Ethan said.

'Sure.' Becca followed him into his office. 'What can I do for you?' she asked.

'I thought you should know that our illustrious patient is leaving this afternoon.'

She froze. Marco was *leaving*? But he hadn't said a word to her.

This was South Africa all over again: he was going without even saying goodbye. Just as well she hadn't let him back into her life, or it would be dump-and-run for the second time.

She schooled her expression into neutral. 'Uh-huh.'

'Which means we're not going to be doorstepped by the press any more, and he'll get the high-level security he's going to need now the story's broken.'

'Of course,' Becca said, trying very hard not to let it show how much she minded that Marco hadn't said a word to her about it in their treatment sessions this morning.

'But,' Ethan said, 'he hasn't finished his physio treatment. Which is where you come in.'

'Me?' She frowned. 'But, if he's leaving, it means he won't be treated here any more.'

'No. He'll be treated at the family apartment.'

She still didn't see what that had to do with her. If Marco was going back to Sirmontane, surely there were physiotherapists there?

'In London,' Ethan clarified. 'And I wondered if you could do it.'

She ignored the flare of hope. 'What about my other patients? I've got appointments booked in between his. And, unless this apartment's literally a two-minute walk away, I won't have time to treat anyone else—I'll be spending all my time travelling between his place and here.'

'Marco needs hourly treatments, which means basically having a personal physio,' Ethan agreed. 'So I can draft someone in to cover the rest of your caseload, if that works for you.'

'He asked for me to treat him?' She really hoped her voice didn't sound as breathless and squeaky to Ethan as it did to herself.

'I didn't give him the chance to ask for you,' Ethan said. 'I wanted to run it by you first. If it doesn't work for you, then I'll tell him he'll have to have a different physio. Royal or not, he can't order you about.' He shrugged. 'But you're good at your job, Becca. You're the obvious first choice, if you're happy to do it.'

Work one-on-one with Marco. No other patients.

It didn't seem real.

She remembered what he'd said. *Seize the day.* Could she be that brave?

'Yes,' she said.

'Ethan told me you'd agreed to treat me at home,' Marco said when Becca called in to go through his next set of exercises. 'Thank you.'

'It was the best solution for everyone,' Becca said, trying to play it cool. 'Sorry I was a bit short with you earlier.'

He shrugged. 'No worries. It always tends to get a bit tense when the press are involved.'

'So...um...do I turn up to your place tomorrow morning at nine? It might be handy to know the address,' Becca pointed out.

He smiled. 'I was rather hoping I could tempt you to come over later this afternoon...say when you've finished work? And maybe stay for dinner?'

'Dinner?' Did he mean just dinner, or would he expect more than that? Her heart rate sped up.

'No pressure,' he said softly. 'I like your company.'

Becca wasn't sure whether to be disappointed that he didn't want to take things further, or relieved that he was letting her off the hook. 'Dinner,' she said again.

He paused. 'If you're not committed elsewhere.'

How could she tell him about her work at the rehab centre? Even if she told a slight fib and said she was volunteering there because they'd helped a close friend, and she wanted to give something back for her friend's sake, he was bright enough to guess that the 'friend' didn't exist—that *she* was the one who'd needed help from the rehab centre to wean herself off vodka and the other stuff Barney had introduced her to.

She really didn't want to tell Marco the truth about the whole sordid mess. She didn't want him to know just how low she'd sunk. She didn't want him to know how she'd been hooked. Even though the therapist had tried to persuade her that none of it had been Becca's fault—that with her mother's addiction and the kind of people who'd surrounded her Becca hadn't stood a chance—Becca had never quite been able to believe that. She still thought she should have been stronger.

'I need to make a phone call,' she prevaricated.

'OK.'

'So why aren't you leaving the clinic in the middle of the night?'

'Why would I do that?'

She spread her hands. 'We've had patients leave in the middle of the night before to avoid the paparazzi.'

He smiled. 'No, I want the press to *see* I'm leaving. Then they'll stop staking out the clinic and you can all go back to normal.'

'What about your arm? If it gets knocked in the middle of the crowd…'

He shrugged. 'That's what my bodyguard's for. He'll clear the way. So… Tonight…' He gave her an address.

Becca blinked, recognising the name of the road and the very exclusive development of houses. It wasn't that far from the clinic, but it was too far for her to go and see him and then come back to see her other patients between his appointments, even if she took a taxi between his house and 200 Harley Street. 'You live on the edge of Regent's Park?'

'Yes.' He didn't look in the slightest bit fazed by the question. If anything, he acted as if it was perfectly normal to live in the sort of house that cost more than a thousand times the average person's annual salary. Yet again Becca was aware of the massive gulf between their lifestyles.

'Come over after work,' he said. 'I'll tell Security to expect you.'

'Security?' she asked.

'There's a security gate. Visitors need to sign in. Are you walking or coming by car?'

'Marco, normal people don't tend to drive in London. It's way too much hassle and parking's a nightmare. You either take public transport or you walk.'

'I could send Rafa, my driver, and the limo for you,' he offered.

'Limo?' She smiled. How incongruous could you get?

'Marco, I'm a physiotherapist, not a rock star or a famous actress. I'll get a taxi.'

'If you insist.'

'I do.'

'OK. Our place is about five minutes' walk from the gate. Just ring the front doorbell and Maria, our housekeeper, will let you in.'

A housekeeper, a driver... How normal he made it sound to have staff. Whereas she did her own housework and if she'd had a car she would've driven herself.

'Right. Now, let's take this hand strap off and see how much mobility you've gained in your hand since yesterday.'

'Yes, ma'am,' he teased.

Face the press. OK. He could do this.

Marco took a deep breath, pinned on his public smile, and walked through the front door of 200 Harley Street, his bodyguard at his side.

What felt like a thousand flashbulbs went off, followed by a babble of excited speech.

'Prince Marco, where are you going?'

'Why are you leaving the clinic?'

'Are you going back to Afghanistan?'

Marco held up his free hand. 'Guys, one at a time, please. Where am I going? To my family's home in London so I can finish recuperating. Why am I leaving?' He nodded at his left arm. 'Because, as you can see, I'm fixed. Or at least on the mend—it was a flexor tendon injury, so it will take a bit of time to heal. Am I going back? I hope so, but not until I'm fit. Because I can't—and *won't*—put my team at risk.'

More flashbulbs. More babbled questions.

'Hey, Marco, thanks for the ice creams and the cold drinks!' someone called.

He smiled back. 'My pleasure. I thought it might be a bit hot for tea and biscuits.'

There was a ripple of appreciative laughter. No doubt half the paps had also been here for the tea and biscuits episode Ethan had talked about.

'Thanks, guys. I'm going home now. And can I ask that you don't jog my arm, please, on my way to the car? My hand's still a little bit fragile.'

'You're a hero!' someone else called.

Oh, how he wasn't.

'I'm no hero,' he said quietly. 'I just did my job. It's not my place to talk politics, but in my view the real heroes are the ones putting their country back together and trusting they can give their children an education and medical treatment. The ones who are fighting for men and women to be treated equally.'

There were heads nodding in agreement as he spoke.

'Marco, will you have a string of beautiful women to mop your brow while you recuperate?' another one of them called.

Marco laughed. 'I'm afraid that's not actually in my doctor's orders. I just have to rest and exercise my hand as I've been taught.' He smiled at them. 'I'm sure you can all understand that I'm a bit tired right now—I'd really like to go home, and I could kill for a cup of coffee.'

There were sympathetic grins all round.

'My father's PR team will issue regular bulletins to tell you how I'm doing,' he said. 'And please remember that my team's still out there in Afghanistan. You were great at keeping them safe before with the media blanket. I'd really appreciate it if you could keep up the good work and keep them safe while I'm here in London.'

And finally, to Marco's relief, the press pack parted and allowed him and his bodyguard to go down the steps to Rafa, his driver, in the waiting limo.

CHAPTER SIX

REGENT'S PARK WAS a place where you'd go to have a picnic by the lake, or to visit the zoo or the gardens. The place Becca had desperately wanted to visit as a child, after reading *The Hundred and One Dalmatians* and discovering that Pongo the Dalmatian was walked there by Mr and Mrs Dearly. The place she sometimes went to in her lunch break, as they had the biggest collection of roses in London, and Becca had always loved the scent of roses.

It definitely wasn't a place where you actually lived. Not unless you were from a seriously wealthy background. The nearest Becca had ever come even to renting a house there was on a Monopoly board.

She went to the security gate, as Marco had directed; to her relief, the staff there were expecting her. She showed them her identity card from the clinic and her bank card, to prove that she was who she said she was, signed in, then walked round the corner to Marco's family home and stopped dead.

The house was amazing; it was part of a long, sweeping terrace. There were four floors, the walls were cream stucco and punctuated by huge floor-to-ceiling windows, and there were actually columns holding up the portico—real fluted two-storey-height columns, like the ones outside the British Museum, except with leafy bits at the top instead of scrolls. There was a wide wrought-iron balcony running along the entire length of the house on the first floor, and wrought-iron railings at the front of the house. Behind the railings were raised flowerbeds, and as Becca got closer she realised that the steps leading to the house were marble.

Wow.

Really, she felt as if she ought to be going to the servants' entrance rather than the front door. After all, wasn't that kind of what she was as the prince's physiotherapist?

Lifting her chin, she rang the doorbell.

A middle-aged woman that Becca assumed was the housekeeper Marco had told her about answered the door. 'Can I help you?'

'Hello, I'm Becca Anderson, the physiotherapist from the Hunter Clinic. I have an appointment with…' Help, how did you refer to a prince? She couldn't just call him Marco, the way she did to his face. His housekeeper was bound to expect a properly respectful mode of address. 'With His Royal Highness,' she finished miserably.

'Ah, so you're Becca—come in. I'm Maria, the housekeeper. I'll take you through to the Prince.'

Becca was surprised and relieved by the warmth of the greeting. She followed the housekeeper through the large black door into the hallway. There were marble floors that reminded her a bit of the ones at Harley Street, but there the resemblance ended.

She was used to discreet luxury from working at the Hunter Clinic, but Marco's family home was something else. Maria showed her into a room where the floors were polished parquet and there was a huge rug in the centre; it looked like silk and Becca was almost too nervous to stand on it, in case she put a mark on it or pulled a thread or something.

'Have a seat. The Prince will be with you shortly,' Maria said.

Everywhere in the room was incredibly neat and orderly. There was a choice of beautiful cream sofas to sit on, liberally spread with thick cushions and augmented by Louis XV tall-back cream-upholstered armchairs. There were also several occasional tables from the same period that Becca suspected were original pieces rather than reproduction, and several beautiful floral arrangements in crystal vases.

The lights were traditional chandeliers, which reminded her of the stunning Venetian glass she'd fallen in love with on holiday one year—the kind of stuff that had been way, way outside her budget. There was a gilt mirror over the mantelpiece, and the reflection had the kind of softness that told her it had to be very old glass—maybe several hundred years old, and handmade by a craftsman rather than mass-produced in a factory.

The floor-to-ceiling windows had cream damask drapes and a view over Regent's Park that took her breath away. *Imagine growing up here*, she thought. It was only a few physical miles away from the grotty seventh-floor flat where she'd grown up, but it was light years away emotionally. Here, everything was beautiful and light and airy, instead of dank and chipped or fraying.

The mantelpiece was marble and held a number of heavy silver-framed photographs. Becca couldn't resist being nosey and taking a closer look at the family portraits. In pride of place was what looked like a relatively recent photograph of the King of Sirmontane with his queen, two sons and a daughter; Becca could really see the resemblance between Marco and his family. Marco had the same dark eyes and hair as his father and brother and the same smile as his mother and sister. His older brother looked more serious, but there was a kindness in his face that Becca knew was part of Marco's make-up, too.

Another photograph showed Marco's sister in a wedding dress, with a man Becca assumed was her husband, and another showed them both in a garden with two toddlers, clearly theirs.

She could imagine Marco as an uncle. He'd be the first one on the floor with the children, building forts out of bricks and settling them both on his lap to read them a story.

Just for a second she imagined Marco as a father, holding his newborn child with a tender expression in his eyes. And she suppressed the thought ruthlessly. She wasn't ever going to have a family, and she most definitely wasn't going to have a family with Marco.

There was another photograph of an older man with the three children, though in this one they were much younger. She had a feeling that the older man was the grandfather who'd been taken ill while Marco was in South Africa—a feeling that deepened when she saw a picture of Marco as a child with the same man and a puppy, laughing and looking totally carefree. A picture that tugged at her heart.

'Good evening, Becca.'

She spun round, feeling the colour flood into her face at being caught snooping. 'I—er—sorry, I was being nosey.' Why hadn't she just sat down politely and waited for him as she'd been told to do?

'No worries. Help yourself.' He smiled at her. 'That's the family—obviously my parents, my grandfather, my sister Arabella, my brother Ferdinand, Bella and her husband Luiz, the twins, and that was my little dog Pablo. He was my sixth birthday present from my grandfather, and I loved him to bits.'

'Uh-huh.'

Marco here didn't feel like the Marco she knew. In South Africa he definitely hadn't been a prince; he'd been just one of the other volunteers at the children's aid camp, super-handsome and yet kind and thoughtful with a heart of gold. And at the clinic he'd seemed just like any of the other patients. But here? Here, Marco was markedly a prince. Even the way he walked seemed different—seemed regal, somehow.

What on earth was she doing here? This place highlighted just how unsuitable Becca would be as a prince's girlfriend. This was so far out of her own experience, it was untrue. She needed to keep that in mind and protect her heart. As soon as Marco was fit to go back to work, he'd leave—and after that one goodbye she'd never see him again.

'Would you like a guided tour?' he asked.

'Um…sure.' Though it felt almost like having a guided tour of an English country house that had been left to the nation by the family years before—a snapshot of the past. Somewhere you could only dream of living. Not somewhere that people actually lived for real.

'I guess I should start with the front of the house. It was designed by John Nash and built nearly two hundred years ago; it's a listed building,' he intoned.

Well, of course—where else would a royal family live?

'It's my parents' base in London—obviously it's big enough for us all to be here together, including Bella's husband and the twins, plus any guests and staff.'

Becca didn't dare ask how many bedrooms there were. This was way, *way* out of her league.

'So, this is one of the sitting rooms.'

One of? Most people she knew had only one, and sometimes not even that; in her own flat the sitting room did triple duty as her dining room and her study, too.

'This is the dining room.'

He took her through to the next room. Again, the windows were floor to ceiling, the large gilt-framed paintings on the walls all looked like original oil portraits, and the dining table was so huge that it could have seated an entire rugby squad and then some. The wood was beautifully polished and there were some candelabra at either end that might have been gilt but Becca had a nasty feeling that they were actually solid gold. There was another beautiful arrangement of fresh flowers in a crystal bowl in the centre.

'This is the library,' he said, showing her into the next room.

She caught her breath. 'Oh, I love this,' she said, unable to hold the words back. Like the other rooms, it had floor-to-ceiling windows, with bookshelves between them and covering one entire wall. There were comfy sofas in the centre, with reading lamps nearby, a low table with a chessboard, a grand piano, and also a couple of guitars on stands which she guessed belonged to Marco. This was a room that made her feel comfortable—where she could actually feel as if she belonged.

He sat down at the piano and picked out a melody with his right hand. 'It doesn't feel right, playing something without the harmony,' he said, 'but I guess this is better than nothing at all.' He stroked one of the guitars longingly. 'So how long will it be before I can play again?'

'You can't even lift a kettle for another six or seven weeks,' she said. 'I'm sorry, Marco. There isn't a nice way of saying this.'

'Tell me straight. I'm never going to play again?'

'Not *never*,' she said, 'but playing guitar means using a lot of pressure. It counts as heavy activity, so it'll be months rather than weeks or days before you can try, and even then you'll have to take it really easy. Play for a couple of minutes, rather than hours.'

'I guess I have to learn to take things slowly, or I'll do more damage that even Ethan Hunter won't be able to fix it.' He looked utterly miserable.

Hating the fact that he was so unhappy and unable to resist trying to comfort him, Becca walked over and hugged him. She knew this was a bad idea—she ought to keep some professional distance between them—but how could she stand by when he was so dejected?

Marco wrapped his good arm round her and rested his forehead against hers. 'Thank you. I needed that. I just hate being so helpless and having to rely on other people to help me. I'm used to doing things myself.'

'Action hero,' she said softly.

He shook his head. 'I'm no hero, Becca. I just do my job, and I try to do it well.'

She guessed that Marco would be good at just about anything he did. Second best would never be enough for him.

'And this time I messed it up,' he said, confirming what she'd just thought.

He was so hard on himself. Why?

'I could hold the guitar for you,' she suggested. 'If you told me what notes to play, you could still do the strings with your right hand.'

His lips brushed against hers, a feather-light touch. She thought it was probably meant to be a token of gratitude, but all it did was make her tingle all over and want more. To the point where she could feel herself on the cusp of hyperventilating.

'That's such a sweet offer. Do you actually play the guitar, Becca?'

'Um—no,' she admitted. 'I never learned to read music or anything like that, and you're the only person I've ever met who actually plays an instrument.'

'Then I'd probably end up barking orders at you and getting frustrated because I couldn't explain myself well enough to you, and—well, I'd be horrible,' he said. 'And I don't want to be horrible to you. But thank you for offering. I appreciate it.'

He held her just a little bit closer, then released her. She guessed that he was just as confused about this as she was. Wanting to touch, to kiss, to lose themselves in each other; yet at the same time knowing it wouldn't be sensible.

When they went to the next room Marco took Becca's hand on the way, lacing his fingers through hers. Her skin tingled where he touched her.

Oh, help. This wasn't the deal. She was his therapist, not his girlfriend. South Africa was in the past, and it was staying there.

The study held more bookshelves and a polished oak desk with more family portraits in pride of place.

'This is Papá's, but Ferdy and I use it sometimes if we're here and he's not,' Marco said. 'The next two floors are just bathrooms and bedrooms,' he told her, leading her up the stairs again. 'But this is my favourite bit of the house.'

He led her up a last flight of stairs, released her hand and opened the door for her.

She gasped as she realised what it was. 'A roof garden. How amazing.'

It was stunning—flagged stone, with terracotta pots of sweet-smelling herbs and bright flowers, comfortable chairs and even a hammock. But the bit that took her breath away was the view: not just the whole of the park, but the middle of London itself, including iconic structures such as the London Eye and the Shard.

They were right in the centre of London, with thousands of people around them; and yet at the same time the garden was incredibly private. She assumed that the other houses in the sweeping terrace had some kind of roof gardens, too, but this one didn't seem overlooked in any direction.

'And then there's this. You don't get the same kind of view of the stars that we did in South Africa,' he said, 'because there's too much light pollution in the city, but it's still good to sit out here and look up at the sky on a summer's night.'

'This' referred to a spa pool, screened off from the rest of the garden by a trellis covered in wisteria.

'I thought maybe we could have dinner up here tonight,' he said.

'I've never had dinner on a roof garden before,' Becca said.

'Good. I think you'll enjoy this. Excuse me a second.' He took his mobile phone from his pocket and made a swift call in Spanish.

'Chef would like to know if you have any allergies or if there's anything you don't like?' he asked.

Becca couldn't quite process this. He had a personal chef? 'No allergies. I'm happy to eat anything.' And then a nasty thought hit her. 'But I'm not keen on puddings with alcohol.'

'That's fine. I'll make sure he knows.' He spoke rapidly into the phone in Spanish again. 'OK, Miguel. *Talué*.'

'What does that mean...*talué*?' she asked.

'It's bye-bye.' He wrinkled his nose. 'Basically it's slang, running the words *"hasta luego"* together. I guess it's like saying *ciao-ciao* in Italian instead of *arrivederci*.'

'Right.' She didn't speak Italian, either, apart from with the aid of a phrasebook.

He grimaced. 'Sorry. I didn't mean to show off. Chef will, though.' He grinned. 'I told him he can show off as much as he likes and do you a real Sirmontanean meal.'

She was still trying to get her head round this. 'You have a personal chef?'

He rolled his eyes. 'You make it sound far more snooty than it is. My parents have to entertain when they're here, and visiting dignitaries kind of expect their full attention rather than having my mother rushing off in the middle of dinner to check something in the kitchen.'

His parents. His family. Ice trickled through her veins. What if his family came over to be with him now he was out of the clinic? Would they think she was suitable to be his physio? They definitely wouldn't think of her as suitable in any other way.

The panic must have shown in her face, because he sighed. 'Relax, Becca. It's just you and me. My family is under strict instructions to stay away because I need to rest.'

Even though part of her was relieved, part of her felt a bit guilty. 'Isn't that a bit unfair to your mother? She must be worried about you.' In her shoes Becca would have been worried sick and desperate to see her injured son for herself.

Not that Becca thought she'd ever get married and have a family of her own. Her experiences with family had pretty much put her off taking that particular risk.

'I love my mother, I really do, but she drives me totally *loco*,' Marco said. 'She frets and she thinks up all the worst-case scenarios. If she had her way she'd wrap me in cotton wool, and that doesn't sit well with me—and then I end up rebelling and snapping at her, and then she gets upset, and then I feel guilty for being mean because I know she loves me as much as I love her, and...' He grimaced. 'Like I said, *loco*.'

It must be nice, Becca thought, to have a parent who cared that much about you instead of one who always put herself first and dumped you when the going got tough. Not that she had any intention of telling Marco about any of that. She didn't need his pity.

'We should do your physio,' she said.

'So when do I get to do the next stage of exercises?' he asked. 'The ones where I can start doing light work with my hand?'

'The next stage of exercises will be in about another

fortnight. And another month after that before you do light activities.'

He groaned. 'Surely I can start using my hand *soon*?'

'Not even to read a newspaper,' she said. 'And using a knife is totally out of the question. That counts as heavy use, and that won't be until three months after the operation. Light use you can start two months after the operation. *Provided* you don't push it and set your progress back before then.'

'Excuse me a second.' He took out his phone and made another call in rapid Spanish.

She gave him an enquiring look.

'I asked Miguel—Chef—to make food I can eat with a fork,' he said, looking grumpy. 'This is worse than being a toddler. I hate the idea of someone cutting up my food for me.' He sighed. 'It's the lack of independence that's getting to me. Not being able to do things I've taken for granted for years.'

'Patience,' she counselled.

'Something I'm not very good at.'

'You were patient with the children in South Africa.'

'That was different.' He shrugged off the compliment. 'Ferdy—now, *he* has patience. Which is why it's so good for Sirmontane that he's the elder son and not me.'

'Do you mind that you won't be king?' she asked.

'No. I have so much more freedom than Ferdy.' He sighed. 'Though obviously I have royal duties. Things I can't neglect. Things that have to come first no matter how I feel about it.'

'It's the same with your hand,' she said lightly. 'You're desperate to use it again—but you have to wait and the healing has to take place first, no matter how grumpy and frustrated you get.'

'Point taken,' he said dryly.

'Time for your exercises.' She talked him through them,

watching him and making sure that he didn't push too hard, yet at the same time pushed himself hard enough to make progress.

They were halfway through the physio session when Maria came up onto the roof garden, carrying a tray bearing a silver teapot with a matching jug and sugar bowl, two porcelain cups, and a plate of delicate almond biscuits.

'Miguel's so happy to have you home, Marco—he's enjoying having someone to cook for other than just the two of us and Rafa,' she said with a smile. 'I'm happy to have you home, too, *hermoso*.'

He smiled at her. 'Thank you, Maria. Though I can assure you that they looked after me well at the Hunter Clinic.'

'It's not Harley Street that worried me,' she said pointedly.

Marco rolled his eyes. 'If Mamá has asked you to nag me about my job, I'll take that as read and you don't have to do it. I'm still in one piece, just a little bit battered, and Becca's fixing me up. She's bullying me, mind.'

Maria laughed and patted Becca's shoulder. 'Bully away, *hermosa*. He needs taking in hand. I brought tea, but if you'd rather have coffee I can bring you some—no problem.'

'Tea's lovely, thank you. It's very kind of you.' Becca smiled at her. 'Though, to be honest, I'd normally make my own tea, and I feel a bit guilty, having you wait on me.'

'Nonsense. That's what I'm here for.' Maria smiled again. 'Call me if you need me.'

'Thank you,' Becca said.

The almond biscuits were lovely.

'These are gorgeous. Can you tell Miguel for me?'

'Sure. They're traditional Sirmontane biscuits,' Marco said. 'They're usually served with coffee after dinner, or sometimes with morning coffee.'

'The tea looks more like an English tradition, though.'

He grinned. 'Yes. Like our neighbours, Spain and France, in Sirmontane we prefer coffee to tea.'

'Just remember you're not to lift anything with your left hand at the moment, even a cup as light and delicate as this,' Becca said, and took charge of the teapot.

Serving tea to a prince, with fine porcelain and silver. If anyone had told her a couple of weeks ago that she'd be doing that she would have laughed. How far away this felt from her real life.

They finished off the physiotherapy session after their tea, and then she was content to sit with Marco in the sunshine and chat about nothing in particular. Just being with him felt so good. And as long as she didn't let herself remember that she was in a multimillion-pound house with a prince, it felt *real*.

Dinner that evening started with tapas. 'Obviously, because we're on the Spanish border, we have similar dishes to Spain,' he said. 'And I like tapas. Lots of little tastes.'

There were dishes of olives, ham, cheeses she didn't recognise but which were totally delicious, and fresh bread. 'This is very nice,' she said, tasting each one in turn.

'And, best of all, I can eat it one-handed,' he said wryly.

The next course was a tender lamb stew, with saffron-scented rice and baby vegetables.

'Fork food at its finest,' Marco said with a grin. 'Miguel's done us proud.'

And then Maria brought up cinnamon-spiked *churros* with the most amazing chocolate sauce.

'Oh, my God. I've never eaten anything as nice as this,' Becca said.

He grinned. 'I told you Sirmontane chocolate's better than Swiss.'

'Lizzie's going to beg you for some of this,' she said, taking another bite.

'I'll get some delivered as a welcome-back present.' Marco laughed.

Finally they had bitter coffee, with the nicest dark chocolate thins she'd ever had in her life, and watched the lights come up over London.

'We could,' Marco suggested softly, 'have a spa bath.'

She shook her head. 'Nice idea, but I'm afraid I don't have a swimming costume with me.' Hers was back in her locker in the clinic.

He pursed his lips. 'What if I said you don't need a costume?'

Oh, the very idea of sharing a spa bath with him— skinny-dipping under the stars… It sent a shiver of desire through her.

'Marco, this—we can't—we shouldn't…' Her voice faded.

'I have no idea what you're trying to tell me, *hermosa*.'

'Oh, yes, you do. I'm your therapist. I can't be anything else.'

He took her hand. 'We're not at the clinic, now. Technically, you're not at work. You're having dinner with me.'

'A platonic dinner.'

'It doesn't have to be.'

'Marco, I'm not going to be just a distraction for you. I'm worth more than that.'

'I know you are.'

But he didn't relinquish her hand. Instead, he raised it very slowly, turned it over so he could see her wrist, and pressed his mouth against her pulse-point. And she knew that he'd be aware of how much her heart-rate was speeding up—and precisely why.

'Remember what I said before?' he whispered. 'Forget the past. Don't worry about the future. Just enjoy the here and now.'

She wanted to. So very badly. It had been driving her crazy, keeping her distance from him and trying her best to be professional when all she wanted to do was rip his clothes off.

But…

'How can I?' she burst out.

'Becca,' he said, 'will you please just shut up and kiss me?'

She narrowed her eyes at him. 'Is that an order, Your Royal Highness?'

'No. It's a polite request. And I did say "please",' he pointed out. 'Or do you want me to beg?'

Oh, help. The pictures *that* put in her head. She dragged in a breath. 'I know I'm technically off duty, but you're still my patient.'

'Then consider me signed off, as of now,' he said.

'I'm afraid I can't do that. Only Ethan can sign you off, as your surgeon. Or maybe Declan, as the acting head of the clinic. And you'd be stupid to sign yourself off. Your hand…'

He groaned. 'Right now I don't care about my hand. This is driving me crazy, Becca. I can't stop thinking about you.'

The confession seemed dragged from him, and it made it easier for her to admit to him, 'I can't stop thinking about you, either.'

'I need to be honest with you. I'm not sure I can offer you a happy-ever-after. I have…well, responsibilities. I still have to finish my tour of duty as a soldier. How do I know that the next bomb won't be directly under my Jeep instead of the one in front of mine?'

'Marco.' She stroked his face. 'Don't talk like that.' She hated to think of him being badly hurt, or even killed.

'I'm not trying to manipulate you, Becca, or bully you into having a fling with me.'

'Is that what you're offering? A fling?'

He blew out a breath. 'Right now it's all I can offer. Maybe—I don't know. Maybe. I don't want to make any promises I can't keep. That wouldn't be fair to either of us. But I can offer you happy-for-now.'

Was that enough?

Either way, she knew that he was going to walk out of her life in a few weeks' time.

If she said no, all she would have were regrets. In years to come, would she wish that she'd been brave?

If she said yes, they could have some time together. Build memories. Things that might sustain her and might just stop her spiralling back into addiction again when he left.

'Seize the day,' she said softly, and leaned forward to kiss him.

How good his skin felt under her fingertips. How good his mouth felt as it teased hers, tempted her, incited her to bite his lower lip and kiss him back.

Despite only having one working hand, it took him seconds to loosen her hair.

'That's what I wanted to see,' he said softly. 'Your hair falling over your shoulders, just like it used to. Fire over cream.'

Oh, God. How had she forgotten how damn sexy he was? Even the way he talked to her made her feel wet. Hot. Needy. Nobody else had ever made her feel this way. It had been so easy to refuse dates, because the men in question hadn't made her feel a fraction of what Marco made her feel.

He brushed a kiss against her mouth. 'Becca. I want to sit with you and drink champagne and look at the stars— well, as much as you get to see of the stars in London.'

'You're on antibiotics,' she pointed out, 'so that's not a good idea.'

'OK. You can drink champagne and I'll watch you,' he said.

Oh, help. She didn't want to explain all this. She didn't drink. Ever. She couldn't risk even one sip in case it pushed her straight back down the slope of addiction. 'No, it's fine. I'm not one for champagne,' she said hastily.

'Pimm's, then?' he suggested. 'Or a cocktail? Miguel makes wicked cocktails.'

Worse and worse. It looked as if Becca was going to have to tell him a certain amount. But she had no intention of letting him push her into a more detailed explanation. 'Actually, I don't drink,' she said. 'Sorry.'

Marco looked intrigued.

The only way she could think of to take his mind off the subject and stop him asking questions was to kiss him. And she was quivering by the time Marco broke the kiss.

'Let's get in the pool,' he said.

'You're not going anywhere near that water without a plastic bag over your arm. You can't get the splint wet. Or the dressing.'

He laughed. 'You're so bossy.'

'Someone has to be. Right now you're exuberant, bored, and full of bright ideas,' she said.

He kissed her lightly. 'Guilty on all three counts. But my bright ideas are great.'

'Another day,' she said. 'When I can make sure I tape up your arm properly and I have something to wear.'

'I'll hold you to that,' he said, and the expression in his eyes made desire lick all the way down her spine. 'OK. Second bright idea. How about you stay here tonight? I remember what it was like, waking up with you in my arms. It might be nice to do that in a comfortable bed instead of a sleeping bag.'

Becca was tempted. Deeply tempted. Though she knew it was a bad idea. The closer she let him get now, the more she was in danger of getting in too deep and ending up hurt again. Making love with him would be one thing; but allowing him a deeper intimacy, like she had in South Africa—that was one risk too far.

'I don't have so much as a toothbrush with me.'

'Not a problem. Our guest bathrooms are well stocked.'

'I don't have any clean clothes, either.'

'Maria can laund—'

She stopped him by pressing one finger gently against his lips. 'Marco, I'm not used to this way of life. I don't have staff. I've always looked after myself. I'm not comfortable with making other people clear up after me. And I don't expect anyone else to launder my clothes for me.' Colour crept into her face. 'Plus...I don't want her to think...well.'

'That you're my lover?' He raised an eyebrow. 'Maria's a woman of the world. Married, too. You've probably guessed that Miguel's her husband. And, despite me teasing her earlier, she's not my mother's spy. She's the soul of discretion. She's been with my family for years—since before I was born.'

'Was she the nanny you told me about?'

He smiled. 'Yes.'

That certainly explained Maria's easy relationship with the Prince and the way she teased him and fussed over him.

'I just feel awkward about it, Marco,' she said.

'OK. So how about,' he said, 'I see you tomorrow—you stay for dinner and bring a swimming costume with you?'

She bit her lip. 'I need to be somewhere tomorrow evening.' To do the volunteer shift she'd skipped tonight.

He stroked her face. 'I don't want you thinking I'm just bored and using you to distract me. Because I'm not. I want to be with you, Becca.'

It was so very tempting.

'I'll sort it out,' she said. He wouldn't be in London for much longer. She'd make the most of the time they had together. 'But I need to go now, Marco.'

'I'll ask Rafa to drive you home in the limo.'

She shook her head. 'I don't need a limo. I'll get the tube. The station's not far from here.'

He sighed. 'I'm not trying to control you, you know. I just want to make things easier for you.'

'I'm fine.' She smiled. 'Don't fuss. I'll see you tomorrow.'

'Mañana,' Marco said, and kissed her, taking his time and heating her blood to the point that she almost, *almost* changed her mind and agreed to stay.

'I'll see you out.'

As Marco closed the front door behind Becca, so he didn't have to watch her walk away, he knew she was right. If a limo with blacked-out glass took her home the neighbours would ask questions, maybe start talking. A word to the press here, a car number plate given there, and connections would soon be made.

He needed to keep his links with her out of the public eye and out of the press. Not because he was ashamed of her—of course he wasn't. She'd always been cagey about her own background, and had been even cagier since she'd discovered he was a prince, so he was guessing that she came from a very modest family. But money didn't bother him. It was how people treated others that mattered to him. You could be as high-born as you like and still be a low-life.

No, he wasn't ashamed of her. It was what the press could do if they found out about her that bothered him. He'd seen for himself how easily the press could hurt people—how public criticism had chipped away at the confidence of his sister-in-law-to-be Marianna. He didn't want that to happen to Becca. So keeping her secret would be the best thing he could do for both of them.

CHAPTER SEVEN

MARCO FOUND HIMSELF looking forward to seeing Becca, and he loved the fact that she'd talk to him about everything under the sun. Except one thing: she was seriously secretive about her past. She changed the subject every time he asked a question about her. He knew absolutely nothing about her family—were her parents still together, still alive?

'You're a puzzle,' he said.

She frowned. 'I'm not with you.'

'I know nothing about you.'

'There's nothing much to know.' She shrugged. 'I'm a physiotherapist, I specialise in treating hands, and that's about it.'

'So this thing in the evenings that you do—is it a course? You mentioned that you were thinking about studying acupuncture.'

'No, I'm not studying acupuncture yet—I'm still in the process of choosing a course.'

He noticed that she'd switched the subject again, and she hadn't told him what she was doing in the evenings. Why wouldn't she open up to him? Did she think he'd hurt her? And how could he get her to trust him?

Though at the same time he knew she was right: he couldn't offer her a future because his duty to his family and his country had to come first.

Yet he needed her.

And he thought that she might need him.

Somehow they'd manage to find a way to make this work.

Somehow.

'I can't stay for dinner, but is the offer of the spa pool still open?' Becca asked, later that day.

'It most certainly is—OK, so it means we don't get to see the very few stars you can see in the London night sky, but we can watch the clouds going past instead. How about after lunch?' he suggested.

'That'd be great.' She gave him a shy smile that left him tingling. 'I brought my costume with me. And a bag for your arm, and tape.'

'That's good.'

'But, for now...'

'I know, I know,' he said. 'Exercises.'

In the middle of the afternoon Marco changed into his swimming trunks and Becca taped up his arm to make sure that his splint wouldn't get wet. He climbed into the pool and settled back next to her with a contented sigh.

'This,' he said, 'is paradise. I love London.'

'Wouldn't you rather be in Sirmontane, in the mountains?' she asked.

'Not when I can't ride a bike or go skiing,' he said wryly. 'Of course I love my country, but there's something special for me about London. There's music, there's drama, there are museums and art galleries—you can eat foods from practically any country in the world, walk in the park, dance in the middle of a fountain. . .'

'Well, *you* can't dance in the middle of a fountain— not unless you bag your arm up like that, and I think that might cramp your style a bit,' she teased.

He laughed, pulled her close with his good arm and kissed her. 'I don't think it cramps my style at all.'

'No?' she teased.

God, he couldn't resist her. 'No.' His expression grew hot, and this time his kiss wasn't all sweetness and gentleness. It was demanding and enticing and promising, all at the same time. He needed her to know how he felt. Needed her to feel the same way.

Nobody else had ever made Becca feel this way—as if she were going up in flames every time his skin touched hers. It had been so easy to refuse dates because the men in question hadn't made her feel a thousandth of what Marco made her feel.

'I need to see you, Becca,' Marco said, tracing the edge of her swimming costume with the tip of his forefinger. 'And nobody's going to interrupt us. This is just you and me.'

She couldn't resist him any more. 'Yes,' she whispered.

It took him a second to slide the straps down her shoulders. And then he was cupping one breast, his thumb stroking her nipple and making her gasp.

He dipped his head and took her nipple into his mouth.

Becca shuddered as he sucked. 'Oh, my God.' It had been way too long since she'd felt anything like that. Since she'd let anyone touch her in this way. And how strange it was that they were both older, changed by their experiences—and yet their bodies reacted the same way they always had.

'You like that?' he asked.

'Yes,' she breathed.

'Good.' He stroked her abdomen and she knelt up, arching against him.

'I'd forgotten how good we are together,' he whispered. 'How you feel. Like warm silk.'

He slid one finger underneath the lower hem of her swimsuit and drew it along the length of her sex. The second time he did it she was quivering. And when he pushed a finger deep into her, she was glad that he'd jammed his mouth over hers again because she couldn't help whimpering in sheer need.

All coherence left her as her body began to tighten round him.

'Better?' he asked softly when she'd come back down to earth.

She felt the colour flood into her face.

He simply grinned. 'It's good to know that it's still like that between us.'

'I…' She shook her head. 'I don't know what to say.'

He kissed her softly. 'Then don't say anything.'

But she didn't want him thinking that she was cheap. Because she wasn't. 'I don't normally do this sort of thing.'

'Neither do I,' Marco said dryly, 'no matter what the press like to think.' Then he frowned. 'Are you telling me you haven't made love with anyone else since we were together?'

'No.'

Guilt flooded through him. 'Because of me?'

'Partly,' she said, but he had a feeling that she was trying to let him off the hook.

'I hurt you that much?'

She shrugged. 'I was young. I guess we both were. And in a way you did me a favour. It meant that I concentrated on my studies instead of letting someone distract me.'

Even so, he'd hurt her to the point where she hadn't trusted anyone else. Maybe she'd dated, but she hadn't let her boyfriends go anywhere near this far.

'I'm sorry,' he said. 'I didn't mean to hurt you.' And wasn't he in danger of doing that all over again? Only offering her the here and now? He dragged in a breath. 'Becca, I...'

'"Seize the day", you said.'

'But that isn't who you are. You're careful. Guarded.'

'Now who's overthinking it?'

Her tone was light, but he was sure she was masking something.

How was he going to persuade her to trust him with the rest of her, not just her body? When they made love they were on the same page. But Marco knew that wasn't enough.

'I have to go,' she said.

He wasn't so sure that she really needed to go, but he also knew if he pushed her now he'd lose any chance of getting close to her and really finding out what was in her head.

'OK. I'm not going to push you.' He paused. 'Will you stay for dinner tomorrow?'

'I'll see what I can do.'

'And maybe,' he said, 'you could stay over.' At the panicky look on her face, he said, 'No pressure. You can stay in one of the guest suites, if you prefer.'

Though he really wanted to spend the night with her in his arms. He wanted to wake up with her and know that the day would be better because she was in it. Or maybe he was asking too much.

'I'll see,' she said, and left to do whatever mysterious thing she did in the evenings.

The next morning, doing the limited exercises he was allowed to do in the gym was a form of torture, Marco decided. So was sitting in the library. Usually it was his favourite room in the house, but not when the guitars he couldn't play right now were in full view, reminding him just how limited his movements were.

The only bright spot in his day was the fact that Becca would be spending it with him; and there might be a chance that she would stay for dinner as on the first night.

Whether he could persuade her to stay overnight was another matter. She'd been reluctant, the night before, and she kept mentioning these mysterious commitments, but clammed up if he asked her about them.

He could put tabs on her easily enough, and find out what she did that way. But having her followed like that would feel wrong. He'd much rather she told him herself, of her own free will.

Clearly she didn't trust him. Now he'd got to know her again he could understand why. He'd left her before, in South Africa, not wanting to explain because everything was too complicated. And he'd been too young and thoughtless to realise just how much that had hurt her.

Now they were both older. Wiser, maybe.

Except Marco knew he was in danger of really losing his heart to her. He liked the woman Becca had become—kind, yet at the same time efficient and good at her job.

If only she'd been born royal. Then it would have been so easy for both of them.

It had always been made clear to him that he had a responsibility to his country. That he should marry royalty and consolidate his country's relationship with that of another country. Royal marriages were based on duty first: respect and love had to learn to grow later.

With Ferdy being engaged to Princess Marianna, it had taken the heat off Marco; but Marco also knew that it wouldn't be too long before the pressure was back. Especially as this tour of duty with the army was likely to be his last.

Whatever this thing was between him and Becca, it couldn't last. He'd have to give her up. Even though it would feel like ripping part of himself away.

* * *

Marco seemed thrilled when Becca told him that she could stay for dinner. And even more thrilled when, just after lunch, she mentioned that she'd brought an overnight bag with her.

'You're really going to stay?'

'If the offer's still there.'

He kissed her soundly. 'It is. Though I meant what I said about no pressure. You don't have to spend the night in my bed.'

She felt the colour flood into her face. 'What if I want to?' she whispered.

His eyes went really dark and he caught her lower lip between his. 'That,' he said huskily, 'would be a bonus.'

She'd already noticed that his accent changed when he was excited; he sounded much less English and much more Spanish.

Right now, she really wished he had two good arms. She loved the idea of him carrying her to his bed. And she had a feeling that he'd like that idea very much, too.

'Exercises,' she said, more to calm herself down than anything else. Marco tempted her too much.

'Sure.'

But she noticed he winced slightly.

'Let me see,' she said, and checked his palm. 'If that gets any redder over today, you're going back into the clinic to let Ethan have a look at it, and the paparazzi can do what they like,' she said.

'You think it's infected?'

'I think,' she said, 'we need to be careful.'

And not just with the condition of his hand.

He lay with his head in her lap while she massaged cream into his hand, taking care to be gentle enough not to hurt him yet firm enough to make a difference to the sore, tight skin.

'Thank you,' he said softly when she'd finished, and pressed a kiss to the tips of her fingers.

'Any time,' she said, stroking his cheek.

Even without Marco carrying her to his bed, Becca found herself swept away by the whole romance of sleeping with him. This time it was nothing to do with canvas and a slightly lumpy sleeping bag and everything to do with a four-poster bed, the softest and deepest pillows she'd ever seen, and cool cotton sheets with a thread count so high that the material felt softer than silk.

And, more to the point, she'd brought condoms. So this time they could really make love. Recapture the old closeness.

'I can't stop thinking about you, Becca,' he said, the admission ripping from him. 'About us. And it's driving me crazy.'

In answer, she leaned forward, just far enough to touch her mouth to his. Gently, softly. It started out all sweet and reassuring, but Marco wrapped his good arm around her, drawing her closer, and the kiss spiralled into hot, aching need.

She wasn't sure who started undressing whom, or how much help she gave him, but it seemed to take seconds until they were both naked.

'Do you have any idea how lovely you are?' he asked huskily.

She felt the colour bloom in her cheeks. 'I'm ordinary.'

He stole a kiss. 'Your judgement's off. There's nothing ordinary about you. You're beautiful, Becca.'

'You're not so shabby, yourself.' Her voice sounded husky to her own ears.

Marco traced the line of Becca's collarbones with his fingertips; she shivered, arching her back and tipping her head so he could kiss the hollow of her throat.

He needed her so much. He wanted to touch her. Taste her. Make her feel as desperate as he did.

She shivered. 'Marco...'

He wanted her all wide-eyed and flushed with passion. Like she'd been when he'd touched her in the spa pool. When she'd fallen apart in his arms.

'I'm having a hard time taking this slowly,' he warned.

She traced his pectorals with the tip of her forefinger. 'Me, too.'

'Good.' He was so dizzy with need for her, he couldn't think straight. 'I'm in your hands,' he whispered. 'All yours.'

'All mine,' she repeated, and her mouth and eyes turned so sensual that he caught his breath.

She smoothed her hands across his bare chest and the pads of her fingertips teased his skin, making him ache. He wanted more. Much more.

She leaned forward and pressed a hot, open-mouthed kiss against his throat; he arched his head back, giving her better access, and closed his eyes in bliss as she nibbled her way across his skin. God, her mouth felt so good. And he wanted her to dip lower. To take him into her mouth and ease the ache.

Her hands stroked over his pecs, his abdomen. 'You're gorgeous.'

'And I'm aching for you.'

'Are you, now?' She looked incredibly pleased with herself. 'I need you to put that sling back on. Your hand needs support.'

He couldn't help groaning with impatience. 'You drive me crazy.'

'Oh, I intend to,' she said, her voice husky and making his pulse kick up a notch. 'But I don't want you undoing all the hard work we've put in so far. Sling. *Now.*'

He sighed, and let her put the sling back in place. 'I

could really do with two hands to do what I want to do with you.'

'Tough. You've got one. Improvise,' she said, giving him a wicked look from under her lashes.

Slowly, slowly, he dropped to his knees, stroking her abdomen. 'You feel nice.' He moved closer and nuzzled her skin. 'You smell nice.' He traced a circle round her navel with the tip of his tongue. 'And you—' He was aware that she was shaking, and stopped. 'What?'

'I'm trying to work out if you're doing the three monkeys or the three bears.' Her eyes were lit with amusement.

She'd been *laughing*?

'That was supposed to be sexy,' he said, giving her a pained look.

She just laughed at him. 'You should've worn the domino, Zorro,' she teased.

'You like the idea of being seduced by a masked hero?' he asked.

She stopped laughing then and caught her breath. And then she traced his lower lip with the tip of her index finger.

He moved to catch her finger between his lips and sucked. Hard.

'Ohhh.' It was a high, breathy sound. Sheer desire. And his whole body responded to it.

He kissed her throat, nuzzled the hollows of her collarbones; she quivered 'Your *hand*,' she said, looking at him and then looking at the bed.

'Then I guess you get to be in charge,' he said, and pulled back the covers and lay back against the pillows.

She swallowed hard, then retrieved a condom.

'Marco, I...haven't done this for a while,' she said.

'It doesn't matter.' But he was glad she'd reminded him. So he could hold himself back, take it slowly for her. Make sure that she was ready for him. 'Come here.'

Looking suddenly as shy as she had all those years ago, the very first time they'd done this, she walked over to the bed. Sat down.

He sat up again and stroked her face. 'Stop worrying,' he whispered. 'I think we both need this.'

'Yes.' Her green eyes were huge.

He kissed her, very slowly, lingering until he felt her breathing change. And then he lay back, drawing her with him.

She straddled him, and he could feel the heat of her sex against his skin.

'Now?' he whispered.

'Now.' She rolled on the condom with shaking hands, then slowly eased herself down on him.

This felt perfect. 'You feel amazing,' he whispered, pushing deeper. 'It's like the very first time.'

'Yeah.'

Her voice sounded shaky. Was she crying? He stopped moving and shifted slightly so he could look her in the eye.

'Are you OK?' he asked softly. 'Really OK?'

She nodded, clearly not trusting herself to speak.

'If you want me to stop, Becca, then I'll stop. It's fine to change your mind.' He touched her cheek with the backs of his fingers.

'It's just—it's been a while for me. And I wasn't expecting...' Her voice trailed off.

'Neither was I,' he said. And although he wanted her, very badly, he knew she needed reassurance before anything else could happen. 'Do you want me to stop?' he asked quietly.

She shook her head. 'I don't want you to stop.'

'I don't want to stop, either.' He lowered his mouth to hers in a warm, sweet, reassuring kiss. He could feel the softness of her breasts against his skin, the hardness of her nipples—and he loved being wrapped in her warm, sweet depths.

Pleasure spiralled through him and he slowed everything right down, focusing on the pleasure; he could tell it was the same for her because she gasped and bore down on him, letting him push deeper.

And then he felt her body tighten round his, pushing him into his own climax—and it was sweeter than anything he could ever remember. Sweeter than even their first time. It felt as if he'd just found something he hadn't even known was missing—but now he knew what it was he was complete.

'My Becca,' he whispered, and sat up so he could wrap his good arm round her and hold her close.

She rested her forehead against his shoulder. 'Marco.'

They just stayed together for a while, holding each other close, enjoying the closeness. And then finally he said softly, 'I need to deal with the condom. But I'm telling you now: I want to go to sleep with you in my arms. I need you close.'

'That's fine by me,' she said softly.

Becca woke the next morning, curled against Marco's side. He was lying on his back and her head was resting on his right shoulder. She gently eased herself away so she didn't wake him, and propped herself on one elbow so she could watch him sleeping.

Asleep, relaxed, he was beautiful—and he was all hers. She didn't have to share him with anyone. It was better even than in South Africa, because there they'd both been busy and had been needed by other people; here it was just the two of them in their own little bubble.

She knew it was going to end and she ought to keep her heart more guarded, but at the same time she knew she still loved him. She needed to be with him for as long as she could.

If only things could have been different. If only she'd had a different life growing up. Maybe if her past had been squeaky clean his family might be able to overlook the fact that she didn't have royal blood—but her past was far from squeaky clean. She'd been in a rehab clinic at sixteen. And you couldn't change the past—you could only do your best to hide it.

Later that day, Becca noticed Maria wincing in pain as she put the tray on the table.

'Maria, would you sit down for a moment, please?' she asked.

The housekeeper looked slightly worried. 'Is there a problem? Something wrong?'

'I think that's what you could tell me,' Becca said gently. 'Remember what I do for a living—OK, I'm a hand specialist, but before I specialised I learned about the rest of the body's systems, and I think right now you're in pain.'

Maria gave a dismissive flap of her hand. 'It doesn't matter. This sort of thing happens when you get older.'

'Arthritis?' Becca guessed.

'My hip. And the tablets don't work as well as they used to,' Maria admitted. 'Maybe I should go back to the doctor and see if he can give me something else. But, please—don't tell Marco. I don't want the family to think I can't do my job and pension me off. I love working here.'

'Marco's in the gym and, knowing him, he'll be there for a while,' Becca said. 'If you wouldn't mind me examining you, I might be able to give you some exercises to help with the pain.'

'Really?'

'Really. One of my favourite patients has arthritic hands. I give her exercises to help with the mobility and the pain, and I've seen a big difference over the last six months. I can do the same for you.'

Maria looked close to tears. 'That's so kind of you, *hermosa*.'

'It's the least I can do, seeing how you've spoiled me since I've been here,' Becca said.

Gently, she examined the older woman, getting her to go through a range of movements so she could see where the trouble spots were. She'd just finished teaching Maria some exercises when Marco came back into the room.

'Good morning, Maria,' he said. 'Am I too late for coffee?'

'It's cold now. I'll get you some more,' Maria said.

'It's my fault. I made her sit down and talk to me,' Becca said with a smile. 'She's told me loads of scurrilous stories about you as a child.'

'I was a perfect child,' Marco protested, laughing.

'A perfect monster, yeah,' Becca teased. 'You told me yourself how your mum had to apologise for you all the time. Making little princesses kiss your pet frog.'

'I didn't make them kiss my pet frog. I just put him on the chair next to them.' He grinned. 'They were annoying. And it stopped them pestering me to play dressing-up games when I would rather have been climbing trees.'

Maria laughed. 'He was a bit of a tearaway.'

When Maria had left, she looked at Marco. 'Can I talk to you about something?'

'Sure.'

'And it won't go any further than you?'

He frowned. 'What's wrong?'

'I need that promise first.'

'OK. I promise.'

'Thank you. There's just something I've noticed. Maria doesn't have a lot of help, and her job's physically quite demanding.'

He looked at her. 'Are you saying this with your work hat on?'

'Pointing out that some work systems might need improving? Yes,' she said. 'Though don't you *dare* say a word to Maria.'

'Patient confidentiality?' he asked softly.

'I,' Becca said crisply, 'am not answering that. But I was just thinking there must be a way to make things a bit easier for her, but doing it tactfully, so she doesn't feel that you all think she's no longer competent.'

'I think,' Marco said, 'I get what you're saying—and also what you're not saying. And, yes, in that case, we need to be tactful. She's been with the family since Ferdy was a baby. She's part of us. That's not ever going to change and I'll make sure she knows it. But I agree, she needs more help. I should have noticed.'

'Why would you notice? You're a prince.'

'I'm a soldier,' he corrected. 'And I look at systems all the time. How things work. I should take more notice in my own home instead of being complacent and thinking that this is the way we've always done things, so this is the way it's always going to be. I'll talk to Mamá and get it sorted.'

'Good.'

'That's teamwork,' Marco said, and gave her a high five with his right hand.

'Talking of work,' Becca said, 'now you've finished being a gym rat, time to do your hand exercises.'

'Yes, boss,' Marco teased, and let her release the hand strap on his splint.

Whatever Becca's mysterious commitments were, she'd clearly managed to change her schedule because she actually agreed to stay overnight every night for the next week. Though Marco noticed that she insisted on going home before dinner and doing her own laundry. Although in some respects it annoyed him, because it was so unnecessary, at the same time he liked Becca's sense of independence and the fact that she wasn't afraid to say no to him.

It made him realise that he was falling more and more deeply in love with her. And that wasn't fair to either of them, because he still hadn't worked out how he could fit her into his life along with his royal duties.

Or maybe, he thought, he was just getting a bit stir-crazy at being cooped up here. Maybe they needed to go out and escape all the worries and just have a bit of fun. It couldn't be somewhere too public, because they'd be caught on a camera lens, but he knew somewhere they could go.'

'Tomorrow night,' he said, 'let's go dancing.'

She looked surprised, then wary. 'Dancing?'

'At a club.'

'But—isn't that a bit, well, public?'

'It's an exclusive club in Soho, owned by friends of mine.' He smiled. 'Mardi's. Short for Mardi Gras—they play mainly Latin music. Samba, salsa, tango.'

'Your kind of music?' she guessed.

'Absolutely. And it's somewhere that our privacy will be respected, because my friends will be careful for us.'

She smiled. 'You're asking me out on a date, Prince Marco?'

He shrugged. 'If you like.'

'You and I—we've never been on a date,' she said thoughtfully. 'Not even in South Africa.'

'Then maybe it's time we did.'

She bit her lip. 'Marco, we…'

He pressed the tip of his forefinger to her mouth, very gently. 'I know. But we agreed—we'll live for the moment. And I want to dance with you, Becca.'

She looked thrilled. And then wary again. 'I, um, don't really do clubs normally. So, um, I don't think I have anything suitable to wear.'

'That's easily sorted. What size are you?'

He eyes widened. 'What?'

'What size are your shoes, your clothes?'

'No way am I going to wear a dress that one of your women left behind,' she said, sounding disgusted.

He laughed. 'I wouldn't insult you by suggesting anything like that. Apart from the fact that I don't normally bring women here, the only women within twenty years of your age who leave stuff here are my sister Bella or Ferdy's fiancée Marianna. Although they're both about the same size as you, their styles aren't the same as yours.'

'Uh-huh.'

'And, just for the record, the press exaggerates hugely. I don't date anywhere near as much as they like to make out, and I'm quite picky about who I sleep with, too.'

'Sorry.' She sighed. 'I'm not good at this relationship business.'

'Neither am I,' he said softly. 'I've made my share of mistakes. Look at what happened when I rescued my men. I made the most stupid tactical error. And other people paid for that.'

Mistakes.

This was her cue to tell him about the massive ones she'd made.

But she knew that if she told him the truth about her past, he'd start to despise her. Besides, she'd moved on from those grim, dark days. It was better to keep her own counsel.

'I'll sort you out something to wear,' he said. 'I need your dress size and your shoe size.'

'So, what? We find something on the internet and you get the stuff delivered here?'

'Better than that,' he said with a grin. 'Leave this with me.'

It wasn't until the next morning that she discovered what he meant, when Maria showed a couple of men holding armfuls of bags into the sitting room.

'Your Highness—I hope we've come up with a selection you'll like,' the first man said, bowing.

Marco had organised a shop to come to them?

And then Becca recognised the logo on the bags. A luxury department store. A place where the celebrity clients of the Harley Street clinic all had accounts, no doubt, but it was way out of Becca's league. She was too stunned to say a word.

'I'm sure you've covered everything,' Marco said with a smile. 'Thank you for being so accommodating. As you can see, I'd find shopping a little tricky at the moment.' He indicated his strapped-up hand.

'We're always happy to help, Your Highness,' the man said. 'Shall we call by this afternoon to collect what didn't suit?'

'That would be perfect. Thank you so much.'

No wonder the newspapers called him Prince Charming. Because he was.

When the shop's staff had left, Becca sat down on one of the sofas. 'Marco, please don't think I'm ungrateful, but I wasn't expecting this. I'm afraid my salary doesn't run to designer originals.'

'It doesn't have to. This was my idea, so it's my bill.'

She frowned. 'I don't expect you to buy my clothes, Marco.'

'Becca, this isn't about being a control freak and telling you what to do—I just wanted to do something nice for you, buy you a dress and shoes so we can go dancing. Is that so very bad?'

She grimaced. 'Sorry. Now I feel like a spoiled brat having a tantrum.'

He laughed. 'Trust me, I've seen spoiled women having a tantrum—and that didn't even come close.'

'It just feels weird, having a shop come to me instead of the other way round.'

'My mother and my sister do this all the time,' he said.

'Royal privilege?'

'More like valued customer privilege—they spend a lot of money at this particular store, and the store looks after them so they don't take their custom to a different store. Either they get stuff brought here, or the store opens for them outside normal shopping hours so they can go shopping in peace. I'm pretty sure they do that for other customers who spend a lot of money with them, too.'

'I guess,' Becca said, still feeling awkward.

He shrugged. 'If it makes you feel better, this way it's safer for me—if we go shopping in actual shops, supposing someone knocks into me and damages my hand?'

She coughed. 'Right, and that's not going to happen at all if we go dancing tonight?'

'It's not,' he said, 'because we're going to a small and fairly exclusive club.'

The one owned by his friends. No doubt from the moneyed set. Where she wouldn't fit in.

As if he guessed her fears, he said softly, 'Becca. This is just you and me, getting away from it all for an evening. Besides, I loathe shopping. I hate dragging round the shops. The chances are there will be someone tailing me in the hope of getting a story, and would you really want pictures of any underwear you bought splashed all over the tabloids, along with a lot of speculation?'

She'd hate being in the spotlight. And the idea of the

press finding out anything about her made her bone-deep terrified. 'No.'

'Come on. Let's have a look at what they brought.'

The bags contained dresses, underwear, shoes, and accessories—in lots of different styles and colours. 'This is amazing.'

'So do I get a fashion show?' he asked.

She raised an eyebrow. 'Does this mean you're going to choose my dress?'

'No, *you're* going to choose the dress, but I want the fun of seeing you in every single one of them.'

Becca was surprised to discover just how much fun it was, dressing up and walking up and down the sitting room while Marco looked on thoughtfully.

Finally she chose a classic little black dress, shoes that were high enough to be elegant and yet low enough to dance in, and a small evening bag that was just big enough to contain her phone, keys, and some money.

'There's something missing,' he said. 'Ah, here we go.' He took a pile of boxes from another bag and started opening them. 'Diamonds—no, they're cold and you're all about warmth.' He opened another box. 'How about this set of black pearls? Look at the lustre; you can see your reflection in them.'

Diamonds and pearls? This didn't seem real. Becca rarely wore jewellery, but when she did it was costume jewellery.

Then Marco opened another box. 'No, this is the one. Just like your eyes.' He held up an emerald choker.

A chill ran through her. 'Aren't emeralds supposed to be unlucky?'

'No. That's just because they're more fragile than other stones and are more likely to chip.'

She narrowed her eyes at him. 'And how do you know so much about jewellery?'

'I had a misspent youth.' He grinned. 'OK, my grand-mother has a few emerald pieces and she told me.'

Again, Becca was reminded of the differences between them. Nobody in her family had ever had jewellery, let alone 'a few emerald pieces'. As far as Becca knew, her mother had pawned her engagement ring and wedding ring so she could spend the money on alcohol.

She pushed the thought away. They'd agreed to live for the moment. And this was a night out at an exclusive club where they'd be safe from the crowds. 'Thank you.'

CHAPTER EIGHT

THAT EVENING, WHEN Becca emerged from the bathroom with her hair pinned up and the emerald choker round her neck, Marco looked at her, his eyes widening.

'You look stunning. Not that you don't look beautiful every day,' he added swiftly, 'but I've never seen you all dressed up to go out before. That dress suits you.'

'Thank you.'

'I've been thinking—it's probably easiest if I go first, then send Rafa back for you.'

She frowned. 'Why are we going separately?'

He grimaced. 'Because it's easier.'

'How? We're leaving from the same place and going to the same place, so it makes sense to share the transport.' Then understanding dawned. 'Marco, you said we were going dancing—on a real date. Have you changed your mind? Am I not good enough to be seen with you in public?'

'It's nothing to do with that.' He sighed. 'Look, my life is pretty much like a goldfish bowl. There was a media blanket when I was in Afghanistan but it's back to the usual free-for-all now. I just want to spare you from that.'

She went cold. Did he know about her past? Had he found out, somehow? His family's security team had probably investigated her and discovered the truth.

'It's just not much fun being hounded by the press,

that's all,' he said softly. 'I've seen how much it's knocked Marianna's confidence. I guess I'm trying to protect you.'

So maybe he *didn't* know the truth about her, then. She just prayed she could keep her secrets until their fling was over.

'I'll go first, then meet you in there. Rafa will drive you,' he said, and kissed her swiftly. 'You look lovely. And I can't wait to go dancing with you. See you shortly.'

Was this the right thing to do? Becca wondered. Plus it would be really intimidating, meeting him in a strange place where he knew everyone but she would know nobody.

But Marco had been getting twitchy for the last couple of days. Maybe it would settle him, seeing his friends.

She went to chat with Maria in the kitchen while Rafa drove Marco to the club.

'Look at you, *hermosa*! Gorgeous,' Maria said, resting her hands on Becca's shoulders and looking at her.

'Thank you.'

'You're good for Marco, you know,' Maria said. 'Not like those fluffy women who chatter on about nothing and only care about their clothes.'

If only. Becca wrinkled her nose. 'I'm not under any illusions that it's going to last, Maria. I'm not from the right background.'

'Love always finds a way,' Maria said. 'And you love him, don't you?'

'I've loved him for years,' Becca admitted. 'I never got over him when he left me last time.'

'This time,' Maria said, 'it will be different.'

Becca knew it wouldn't be—how could there possibly be a happy ending for her and Marco when they came from such different worlds?—but she smiled at the older woman and pretended to agree.

Then Rafa came into the kitchen. 'I'll take you to the Prince,' he said.

Becca baulked when he opened the door at the back for her. 'Would you mind very much if I sat with you, instead?'

'It's a scary lifestyle the Prince leads, yes?' Rafa smiled at her. 'Sure, come and sit with me. I don't mind.'

He drove her to Soho and parked just outside the club.

'Are you going to be all right? Would you like me to walk you in?' he asked.

'No, I'm just being pathetic. I'll be fine. But thank you for being kind, Rafa.'

'No problem, *señorita*. Have a good time and I'll see you when you're ready to go home.'

She nodded. 'Marco will ring you?'

Rafa smiled. 'I wait here until you're ready.' Clearly he could see that she was about to protest that he shouldn't have to hang around, because he said gently, 'I have the radio for company. It's fine.'

'Then thank you. I'll see you later.'

She walked up the stairs to Mardi's and took a deep breath. It was ridiculous to feel so nervous; but at the same time she knew that she didn't fit into Marco's world.

He'd said the club was owned by friends of his. She hoped that they would at least be polite to her on the surface, for his sake. It would be awful if they were mean and sneered at her.

She took another deep breath and pushed the door open.

The club was amazing. From outside it was a nondescript building, but inside the walls were painted a deep burgundy, and there were fairy lights everywhere. It made the place look magical.

There was a band playing on the small stage—a singer with a guitar, another guitarist, a double bassist and a drummer—and people were dancing. The floor was shiny black with lots of tiny lights set into it so people could see their feet as they danced.

She scanned the room, looking for Marco. He was over by the bar; he lifted his good arm in greeting, and she nerved herself to walk over to him, knowing that the people standing with him would be scrutinising her.

'Good evening, Becca,' he said softly, and kissed her. 'I did wonder if you'd chicken out.'

She shook her head. 'I couldn't do that—what if you knocked your arm and needed urgent physio?'

He laughed. 'No, I just need you.' He stroked her face. 'Come and meet my friends. This is Rupert and Henry—they own the club. They were at school with me,' he explained.

'Hello, dear girl,' Rupert said. 'Delighted to meet you.'

'*Enchanté,*' Henry said, and kissed her hand.

'And this is Seraphina and Talia.'

Rupert and Henry's girlfriends? she wondered. They were incredibly elegant—reminding her of Audrey Hepburn on a really stellar day—and she felt totally out of place.

'Oh, I love your shoes,' one of them said.

'And your nail polish. Such a gorgeous colour.'

They both smiled at her—and then suddenly everything was all right. She'd been worrying about nothing.

She learned that Seraphina and Talia were both Rupert's sisters, and that Rupert and Henry were life partners as well as business partners.

'Marco bailed them out last year when the club was about to go into receivership. He won't let them pay him back until they're totally on their feet again. He's really one of the good guys,' Seraphina confided.

'He certainly is,' Rupert said, clearly overhearing the last bit. 'We used to call him El Príncipe at school—The Prince.' He smiled. 'Though when he met my sisters and

everyone else's we changed that to El Príncípe Azul—
Prince Charming.' He grinned. 'He was a hero to the rest
of us, though—he stopped one guy bullying one of the little ones, even though he was four years older than Marco.
Nobody's quite sure exactly what he did or said, but we
know it involved a sword.'

Becca blinked. 'A sword?'

'And the school needed to buy a new mattress,' Henry
added.

'You're telling me Marco killed someone?' she asked
in a shocked whisper.

'Not quite, dear girl—wrong fluids. The guy wet himself to the point where the mattress was ruined.' Rupert
smiled. 'Mind you, he never bullied anyone again after
that.'

'Did he get into trouble?'

'Marco?' Henry grimaced. 'Um, yes—you can't exactly
go round threatening people with swords, even if you *are*
being a hero. The head confiscated his sword and banned
him from fencing practice for the rest of the term—but we
all knew the teachers were on his side about it.'

'Interestingly,' Rupert added, 'the bully left at the end
of term and never came back.'

Becca wasn't surprised that Marco had helped a bullied child. It was totally who he was: protective and kind-
hearted.

'You do know he's a serious fencer—that he's an international champion?' Henry asked.

Becca looked at Marco. 'I had no idea. You never said.'

Marco rolled his eyes. 'Honestly, it's not that big a deal.'

'A gold medallist, no less.' Rupert described a huge
circle on his chest. 'Only our Marco would say it's no big
deal. And you know when celebs open things by cutting
ribbons? Well, El Príncípe here does it with a sword.'

'Sabre,' Marco corrected dryly.

'It's still awesome—and he wears a dress uniform and looks…' Rupert fanned himself and grinned. 'Well. Such a shame you only like women, El Príncipe Azul.'

''Fraid so.' Marco grinned back.

Becca smiled. 'Hey, Rupert, do you know what his surgeon called him at the clinic?'

Marco groaned. 'If you tell them that, Becca, they'll never let me live it down.'

'Too late, dear boy,' Rupert said. 'You have to tell us now, Becca, or we'll come and criticise your curtains.'

She couldn't help laughing; she liked Marco's friends immensely. 'I'm sure you'd never be so mean.'

'Come on, what did the surgeon call him, Becca?' Rupert asked, wagging his finger at her. 'Tell us. Tell us now.'

She paused for maximum effect. 'Zorro.'

Henry hooted in delight. 'How *perfect*. Wait a second.' He disappeared, and came back with a domino mask. 'Come on, dear boy, put it on.'

Marco gave him a pained look, but did so.

'Doesn't he look perfect? El Príncipe, the freedom fighter—Zorro.' Henry looked pleased with himself.

Rupert looked at Marco. 'Hmm. Does the surgeon know about the medal, I wonder?'

'No—and you're not going to say anything to him, are you, Becca?' Marco said.

Becca just smiled. 'Tell me more, Henry.'

'Ferdy, now, he was the serious one who was top of the class at everything, but Marco here was the cool guy—the one who managed to make his uniform non-regulation, and he played lead guitar in a band,' Henry said.

That didn't surprise Becca in the slightest.

'Everyone's sister fell in love with him,' Rupert said, with a stern look at his own sisters, 'and he had hordes of girls trying to sneak into school to see him.'

'He's good at everything he does,' Henry said. 'If he wasn't such a nice guy, you'd have to hate him for it.'

'Oh, enough.' Marco flapped a dismissive hand. 'I'm going to get drinks. What's everyone having? Rupert, Henry, look after my girl,' he said, once he'd taken the list of what everyone wanted to drink.

Becca found herself surprisingly happy to be left with his friends. They weren't being nice to her for Marco's sake; they were being nice because they *were* nice.

'I haven't seen him smile like that for a long time,' Rupert said. 'You've made a difference to him, Becca.'

She gave him a rueful smile. 'We don't come from the same world. I'm under no illusions here.'

'It doesn't matter where you come from,' Henry said, 'it's who you are that matters, how you treat other people. Marco believes that, too.'

Becca thought, *If only that could be true.* But her past was always going to get in the way. The only thing she could do was to make the most of now, store up the memories for the rest of her life.

'So we're dancing the tango tonight?' Marco asked when he returned with the drinks.

'You can't do it with one arm, Marco,' Rupert said.

'Yes, I can.'

Rupert rolled his eyes. 'Not if Becca hasn't done it before—unless you take the girl's part and let her lead, that is.'

Marco just grinned. 'Yeah, right. That's *so* going to happen.'

'Can I show you the steps, Becca?' Rupert asked.

She looked at Marco, who sighed. 'Rupert teaches this stuff for a living, so I guess he'll do a better job than I would.'

Rupert laughed. 'I should jolly well hope so. Especially as right now you only have one arm! Come on, Becca, darling. Now, the tango is all about stalking. See how El Príncipe here is looking daggers at me right now? That's how a man's meant to look in the tango. And here we go. Slow-slow, quick-quick.' He talked her through the basic steps. 'And at the end, when you turn round, you stamp your feet—it's great when someone has spent all day annoying you and you can stomp about like this.'

She laughed. 'You think Marco spends all day annoying me?'

'Dear girl, he's a soldier and he orders people about. Of *course* he's annoying.'

And to think she'd been worried about coming here tonight. Marco had been right, after all—she was enjoying this, had relaxed, and was really having fun.

'And there's a lovely little move where you snap your head to the side—oh, but wait, the sling.' Rupert grimaced. 'It might not be kind to him. I don't want to hurt him.'

'Perhaps we'll leave that one for now,' she said.

'OK. But you can do the corner. Marco, no promenades, OK?' Rupert instructed.

Marco just rolled his eyes.

'Let's go through it again, dear girl. Marvellous. Now he can dance with you holding you only with his right hand.' He looked thoughtful. 'But the tango is special. We're not ready to dance that yet. We'll warm everyone up with some salsa first.'

Marco took off the domino mask and put it in his pocket.

'You have to wear it for the tango,' Henry said. 'I ought to see if I can find you a cape.'

'Great idea. Then we can make him do the Paso and wave the cape about,' Rupert agreed.

'Oh, please.' Marco rolled his eyes. 'Next thing you'll have me waving a sword about.'

'Now, there's an idea,' Rupert said with a grin.

'Becca, tell them I'm unbalanced with my arm like this,' Marco pleaded.

'Unbalanced, hmm?' Henry made a mocking circle with his forefinger on his temple.

Becca couldn't help laughing.

'I give up,' Marco said, and kissed her.

Becca was having a great time. Marco taught her the basic salsa steps, and she even recognised the music— *Living la Vida Loca* and *L'Americano*.

'Now, Rupert would tell you that the salsa is a party dance. Obviously if I had both arms working properly I could teach you different steps and the arm movements, but...' He grimaced. 'Not tonight.'

She smiled. 'I'm glad you realise that will have to wait, bec—'

'Because it's not light work for my hand,' he cut in, using his good hand to make the sign of someone talking too much at her. 'Yeah, yeah. Heard it a thousand times.'

'Ah, so he's finally listening,' she teased back.

She was so glad he'd brought her here. This wasn't her usual kind of scene, but she enjoyed it, and nobody commented or tried to push her into having alcohol when she asked for sparkling water. She liked his friends, too; they seemed warm and genuine and really cared about him. And they were interested in her job, too; although when one of the girls asked for her advice about RSI Marco cut in gently, 'Hey, guys, she's off duty.'

'I don't mind. Call me at work,' Becca said, 'and I'll sort it out for you.'

They were taking a break from dancing when a woman sashayed over to them. She looked familiar, though Becca couldn't quite place her.

'Darling, how lovely to see you,' she said to Marco, and draped herself over him.

'Anastasia.' Marco was polite but seemed distant.

Anastasia kept glancing at Becca, but didn't ask to be introduced and pretty much ignored her, concentrating all her energies on Marco.

That was when the penny dropped. Anastasia must have dated Marco at some time in the past. Becca was about to make an excuse that she needed the toilet, but Marco's fingers tightened round hers, as if he'd guessed that she was desperate to go and was asking her to stay.

Eventually Anastasia gave up trying to persuade Marco to dance with her, and left in a bit of a huff.

'Sorry about that,' Marco said. 'I didn't know she was going to be here tonight.'

'Is she an ex?' Becca asked softly.

He nodded. 'It was over months ago, but she wasn't too happy when I ended it.'

Becca knew how that felt—and she also knew she'd feel that way again.

'Becca—don't overthink this,' Marco said. 'I liked her when we dated, but there wasn't a real spark between us. It's not like how…'

She caught her breath—was he going to tell her how he felt about her?

Did he feel the same way about her as she did about him?

'Not like how things are between us,' he said softly. 'You're so different from the other women in my life.'

He could say that again, she thought wryly.

'There's something about you,' he said, 'something pure and innocent.'

Oh, help. He couldn't be more wrong.

'That's what drew me to you in South Africa, I think,' he said. 'You're not tarnished by life.'

Yes, she was. She'd been in rehab at sixteen. She'd seen the darkest sides of life. She'd watched people pour their lives away.

'I admire you,' he said, his eyes dark with sincerity. 'Really I do.'

How would Marco react if he knew the truth about her—if he knew that every day she had to remind herself to breathe and never, ever let her life spiral back to where it had been? He wouldn't admire her then. Nobody in their right mind would admire someone who'd skipped school in favour of vodka.

Maybe she should break it off now, before he could find out the truth about her and she saw his feelings change and crumble into dust.

And yet they'd agreed this was happy-for-now. They both knew their fling would have to end when he healed enough to go back to his royal duties. Was it so wrong of her to want to cherish these last few days together, to eke out every precious moment?

'Becca?' he asked softly. 'What's wrong?'

She was saved from having to answer when Henry came over and patted them both on the shoulder. 'It's time to tango. You need to wear your mask.'

Marco rolled his eyes but put the domino on.

When the music began, they went onto the dance floor.

'It's not the same with only one arm, but one day I'll dance with you properly,' Marco promised. 'For now, I'm afraid this will have to do.'

The music was incredibly sensual. Becca found herself picking up the beat easily after Rupert's earlier tutorial, especially as Marco guided her with his good arm and used his body to make her move the right way. He talked her through the steps: slow-slow, quick-quick, swaying along.

Then a spin. 'Quick-quick, turn; quick-quick, stamp— and we do it again,' he said.

Then they found themselves in the corner of the dance floor. Marco leaned over her and drew his hand into the small of her back, making her arch backwards. For a moment Becca's heart skipped a beat and she thought he was going to kiss her. But then he pulled back, guiding her with his good hand to lean over him, before repeating the move so that he was leaning over her and his lips were just millimetres from hers.

It took her breath away and the mask made everything ten times worse, because it made him look like a movie star. Sexy as hell.

He danced her round the corner and along the next side of the room, keeping her close and his thighs thrust between hers.

'Oh, my God, Marco—I had no idea you could dance like this,' she said.

'I love the tango,' he told her. 'It's the same stance as boxing—but I'm more of a lover than a fighter.'

He was both, she thought. A lover and a fighter—for freedom and truth and decency.

And she loved every single bit of him.

She was shocked by how hot the dance made her feel—how much she wanted him. And it decided her: no, she wouldn't tell him about her past. She'd take these sweet, stolen moments as they were and not spoil them.

When the dance ended, he kissed her lingeringly.

'Marco—can we go home?' she asked.

He gave her a slow, sensual smile, as if he knew what she was really asking. 'Great idea. Let's go home.'

CHAPTER NINE

MARCO AND BECCA said a quiet goodbye to Henry and Rupert, then left the club wrapped in each other's arms. But the second they stepped outside the front door flashes started popping in their faces.

On instinct, Becca covered her face. This was just like the press pack outside the clinic when the news of Marco's injury broke. Except this time they appeared to be focused on him.

And on her.

Panic flooded through her. She prayed they hadn't caught a picture of her face. If they found out who she was they'd reveal her past to the world and, worst of all, to Marco. The man she'd lied to.

She had to get out of here.

Now.

Just as she was about to run, Marco clamped her to his side. 'Keep your head down and don't worry—just walk. I'll protect you.'

No, you can't protect me, she thought. *Nobody can protect me. Not now.*

Marco's bodyguard—who'd been so discreet that she hadn't even noticed him at the club—materialised on the other side and cleared a path to the car.

The noise levels were unbelievable. People were all talking and yelling at once, and she could barely make out the words; it was just a babble of noise. Flashbulbs were still going off, lighting up every step they took. What? Were they waiting for her to trip and fall over? For her skirt to fly up and show her knickers? They were like a crowd of teenage bullies, going on and on and on, and never shutting up. Pushing and pushing and pushing.

'Who's the girl, Marco?'

'Who's your lady friend?'

'Are you going to leave us a glass slipper, Cinderella?'

And the comments were interspersed with mocking catcalls and whistles, no doubt designed to make her look them in the eye so they could get a clear picture of her face.

'Ignore them. They're simply trying to get a reaction,' Marco said.

Just like playground bullies, she thought.

Except Marco wasn't going to be able to protect her as he'd protected the little boy at school by facing the bully down, because you couldn't face down the press. They'd find their story and twist it and twist it until they got their sensational headlines and their sales, not caring whose lives they wrecked in the process.

They just about made it to the car.

'Take me home,' she begged as she closed the car door on the rabble outside. 'Please take me home.'

'Rafa, back to Regent's Park, please,' Marco said.

'No, I want to go to *my* home,' Becca said, close to tears. 'They'll follow us to your place—if I go back to mine I can disappear and they won't find me. They don't know who I am so it'll all blow over.'

He took her hand. 'Becca, even if Rafa breaks a few speed limits, it won't make a difference. Some of the paps have motorbikes, so they will be able to keep up with us. And do you really want to be doorstepped at your place?'

She thought of how the paparazzi had been at the clinic, blocking the whole street to get a picture or a quote about one of their celebrity patients. That would be unthinkable in her quiet little street.

'At least at my home you'll be protected. You won't be out there on your own.'

She felt sick. Maybe she ought to tell him the truth about her past, right here and now—but she just couldn't face seeing the disgust in his eyes if he knew what she was and what she'd done.

She hadn't cried since the day she'd found out Marco had abandoned her without a word in South Africa. She'd thought she'd cried out all her tears then—but now she found herself sobbing, unable to stop.

Marco hated feeling so useless. There was nothing he could say or do to make this right for her. He knew she'd seen the paps in action before, given that the Harley Street clinic where she worked treated celebrities, but nothing could prepare you for actually having it happen to *you*. He'd been used to it all his life, but he knew it must be overwhelming to someone who wasn't used to living in the public eye.

When they got back to Regent's Park, he made her a mug of hot milk and shooed Maria away. 'No, of course I haven't done anything to make her cry. It's shock because the press followed us. Don't worry, I'll look after her.'

Becca didn't drink the milk. All she did was cry silently.

'Talk to me, Becca,' he begged, seriously worried. 'You're blowing this out of proportion. Once they work out who the mystery girl is they'll have their story. They'll run on for a bit about the prince and the physio, and then it'll die down. There might be a couple of headlines—*Who's that girl?* or something like that—and then they'll find someone else to annoy.'

She shook her head and just looked at him in mute appeal.

He didn't understand why she was reacting this badly.

What did she have to worry about? It didn't matter that she wasn't a socialite.

'Come on, let's go to bed,' he said. 'And, no, this isn't me trying to take advantage of you. It's me saying I want to hold you and make you feel safe until you fall asleep.'

To his horror, more tears streamed down her face.

'Becca, talk to me. What's wrong?'

She shook her head, clearly unable to get the words out.

'If I didn't have a busted arm, I'd carry you,' he said.

She looked horror-stricken at that, no doubt worried that he'd hurt himself.

He brushed his mouth lightly against hers. 'Come on, let's go to bed. Everything will be fine in the morning.'

He lay there with her curled against him. He knew she was still crying because he could feel the warmth and wetness of her tears against his skin, but he didn't know how to fix this, what to do or say. He just held her and hoped that he was right about the press and all would be fine in the morning.

All the same, he slept badly. Becca was clearly exhausted as he could hear her breathing, slow and deep; she wasn't faking sleep.

Unable to settle, he got up early, without waking her, and checked the news sites on the internet.

As he'd expected, there were a few *Who's that girl?* headlines.

But then he hit 'refresh' and saw the headlines of the story change.

My Nights of Shame with Prince's Lover...

What?

Marco flicked through the reports. They seemed to be focused on a guy called Barney, telling how Becca had been drunk out of her mind on vodka. According to him, she'd taken tablets to get high, then spent a sordid night with him.

No, this had to be some kind of mistake. Becca wasn't like that. She wasn't a wild child. The girl he'd met in South Africa had been sweet and shy. She'd been a virgin, for pity's sake. You couldn't fake that…could you?

And Marco knew for a fact that Becca didn't drink. He'd offered her champagne and cocktails and Pimm's, here on the roof garden, and she'd told him straight that she didn't drink. She'd drunk only mineral water last night at the club.

Then again, this could explain why she was teetotal. Because she'd had problems with drink before, now she couldn't trust herself with so much as a single sip of alcohol.

More news reports were coming through, all saying the same. Some had different levels of detail, but all of them said she'd been a wild child as a teen.

Why hadn't she told him?

Did she really think he would judge her for something that had happened years ago, when she was still little more than a child? Did she really think that he hadn't made some stupid mistakes himself?

He scanned another page and a fact leapt out at him.

Barney was in his late forties.

And if this had happened when Becca was sixteen, ten years ago…

What the hell had a man in his late thirties been doing with a teenager less than half his age?

Something about this wasn't right. Had the guy been grooming her? Had he been the one who'd given her the drink and the drugs?

Right at that second Marco wanted to hunt this Barney down. He wanted to pin the guy to the wall, with the tip of his sword at the scumbag's jugular vein, and demand some real answers.

And he was furious for himself for not protecting Becca.

Why had he been so stupid and pushed her into going out for a night of fun at Mardi's when she'd been reluctant to go in the first place?

Henry and Rupert were loyal to him, he knew, and would have been more likely to create a diversion for the press to keep their attention off him rather than rat him out. But there had been someone else at the club who'd had an axe to grind, especially given that he hadn't gone there alone. He was pretty sure he knew who'd tipped the press off. There was nothing he could do about it now it had happened, but he could make Anastasia apologise to Becca and then warn everyone that he knew what she'd done, so they knew Anastasia couldn't be trusted and they'd need to be careful what they said and did around her in future.

He felt as if he'd been sucked into the middle of a seething cauldron of guilt, anger, and despair. He was guilty and angry with himself that he hadn't been able to protect Becca from all this spite and that she'd been hurt; he was angry with Becca that she'd kept something so huge from him; and he was despairing because he realised now that he'd been working towards the idea that his family might accept her as his life partner, but he knew all this mess would close the conservative royal circles to her. Anyone involved with the monarchy had to be totally squeaky clean. And even though Becca had been very young at the time it had happened—and he was damn sure she hadn't been the instigator of the drink, drugs and sex stuff—the mud was still going to stick.

He heard the door to the library close and looked up. Becca was standing there, fully dressed, looking pale and drawn and incredibly nervous.

Becca could see that Marco was reading something on the internet. If her phone hadn't been out of charge she would have checked the news herself. But she had a nasty feeling that the truth was out now. All of it. In every deeply shameful detail.

She couldn't tell from his expression how he felt about it. He'd said last night that he admired her. Now, would he despise her?

'Are you all right?' he asked.

She nodded, and swallowed hard. 'It's in the papers, isn't it? Everything?'

'Yes.'

The story must have travelled round the whole world before breakfast. And now everyone knew just how bad her past had been.

'Why didn't you tell me?' he asked.

'I couldn't—I was…' The words stuck in her throat. 'I was ashamed,' she whispered. 'So ashamed.'

Just as she could see now that he was ashamed of his relationship with her—and she couldn't blame him for it. After all, she'd just dragged his name into the mud along with hers.

'You should have told me,' he said.

Becca knew she was being unfair, taking out her shock and fear on him, but she couldn't help the anger bubbling over. 'Why? So you could judge me and find me wanting?'

'No. I'd never do that.' He stared at her. 'But I'm hurt that you didn't trust me. That you didn't feel you could tell me the truth.'

'It wouldn't have changed anything, would it? You can't change the past. I was a drunk and I went to rehab. Telling you wouldn't make me *not* have been a drunk. And I'm not a drunk any more. So what was the point of rehashing the past and telling you?'

'Because at least then I would've heard it from you. I wouldn't have had to find out from some spiteful, scurrilous article.'

That was true. But right now she couldn't think straight.

The fear and the misery were uppermost. 'What's the point?' she asked. 'This thing between us—it's always been a fraud. Right from the start, in South Africa, when you lied about who you were. And this time round we couldn't even conduct a relationship in the open—it had to be kept a secret.'

'That's not fair,' Marco said. 'I wasn't the only one who wanted to keep it quiet. It suited you, too.'

Because she'd been an idiot and tried to hide from the truth. She should have known better.

'And,' he said, 'I might point out that I took you to meet my friends.'

She scoffed. 'We didn't even go to that club together. You went first, and I followed.'

'Because it was easier that way.'

'Easier for *you*. Do you have any idea how it felt, having to walk into a room on my own where you knew loads of people and I knew nobody?' Her eyes met his. 'You've lived such a privileged, pampered life—you have absolutely no idea what the real world's like.'

'Says the woman who works in a clinic catering to the rich and pampered,' he snapped back.

She flinched. 'We do a lot of charity work at 200 Harley Street. It isn't all facelifts and cosmetic procedures.'

'No?'

'No, it damn well isn't! You should know—they treated *you*. And I might not even have a career there any more.'

The one thing that had been certain in her life and now it wasn't. Fear of what was going to happen next made her bones feel as if they'd turned to liquid.

'Now all my past's been dragged up people aren't going to want me to treat them. I might even be struck off the register for unprofessional behaviour. It's all right for someone like you—you've got a family behind you, people who have your back. The only person I can really rely on is me—and I'm not going to be able to save myself from this.'

She shook her head.

'I can't stay here any more.' Not being so close to him, and knowing that he could never be hers any more. It was too much for her. She wanted out.

'You can't go. The paps are knee-deep outside,' he said wearily.

Not *Don't go because I love you and I want you to stay,* she noticed. He was worried about his *reputation*, not her. How had it come to this? How had all the love just leaked away overnight to leave them with nothing?

'I'll take my chances with them.' She lifted her chin. 'You know as well as I do it could never have worked out between us. We would never have got together in a million years. A prince can't date an addict—even a reformed one. But this time, Marco, this time *I* get to be the one to walk away.' Even though walking out on him was going to be like ripping her heart out.

How stupid she'd been to let herself fall in love with him all over again. With a man she knew was out of her reach, a man she could never have. They'd been living in a bubble, and now it was time to face the truth. It was over.

'Don't bother sending my stuff after me,' she said. 'Just throw it away. I don't want it any more.' Not when everything would be soaked in memories of him.

As Becca walked out, Marco was too shocked to stop her or follow her.

She clearly wasn't going to listen to his side of things.

Just when he'd been sure that he'd found someone who actually loved him for himself—someone who'd loved him before she even knew that he was a prince—he realised that he hadn't.

If she'd really loved him then she would have known she could tell him anything and it wouldn't matter.

The fact that she'd kept such a dark secret from him just proved that she didn't trust him—and if she didn't trust him, then how could he trust her?

So maybe she was right and it was better this way.

Maybe he should just let her go.

Because you couldn't give someone a royal order to love you. You couldn't order them to feel something they didn't feel.

And she was right, too, about them never getting together in a million years—they came from such different places. This was a reality check. The bubble had burst.

The only thing was, he didn't want it to be over.

And he didn't see how it could be anything *but* over.

Angry, hurt and just a tiny bit bitter, Marco sat at the piano and, one-handed, played all the saddest music he knew—music of pain and heartbreak and misery. And even then it couldn't express how he felt because he couldn't add in the bass, the deep notes of despair.

Becca left everything behind in the house at Regent's Park except her handbag.

Marco hadn't come after her. How stupid she'd been to hope that he'd care enough to follow her, that he'd ask her not to go and tell her they could work something out. The fact that he hadn't just proved that she'd just been a diversion for a bored prince while he waited for his hand to heal.

The press were waiting outside for her.

This time she wasn't going to let them make her cry. Or run. They could all go to hell, as far as she was concerned. Because she really didn't care any more. She didn't care about anything. Because she didn't have a heart left to care.

She just ignored the cameras flashing and the questions being yelled at her and strode through the park until she got to the Tube station. She was relieved that she already had a season ticket and didn't have to worry about buying a ticket. She lost some of the press pack in the morning rush hour as she went through the ticket barrier, then quickened her pace and took the left-hand side of the escalator so she could rush down in the middle of a pack of commuters instead of being trapped in one place. As she was halfway down the escalators, she felt the cool breeze signalling that a train was coming in and quickened her pace again. It didn't matter that the train was going in the wrong direction; she could sort that out later. She heard the station announcement telling passengers to mind the doors, and managed to squeeze on to the train.

Thank God none of the press pack was quick enough to follow her. No doubt they'd all been barged out of the way by irritated commuters.

Becca stayed on the train until it stopped at Embankment. Then she joined the throng of commuters, changed over to the Circle line, and caught the Tube through to Paddington. Hopefully the press wouldn't have managed to dig up her address yet.

She kept her head down as she left the train, but there was no sign of waiting paparazzi. Relieved, she headed for her flat and locked the door behind her.

Safe at last.

But just what did she do now?

Technically, she was still working one to one with Marco, so her caseload at the clinic was still being covered and she didn't have to worry about missing any appointments. But she knew that the rest of the staff would have seen the news. She couldn't just pretend that nothing had happened; she had to face it.

Just…not quite yet.

It was still early, officially before the start of the main day at the clinic, so with any luck she'd get the answering machine instead of the receptionist and could leave a message to buy herself a little more time and work out what to say. How to explain. How to apologise.

To her relief, the answering machine kicked in. 'Sorry, it's Becca,' she said. 'I'm not feeling well. I'm not working today. I'll keep you posted. Sorry.' Aware that she was gabbling, and not wanting to risk that someone would hear the message as she was speaking and pick up the phone, she hung up.

A few moments later the doorbell rang. Marco? Her heart leapt at the thought.

She picked up the Entryphone. 'Yes?'

'Becca Anderson?'

It was a voice she didn't recognise—and there was the kind of hubbub in the background that told her some of the journalists had managed to get hold of the electoral roll and found her details on it. Of course it wouldn't be Marco. He didn't even know where she lived.

She didn't answer the journalist, and hung up without pressing the button to let anyone in.

The doorbell rang again and again, but she ignored it.

No doubt now they were after her side of the story, to see if they could fill in any juicy details that Barney had left out.

Well, tough. They weren't going to get it. She had nothing to tell them.

Becca spent the next three days holed up in her apartment, not answering the phone or the door or emails, and keeping her mobile phone turned off most of the time. When she did turn it on, she deleted all messages from Marco without reading them and just ignored the ones from work. She still couldn't face talking to anyone. Not even Lexi, who'd left several messages before Becca's answering machine was filled to the max, and then texted her saying she was there whenever Becca needed to talk.

What should she do now?

The first thing would be to resign. The stories about her were just too awful; if she stayed, her reputation would drag down the clinic. Patients wouldn't want to be treated by someone like her. But leaving the clinic meant she'd have to give up her flat, too. She wouldn't be able to afford it without a job. And where was she going to find another job? She still wasn't sure if she'd be struck off the register for unprofessional conduct, but even if she wasn't she could hardly ask for a reference. Without a reference she'd be unemployable. All her dreams, all her future—gone.

And the worst bit was how much she missed Marco. Last time round she'd been a naïve teenager. This time round she was a strong, independent woman. She'd made exactly the same mistake. And, this time it hurt more. Missing him was a physical ache. The rest of her life stretched out in front of her, and there was nothing left to fill it. Just a black hole where she wished Marco could be.

And all the time the press remained camped outside the block of flats. In the end, she disconnected the Entryphone because she was tired of the constant calling.

When Becca finally managed to slip out of the back entrance to her block of flats, without the paparazzi following her, she went straight to Harley Street.

'Is Ethan in?' she asked Helen, the receptionist on duty.

'Yes, he's in his office,' Helen said. 'Are you all right, Becca?'

No, she wasn't all right, and she didn't think anything would ever be all right again. She gave the receptionist a sad little smile in answer, went to Ethan's office and rapped on the open door.

He looked up from his desk. 'Becca, you look like crap,' he said bluntly.

'I'm sorry I let you down and went off sick,' Becca said. 'I wasn't really sick. I just couldn't…'

'It's OK. I understand,' he soothed her.

She took a deep breath. 'I'll resign.'

'You most certainly will not,' Ethan said. 'You're an excellent hand therapist and we don't want to lose you. Your resignation is not accepted.'

'But all the stuff in the papers…'

'I don't care—well, I do,' he said, 'because I hate to think that you had such a rough time growing up, and I'd like to scoop out that Barney's heart with a rusty blunt scalpel.' He smiled at her. 'And, believe you me, I'd have to fight for my place at the front of the queue to do that.'

She stared at him, not quite believing this.

'Look, I know what it's like to have a parent who drinks.'

She nodded. She'd heard the rumours, even though it had all happened years ago—which was also why she knew the stories about her would run and run and run.

'It's not pleasant. And look at you now—you've pulled yourself out of that world. It all happened years ago, and it's totally not relevant to what you do now.'

'But won't the patients—well—prefer not to be treated by someone like me?' Becca asked.

'Are you kidding? Mrs van der Zee has been ringing every day to see if you're back yet, and she's not the only one—they're all worried about you.'

Becca felt the tears well up and blinked them back.

'You belong here,' Ethan said, 'and we've got your back, Becca. You're one of us.'

She really belonged?

Really, *really*?

She couldn't trust herself to speak, at first, but eventually she managed a broken 'Thank you.'

'Anyway, where the hell is Zorro? Why hasn't he protected you from the monsters in the press?' Ethan demanded.

'We— It's over,' she said in a whisper.

Ethan said something very pithy about what Marco was lacking.

'That's not quite fair, Ethan. I was the one who walked out on him.'

'But he should've come to get you back. He's an idiot and he doesn't deserve you.' Ethan narrowed his eyes. 'And I told him not to flirt with my staff. I thought he'd understand that meant anything further than flirting was way off limits.'

Becca couldn't say anything to that.

'Right. Lexi will help deal with the press—we'll get this sorted and minimise the damage. And we want you back to work, so go and scrub your face. When did you last eat?'

'I can't remember,' she admitted. Since the story had broken, she hadn't felt like eating.

'Well, you can't live on fresh air. Go down to the buffet and grab some breakfast—I don't want you fainting on anyone—and then get in that white coat and back in your office, OK?'

'OK.' It was so, so much more than she'd hoped for. So much more than she thought she deserved. 'Thank you.'

Funnily enough, eating breakfast did make her feel better. And so did the fact that every single member of the clinic dropped in to see her, give her a hug, and say that they were on her side.

'You idiot. Why didn't you tell me?' Lexi hugged her. 'You know what I do for a living. You know I could've spun this for you and saved you from all the nonsense.'

Becca was too close to tears to answer.

Lexi hugged her again. 'And we're friends, right?'

Friends. This time, a tear trickled down her cheek. 'I think so,' she whispered.

'I know so,' Lexi said. 'Even though you always keep so much of yourself back.'

'I'm not used to having friends,' Becca said. 'When I was little…' She dragged in a breath. 'People got sick of my mum being late to pick me up from playdates. And they noticed that she smelled of drink. So they didn't encourage their kids to be my friend. I was always the child in the class who didn't get invited to any of the birthday parties.'

Lexi stroked her hair. 'That sucks.'

'It's how it was. It was my life.' She dragged in a breath. 'It wasn't so bad when I was a teen. You know how kids like to rebel against their parents—so my home life didn't stop them being friends with me. Or *trying* to be. Nobody ever taught me how to make friends. I wasn't very good at it.' She looked away. 'Then I started drinking. I wasn't nice to be around. I was an embarrassment to everyone.'

'The teen years are hard,' Lexi said softly. 'Harder still if you don't get support from your parents.'

Becca narrowed her eyes. 'That sounds personal.'

'It is. The way you look…' Lexi shook herself. 'Enough of that. But the important thing is not to stop believing in yourself. Look what you did. You were dragged into the kind of world a teenager should never be dragged into. And you got yourself out of it. You studied hard, and you got yourself a really good job. You're stronger than you think.'

'Right now I don't feel strong. I feel stupid.' Becca blinked away the tears. 'What was I thinking, having an affair with Marco? He's a prince. Of course the likes of him aren't for me.'

'Why not?'

Becca found herself telling Lexi the whole messy story. How she'd fallen in love with 'Seb' at the camp and he'd broken her heart. How she'd met Marco again at the clinic and they hadn't been able to stop themselves falling all the way back in love. And now… 'He didn't ask me to stay or say he'd help me fix things.'

'Did you give him the chance to ask you to stay?' Lexi asked.

'Maybe not,' Becca admitted. She bit her lip. 'He was pretty angry because I hadn't told him the truth.'

'Angry because you hadn't trusted him, maybe,' Lexi said.

'That night, just before the press lay in wait for us, he said he admired me. That I was sweet and innocent and untarnished.' She closed her eyes. 'Now he despises me.'

'Did he say that?'

'He didn't have to.'

'Does it not occur to you that there's a lot to admire about you?' Lexi asked. 'Look at the way you've overcome your past.'

'That's just PR spin,' Becca said.

'No. It's the truth. Look at yourself properly, Becca. You've got so much to give. And Marco has a point. What happened wasn't your fault. You were a child. People were supposed to look after you, not drag you down into the mire.'

'I could've said no.'

'When was the last time you had a drink?'

Becca thought about it. 'Before rehab.'

'Years ago. Exactly. You're strong, Becca. You're amazing. And that's what Marco would've seen if you'd trusted him with the truth. I don't know him that well, but what I do know is that he has integrity. Give the man a chance. Trust him—and then you can really move on from your past.'

'I think it's too late for that.' Becca shook her head. 'I'm totally unsuitable for him. His parents would never approve.'

'His parents,' Lexi said, 'are surprisingly down to earth.

And they're very easy to work with in PR terms. You need to take that step forward, Becca. Trust yourself. And trust him. I know it's easier said than done, but think about it.' She hugged Becca again. 'I'll see you later, with my PR hat on, and we'll get a few things sorted. But, for now, just remember I'm here. As your friend.'

The lump in her throat was so huge Becca could hardly speak. 'I will,' she whispered.

Becca's first patient of the day was Mrs van der Zee.

'Are you sure you still want me to treat you?' Becca asked. 'After all the stuff in the press?'

'Which no doubt they exaggerated to sell more filthy copies.'

'Not that much,' Becca said. 'I was addicted to vodka and E.'

'You were sixteen, still a child, and it wasn't your fault,' Mrs van der Zee said. 'That man has a lot to answer for. I think every parent in the country wants to find that man and make quite sure he can never do anything like that again.'

Becca felt the tears well up again. She hadn't expected people to be so kind.

And it made it hurt even more that the one person she'd wanted to believe in her, root for her, had just abandoned her and left her to it.

Mrs van der Zee hugged her. 'It'll work out, love—don't you worry. And I think that prince of yours needs a good kick up the backside, war hero or no war hero.'

That earned her a watery smile. 'He's one of the good guys.'

'Well, he should be here protecting you and making the press go away,' Mrs van der Zee said. 'Now, shall we get started?'

* * *

Becca wouldn't answer a single one of Marco's calls, and either the clinic was protecting her or she'd totally gone to ground. All the curtains in her flat were drawn. The door hadn't been answered when he'd sent a discreet box of chocolates to apologise—because he knew damn well that the press would make a big deal of it if he sent a huge bouquet that she refused to accept. Being Becca, she *would* refuse to accept it.

The only reason that he hadn't gone to get her himself was because he knew that it would make the press speculation much, much stronger, and they'd make her life even harder. At times like this he really hated his background and wished that he was just an ordinary man who wouldn't be noticed going about his day-to-day business—that he could put things right without every movement being scrutinised in the public eye.

But the worst bit was the huge hole in his life now Becca wasn't here. He hated being without her. The future was just lonely and bleak, stretching out for eternity. Nothing but his duty to sustain him. And that would be his royal duty; he had to be honest and admit that the injury to his hand would make it next to impossible to go back to active service in the army. Anything less than full fitness would put his men in jeopardy, and he wasn't prepared to be that selfish.

Just his royal duty, and no Becca to help him through it.

Then again, if he had Becca in his life it meant he couldn't have his family. He couldn't bring disrepute on the monarchy and the mud would most definitely stick, even though Becca was clearly clean of drink and drugs now.

If he stayed as Prince Marco, he'd be without the love of his life.

If he became an ordinary man, he'd be without his family.

Why couldn't he have come from an ordinary family so none of this would matter? What was so wrong with wanting love *and* your family? Why couldn't you have both? There had to be a way. There just had to be.

And he couldn't sort it out in England. He needed to be back in Sirmontane and talking it over with the two people who could help him make it happen. He needed them to understand how he really felt. And maybe, just maybe, they could work it out.

Four hours later, Marco walked into his parents' drawing room in the castle.

'My son.' Elena, his mother, greeted him with a hug. 'You look absolutely terrible.'

He rolled his eyes. 'Thanks, Mamá.'

'I'm your mother. I'm not going to lie to you.' She hugged him again.

Alfonso, too, hugged Marco. 'Your mother has been worrying about you.'

'I'm healing.' He indicated his left hand. 'I get to do more this month.'

'Not just about your injury. We've read the papers,' Elena said.

And no doubt they thought the worst of Becca. 'She's not like the press paint her,' he said. 'She's not a wild child at all. She's brave and she's managed to overcome her past—she's worked hard and made a good career for herself. There's a lot to admire about her.'

'I agree, the press are spinning it,' Elena said, surprising him. 'She was vulnerable when it happened. Still a child. And it wasn't her fault that she was led into the darker edges of life.'

'I agree, too. And as for Barney, I'd horsewhip him myself,' Alfonso said.

The guy who'd groomed her. 'I'll kill him,' Marco said.

'No—and we don't want another incident like that one with the sword at school,' Alfonso said. 'You're not a hothead in the army. Don't be a hothead outside it. Think before you act. How many times have I told you that?'

'And how many times haven't I listened?' Marco asked wryly.

'You are who you are.' Elena smiled at him. 'So you knew Becca before you met her at the clinic?'

'I first met her in South Africa, at the children's aid camp.' Marco grimaced. 'Then Abuelo was taken to hospital. I went back for her when the doctors said he would pull through, but she'd already left South Africa. Vanished.'

'And you didn't tell her where you were going in the first place, did you?' Elena asked, rolling her eyes. 'Why are boys so hopeless when it comes to communicating?'

'That's why we get married, *cariña*,' Alfonso said, kissing her. 'So our wives can do it for us.'

She flapped a dismissive hand. 'This is about our son, not you.'

'Though Papá has a point,' Marco said dryly.

'Yes, I suppose he does.' She sighed. 'Sometimes, Marco, for a man who can be so bright, I wonder how you can be quite so stupid. Do you know that Becca is still involved with the rehab centre that helped her?'

'How do you know that?' he asked, surprised that his parents seemed to know a lot more about the situation than he did.

'We've been working with Lexi at the clinic,' Alfonso said.

'Becca's a volunteer at the rehab centre,' Elena explained. 'She talks to young girls like she was, girls who are addicted to drink and worse, and helps them find their way back to a happier life.'

The penny suddenly dropped. That was the 'commitment' Becca had been so vague about. And of course she wouldn't have been able to tell him about it, because then she would have had to explain why she helped there.

And now for the crunch issue. The one that could divide him from his family. But he needed it to be out in the open.

'Becca's the only woman I've ever really loved. The woman I want to spend the rest of my life with. I know it's all a mess, and lots of people are going to think she's totally unsuitable to be a princess. But I'm so miserable without her.' He bit his lip. 'I've been thinking about it. I'm prepared to give up being a prince, if that's what it takes to make her acceptable as my wife. But I don't want to lose my family. I don't want to have to choose between you. And that's why I came home. To talk to you. To see if there was a way I could still be your son but be with the woman I love.'

'My darling boy, you would *never* have to choose between us. We're your parents and we will always love you, no matter what you do and even when you make us worried sick. We want you to be happy,' Elena said. She tutted. 'Alfonso, I told you he was stupid. How could he think such a thing?' She cuffed Marco's good arm.

'So you would accept Becca,' he said carefully, 'as my wife?'

'We think she's a shining example of strength and grace, someone who's lived through hard times and come out the other side to help others who fall into the same traps,' Alfonso said. 'And other European princes have married women who are not of royal birth. This is the twenty-first century. There isn't the same issue over class that there was for my father, or my father's father.'

Hope flared in Marco's heart for the first time in days. 'With Becca at my side I'll be a better man. A better prince.'

'A better soldier?' Elena asked dryly.

He shook his head. 'I have to be honest. My hand will

heal, but I might never regain the full range of movement or grip. I won't be able to do my job properly, and I won't put other people at risk just for the sake of my pride. I'm prepared to accept an honourable discharge, or just finish my tour of duty as a pen-pusher. And then that's it. I'm back in the fold and ready to begin my royal duties.'

Elena hugged him. 'For that alone I would gladly accept Becca. Because having her in your life will take you out of danger.'

'Small problem,' Marco said. 'She's not talking to me right now.'

'So you think she'll turn you down?'

'I'm going to eat humble pie,' Marco said. 'And I'm going to tell her how I really feel about her. And then, with luck, she'll agree to make me the happiest prince in the world.'

'Go, *niño*,' his father said, 'with our blessing.'

Elena coughed. 'We'll be going to London, too.'

Alfonso frowned. 'Why?'

'To meet our future daughter-in-law.'

'Mamá, much as I love you, I'm not having that conversation with Becca in front of you,' Marco said.

Elena laughed. 'Of course not. But I'm looking forward to meeting her. And you can tell her that, too—not in an intimidating way, but in a welcoming way.'

Marco smiled. 'That's a royal order I'd be very happy to carry out.'

'I'll call Carlos and have the plane sorted out,' Alfonso said. 'And you need to do your exercises and then rest your hand, *niño*.'

CHAPTER TEN

FIRST THING THE next morning, Rafa drove Marco to the back entrance of the Hunter Clinic, and Marco slipped inside.

The receptionist looked at him. 'Can I help you, Your Highness?'

Either she recognised him from his stay at the clinic, or she'd seen the newspapers. Given the slight coolness of her tone behind the politeness, he had a nasty feeling it was the latter. Of course everyone here would be protective of Becca.

'I was, ah, hoping to see Becca Anderson.' He indicated his strapped-up arm. 'I'm due a physiotherapy session.'

'I see. If you wouldn't mind waiting over there, Your Highness, I'll see if I can find her for you,' the receptionist said, gesturing to the waiting area.

Marco sat down on one of the plush white leather sofas. He ignored the glossy magazines on the low coffee table; right at that moment he couldn't concentrate on anything. He just needed to see Becca.

But would she agree to see him?

He looked up hopefully as he heard someone come down the corridor. Except the tall male figure wasn't the one he wanted to see.

Ethan Hunter looked grim. 'Shall we go to my office, Your Highness?'

Oh, hell. He wasn't here to have a fight. He was here to make things right.

'Sure,' he said, and followed the surgeon to his office. Though he declined to have a seat.

'So what you do want, Your Highness?' Ethan asked.

Marco sighed inwardly. It wasn't just his relationship with Becca that he'd messed up; he'd crushed his burgeoning friendship with the spiky ex-army doctor, too. 'I need to see Becca,' he said.

'Uh-huh.' Ethan gave him a level stare. 'I told you not to flirt with my staff, but you completely ignored me. In fact, you did more than that. So, tell me, why the hell should we even let you back here?'

'Because I need to see Becca.'

'I don't give a damn who you are—prince or no prince, you hurt Becca, and that's not acceptable. We have a zero tolerance policy and no money or celebrity or royal status will ever change that.'

Marco knew he deserved every bit of the reprimand. 'I screwed up,' he said softly. 'But, hand on heart, Clavo, can you tell me you've never made a mistake? Can you tell me you've never hurt a woman? Someone you loved? Because everything around you got messed up and the right words wouldn't come out?'

Ethan said nothing, and Marco knew he'd hit home. Whatever Ethan Hunter had done probably wasn't quite in the same league as the way Marco had messed up, and it certainly hadn't been done on the stage of the world's media circus, but all the same Marco could tell that the surgeon knew what it was like to get it badly wrong.

'I need to see Becca,' he repeated. 'I need to apologise to her properly. I need to tell her that I love her and I don't give a damn about where she comes from or what she's done in the past—it's the present and the future that matters. Who she is now.'

Ethan didn't look convinced.

Marco drew in a breath. 'I know she doesn't have family to look out for her, and the people here at the clinic and the rehab centre are the nearest she has to a family. I'm glad you're all looking out for her—and I can assure you my intentions towards her are completely honourable.'

Ethan was silent for so long that Marco thought he'd blown it.

But then the surgeon nodded. 'Just so you know, if you do anything to upset her or hurt her, I'll come after you myself. Limp or no limp.'

'I'm not going to hurt her,' Marco said. 'I'm going to grovel. And I just hope she can find it in her to forgive me and give me a second—no, a third chance.'

'Three strikes and you're out, I'd say.'

Marco gave him a wry smile. 'I'd better make sure I get it right this time.'

'Yeah, you'd better. She's in her office,' Ethan said. 'I assume you know where that is?'

'I do. And thank you.'

When the surgeon had left, Marco went down the corridor to Becca's office and rapped on the door.

She looked up, as if to welcome in a patient, and her face went white. '*You*. What are you doing here?'

'I believe I have a physiotherapy appointment,' he said. 'Phase two.'

She shook her head. 'I'm not treating you any more.'

'I can understand why you'd rather not treat me,' he said carefully, 'and I'll accept your decision—but will you please listen to me before you make that decision?'

Her eyes narrowed. 'Like you listened to me?'

'Technically,' he said, 'you didn't give me the chance to listen to you. You blew up and stormed out. And, yes, I know I should've run straight after you and stopped you leaving. I was a fool. I let stuff get in the way.'

She said nothing, but at least she hadn't thrown him out.

'I don't care about your background, Becca. I don't care where you came from or what happened in your past,' he said. 'Well, I *do* care—I hate that you were treated so badly when you were a vulnerable teenager, by someone who should've looked after you instead of dragging you down—but what I mean is that the past doesn't matter. I love the girl you were when I first met you, and I love the woman you are now.'

'You love me?' she said. 'But nothing can come of it. You're a prince and I...' She blew out a breath. 'Well. The press labelled me a wild child.'

'Because they know only half the story. Something that someone fed them. By the time I've finished talking to them they're going to see you for exactly who you are,' he said. 'A brave, talented woman. Someone who's a real role model—someone who's come through adversity and built a decent life for herself. I'm proud of you.'

She curled her lip. 'You didn't seem proud the other day. You were angry.'

'I was, but not with you,' he said. 'I was angry with myself. I should've protected you better. And I should've seen for myself that you can fit into my world. You're good enough, Becca. More than good enough.'

'What made you see it differently?'

'Being without you. Because it was like a black hole. I saw my future without you, and it was so bleak and lonely and miserable.' He looked at her. 'My parents have been talking to Lexi. Nobody's broken any confidences—but they did tell me that you volunteer at a rehab clinic. And I'm guessing that's your way of paying back for the way you were helped.'

She frowned. 'Yes—but...' She looked confused, unable to take things in. 'Your parents?'

'They hold you in pretty high esteem,' he said. 'I guess

what I'm saying is if you'll have me, and put up with the royal engagements and media circus that kind of have to go along with me, then…' He had nothing to lose, now. So he'd tell her just how he felt. 'Becca, you make me a better man. I feel complete when I'm with you. I know I've hurt you, more than once, and I'd like the chance to make that up to you. Will you marry me?'

'But—what about the drink and the drugs? I'm totally unsuitable for a prince's consort or what have you.'

He shrugged. 'Everyone makes mistakes. Sometimes they're helped to make those mistakes, dragged into it by someone else. It's in the past. You can't go back and change it. But you can learn from your mistakes, put them behind you—and you've gone one step further than that, because you're helping other people who've ended up in the same trap you were in. And they'll listen to you because they know you've been there and come out the other side so you understand what it's really like. It takes someone really special to do that, to help people like that. So will you marry me?'

She bit her lip. 'Marco, I can't give you an answer. Not while this is all hanging over me.'

'I hope you know that you have my family's backing. And the backing of everyone here. And I'd guess it's the same at the rehab place. You're not alone,' he said softly.

'I was alone for a long time,' she said, suddenly looking very young and vulnerable.

He held out his free arm. 'If telling me the whole story will help you, I'll listen. And I won't judge,' he said softly.

Would telling him the whole story help her?

At least it would mean they had no more secrets. No more lies between them.

She stood up from her chair and walked round to his side of the desk. Let him hold her.

All these years of standing on her own two feet and now, for once, it felt good to have someone to lean on.

She dragged in a breath. 'My dad died when I was tiny. It was an accident. My mum didn't cope very well—she wanted someone who'd look after her and love her, the way he had. I had a lot of "uncles", but she never seemed to find the right one. And in the end she started drinking to help her forget how unhappy she was.' She looked at him. 'And I mean hard drinking. Half the time she forgot I was there, too. I learned to make a jam sandwich before I could even write my name.'

'Oh, Becca.'

She shrugged. 'Plenty of people have it as bad as that. They don't have much money; bread and jam's cheap, it fills you up and it doesn't need cooking.'

He stroked her hair. 'OK. I'm not judging.'

Though she could see in his eyes that he was angry on her behalf.

'It doesn't get better,' she said. 'But I understand why, now. My mum was lost. She couldn't find her way out. I guess she was needy—and it was too much for a new partner. Every time she met someone and I thought it was going all right, because she was going to have a baby and we'd be a family... Well, she found it hard to cope when the baby cried. Then she'd drink. Pick fights. Then her partner would get tired of her drinking and leave. And that would make her feel worse, and the only way she could feel better was to drink enough to make her forget.'

'Hard on you.'

'Not just me. I've got, what, four or five brothers and sisters. Half-brothers and sisters,' she amended. 'Not that I've seen any of them since they were two years old. Their dads got custody—well, what with my mum's drinking, it was probably better they lived with their dads than with us.'

'What about you? Didn't any of them try to take custody of you?'

She shrugged. 'I wasn't their child. They didn't want me.'

'But why didn't you get taken into care? Surely the authorities knew from the court cases that your mum was drinking and not looking after you. Didn't anyone speak up for you?'

'There wasn't anyone to speak up for me.' She shrugged. 'It was OK. I managed. I mean—it hurt that nobody ever invited me to birthday parties, but I understood why. The other mums didn't like my mum. She'd get drunk and try to flirt with every man in sight.' She sighed. 'We did OK until I was fifteen—and then she started seeing Barney.' She bit her lip. 'He started putting vodka in my lemonade. I didn't realise what was happening at first—you can't taste vodka, can't smell it. But it quickly got so I felt I needed something. He talked to me in the kitchen one night, and I must've said something because he gave me a drink. It made me feel better. So I had more. And I...I was horrible when I was drunk. I fell out with the few friends I did have, because of my drinking. And drinking more helped to blot out how miserable I was.'

Marco looked at her. 'You were *fifteen*. Too young to drink.'

'Too young to buy it for myself from a shop or a pub, and too young to drink in a public place,' she corrected. 'But it's harder to police what goes on behind closed doors. There were lots of underage kids at the rehab centre.'

'So he let you drink vodka. He encouraged you.'

'And then one night he kissed me.' She closed her eyes briefly, remembering how disgusting she'd found it. How he'd slobbered over her. How she'd wanted to scream herself sick when he'd put his hands under her clothes but she'd been too scared to make a noise, because Barney had told her to keep quiet or her mum would be upset.

But her mum had been upset anyway.

'My mum caught us, and he told her...' She dragged in a breath, still outraged by how easily Barney had lied, and how her mother had actually believed him. 'He said I came on to him. She accused me of trying to steal her boyfriend, and she threw me out.'

Marco stroked her hair. 'Where did you go?'

'I didn't have anywhere to go,' she said. 'I'd fallen out with everyone at school because of the drinking, so I couldn't ask to stay with anyone. I thought I was going to have to live on the streets. I was just walking round, trying to see a doorway where I could shelter for the night. But then Barney came after me. He said he'd look after me. That I could stay at his flat. And he had a spare room.' She bit her lip. 'I thought he felt guilty about what he'd done and was trying to be nice, helping me out. I thought he was going to soften my mum up a bit so she'd let me go back home and I'd stop crying round his flat. Except...'

She looked away.

'That wasn't quite what he had in mind. He said he had something for me, something that would make me feel better. And he gave me this tablet.'

'You took it?'

'I was drunk at the time. Of course I took it.' She swallowed hard. 'And then a couple of weeks later, when he'd given me more and more, he said I owed him for the drugs I'd taken. And the vodka. I didn't have any money. He said I could—I could pay him in kind. Give him my virginity. And...' Oh, this was so hard to say. 'He was going to film it,' she whispered. 'Make money from it. Sell it to people who wanted to watch.'

Marco held her close. 'Oh, my Becca. I want to kill

him. Very, very slowly. The traditional death from a thousand cuts.'

'He didn't actually do it,' she said. 'Because I told him I couldn't do it, it was the wrong time of the month. And he said as soon as—as soon as I was clean, he'd do it.'

Marco held her tighter.

'But I went to school that day,' she said. 'I'd been skipping lessons. I didn't care about school any more. But for some reason I felt I had to go in that day. We had a Personal Development class. There was a woman there from the rehab centre, giving us all a talk about drugs. After the talk I asked to leave the classroom to go to the loo, but I followed her out to her car, and I asked her to help me get into rehab—to help me get away from Barney. And she told the school I was going with her, and she took me to the rehab centre. They helped me get off the vodka and the drugs.'

'What about Barney? *Please* tell me she skewered Barney. That he was put in prison for what he did.'

She shook her head. 'He said I was lying. It was my word against his. He said I'd tried it on with him and he'd turned me down because I'd only just turned sixteen, and he said I was just trying to get my own back by smearing his good name.'

'How could the police let him get away with it?'

'I had no evidence. It was all circumstantial. Like I said, it was my word against his.'

'But surely your mum stood up for you and told them what he did?'

'She was still angry with me. She said nothing.'

'Oh, Becca.'

'I never lived with her again,' Becca said. 'The rehab centre found me a place to live, and got me made a ward of the court so I couldn't be taken anywhere without their permission. Barney couldn't come and get me. And I was determined I'd prove their faith in me, that I'd make something of myself. I passed my exams—I crammed everything at the last minute and my grades weren't brilliant, because I'd had a year of skipping classes and being drunk, but I passed enough to go on to sixth form. I did better with my A levels, earned a place at university. The rest you know.'

'You truly are amazing,' Marco said. 'And I'm so proud of you.'

She blinked back the tears. 'I'm *not* going to cry.'

'Only happy tears, from now on,' he said. He stroked her face. 'Did you make it up with your mother?'

'Not really. After she split up with Barney she drank even more. She ended up with oesophageal varices. One day, she bled out. It was just before my A levels.' She swallowed hard. 'The emergency department called her neighbour, who called me—I'd given her the details in case Mum ever changed her mind and wanted to see me. So I was there at the end. But she didn't forgive me, Marco.'

'Because she couldn't forgive herself, maybe,' he said. 'She knew she'd let you down, hadn't looked after you properly. And she'd introduced you to Barney. She'd let him do what he did to you. She couldn't forgive herself for it, and she couldn't tell you that, so she just made you feel that it was your fault—and it *wasn't* your fault, Becca.'

'I wish we'd made up,' she said. 'And it scares me. Maybe there's an alcoholic gene in my family. My mum never said why we never saw my grandparents, but maybe one of them was an alcoholic. So was she. So was I.' She took a deep breath. 'And I always said I'd never get married, never have a family, because I don't want to pass that weakness on.'

'Firstly,' Marco said, 'you're very far from weak. You're strong. Yes, you were supported by the rehab centre, but you were the one who took that first step and asked for help. By sheer determination, you got yourself sorted out and away from all the mess of your life. Secondly, you're not your mother. You wouldn't ever abandon your children, and you'd steer them away from drink and drugs.' He dropped to one knee. 'As for marriage? I hope very much that you'll reconsider that and marry me. Be the perfect modern royal escort.'

'I'm not perfect,' she said.

He smiled. 'Don't you see? That's what makes you perfect for the job. You're human. You're brave. And you can move on from mistakes you've made. But…'

Her eyes widened. 'But?'

'This is the third time I've asked you, now. If you don't want to get married, then I'll respect that. Provided that you'll live with me. Be my love. Be part of my family. Because I don't ever want to be without you again, Becca. I need you with me. I love you.'

She dragged in a breath. 'But how can your family ever accept me? I'm from the *gutter*.' She shook her head. 'I love you enough to walk away and let you find someone suitable. Someone who'll make you happy.'

'I don't want to find "someone suitable".' He grimaced as he made quote marks with his good hand. 'I want you. You're the one who makes me happy, Becca.'

'You don't have a choice. You're a prince of Sirmontane.'

'I do have a choice. And, before you even start thinking it, no, I don't have to choose between love and duty. I'm free to choose you.'

She couldn't let herself believe it. Dared not let herself hope. 'There's no way your parents will be able to accept a former addict as your partner.'

'Yes, there is.' He sighed. 'Look, come and meet them. Then you'll see for yourself.'

'Meet them?'

'I'm under royal orders to tell you that they want to meet you. Not to be intimidating, but welcoming. Actually, I have a feeling you'll get on incredibly well with my mother. And then,' he said, 'your doubts will all be put to rest and you can do what we both want and agree to marry me.'

He was right—it was the only way she could be sure. Except she was pretty sure that she was the one who had it right, not him.

'OK.'

Marco grabbed his phone from his pocket and called his mother. 'Mamá ? No, she said no. Not until she's met you and Papá. OK. Yes, here would be good. *Talué*. Yes, I love you, too.' He laughed, and put his phone back in his pocket. 'Righty, Ms Anderson. One bluff thoroughly called.'

'Your parents are coming here?' she asked.

'If we go to Regent's Park we'll have to run the gauntlet of the paps.'

'And so,' she pointed out, 'will your parents, if they come here—and that's not fair. We'll go to them.'

'OK. I'll tell them to stay put.' He rolled his eyes and made two more calls. 'All sorted. Rafa says the back entrance is the quieter one, so we'll use that one.'

So much for quiet. The paparazzi were three-deep. Flashlights popped as Marco helped Becca into the car, and there were ribald comments and calls of, 'Are you giving the prince some *special* treatment, Becca?'

She remembered what Declan and Lexi had told her about dealing with the press: be polite, be gracious, and don't let them see that they've got to you. So she just smiled, said nothing, and got in the car.

She felt unbelievably nervous about meeting Marco's family. What if they didn't like her, after all?

Marco, as if guessing how tense she was, simply held her hand. 'It's going to be fine.'

How could he be so sure?

The drive to Regent's Park was over way, way too soon.

But at least Maria the housekeeper was there to meet her with a hug. 'Lovely to see you back, *hermosa*.'

'You, too, Maria.'

'Your parents are in the sitting room,' she told Marco.

'Thank you, Maria. Maybe we could have some coffee in a little while?'

Oh, help, Becca thought. *Please don't let me spill it all over that expensive silk carpet.*

Her nervousness grew exponentially as they walked up the stairs to the next floor and Marco opened the door to the sitting room.

What on earth did you say to the King and Queen of Sirmontane? She should have asked Marco in the car about formal addresses. Too late, now. Hoping that she was doing the right thing, she swept into a low curtsey when they were standing in front of Marco's parents. If a prince was Your Highness, his parents must be the next rung up. What did people call the Queen of England? Hmm... She couldn't call a king 'ma'am', could she? She was just going to have to wing it.

'Good morning, Your Majesties,' she said.

Marco coughed. 'How come you never curtsey to me like that?'

She looked up at him and rolled her eyes. 'Because you don't deserve it.' The words were out before she could stop them.

Oh, no. Why had she said something so *stupid* in front of Marco's mother?

But, to her surprise, Marco's mother burst out laughing. The Queen of Sirmontane stood up and held her arms open. 'Now I know you're definitely the right girl for my son. I did have my doubts.'

Because of the press?

The question must have shown on her face, because

the Queen of Sirmontane explained, 'When you curtseyed to us. But, no, you're exactly what he needs. A breath of fresh air. He's absolutely right about you. Welcome, Becca.'

Oh, my God.

She was being offered a hug *by a queen*.

This couldn't possibly be protocol.

But the fact that she was being offered a hug proved that Marco was right, that his family had already accepted her. It made the last barriers of fear round her heart melt. So she stood up and hugged Marco's mother right back.

'Sit down with me, *hermosa*,' Marco's mother said, sitting down herself and patting the seat of the sofa next to her. 'Now, I'm Elena, and this is Alfonso.'

First-name terms with a king and queen.

This didn't seem real.

'Maria's been singing your praises,' said the King— Becca didn't quite yet dare to think of him as Alfonso. 'She says you've helped her a lot.'

That business with her arthritic hip. And Becca had been sworn to secrecy about it. 'I don't want to be rude, Your Majesty, but may I plead patient confidentiality?'

Elena smiled. 'Of course you may. But she's told us everything. And I'm cross with her for not saying something before, because we could have sent her for treatment much earlier and got her some more help.'

'There's something about this house and extremely stubborn women,' Marco said, lounging back on one of the tall-back chairs and giving his mother an insolent grin.

Elena gave him a speaking look and ignored him. 'So Maria will have more of a supervisory role in future,' she said. 'Thank you for helping her, Becca.'

'It was my pleasure,' Becca said, meaning it.

'And we would like you to know that we would be very happy to welcome you to the family,' the King said.

'Even though...' There wasn't a way to put it tactfully.

'After all the stuff the papers said about my past?' Becca asked.

'The way you've come through adversity would inspire a new generation,' Elena said, surprising her. 'And your example might also give Marianna—Ferdy's fiancée—back some of the confidence that the press has chipped away.'

'I agree,' Alfonso added. 'I think you'll be good for us, Becca. You've made Marco happy. And steadier than he's been in quite a while.'

'I am *here*, you know,' Marco said, sounding pained.

'And we're your parents, so we can talk about you in front of you,' Elena said crisply. 'Always. Even when you're a white-haired grandfather yourself and we're ancient crones.'

Alfonso coughed. 'Since when can men be crones, Elena?'

'You can be an honorary crone, then. Add it to your titles,' Elena said.

Becca couldn't help laughing. She really, really liked Marco's family. And to think that she'd been afraid they'd be stuffy and formal. Lexi had been right about them: they were down-to-earth. Elena was wonderful. Brisk, no-nonsense, and with a rapier-sharp sense of humour. And Marco had been right, too: Becca had the distinct feeling that, in the future, she and Elena would be good friends.

'Now we've got that sorted, I think Becca and I need a quiet chat,' Marco said, and stood up. 'Excuse us, O ancient crones-to-be.' He took Becca's hand and pulled her to her feet. 'We'll be back shortly. Because I am *not* having this conversation in front of you, Mamá.'

'Spoilsport,' his mother grumbled. 'Becca, I want a full report.'

'You'll get it,' Becca promised with a smile.

Marco took Becca up to the roof garden.

'So can you see it, now?' he asked softly. 'That my parents are very happy to accept you in my life.'

She nodded. 'I like your parents. Especially your mum.'

'Mamá,' he said, 'can be a bit full-on. And she's horrendously bossy.' He smiled at her. 'They say that women marry men like their fathers. I guess it's the same for men.'

She looked at him. 'Are you calling me bossy?'

He grinned. 'I love it when you're bossy. But sometimes I want to be the bossy one.' He dropped to one knee. 'Becca, I don't have a ring to offer you right now, because I want the fun of choosing it with you. But will you do me the honour of being my wife, the love of my life and the centre of my family?'

Being the centre of a family. What she'd always secretly wanted and always feared she'd never have.

And, best of all, waking up with Marco every morning, knowing that it would be a good day because he was there and he loved her as much as she loved him.

She knelt down to join him. 'Yes,' she said, and kissed him.

EPILOGUE

One month later

'READY?' MARCO ASKED BECCA.

'Ready.' She smiled at him and stole a kiss. 'My first ever royal engagement. Well, royal-to-be,' she amended.

'It still counts as royal,' Marco said. 'And I can't think of a better place for it,' he added as he helped her out of the car outside the rehab centre.

'Be careful with your arm,' she said. 'You're only just allowed to do medium activities with that hand.'

'Yes, dear,' he teased. 'You can nag me about the exercises later. Stop worrying. I'm fine.'

Thanks to a donation from the royal family of Sirmontane, the rehab unit had been able to set up a new physical therapy room to help their patients.

Cameras flashed as Becca got out of the car. She waved and smiled at the paparazzi, who'd decided since the news of the engagement broke that she was their darling rather than their demon. Instead of calling her Wild Child Becca and sneering at her, they'd nicknamed her Princess Braveheart and cheered her on.

The fact that at her last press conference she'd spotted that two of the journalists were shaking their writing hand, and taken them to one side and taught them exercises to relieve the pain, had only made them love her more.

Marco was rather less thrilled that the press had also taken to calling him Prince Zorro, but he put up with it for Becca's sake. If she was happy, then his world was all right.

They did the tour of the rehab centre, as agreed—but it took rather longer than planned because Becca stopped to talk with every single one of the young patients. And every single one of them was smiling when she left them, knowing that they were understood rather than judged.

His wife-to-be, Marco thought, was a real shining star.

'I'm delighted to declare the physical therapy room open,' she said, and posed with the oversized scissors in front of the ribbon for the press. Then she smiled and cut the ribbon. 'And may everyone who uses this room find their inner strength, too.'

Like she had.

Marco was so proud of her. She'd come so far. And, just as his parents had predicted, she'd inspired a new generation—across Europe, not just in Sirmontane and England. And politicians finally seemed to be noticing the problem of addiction among teenagers and were setting up more rehab units to help them find their way back.

As they came back to the royal limo, one of the press called, 'Kiss her, Prince Zorro!'

He smiled at Becca. 'I guess that's telling me my royal duty.'

He kissed her, to cheers from the crowd.

'I'd just like you all to know,' he said, 'how proud I am of my Princess Braveheart. And I can't wait to marry her in four months' time.'

In the cathedral next to the palace in Sirmontane where he'd been christened, his parents had been married and his father had been crowned.

He kissed her again. 'I love you, Becca. Now and always.'

She kissed him back. 'And I love you, too.'

* * * * *

200 HARLEY STREET: THE ENIGMATIC SURGEON

BY
ANNIE CLAYDON

MILLS & BOON

Published in Great Britain 2014
by Mills & Boon, an imprint of Harlequin (UK) Limited,
Eton House, 18-24 Paradise Road, Richmond, Surrey, TW9 1SR

© 2014 Harlequin Books S.A.

Special thanks and acknowledgement are given to Annie Claydon for her contribution to the *200 Harley Street* series

ISBN: 978 0 263 90769 8

Harlequin (UK) Limited's policy is to use papers that are natural, renewable and recyclable products and made from wood grown in sustainable forests. The logging and manufacturing processes conform to the legal environmental regulations of the country of origin.

Printed and bound in Spain
by Blackprint CPI, Barcelona

Dear Reader

I've always loved reading continuity stories, so it was a thrill to be asked to write one, and an honour to be in the company of the other wonderful authors who have contributed to this series.

From the moment he came alive on the page for me I knew that Edward was going to be a challenge. He's one of those people who'll shine whatever he turns his hand to. He might not be much of a team player, but give him a problem and he'll come up with a brilliant and imaginative solution. He has his work, his books and his music, and seems to want nothing and no one else. What can you give a man like that?

Well, you can give him Charlotte. Charlotte might not always understand the complexities of Edward's thought processes, but she understands people. And as she gets to know Edward it becomes obvious that there's something missing in his well-ordered life. But she and her son have been hurt once already, and the one thing that Edward needs is the thing that Charlotte has promised herself she'll never give.

I hope that you enjoy Edward and Charlotte's story. I'm always delighted to hear from readers, and you can contact me via my website at www.annieclaydon.com

Annie x

Recent titles by Annie Claydon:

ONCE UPON A CHRISTMAS NIGHT…
RE-AWAKENING HIS SHY NURSE
THE REBEL AND MISS JONES
THE DOCTOR MEETS HER MATCH
DOCTOR ON HER DOORSTEP
ALL SHE WANTS FOR CHRISTMAS

**These books are also available in eBook format
from www.millsandboon.co.uk**

Dedication

To the ladies who lunch: Yve, Nicky and Vicki.

200 HARLEY STREET

Glamour, intensity, desire—
the lives and loves of London's hottest team of surgeons!

**For the next two months enter the world of London's elite surgeons
as they transform the lives of their patients and find love
amidst a sea of passions and tensions...!**

In April, renowned plastic surgeon and legendary playboy Leo Hunter
couldn't resist the challenge of unbuttoning the intriguing
new head nurse, Lizzie Birch!
200 HARLEY STREET: SURGEON IN A TUX by Carol Marinelli

And glamorous Head of PR Lexi Robbins was determined to make gruff,
grieving and super-sexy Scottish surgeon Iain MacKenzie
her Hunter Clinic star!
200 HARLEY STREET: GIRL FROM THE RED CARPET
by Scarlet Wilson

In May, top-notch surgeons and estranged spouses
Rafael and Abbie de Luca found being forced to work together again
tough as their passion was as incendiary as ever!
200 HARLEY STREET: THE PROUD ITALIAN by Alison Roberts

And one night with his new colleague, surgeon Grace Turner, saw former
Hollywood plastic surgeon Mitchell Cooper daring to live again...
200 HARLEY STREET: AMERICAN SURGEON IN LONDON
by Lynne Marshall

Then, in June, injured war hero Prince Marco meets physical therapist
Becca Anderson—the woman he once shared a magical *forbidden*
summer romance with long ago...
200 HARLEY STREET: THE SOLDIER PRINCE by Kate Hardy

And when genius micro-surgeon Edward North meets single mum
Nurse Charlotte King he opens his eyes to a whole new world...
200 HARLEY STREET: THE ENIGMATIC SURGEON by Annie Claydon

Finally join us in July, when junior surgeon Kara must work with hot-shot
Irish surgeon Declan Underwood—the man she kissed at the hospital ball!
200 HARLEY STREET: THE SHAMELESS MAVERICK by Louisa George

And brilliant charity surgeon Olivia Fairchild faces the man who once
broke her heart—damaged ex-soldier Ethan Hunter. Yet she's unprepared
for his haunted eyes and the shock of his sensual touch...!
200 HARLEY STREET: THE TORTURED HERO by Amy Andrews

**Experience glamour, tension, heartbreak and emotion
at 200 HARLEY STREET in this new eight-book continuity
from Mills & Boon® Medical Romance™**

**These books are also available in eBook format and in two
200 HARLEY STREET collection bundles from www.millsandboon.co.uk**

CHAPTER ONE

'So which is it, then?'

'Eh?' Charlotte King was busy trying not to notice that Edward North was currently going through his pockets to find the key to his office, and she had lost the thread of the conversation that was going on around the nurses' station.

'Which do you think? Secret love-life, or no love-life?' Paula craned across the desk to get a better view. 'Wonder if he needs a hand with that?'

Charlotte swallowed a laugh. 'What? You know where he's left his keys?'

'No. But I'm really good at finding things.' Paula's smile left no doubt that she was contemplating a thorough investigation and possibly a body search.

'Too late. He's got them.' Allie grinned at Paula. 'And I reckon he's got a secret mistress somewhere.'

'When does he get to see her? In between here and the hospital, I'd be surprised if he has much time for anything else.'

'He has time to swim.' Allie's blue eyes flashed mischievously.

'Yeah?' Paula's attention was on Allie now.

'Mmm-hmm. I left my trainers downstairs in the gym the other day and went to fetch them after work. He was in the pool, doing laps.'

'Hmm. Perhaps I'll go buy myself a swimming costume. Common interests can be very important in a relationship.'

'So you've thought this through, then?' Charlotte wished that Paula and Allie would keep their voices down. Not that the nurses were in any danger of being heard. It was difficult enough to get Edward's attention even when he was supposed to be listening to you. It just seemed somehow wrong to be talking like this.

'Who hasn't? I reckon he just needs a good woman. And I'll apply for the position if no one else is interested.'

Allie laughed. 'Steady, Paula. Remember there's a queue and I'm in it. Charlotte, too, eh?'

Charlotte considered the prospect. She couldn't get away with a lie that big. 'Yeah, okay. Just to keep you two company, though. I don't have time for dating.'

Or the money. Or the inclination, most of the time. Apart from when Edward... Her gaze wandered over to the glazed wall of his office. He was behind his desk now, deep in thought, a stack of papers and books in front of him.

'Yeah, right.' Paula was laughing now. 'Guess we could share him around.'

Oh, no. Edward wasn't for sharing. He was for being loved, nurtured by one woman, not passed around like a beautifully wrapped, enormously sexy parcel. He looked up, as if somehow the thought had penetrated the walls of his office, his eyes suddenly focussing in Charlotte's direction.

She could feel the flush spreading up from the back of her neck to her cheeks. Edward might be for one woman, but that woman definitely wasn't her.

Charlotte turned, trying to pretend that he hadn't just caught her staring at him. 'I'll leave you to do that. I've got to do my last ward round and my friend is bringing Isaac here soon.'

'Really?' Paula always made a particular fuss of Isaac. 'What do we owe that pleasure to?'

'There's no school today and my friend's been looking after him. Lucy's got a date tonight so she's dropping him off here before she goes on to hit the town. If you see them, will you get them to wait here?'

Paula nodded. 'Sure thing. Take your time.'

Edward North had just got to the complex part. Not that tomorrow's microsurgery wasn't all complex, but this particular section was intricate in the extreme. Running through it in his head was his preferred method of preparation, and the swimming pool in the basement of the Hunter Clinic his preferred place. Working his body seemed to free his mind, but he couldn't be assured of solitude until the clinic was closed for the day, so his office was going to have to do.

'No. Not like that...' He shook his head, muttering in disgust at his own ineptitude. He'd have to start over now. Or at least from the last set of microscopic sutures. Edward took a breath, cleared his mind, and...

The image that floated into his mind was nothing like the one he was concentrating on building. Pale chestnut hair, bound in a tight knot at the back of her head. Light brown eyes. He couldn't see the flecks of gold from this distance, but he knew that they were there. Somehow Charlotte's eyes had impressed themselves on his consciousness when he had difficulty in recalling the names, let alone the eye colour, of most of the rest of the nursing staff.

She'd looked away, then. Blushing.

The exact mechanics of that particular form of vasodilation was child's play alongside the complexities of its causes. Most things were. Edward closed his eyes, cleared his mind, and went back to the matter in hand.

* * *

Lucy was already standing at the nurses' station when Charlotte returned from her ward round.

'Hey, Lucy, you look nice. I won't be a minute. I've just got to pick up my coat.' Charlotte looked around. Just one glimpse of her son after a long day was always enough to lift her spirits.

'Sure. Why don't you leave Isaac here with me?'

'Isn't he with you?'

'No. He ran ahead up the stairs. I called after him to wait for you here...'

For one split second the two women stared at each other. Charlotte almost choked as something squeezed tight around her heart, and then instinct and the sure knowledge that she needed to move *now* took over.

'Go downstairs, Lucy. Make sure he's not slipped out of the building. I'll look for him here.'

She glanced over in the direction of Edward's office. The view inside was partially obscured by a long, low cabinet, running the length of the glass wall and designed to keep the mess of books and other artefacts under some semblance of control, but she could see that he was no longer sitting at his desk. Not that he'd probably notice if a whole horde of five-year-olds started roaming the corridors, but he'd been the only one there and beggars couldn't be choosers.

Isaac shouldn't have gone into any of the treatment rooms. He knew not to do that. All the same she looked, trying not to panic, trying not to cry. Allie hadn't seen him and neither had Paula. She opened every cupboard, every locked door, just in case. And each time her baby wasn't there the agitation in the pit of her stomach grew.

'The receptionist says that he can't have got out of the building. He would have had to have either opened one of the back doors, and they're all alarmed, or gone straight past her.' Lucy arrived back upstairs, red and breathless.

That was something, at least. Mind you, there was plenty of trouble right here that a five-year-old could get into. The swimming pool… Charlotte remembered the swimming pool in the basement and felt suddenly sick.

'I'll call Security…' She grabbed for the phone and then dropped it. Either she was hearing things, or…

Isaac laughed again. That was definitely not a hallucination.

Lucy had heard it, too. 'Where is he?' Lucy looked around wildly.

Another laugh. This time deep, round and rich. The kind of laugh that Edward might have, only Charlotte didn't think she'd ever heard him laugh. Wordlessly she swung round and marched towards the door of Edward's office, opening it without bothering to knock.

For a moment, in the relief of seeing that Isaac was safe, she didn't register the scene in front of her. Somehow she noticed that Isaac's favourite toy, the blue bunny that he carried with him everywhere, was sitting in Edward's black leather chair, and that Edward was on the floor.

'Isaac!' Charlotte gulped out his name. 'What are you doing?'

Her son looked up at her. Innocent blue eyes and dark blond hair framed the sweet smile which never failed to dissolve her anger and dispel her fears.

'Hi, Mum. I'm making water.' He picked up a small red ball from the box in front of him. 'Look, you take one red one. That's…'

'Um…oxygen.' Edward got to his feet quickly, facing Charlotte with a slightly abashed air. 'So you're Isaac's mother?'

'Yes.' She ducked around Edward. She could deal with him later. 'Isaac, come here, please.'

'But, Mum, I haven't shown you. Look…'

'We mustn't bother Mr North any more, sweetie. Where did you get that from?' She looked at the molecule model kit in front of him on the floor. It looked like a great toy and she wished she could afford something like it for Isaac, even if he was a bit young for it at the moment.

'It's Edward's.' Isaac shot a pleading look up at his new friend, who ignored him completely and sat down in his chair, remembering just in time to pull the blue bunny out from under him before it got squashed. He proffered it to Isaac and when he didn't show any inclination to take it propped it up against the phone.

It had been a long week, and Charlotte had just about had enough. You could only take so many small crises, each one popping up hard on the heels of the last, before life became one big crisis.

'Then put everything back in the box and say thank you to Edward. We've got to get home.' Hopefully she could get out of here before the temptation to tear Edward off a strip became too great. Didn't he realise that someone would be looking for the stray five-year-old who had wandered into his office?

Isaac shot her a look which left her in no doubt that he wasn't in agreement with that decision, but complied anyway. One down, one to go. Charlotte turned to Edward, who was arranging the blue bunny into a crossed-legs, hands-behind-the-head posture which gave the impression that he was leaning back against the phone, sunbathing.

'I'm sorry he…interrupted you. We'll be going home…'

The sheer force of his gaze stopped her. Thoughtful. Intensely blue. And at this moment tainted with an uncertainty that was unlike Edward.

'Were you looking for him?'

'Yes. But it's all right, he's here…' Charlotte just wanted

to hug Isaac. As soon as she got out of Edward's office that was the first thing she planned to do.

'I should have let you know he was here.'

He'd recovered himself now. Whatever emotion he did or didn't feel was locked away somewhere, no one's business but his own.

'That's okay. I've found him now...' She was shaking. So tired that she was almost in tears. All she wanted to do was get home. 'Isaac, will you give Edward the box back, please?'

Isaac seemed to have got over his disappointment and carefully collected up the box and laid it on Edward's desk. 'Thank you.'

'You're welcome.' Edward gave Isaac a guarded half-smile and a little formal nod and her son copied the expression in return. 'Don't forget... What's his name?'

'Stinky.'

Edward raised one eyebrow. 'Well, don't forget Stinky, then.'

He looked up at Charlotte and she tried for a smile.

'Will you stay a moment, please, Charlotte?'

This was the last thing she needed right now. She knew that Isaac shouldn't have been running around the clinic on his own. Edward didn't need to tell her that, and it went without saying that it wouldn't happen again. 'Isaac, will you go and sit with Lucy, please? Just for a minute.' She pointed to the patients' seating area outside.

'Here.' Edward leaned forward, towards the boy, proffering a handful of change. 'Get something for yourself and Lucy from the vending machine. D'you think Stinky wants anything?'

'No, he doesn't. He's not a real rabbit, you know.'

'Of course not. Well, something for you and Lucy then...'

Charlotte was about to stop Isaac from taking the

money, but Edward had already put a selection of coins into his hand and Isaac was halfway towards the door. At least he remembered to thank Edward. She straightened herself and prepared for the dressing down that was coming.

'I'm sorry, Charlotte.'

'Eh…?'

'You must have been worried when you couldn't find Isaac.'

Worried? Frantic, more like. 'I…I'm sorry he bothered you.'

'He was no trouble. He seems to like molecules…' Edward almost smiled and then thought better of it. Too bad. In that brief moment his eyes had seemed bluer, and his dark good looks less brooding.

'He's only five. He likes putting things together and taking them apart again…' The rush of relief at finding Isaac had left her feeling like a limp dishcloth. And now this. Instinctively Charlotte put one hand to her brow, as if to shade herself from the intensity of those blue eyes which seemed to hold so much that was unsaid.

'Hey. What's this?'

He was on his feet, his hands on her shoulders. Edward had the worst timing of any man she'd ever known, bar none. Of all the times to choose to be kind, this was the one most likely to reduce her to tears.

'Nothing. It's nothing. I'm okay.' She tried to avoid his gaze.

'Clearly you're not.'

There was a note of tenderness in his voice that she hadn't heard before. Something warm about the arm which wound around her shoulder. Something about his scent that made her instinctively sink into him, even though she knew that this was probably one of the worst ideas she'd ever had in her life.

Under the crisp white shirt there was some serious musculature. Strong arms, and a flat, hard stomach. For the second time in the last few minutes the swimming pool flashed into Charlotte's head, but this time the image was considerably more inviting.

'I'm okay...' Charlotte thought about pushing him away and then decided that putting her hands anywhere near him would be far too much of a temptation. 'Really. I'm fine.'

He seemed to feel it, too. He stepped back quickly, almost as if she'd burnt him, and turned towards his desk. 'If there's anything that's bothering you, you should let someone know.' He thought for a moment, obviously considering himself an unlikely candidate for any kind of emotional disclosure. 'Lizzie, perhaps...I'm sure she'd be able to do...whatever's needed.'

Edward had switched back into professional mode and the relief was almost palpable. 'No. There's nothing. I just had a bit of a scare when I couldn't find Isaac...' She bit her words back. Nothing like blaming the very person who had just tried to help her.

'I'm sorry. It won't happen again.'

That was supposed to be *her* line. She smiled up at him, wishing that she could smooth some of the creases on his brow. 'It's okay. He's safe, and that's all that matters. I'm sorry he disturbed you. He knows he mustn't wander around here.'

'That's all right. It was nice to talk to him.' He gestured stiffly towards the molecule model kit. 'His approach is refreshingly creative, compared with most.'

Was that a joke? It was difficult to tell with Edward, but the possibility intrigued Charlotte. She could see Lucy and Isaac out of the corner of her eye, settling themselves down on the sofa with their drinks. They'd be at least another five minutes, and hadn't Paula always said that Charlotte only needed five minutes to get anyone to open up?

'What's it for? If you don't mind my asking?'

'You can use it for anything. I'm thinking of DNA sequencing.' The way he brushed off the question almost made her believe that everyone had a model of a DNA sequence somewhere in their office.

'Ah. Right. Anyone in particular?'

'Mine, actually. Just a snippet of it, of course. But don't you think there's something rather interesting about actually being able to look at something that's the very basis of your own make-up?'

'I'd never really thought about it.' Now he mentioned it, there was. There was an obscure symmetry about the concept that made her smile, even if she didn't properly understand it.

'You should. It would be interesting for Isaac…' He narrowed his eyes. 'Perhaps when he's a bit older.'

'Yes, I think so. Is that all?' She should go now. She'd managed to stem her tears for the moment, but who knew how long that particular dam was going to hold? Hopefully until after Isaac was safely tucked up in bed.

'Are you going home? I'm going your way. I'll give you a lift. The buses are horrible at this time of day—' He broke off, as if he'd let something slip that he shouldn't.

How did he know she took the bus home? And how did he know which way she went? Charlotte stared at him.

'I've seen you waiting at the two-three-nine bus stop. And the two-three-nine goes almost directly along my route home. Of course you could be catching the number thirteen, but most people who do that walk down to the Oxford Circus stop, so they can get a seat—' He broke off again, obviously wondering whether that was too much information.

'Right. Next time I want to know which bus to take, I'll know who to ask.' She grinned at him. 'But it's okay, really. You must still have work to do and we'll be going in a minute.'

He shrugged. 'I was operating at six this morning, I should have been gone hours ago. And… You look tired.'

Perhaps Edward noticed more than everyone thought.

There was no perhaps about it. He clearly did. Somewhere inside a smile formed at the thought that some of those things were connected with her.

'We…we can't. Isaac needs a proper car seat…' It was a pity. The buses were always packed on a Friday evening and she could have done with a ride home.

'No problem. I have one fitted in my car.'

Something told Charlotte that Edward had worked all of this through before he'd even made the offer. The complex equation balanced two shopping bags, one child and an indeterminate number of full buses, crawling through the traffic, against one child seat, a comfortable car and a lift home. He probably already knew what she was about to say.

She smiled, wondering whether he'd factored that in or not. 'Okay. If it's no trouble. Thanks.'

CHAPTER TWO

EDWARD GAVE NO explanation for the brand-new child's car seat when he opened the back door of his sleek dark blue car and waved Isaac inside. Perhaps the girls at work were right. Perhaps he *did* have a woman somewhere. A woman with a child. So much for Paula's assertions that it couldn't hurt to try to breach Edward's reserve.

All the same, there was nothing wrong with taking a lift from him, and Charlotte couldn't deny that this was a great deal nicer than the bus. Not having to continually grab at her bags to get them out of the way of someone else's feet. Isaac safely strapped in behind her, with Stinky on his lap. Leather seats. The quiet strains of music floating at her from four different directions. She began to relax.

'It would be more convenient for you to drive to work.'

As they passed Regent's Park Edward's customary forthrightness broke the silence.

'Yeah. More expensive, too.' She grinned at him. 'Congestion charge, parking costs.'

He nodded. 'I thought you were going to say you liked the bus.'

'It's not so bad. You meet a lot of interesting people on buses.'

'So it's a social experiment, then?'

Maybe for Edward. It was a matter of necessity for

Charlotte. 'You could call it that. We like it on the top deck, don't we, Isaac?'

'Yeah. You can see into people's windows,' Isaac piped up from the back seat.

'Can you?' Edward paused for thought. 'What do you see?'

'Christmas trees.'

'In July?'

'No, at Christmas.' Isaac's voice took on the tone of patient explanation that he sometimes used with adults. 'We counted how many Christmas trees we could see on the way home.'

'So you're a mathematician. Is that why you're called Isaac? After Isaac Newton?'

Isaac seemed to have succeeded where the combined talents of the Hunter Clinic had failed. That was definitely a joke, even if Isaac didn't appear to understand it.

'Who?'

Charlotte rolled her eyes. 'He's five, Edward.'

He nodded. 'So you're keeping Newton for later.' He made it sound like leaving the best chocolate in the box until last. He raised his voice, speaking to Isaac again. 'So how many Christmas trees did you count?'

'A million.'

'Really? You live on the moon?' Edward's lips twitched and Isaac cackled with laughter. Although neither seemed to be quite on the same intellectual wavelength, they clearly shared the same sense of humour.

'Noooo. Kentish Town.'

'That explains it, then. Are you sure you didn't count any of them twice?'

Isaac shrugged. 'Maybe. It might have been a hundred.'

It seemed so natural to laugh with them. The obvious thing to do. 'It was three hundred and forty-nine, wasn't it, Isaac?'

'That's right. Three hundred and forty-nine.'

Edward nodded. 'Impressive. That's a prime number, you know.'

'What's a prime number?'

Edward shot a helpless glance at Charlotte and she shrugged. All of a sudden this quiet, reserved man had become almost talkative, and against her better judgement she actually wanted to hear what he had to say for himself.

'It's…um…it's a very special number. There are lots of them. I dare say they'll teach you about that at school.'

'When?'

'Er… Pretty soon, I imagine. Ask your teacher.'

'Okay.'

Lucky escape. Charlotte mouthed the words at him and he raised one eyebrow, as if he'd been in complete control all along.

'How many are there?'

She saw the line of Edward's jaw stiffen as it became apparent that she had spoken too soon.

'More than you can count. Even if you ride on the bus all day. The first prime number is two. Then five…'

By the time he'd worked his way up to twenty-nine and shown no signs of flagging Charlotte decided to step in. At this rate they could be driving to Birmingham and back before either Isaac went to sleep or Edward got to the point where he could no longer work out the next prime number in his head.

She turned in her seat to face Isaac. 'Edward's got to stop counting now, sweetie, because he's driving and has to keep his eye on the road. I'll explain all about prime numbers when we get home.'

'Okay.'

It was nice having her in the car. She smelled good—like soap and roses. Rose soap, maybe. Edward ran through

all the possibilities in his head and surprised himself with
how delicious each of them was.

She didn't just smell nice; she *was* nice. Whenever he
saw her with the clinic's clients she was always the same.
Gentle, reassuring, and yet with a hint of fun about her.
She made people smile. But Edward couldn't help but think
there was more. When he'd seen her at the bus stop the
other day, huddled under her umbrella in the pouring rain,
there had been a defeated slant to her shoulders that had
made him want to stop, but his nerve had failed him. Getting involved with people wasn't what Edward did.

'You must like jazz?' She was stretching her legs out
in front of her. Smiling.

'Very much,' he said. 'You?'

'I don't really know. I've not listened to much. I like
this.'

'Good.' He could have left it at that. Would normally
have left it at that. But against his better judgement he
wanted to prolong the conversation. 'Most people just automatically say they love jazz, irrespective of whether
they've listened to any.'

She gave a little laughing nod, as if she knew just what
he meant. 'It's one of those things that you're meant to
like, isn't it? I mean if you admit to not knowing much
about jazz, then it's like owning up to being some kind
of barbarian.'

'I don't think you're a barbarian.' He thought she was
a damn sight more honest that most people.

He was rewarded with one of the smiles that she was
so free with. This one seemed just for him. 'That's all
right, then.'

Charlotte asked him to drop them in the High Street,
but when Edward insisted on taking her all the way home
she directed him to a quiet backstreet. Small houses—
many of them shabby and unkempt. He parked outside

a house with a neat front garden. The front door badly
needed a paint job. Charlotte jumped out of the car, un-
buckling Isaac's seat belt while Edward took her shopping
bags out of the boot.

'Can I carry these in for you?'

'No. No, that's okay, thank you. Thanks for the lift.' She
picked the bags up with one hand and took Isaac's hand
with the other. 'I'll see you on Monday.'

'Bye, Edward. Thank you…'

She shot a glance of approbation in her son's direction
and then turned away. Suddenly it seemed that she couldn't
get rid of him fast enough and a vague feeling of disappointment nudged at him.

'Bye, Isaac. Nice to meet you…'

The boy twisted his head around as his mother marched
him away, and gave him a grin, but Charlotte seemed
caught up with her shopping bags. There was nothing to
keep him so Edward got back into his car. As he turned
in the road he noticed in his rearview mirror that the front
gate was sticking and that she was struggling with it. He
almost stopped the car and got out again, but then she
kicked it and it snapped open, and she walked up the front
path without looking back.

Charlotte slammed the front door closed behind her and
dropped her shopping, leaning back against the door.
Home. Half of her wished she was still in Edward's car
and that they really had been driving to Birmingham and
back. Newcastle, even. The other half was glad that he
was gone before he'd had a chance to see the threadbare
carpet in the hall and the second-hand furniture in her
sitting room.

'Is Edward your boss, Mum?'

'He's a surgeon. At the clinic.'

'So he makes people well? Like you do?'

'Yes, darling.'

Isaac nodded. 'He's nice'

Charlotte found herself smiling again. 'Yes, he is, isn't he?' She picked up her shopping bags. 'Now, let's see what we've got for supper, shall we?'

It was only a short drive from Edward's house back to Charlotte's, but it was like travelling from one world to another. The trendy shops and cafés gave way to houses which seemed even more run-down than they had yesterday evening, and when he drove slowly along Charlotte's road it didn't seem any more salubrious than the last time he'd been here.

Perhaps he shouldn't have come. At ten o'clock on a Saturday morning she could be out, or having a lie-in… anything. But he was here now, with Stinky sitting next to him on the front passenger seat. If she wasn't there, then maybe Stinky would fit through the letterbox.

Cars lined the pavement, and he had to drive past her house to find a parking spot. As he did so he caught a glimpse of her on the doorstep, between the broad backs of two men who seemed to be crowding close in on her. What he could see of her stiff, upright frame, screamed that there was something wrong.

Edward accelerated into a free space. 'Don't move, Stinky. I'll be back in a minute.' He lunged out of the car, and down the road, to where her front gate stood open.

'Charlotte!' Now that he was closer he was sure that he was right. She was dressed in sweat pants and a tee shirt, bare feet on the doorstep, but she stood as tall as she could, the door almost closed behind her, her face fierce and determined. 'What's going on?'

She stared at him as if he'd just landed from another planet. One of the men swung round to face Edward, his pudgy face harsh. 'Nothing to concern you, sir. Just a bit of business with the lady.'

Her face had flushed bright red. Tears rimmed her eyes, before she quickly brushed them away. These guys were bad news. They stank of the kind of aggression which dressed itself up in cheap suits and a nasty attitude.

'Then you have business with me.' Edward pushed in between them and stood next to her on the step. He wanted to put his arm around her, ask her if she was all right, but this wasn't the time. 'Step back. Now.'

They stepped back. The anger that was raging in his chest must have been showing in his face, because the expression on the face of the larger of the two became slightly less belligerent. Edward pressed his advantage. 'Now, what's all this about?'

'Are you this lady's husband, sir?'

'I'm her legal advisor.' Suddenly Edward was mightily glad that he'd left Stinky in the car. This was rapidly beginning to look like a confrontation of some sort, and holding a battered blue rabbit in his hand wouldn't have helped.

He felt Charlotte's fingers on his arm. 'No, Edward. Please.' Her voice was almost a whisper.

If she wanted him to go, she had another think coming. Edward didn't shift his gaze from the two men. 'Who are you? Do you have some identification?'

One of the men reached slowly into the inside pocket of his jacket and drew out a wallet. Opening it, he held it out for Edward to see.

Debt collectors. What had Charlotte got herself into? No time for that now. A child's whimper sounded from the other side of the door and he felt Charlotte's small, convulsive movement against his arm. 'Go inside, please, Charlotte. Close the door.'

She looked up at him. Cheeks pink, her lovely eyes still brimming with tears. She hesitated, obviously torn between going to comfort her son and dealing with the men on her doorstep.

'Go and make sure Isaac's okay.' He spoke gently to her and she nodded quickly, disappearing inside the house.

One down, two to go.

He turned to the two men. 'I assume you're not in possession of a court order with regards to this property?'

'No, sir.' Somehow the man made that sound like a threat.

'In that case I'm asking you to leave now. I'll speak to you when you're standing on the pavement.'

The men exchanged a look. Obviously they considered that browbeating him was a different matter from a lone woman and a child, and Edward didn't bother to conceal his disgust as they turned and took their time in walking down the path.

'There is the matter of an unpaid debt, ma'am.'

Edward looked round and saw Charlotte back in the doorway, pulling a pair of sneakers on. She must have settled Isaac and come back out again.

'You don't speak to her. If you've something to say, then say it to me.' Edward had just appointed himself, unasked, into the role of protector, but he didn't care. No one else was around to do it.

'I need to speak to the lady.' The man's voice suddenly became gentle. He'd seen a way in and was trying for it. Be nice to her, then divide and conquer.

Edward looked round at Charlotte. It was one thing to expect her to go along with his instructions at the clinic, but here… Here she had Isaac to think of, and she wasn't going to give that responsibility away too easily.

'You can speak to my…' She walked down the path and stood next to him. 'My legal advisor.'

The man pressed his lips together. 'In that case…' He

turned to Edward. 'We're looking for this lady's husband. We have reason to believe he's here—'

'He isn't,' Charlotte broke in vehemently. 'I haven't seen him for over a year.'

'We'd like to check, madam.' Deftly the man had turned back on Charlotte.

'You have no right of entry to this property. The lady's already told you that the person you're looking for isn't here, and that she doesn't want you in her home.' Edward folded his arms to indicate that this was now an end to the matter.

'Fair enough. But do you know where he is?' The question was aimed at Charlotte again.

This time she gave her answer to Edward. 'I don't...'

He nodded, laying his hand on her arm with as much tenderness as he could muster. 'They're allowed to ask you whether you know where the person they're looking for is. It's entirely up to you whether you answer or not.'

'We haven't lived together for eighteen months. I have the name of his solicitor.' Her voice was almost a whisper, her eyes pleading. Not just for him to help her get rid of these men. For him to understand.

'Can we have that at least...please?' The word *please* seemed to stick in the man's throat and he took another step forward, as if this was an invitation into the house.

'Wait there.' Edward turned to Charlotte and she nodded. She knew as well as he did that if she could give these men something it might get them off her back. 'Go and get it, then.'

She hurried inside and Edward indulged in a staring contest with the men, open hostility buzzing between them. She returned, clutching a piece of paper with a hastily scribbled address on it, and gave it to Edward. 'Here it is.'

Edward turned back to the men on the pavement.

'Right. The lady hasn't seen her husband in months, and she doesn't know where he is. She's given you every assistance she can in locating him, and this ends her involvement in the matter.'

'All right.' The man snatched the paper that Edward proffered. 'And you're sure you don't know where he is?'

'Doesn't sound very likely to me,' his companion sneered, forcing home the point. 'Doesn't he want to see his own kid?'

Edward heard Charlotte's sudden intake of breath and fought to stay in control of the fury that swept over him in a red-and-black wave. Much as he'd like to, getting into a fight with these guys wasn't going to help. 'You've asked your question and you've got your answer. You know full well that the law prevents you from harassing this lady any further or from speaking to a minor.' He pulled his phone out of his pocket. 'You've got ten seconds to get going before I call the police.'

The two looked at each other, grins on their faces. Edward wondered how many people actually followed through with that threat. He started to thumb the numbers on the screen.

'All right, mate.' The larger of the two, who was obviously the lead man, held up his hands in surrender. 'We're going.'

'Tell your head office to expect a letter, confirming the information that this lady's given you. She knows nothing more which will assist you, and she wants no further contact with you.' Edward pressed his advantage home.

The two turned without a word and Edward watched them lumber off down the road and climb into a shiny SUV. Business was clearly booming for them.

'Go and see to Isaac. I'll just keep an eye out here for a couple of minutes.' The SUV roared past them down the road, with the engine being gunned so that it made as much noise as possible.

He looked around. Charlotte was still there, her face burning so red that he probably could have warmed his hands on it if he'd needed to.

'Thanks, Edward. I'm sorry you had to see that.'

'It's not your fault. Those guys had no right to act the way they did.'

Her gaze dropped to the cracked paving stones at their feet. 'Yeah, I know. It was such a shock to see them on the doorstep, and they were so intimidating...' She looked as if she was about to burst into tears and then visibly pulled herself together.

Turning, she hurried back up the path and opened the front door. 'I'm really grateful to you, Edward. I'll...' She had the grace to flush an even deeper red before she gave him his marching orders. 'I'm sorry, but I need to go and see how Isaac is. Will you excuse me? I'll see you on Monday.'

The door closed, and Edward found himself standing alone. What was he supposed to do now? Charlotte had made her intentions more than clear, and he supposed he should leave. But he was damned if he was going to leave a woman and child alone in this situation.

Edward strode to his car, snatched Stinky up from the front seat, and walked back to her front door.

CHAPTER THREE

ISAAC WAS WHIMPERING in her arms. He was trying to be brave, but his little body was shaking as he clung to Charlotte. She wanted to go and find those men and punch them. More than once.

There was a noise at the letterbox and she tried not to jump. Isaac fell silent, staring at the door.

'Charlotte? Charlotte, I have Stinky here. That's what I came for this morning. He's too big to put through the letterbox.'

She thought about telling Edward to leave him on the doorstep. She might possibly have been able to, whatever the consequences later on, if she hadn't seen the look on Isaac's face. It was as if he'd just seen the cavalry, riding hell for leather over the horizon.

Perhaps he was right. Maybe his five-year-old mind was able to see a little more clearly than hers. She wouldn't be all that surprised. Edward engendered such a plethora of different emotions in her that her judgement wasn't to be trusted where he was concerned.

'I'm coming…' she called out to him, and took Isaac's hand, leading him to the door. She took a deep breath and opened it.

She had hardly registered it before, through her tears and her panic, but Edward's eyes looked a brighter blue than usual. His hair darker. There was less of the suit and tie about him and a great deal more of the enigma, with his dark shirt and jacket giving him an almost dangerous look. Even the blue stuffed toy, grasped lightly in his long fingers, couldn't dispel the feeling that here was a hero, come somehow to save her.

'Hey, Isaac.'

He might only have been able to spare her son a half-smile, but it would have melted an ice hotel, launched a battleship, and cracked a grin on the face of a statue.

'I brought Stinky for you.'

Isaac looked up at him and wiped his nose on his sleeve. Charlotte resisted the impulse to tell him to use a tissue on the grounds that she'd been doing the same herself just a moment ago. This morning Isaac could do anything he liked, as long as she could see just a glimpse of his smile.

'Thank you.' Isaac's voice was small, quavering, and it tugged at Charlotte's heart.

'Bit of a morning, eh, little man?' Edward suddenly seemed to realise that getting down onto Isaac's level would be a good idea and dropped to one knee, proffering the boy's toy.

Isaac nodded, reaching for Stinky. Charlotte felt his hand slip out of hers and he walked uncertainly towards Edward, then seemed to throw all caution to the winds and flung his arms around Edward's neck.

'Hey… Hey, there.' For a moment Edward's hands fluttered awkwardly. Then he wrapped his arms around Isaac, hugging him as if he could hold him tightly enough to make everything all right.

For a moment all Charlotte wanted was to be in on that hug.

'You know what?' Edward had got to his feet, taking Isaac with him. Safe and sound in his arms. 'You and I have a job to do. We're going to tell your mum that everything's going to be okay. That we'll look after her.'

Isaac nodded sagely.

'I think we could all do with a cup of tea. What do you say?'

'I want milk.'

'Good idea. I'll have some milk, too. And we'll make your mum a cup of tea.'

'She likes coffee. The kind with the froth on top.'

Isaac had a tight hold of Edward's jacket collar, his other arm wrapped around Stinky. Charlotte knew that his tears weren't too far below the surface, but Edward seemed to be reassuring him with his sheer bulk and unflappability.

'Okay. Tell you what—we could go out for coffee, if you'd like.' His gaze moved from Isaac to Charlotte. 'What do you think?'

'I…' She wanted his arms around her so much. His comfort. Charlotte pulled herself upright, squaring her shoulders. 'We're all right. Really.'

'Yeah. I can see that.' He reached forward, touching her cheek so lightly that she shivered. As his hand dropped to his side his fingers skimmed his thumb, as if he wanted to test the exact nature and volume of the tears he'd brushed away.

'We can manage, Edward. I don't know what I would have done if you hadn't turned up just then, and I can't tell you how much I appreciate it…' Good start. That was really going to make him feel that it was okay for him to go away now, wasn't it?

'But…?'

'But I can't keep you. You must have things to do.'

Edward always had something to do. His head was always buried in a book, or some papers. Even when she'd chanced to see him in the street he was always deep in thought, and half the time he didn't even acknowledge her, either because he hadn't seen or didn't want to see.

'I don't think so. In fact I've nothing to do today. It's

only fifteen minutes over to my place.' He pursed his lips, as if he'd surprised himself by the invitation as much as he'd just surprised Charlotte. 'We'll get coffee on the way, and we can talk…privately. Perhaps I can help.'

She could have turned his help down for herself, but she had Isaac to think about, and Charlotte had no choice but to grab at any and every offer that came her way. And there was the matter of that nagging need at the back of her head, which wanted her to explain to Edward, tell him that she wasn't the person that all of this made her seem. She was going to have to swallow her pride and go for coffee.

Edward had waited in the hallway while she dragged on a pair of jeans, shoved her feet into her sandals and splashed her face with water. Her eyes had looked puffy in the mirror, but she hadn't wanted to keep him waiting for too long, so she'd dropped her make-up bag into a canvas holdall along with a few of Isaac's favourite toys to keep him occupied.

They'd stopped at a coffee shop and Edward had ushered them in. Isaac had slipped his hand into Edward's, tugging at his jacket until he'd lifted him up to see over the counter. He seemed to trust that if he stuck with his new friend no harm would come to them, and Charlotte hoped that her son was right.

Now they turned into a wide street, dappled by sunlight shining through the branches of the trees. Turned again into a short drive, behind a high wall hung with greenery, and came to a halt outside a double-fronted Georgian house, white-painted with slim, elegant lines.

It was quiet here. Far enough from the main road for them to be able to hear birdsong. Charlotte handed Edward the cardboard coffee holder and busied herself with getting Isaac out of the car.

The silence between them was oppressive. Edward

seemed awkward as he opened the front door, walking inside without even asking them in, and Charlotte began to wish that she was anywhere but here. Apart from being at home, that was, waiting for the phone to ring again.

'Well…' He clapped his hands together awkwardly, like a man who was unused to guests. 'Here we are.'

'Yes.' Charlotte stepped tentatively over the threshold, holding tightly onto Isaac's hand. Inside the house it was tranquil—a cream-painted hallway, pictures on the walls, green plants everywhere.

'Let's go into the sitting room.' Edward seemed to galvanise himself into action and opened a wide panelled door, ushering them through it.

Sunlight streamed through the front windows onto pale oatmeal-coloured sofas at the front. A TV, nestling unobtrusively in one corner, conceded pride of place to a state-of-the-art sound system. The room ran the full depth of the house, and next to the French windows at the back stood a grand piano.

'What a lovely room.' She gave her son's hand a squeeze, although whether it was to give or receive confidence she wasn't quite sure. 'Isn't it, Isaac?'

Isaac was too busy looking around to reply. At the lines of glass-fronted cabinets, heavy with books. The green plants, arching gracefully around the windows.

'Come and meet Archie.' Edward beckoned Isaac over towards the French windows, where a ginger cat lay stretched out on the carpet, basking in the warm sunlight.

'Is he a lion?' Isaac looked up at him gravely.

Edward laughed. 'Well, he's not very fierce. You won't need that.' He gestured towards Isaac's plastic ray gun, which he'd insisted on bringing along with him.

Isaac stowed the ray gun in his pocket, just in case he'd need it later, and followed Edward over to where the cat lay. He watched solemnly as Edward tickled its ears and then its tummy as it rolled over, luxuriating in his touch.

'Do you want to stroke him?'

Edward was letting Isaac approach the creature in his own time, and Charlotte smiled as Isaac slowly reached out.

'He's growling.' Isaac snatched his hand away.

'No, that's purring. It means he likes you.' Edward drew back a little, letting Isaac stroke Archie.

'Be gentle with him, sweetie. Remember that he's much smaller than you are.' Charlotte stayed at her post by the door, still not sure whether to accept the quiet welcome of this place.

'Would Isaac like to watch some TV? While we talk?'

'Oh. Yes, he might do. Thank you.' Charlotte took the remote that Edward proffered and found a channel that Isaac liked, turning the sound down to a quiet murmur.

Edward set a low coffee table in front of the screen, put Isaac's frothed milk onto it and opened a cupboard, drawing out the molecule modelling kit.

Charlotte grinned. 'You're going to let him play with your toys?'

'If I share, then maybe he'll let me have a go with his ray gun. Will he be all right here?'

'He'll be fine. Look, he's already made a new friend.' Charlotte nodded towards Isaac, who was talking confidingly to Archie, stroking him carefully.

'Good. Well, we can talk through here.'

There was a door at the far end of the room, by the piano, and Edward disappeared through it, leaving Charlotte to get Isaac out of his jacket and settle him in front of the television.

She took one last look at Isaac, and then took a deep breath. Time to face Edward now. Now that keeping up appearances was no longer an option it was going to have to be the truth. She just hoped that he would understand.

He was sitting at a table in the large kitchen, studying the coffee in front of him as if there was some solution in there. She could tell him the answer to that. She'd tried it enough times herself. She mustered a smile, and sat down opposite him.

'So who's Archie named after? Archimedes?' She pulled her own coffee towards her and peeled off the plastic lid. It was smooth and strong and the caffeine hit her straight between the eyes.

He looked up, suddenly aware of her presence. 'Yes, actually. Although it's a mispronunciation, of course. Am I that predictable?'

'No. I thought of the most unlikely thing I could and suggested that—' She broke off as he smiled at her. That smile did all kinds of things to her, none of which were going to be of much help at the moment.

'So.' His gaze dropped to his cup again. 'You're in trouble, aren't you?'

'Yes. I am.' She should have realised that Edward would cut straight to the point. He wasn't much for small talk. Charlotte hadn't anticipated how much of a relief it would be. 'It isn't what you think.'

He looked up at her. Those deep blue eyes were almost irresistible. 'I'm not thinking anything.'

'You're always thinking something, aren't you?'

A trace of a grin tugged at his lips. 'Yes, I suppose I am.'

Suddenly she wanted to defend herself from all the implications of what Edward had seen and from whatever conclusions that agile, razor-sharp mind of his was working its way towards. 'The debts aren't mine, Edward.'

'I know. It was your husband they were looking for...'

'He'll be my ex-husband soon. Very soon, if everything goes as planned.'

Maybe she should have been a little less vehement about that. Said it a little more as if it was a matter of fact rather than an avowal of innocence. Edward seemed far more at home with facts than emotions.

'Have you asserted your separation financially?'

'Yes. There are no more joint accounts and credit cards. The house and the mortgage are in my name.'

'Then you have nothing to worry about. As long as you've applied for a Deed of Separation, and you're not jointly liable for any of his debts…'

'How do you know all this?' The question had occurred to Charlotte on her doorstep, but she'd pushed it to the back of her mind.

'I have a degree in Law.'

'As well as being a surgeon?'

'I…um…I was advised to wait until I was eighteen to go to medical school. I was at a loose end.'

'So…' The gossip was correct, then. 'You *are* a genius?'

'They called it "gifted" when I was a kid. Now it's called High Learning Potential.'

The twitch of his lips told Charlotte that they were just labels, which Edward didn't set much store by.

'I don't need to be a genius to know that there's more to your situation than what you've told me.'

There was a lot more. Charlotte grinned at him almost automatically, the way she did whenever anyone offered anything that sounded a bit too much like sympathy. 'Really?'

'Yeah, really. And you're not going to convince me otherwise with that smile, either. Even if it is a very nice one.'

Stop now. One thing at a time. Having Edward as a concerned friend was already turning her universe upside down. It was a bit too soon for compliments.

'You're right, that's not all. My husband had…I think it's probably fair to say *has*…a gambling addiction.'

'And that's why you left him?'

'I wasn't that smart. I didn't know about it until the bailiffs started calling. The first one was the day after Isaac's second birthday.' She sighed. She didn't need to go into details; he was getting the gist. 'I started out by paying his debts. He promised me that he'd stopped, and I believed him.'

'But he lied?' He was blunt, but there was no brutality there. Just the truth.

'Yes, he just kept on racking up the debts. Internet gaming sites, card games… He maxed out our credit cards and I dipped into the money I'd inherited from my parents just to keep a roof over our heads.' Charlotte gulped in a breath of air. This time she was going to do things better. She had to for Isaac's sake.

'But you couldn't hold it together.' Another flat, emotionless statement of the inevitable facts.

'I did for a while. Then he left. That was eighteen months ago. I sold the house, paid off all the debts, and managed to scrape enough together for a deposit on a smaller house. Made a new start for Isaac and me.'

Edward just nodded.

Caught in the force of his concentration, Charlotte realised that Edward was not an absent-minded, otherworldly creature. He was thinking things through, his ruthless single-mindedness not allowing a single detail to escape.

'Does your husband know where you are?'

'Yes, he knows. I was hoping that he'd come and see Isaac but he never has.'

Charlotte heaved a sigh. She didn't need to tell him about the thing that had damned her the most—it didn't affect the problem at hand. Anyway, it was humiliating.

Even more so than having to admit she was being chased by her husband's debtors.

She met those blue eyes again. Ever questioning, but not as judgemental as she'd feared.

'And you said your divorce is in the pipeline?'

'Yes. I have the Decree Nisi and I'm waiting for the Decree Absolute. I'm hoping that he won't throw any spanners into the works and put in a last-minute objection.'

'Do you have any reason to think he will?'

'No… Maybe… I don't know. Peter's not exactly the most predictable of people.' Charlotte sighed. 'He's not strong. He'll do whatever gets him through the day and forget all about the consequences for tomorrow.'

'You don't trust him.'

Damn right she didn't. She had very little reason to. 'No, I don't. The men who called this morning aren't the only people looking to get paid. I had a telephone call last night from someone who said I owed money for a mobile phone bill.'

'Do you?'

'No!' She was protesting too much again. 'My phone's a pay-as-you-go…'

Charlotte reached for her handbag to show him the phone and Edward stopped her, laying his hand on her wrist.

'It's okay.'

'It isn't. The divorce won't protect me if he's managed to raise a line of credit in my name, and I've no money to pay off any more of his debts.'

It was as if she and Isaac were being dragged back into the nightmare that she'd worked so hard to get out of, and there was nothing she could do about it. Charlotte gulped back the tears, pulling her hand away from his grasp.

'What did you tell them?' He was still calm, almost icy cool. Still focussed on the facts.

Charlotte took a deep breath. She should try to sound a little more grateful, Edward had already helped her more than he had any reason to. 'I said that I had no knowledge of the account in question and asked them to put everything in writing and send it to me.'

'Good. We can start making enquiries on Monday. In the meantime, is there anyone that you and Isaac can stay with?'

'Not really. My parents are dead and I don't have any brothers or sisters...' She tried to smile, make light of it, but Charlotte had never felt so alone. 'We'll be okay. I'll take the phone off the hook and lock the door...'

'You'll stay here.' Even Edward seemed surprised at his uncompromising words.

'No! I mean...Edward, it's kind of you to offer, but I couldn't think of it.'

'What about Isaac? I gather that Sunday mornings are a favourite time for debt collectors to make their calls. He's old enough to know what's going on now.'

Low blow. He'd found the spot where her guilt was almost unbearable. 'I thought he was too young to remember. But when those men called this morning...'

Isaac had understood exactly who they were and had launched himself at them, trying to drive them away, trying to protect her. Charlotte had managed to keep hold of him, and the men had smirked at each other as she bundled him back into the house.

She heard Edward sigh.

'Look, you need to get yourself and Isaac out of the firing line for a few days, until you have a chance to sort this out. I've plenty of room here—there are two spare bedrooms upstairs—and you'll both be safe.'

He didn't mince his words, or dress it up to make it sound as if she had a choice, but he was right. She *did* need to get her son away from this nightmare, and she had no-where to take him.

'Charlotte.'

He reached out to her, his finger tipping her chin up-wards. His shrewd blue eyes saw straight through her. There were no excuses, no way that she could just fob him off with something.

'Where else are you going to go?'

CHAPTER FOUR

HE HADN'T MEANT to be cruel, just to look at the situation rationally. But when she finally gave way to her tears, her forehead sinking until it almost touched the surface of his kitchen table, her body trembling with the effort that it seemed to take her to cry, Edward realised that she wasn't the only one who was in over her head. He didn't feel equal to this—not the crying woman at his kitchen table, or the vulnerable child on his sofa—and the knowledge that he was way past the point of dispensing some good advice and leaving them to it wasn't helping much.

'Hey.' He reached out, touching her arm tentatively with the tips of his fingers. 'Charlotte, please don't.'

She ignored him, and it had been a stupid thing to say anyway. Charlotte was at perfect liberty to do whatever she wanted. It was him who didn't want her to cry, because it wrenched his heart so much to see it.

'Okay. Well, you can cry as much as you like. But I'd appreciate it if you'd keep it down a bit or Isaac will be in here, blasting me with his ray gun for upsetting you. Which I didn't mean to do, by the way.'

Her shoulders stopped shaking. Slowly she raised her head. For a moment Edward was unsure about whether she was going to burst into laughter or start crying again. He decided to wait. He'd probably said more than enough already.

'I'll pay you rent.' Her voice was low, a little unsteady, but there was no doubt that she was back in control of herself.

'No. I won't accept it.' She opened her mouth to protest and he silenced her with a look. 'That's not negotiable.'

'I could clean for you.'

'That's not going to work either. I have a cleaning lady and there will be hell to pay if you put her out of a job.'

Somehow, from somewhere, she managed to find a smile. It was like basking in a ray of sunshine on a rainy day. 'I wondered whether it was you who kept all these plants watered.'

'We have an…understanding. She looks after Archie and the plants, doesn't move anything that I'm working on, and I keep out of her way and don't forget to pay her. Works like a dream.'

'I'm sure it does. Does she cook?'

'I imagine so. Not while she's here, though.'

'I'll cook for you, then.'

She narrowed her eyes obstinately and a sudden flood of longing gripped him. He hadn't counted on these sorts of complications, and wondered whether what he was about to do was wise.

'Okay. Deal.'

She bit her lip. 'Isaac won't be any trouble. He won't touch any of your things. I'll make sure of it…'

That sounded a bit dull. 'I can put anything that I don't want touched away out of his reach. And he can be as much trouble as he likes.'

She gave a tremulous laugh. Charlotte wasn't just a pretty face; she was tough, too. And brave. And about a million other things, all of which he felt inexplicably driven to find out more about.

'You have no idea how much trouble a determined five-year-old can be and, trust me, you don't want to find out.'

'Well...I'll leave that to you. What I mean is that you should make yourselves at home.' His mother was always telling him that this house was far too big for one. Granted this was not what she'd had in mind, but the principle was a good one. There was more than enough room for him to carry on with his life, undisturbed by two house guests.

'Thank you. I really appreciate this, Edward. And it'll only be for a few days, while I get everything sorted out.'

'You can stay as long as you like.'

He knew that it would take longer than a few days to work this out, and he didn't want her or Isaac going back home until it was. They'd both been through too much already.

After he'd taken them back to Charlotte's house, to pack what they needed, Edward had left them to their own devices. They had their own routine, which clearly involved eating and sleeping at regular intervals, and he had his, which disregarded any such practical activities in favour of whatever he happened to be doing at the time.

When he parked outside his house on Sunday evening his mind was still racing from the concepts that had been explored in the afternoon seminar he'd attended, and then endlessly again afterwards over sandwiches. The house was dark, and as he slipped his key into the lock on the front door it occurred to him that Charlotte might have taken her son and left, leaving a note on the hall table for him to find when he got back.

'Oh, no, you don't...' He muttered the words to himself, since she wasn't around to hear them.

He slid the key into the lock and the door gave by six inches, then caught. The chain, which usually hung unused from the frame, barred his entry. At least he wasn't going to have to get back into his car and drive over to Charlotte's house, to make sure that she and Isaac were all right.

All the same, there was the small matter of being locked out of his own home. Ringing the bell would probably wake Isaac up, as would bellowing through the letterbox, so Edward pulled the door to, twisting the key to relock it.

He seldom took the path around the side of the house, and he jumped as a pair of iridescent orbs appeared from the bushes. 'Locked out as well, eh?' Archie swished his tail. 'Yeah, I know. It's a bit much.'

Discomfiture that his arrival home hadn't provided the usual well-ordered release from the complications of the world began to swell into anger.

He didn't need to find the key for the French windows; they were standing open. She was there, in the failing light, curled up in a chair on the stone-flagged patio.

'Charlotte!'

She jumped, throwing off the woollen jacket that was wrapped around her shoulders and twisting around. When she saw him she smiled, and Edward felt the hard edges of his anger melt.

'It's you…' She rubbed her eyes with her hand, as if she had been dozing.

It occurred to Edward to make the point that there wasn't much to gain by locking the front door if she was going to fall asleep with the doors to the patio wide open. But that sounded rather too much like criticism, and he'd already seen her flinch enough times when she or Isaac did something that she thought he might disapprove of.

'Did I wake you?'

'I must have just dropped off…' Her gaze swung from him to the house and then back again. 'Ohhh. I locked you out…'

That didn't seem so much of an issue as it had a moment ago. 'Putting the chain on the front door's a sensible precaution at night.'

'And falling asleep with the patio doors open isn't.' She gave a little self-deprecatory smile.

He shrugged, as if he'd not thought about that. 'Why don't you give yourself a break? You're safe here. No one can find you.' No one apart from him. He liked that thought so much that he dumped his briefcase on the stone flags and pulled up a chair, sitting down next to her.

She nodded. 'Thank you. Having a safe place to stay has meant a great deal to me and Isaac.'

'So you've had a good day?'

'Yes, thank you. We had lunch and then went to the park. They've got a great playground there, and a lovely cafeteria. We played football, as well.'

She made it sound like a real treat, and Edward found himself smiling, wondering whether football wouldn't have been preferable to a dark, humid lecture theatre. She and Isaac were a small, self-sufficient unit, though. They probably wouldn't have wanted him along.

'Sounds nice. Have you thought about what you're going to do yet? With regard to your situation?' He tried to put it delicately.

'I called Paula and she's going to lend me her laptop tomorrow. I've drawn up a list of things I need to find out about, and then I can start in on sorting everything out.'

Edward had left his own laptop on the coffee table, specifically so she could use it if she wanted to go on the internet. He should have thought that she wouldn't touch it, or allow Isaac to either, without asking. 'No need for that. Mine's right there.'

'Oh. Thank you.' There was a hint of awkwardness in her manner as she slid to the edge of her seat. 'Would you like something to drink? There's some hot chocolate…'

Her determination to pay her own way seemed to know no bounds. Everything he did for her—things that he gave without expecting anything in return—was entered on a balance sheet in her head to be repaid at a later date. Edward was debating whether he should tell her that she really didn't need to wait on him like this, but she was on her feet already.

'Hot chocolate would be great. Thank you.'

Since she so much wanted to do something for him, he supposed he should let her, and Charlotte's bright smile as she disappeared into the house tentatively proved his theory.

She brought him a mug of creamy hot chocolate, along with a plate of home-made biscuits.

'Thank you.' He took a sip and nodded his approval. Archie materialised from his nightly tour of the garden and curled up under her chair. If she'd been feeding him as well as she seemed intent on feeding Edward he couldn't fault the animal's change of allegiance. 'There's something I want you to do for me.'

She brightened noticeably. 'Yes, of course. What is it?'

Too late, Edward realised that he should have chosen his words more carefully. The impression that she was about to do him a favour was accurate enough, in the context of the amount of thinking time he'd already given to her plight, but Charlotte probably wouldn't see it that way.

'My father has his own practice at law, and I want you to consider making an appointment to go and see him. He can advise you and get his investigative team to find out exactly what's going on. With my dad on your side, you can get things sorted out quicker and more efficiently.'

'But I can't afford to pay a lawyer, Edward.'

'You won't need to. If I ask him, he'll do it for free.'

She hesitated. For a moment Edward thought that her pride was going to let her see sense and give in to expediency. Then she shook her head.

'No, I can't do that. It wouldn't be fair. Please don't mention it to him.'

He sighed. 'What isn't fair is that you're spending time on researching and fighting your own battles when there are people who will happily help you out. It's not just you that it makes an impact on—it's your work at the clinic.'

That particular argument didn't stand up to much scrutiny. Charlotte must have been worried sick over the last couple of weeks, but she'd never shown any evidence of it on the job.

She frowned at him. 'I wouldn't let anything get in the way of my work.'

'I know you wouldn't mean to, but none of us can be expected to give a hundred per cent when we're under the kind of pressure that you're facing at the moment.' He was pressing hard, exploiting every chink in her armour.

She hesitated. 'Edward, I… You're confusing me.'

Well, now she knew how *he* felt. 'It's very simple, Charlotte. Trust me.'

Two little words, spoken almost as a throwaway to emphasise his point. He should have known better. If he'd thought about it for two seconds he would have realised that trust was something she had a lot of difficulty with.

'I'm sorry.' Without another word, she got to her feet and disappeared into the house.

Edward leaned back in his chair and stared out into the evening shadows. Archie slid past his legs, waiting to be stroked, and he ran his fingers thoughtfully along the cat's back. Adjusting to the complex myriad of emotions that Charlotte and Isaac had brought to the quiet peace of his home was proving more difficult than he'd imagined.

The green reflective eyes seemed for a moment to understand his frustration, and then Archie was off again, his instinctive urge to chase shadows getting the better of him. Edward silently wished him better luck than *he'd* had tonight.

* * *

Edward had left the house before she was up the following morning. Charlotte went through the routine of getting herself up and ready for work, and Isaac ready for school, almost on autopilot. She was well aware that she'd walked out on Edward in the middle of a conversation last night, and common courtesy demanded that if he decided to broach the subject again she should have some kind of reasoned answer for him.

'Mum…?'

'Yes, Isaac.'

'Is everything going to be all right?'

She sat down opposite him at the kitchen table. 'Of course it is. What makes you ask that, sweetie?'

Some kind of understanding of the situation they were in, perhaps?

Isaac shrugged. 'I don't know.'

His brow was still furrowed, perhaps as a result of the unerring radar that seemed to alert him whenever something was wrong, even though he didn't grasp quite what it was.

'Look, sweetie. Those men came to our house by mistake on Saturday—they weren't looking for us. We're staying here with Edward for a few days, while I get everything sorted out, but that's going to happen very soon. Everything's going to be okay.'

'Do you promise?'

He still lived in a world where she could make everything right. Those trusting eyes would give Charlotte the courage to face anything that the world could throw at her. They'd even give her the courage to ask just one more favour from Edward.

'Yes. I promise. Cross my heart.'

She'd gone straight to Edward's office when she'd arrived at work and left a note for him on his desk. As luck would have it, he returned from his morning's surgery just as Allie and Paula were both within range of the nurses' station, beckoning Charlotte into his office in full view of both of them.

She was aware that two pairs of eyes were following her every move, so knew she'd better make this quick. 'I wanted to apologise. For last night…'

'You have nothing to apologise for. Why don't you sit down?' He threw himself into his leather chair.

'Because…' Charlotte shifted uncomfortably from one foot to another. 'We said we'd be discreet about our current living arrangements. And we're being watched.'

'Really? By whom?' He glanced around his office, perfectly oblivious of the stares that were homing in on them through the glass.

'Don't look…'

His attention swung back to her, and Charlotte began to wonder whether it wouldn't have been better to leave well alone. Edward's gaze made her feel as if he were undressing her. Taking his time and getting it absolutely right.

'There—will that do?'

As long as he didn't keep it up too long. 'That's fine. Allie and Paula are at the nurses' station. Watching us.'

'Ah. Well, in that case, I'll just pretend to show you this…' He flipped through the pile of journals on his desk, pulling one out and opening it. 'Then you can sit down and pretend to read it.'

His lips twitched slightly as she took the journal from his hand, and Charlotte suppressed a grin. His sense of humour might be an acquired taste, but it was well worth the journey.

'You wrote this?' She read the title of the paper slowly, just about getting the gist of it.

'Yeah.' He leaned forward across his desk. 'What do you think?'

'I don't know. Give me a couple of months to work my way through it…'

'Then you'll need to sit down.'

Charlotte gave up the unequal struggle and plumped herself down on one of the deep-cushioned leather easy chairs which were reserved for guests. Edward swung around in his own office chair, making sure that his back was to the glass wall, and shot her a conspiratorial look.

'So what do you want to speak to me about?' His finger nudged at the note on his desk.

Charlotte took a deep breath. 'I was being pig-headed last night. I'm sorry.'

'You have nothing to be sorry for. I'm not…' His intent blue gaze found hers and held it fast. 'I'm not great with certain kinds of solutions.'

What did he mean by that? Edward's usual forthright way of expressing himself seemed to have deserted him for the moment. 'I don't understand what you're saying…'

He sighed. 'I'm saying that I'm not as good with people as you are. I can be insensitive at times.'

'No, Edward…' She wanted to take him by the shoulders and shake this nonsense out of him, but she was being watched. She had to stay still and pretend this was just a conversation between two work colleagues. 'You've shown me and Isaac nothing but kindness.'

His eyes betrayed his confusion. 'Is this your way of letting me off the hook?'

'No. I'm paying you the respect of being honest with you. The way you've done with me.'

His slow smile penetrated every dark corner of her being. Filled her mind with the kind of ideas that she'd been trying not to think about for the past three days.

'Thank you,' he said.

'You're welcome.' Charlotte was sure that there was a more appropriate response than that, but she couldn't fathom what it might be at the moment. Not without the kind of body language that would get her into deep trouble. 'Look, what I wanted to say was that I'm over trying to make out that I can do everything by myself. If the offer's still open, I'd be really grateful if your father could spare a little of his time—perhaps just to talk to me and give me some general advice.'

He nodded. 'The offer's still open; there was no time limit on it. I'll give him a call.'

'Thanks, Edward. I really appreciate it. You'll tell him that, won't you?'

'I will.' He pointed to the journal in her lap. 'You know, if you're going to do this properly you should at least look as if you're reading.'

She picked up the journal and looked at it. 'Better?'

'Much. If anyone asks, what's our excuse for talking to each other?'

'I've probably been disputing some of the conclusions you came to in this article.' Charlotte jabbed her finger at the page in front of her and threw the journal down onto his desk.

'Very theatrical.' His eyes flashed as he leaned forward, picking up the journal and clipping something to the pages before he passed it back. 'Here's my father's card. I'll give him a call right now and tell him to expect your call this afternoon.'

'You're enjoying this, aren't you?'

'I wouldn't say *enjoying*. I think you've made the right decision....'

'I meant the secret rendezvous stuff.'

'Oh. Well, that adds a certain frisson. D'you think it's working?'

'Probably not. But at least I've got a measure of deniability.' Charlotte slipped the business card into her pocket and closed the journal, passing it back to him. 'Will you be working tonight?'

'No. Do you want a lift home?' He grinned. 'You could wait for me by the park gates if you like. With a wig and a pair of sunglasses, no one will think it's you...'

'I'll wear a pink carnation in my buttonhole.'

'Yeah. That would be a nice touch. Match your ears.'

Her ears weren't the only things which felt as if they were burning up when Charlotte walked back past the nurses' station.

'Not so fast.'

Paula's murmured words stopped her in her tracks.

'Sorry?' She was going to have to brazen it out.

'So what's the story, then? You and Edward North?'

'He was just showing me a paper he'd written. In one of the journals. Something that came up.'

Charlotte pushed her hands into her pockets and curled her fingers around the business card, just to check that it wasn't about to leap out of her pocket and embarrass her even further.

'Well, make sure that something comes up more often. After all...' Allie shrugged '...one thing might lead to another.'

'I don't have time for anything like that. Isaac's the only man in my life at the moment.' It would be as well if *she* remembered that, too.

'Spoilsport. Surely you get time for a night off once in a while?'

Paula's tone was edged with concern. She might tease, but underneath it all she had a good heart.

'Edward North...he needs someone like you. And he *is* gorgeous.'

'And headed this way...'

Charlotte had been deliberately not looking in the direction of Edward's office and it was Allie who raised the alarm. Edward was striding towards them, and Charlotte caught the quick exchanged glance between Paula and Allie as he passed behind her. A little too close.

'Charlotte.'

There was something intimate about the way he said her name. Or maybe it was just her imagination. Charlotte didn't dare to look in Paula's direction.

'Mrs Ashe is here a little early with April. If you're free, then I'll see them now.'

'Yes, of course.' Charlotte reached over for the notes and followed Edward into the plush, comfortable consulting room.

The seventeen-year-old took a nervous breath as Edward began the careful, precise work of taking the dressings from the side of her face. The previous week he had used skin flaps to revise the scars that a road accident had left, and today April was to see the result. His small nod, and a fleeting glance in Charlotte's direction, revealed that he was pleased with his work.

'Does it look horrible?' April was chewing her lip.

'No. Mr North's got to take a careful look, but so far everything's fine.'

The other nurses sometimes complained that it was pretty much impossible to gauge Edward's reactions to anything, but today he seemed more transparent than usual.

She ventured a little more reassurance for April. 'It's a little raised at the moment, but that's normal. It'll settle over time.'

'Yes.' Edward was taking her lead. 'I'm very pleased with the way it's healing.'

Charlotte laid her hand over April's, feeling the tremor of her fingers. 'When you look at yourself in the mirror, remember that we're at the very early stages of healing right now. Your procedure went well, and everything's going just as it should. You'll see a lot of improvement in the coming months.'

'That's okay.' April managed a smile. 'I know.'

She might be young, but April was much more pragmatic than some of the clinic's clients, who seemed to expect that the miracles Edward performed should take effect immediately. Charlotte reached for the mirror, but Edward already had it, and was handing it to April.

'Everything's looking good, April. There's very little swelling, and I can see you've been doing all the things that Charlotte told you to do when we saw you last. Keep up the good work.'

'Thanks.' April took the mirror and looked at her reflection. 'That's not so bad.'

Charlotte grinned at her. 'No. Not so bad at all. Now, I'll show you how to massage it gently. With just a little more work, we can make it even better.'

CHAPTER FIVE

THE SMELL COMING from the kitchen was gorgeous. Mouth-watering. Edward wondered how he could possibly be so hungry when normally he ate far later than this, and sometimes not at all if he got involved with what he was doing.

'Do you know what's for dinner, Isaac?' He sat down on the sofa next to the boy, who was fidgeting restlessly.

'Yes. Mum made it yesterday.'

'Would you like to share?'

Isaac thought for a minute, and Edward wondered if he ought to rephrase.

'Lasagne.'

'Sounds great. I like lasagne.'

'Me, too. I like it here, too.' Isaac thought for a moment. 'When are we going home?'

Edward glanced towards the open door of the kitchen. No Charlotte. She must be able to hear their conversation, but it didn't appear that she was going to help him out.

'Whenever you and your mum want to.'

'Can we stay until next weekend?'

'Yes, if you'd like to. What's happening next weekend?'

'The men are coming again.'

'No, Isaac…' Where was Charlotte when he needed her? She didn't seem to have any difficulty in turning up almost like magic whenever she was needed at a patient's bedside. 'Your mother's done nothing wrong. Those men aren't allowed to come back, and I'm going to make sure they don't.'

'How?' Isaac slipped off the sofa and approached Edward, laying both hands on one of his knees, clearly intent on a man-to-man talk.

Edward took a deep breath and leaned forward. 'That's a secret. But I promise you that we'll stop them from coming back.' He held out his right hand. 'You want to shake on it?'

Isaac gave him a puzzled look.

'Here.' Edward picked up his right hand and gave it a gentle shake. 'That means that I've made a promise to you and I can't break it.'

'Like that?' Isaac proffered his right hand and shook Edward's again.

'That's right. Just like that.' This was going better than he'd thought it might.

Isaac proffered his hand again. 'I promise I won't touch your piano any more.'

A noise from the kitchen door made Edward look up and he wondered how long Charlotte had been standing there.

'I'm sorry. He only played a couple of notes and I wiped the fingermarks off...'

'Don't worry about it.' He turned back to Isaac. 'How does not touching my piano unless you ask your mum or me first sound?'

'I won't touch your piano unless I ask Mum or you.' Isaac sealed the bargain with a handshake and then ran over to the piano stool. 'Can I touch it now?'

'No, Isaac, it's time for dinner. Go and wash your hands.'

Isaac pulled a face, but ran out of the room. Charlotte's eye was on him all the way.

'How do you do that?'

She'd picked up the lasagne, newly out of the oven, and was carrying it through into the dining room. Edward followed with the salad.

'Answer all the questions? I just tell him the truth.' She laid the dish down onto a padded table mat, her shoulders drooping suddenly, as if someone had loaded some extra weight onto them. 'Well, most of the time. I still want to shield him, but he's getting to an age when that's not so easy.'

Edward wondered whether he should mention the fact that Isaac plainly wanted to do the same—to shield his mother. Probably not. He shouldn't interfere.

She'd put a small glass vase of flowers on the over-large oval table, which Edward had never managed to fill but had bought because it balanced out the proportions of the room. He liked balance. Order and proportion helped him to think. Charlotte had laid a place for him at the head of the table, and he sat down.

It was the strangest feeling. Charlotte on one side of him, helping him to a generous portion from the dish and pushing the salad bowl towards him. Isaac on the other side, sitting on a cushion so that he could reach the table. It was almost as though they'd taken him in, rather than the other way round.

'Would you like some water?' Charlotte was still on her feet, leaning across the table to place a beaker of water in front of Isaac.

'No, thank you. Why don't you sit down? I'll get some wine.'

She hesitated. Clearly debating whether or not she was going to allow him to contribute to the meal even in this way. 'Um…yes. Thank you. That would be nice.'

Edward got to his feet and went to the kitchen, fetching a couple of glasses and a bottle from the chiller. When he returned he was gratified to find that she'd done as he'd asked, and was sitting, her hands in her lap.

He placed a glass in front of her, uncorked the bottle and poured.

'Thanks. That's enough.'

She'd only let him half fill the glass but that was okay. It was the principle of it. Something had been accepted into the routine that they were building.

Isaac was watching his every move, eyes wide as saucers. 'Can I have some?'

'No, sweetie, this is for grown-ups.' Charlotte quietened him with a quick look.

'Pleeeease.' Isaac was obviously unused to not sharing everything with his mother.

'I've got something better for you.'

Edward gave him a conspiratorial grin and the boy quietened. He went to fetch a sturdier glass from the kitchen cupboard—not the fine crystal that he'd given to Charlotte, but a nice-looking faceted tumbler—and grabbed a bottle of sparkling raspberry cordial from the fridge.

'Here you are.' He set the glass in front of Isaac and filled it. 'Try this.'

He sat down, aware that Charlotte's smile was on him. It seemed to slide into his senses, warm and tingling, like fine brandy. Isaac took a sip from his glass and gave the same nod of approval that his mother had given when she'd tasted her wine. He was a part of this little treat.

Funnily enough, Edward felt a part of it, too. Eating together…praising Charlotte on the meal. Hearing the silly jokes passing between Isaac and Charlotte, which both of them expected him to laugh at, too. He was probably expected to tell a few, as well, but he couldn't think of any that they might like at the moment. But even that didn't seem to matter.

The doorbell rang.

Isaac jumped and would have spilled his drink if Edward hadn't put out a hand to steady it. Instead his fork slithered to the floor, bouncing across the rug and clattering noisily on the wooden parquet.

'Let's not answer that.' Edward shot a grin at the boy. Doorbells didn't appear to be his favourite thing at the moment, and who could blame him?

'It's okay.' Charlotte passed her own fork over to Isaac and bent to retrieve his. 'It might be something important.'

Isaac's gaze pleaded silently with him.

'So what if it is? We're eating.' A feeling of bravado, quite out of proportion with the deed, sparked in Edward's chest.

'But it could be a friend. Someone you know.'

Unlikely. And if it were they'd know him well enough not to give up after the first ring. Opening the door when the bell rang was one of those things that Edward classed as optional.

'If it is they'll ring again. Or phone me.' Edward generally picked up the phone. Unless he was in the middle of something really interesting.

She laughed. 'Aren't you even curious?'

Edward shrugged. 'It's probably someone wanting to sell me something.' And, anyway, he was making a point.

'And a man's home is his castle, eh?'

'Er…possibly. In a manner of speaking.' It was certainly somewhere that his mind could wander freely. Explore the nuances that everyday life seemed to ignore so heedlessly. He hadn't thought about the aspect of fortification, though…

Charlotte leaned towards him. 'It's just an expression. One size fits all.'

She was smiling at him, and that smile seemed to banish all thoughts of whether, either in truth or in paradigm, his home really was a castle. All he could do in the face of such unarguable persuasion was smile back.

'Yeah. Well, then, whatever size my home is…' he flipped a glance towards Isaac, hoping he'd get the point '…or I am, it's definitely a castle. Which means I don't have to answer the doorbell if I don't want to.'

Isaac seemed to understand and turned his attention back to his meal. Charlotte was more difficult to satisfy.

'So… Don't you think you're missing out on something?'

'Like what?' Like the world that she seemed to inhabit? The one where she seemed to navigate chance meetings and random conversations so easily.

'I don't know. That's the thing, isn't it?'

He shook his head. 'It's no one. And, anyway, we're eating.' He turned back to the plate in front of him. 'And this is very good.'

CHAPTER SIX

CHARLOTTE HAD STACKED the dishwasher, sat with Isaac until he started to yawn, and then taken him up to bed. She tucked him in, along with Stinky, in the small second guest room which adjoined her own, and closed the connecting door between the two. Isaac had slept soundly for the last two nights, and showed no signs of doing anything else tonight.

Edward had seen to it that Isaac should feel at home here. When he'd taken them both back to the house on Saturday afternoon he'd filled the boot of his car with Isaac's things—toys, games, clothes—so that he shouldn't wake in the night and find himself in a completely strange place. Somehow the molecule modelling kit had found its way up here, too, and Charlotte wondered whether Edward had put it there. The thought made her smile.

When she got back downstairs the room was silent. Edward was in an easy chair with his nose in a book. Not wanting to disturb him, Charlotte retreated to the kitchen and set about cutting sandwiches for Isaac's lunch tomorrow.

It was awkward being alone with him. At work, and when Isaac was around, she had a reason to ignore the desire to touch him. Now it was just him and her, and the empty space between them seemed almost to be daring her to breach it.

She'd finished the sandwiches, and was sitting at the kitchen table wondering what to do next, when the door opened quietly.

'Hey.'

'Oh…' She jumped, almost spilling the cup of coffee in front of her. Suddenly she noticed that the deep blue open-necked shirt he'd pulled on when he got home emphasised the colour of his eyes. 'You're busy. I didn't mean to disturb you.'

He shook his head, as if the concept were new to him. It probably was. Short of a nuclear explosion, it was practically impossible to divert his attention away from what he was doing at work. 'You don't need to sit in here, you know.'

'Yes… I mean, no. I mean… I don't want to get in the way.'

'You aren't. I'd appreciate the company.'

He meant it. Edward who had always seemed so aloof at work, so self-sufficient. And yet he'd surprised her by seeming to understand just how she and Isaac felt. There was a great deal more to Edward than met the eye.

'Me, too. I'll…make some coffee, shall I?' She looked at the mug of instant in front of her. 'Some fresh coffee.'

'That's okay. I'll do it.' His mouth quirked. 'Refreshments and snacks don't count as cooking.'

His quiet, dry humour curled around her like a delicious full-bodied chuckle. 'Oh. So you're beginning to chip away at our bargain, are you?'

'I don't think so. I don't remember any mention of brewing, looking in the fridge, or pouring.' He measured the coffee into the machine and switched it on. 'And I certainly don't recall having covered electrical appliances.'

She smiled at him. 'I'm going to have to watch myself, aren't I? Next time I make a bargain with you, I'll make sure I read the small print.'

Did that sound a bit too forward? Hopefully everything would be settled in a few days' time and she would be on her way back home. Edward would forget her as he moved on to his next project of interest.

'Yeah. Always read the small print.'

He flipped open the cupboard doors and pulled out two cups, his long fingers placing them precisely on the counter. He had a delicate touch. He had to have. Micro-surgery was one of the most challenging disciplines in a challenging world. And Edward was the best at what he did—just like everyone else at 200 Harley Street.

He made the coffee and picked up her cup with his own, taking it into the sitting room, as if unsure whether she might follow otherwise. Charlotte perched herself on the sofa, casting around for something that she could make conversation about.

'This is a lovely room.'

He nodded. 'Thank you.'

'Do you play the piano much?' From the wide-ranging collection of CDs on his shelves, and the grand piano, Edward was obviously passionate about music. In the three days that she and Isaac had been here, though, he'd never once opened the piano. Never once switched on the high-end audio equipment.

'Most days. Do you play?'

'No. I love listening, though.'

He must have changed his routine because of her presence. Maybe she could encourage him to change it back again.

Edward didn't move. 'I wouldn't want to wake Isaac.'

'You won't. He's upstairs and he's fast asleep.'

Maybe she shouldn't have asked. Maybe this was something private, that Edward didn't like to share.

It *was* something private—she could see it in the way he hesitated. But then he made his decision, jumping up and striding across the room. Charlotte tried not to notice the ease with which he lifted the heavy lid, or the way that his shoulder flexed as he propped it open. Suddenly his mastery over the large, shining instrument was physical, as well as just a matter of the mind.

Sitting down, he raised the lid from the keyboard and lowered his fingers onto the keys. 'Any requests?'

For a moment she couldn't think. Then Charlotte knew what she really wanted to hear. 'Something *you* like.'

He nodded. Charlotte was expecting something classical, but the soft strains of *Ain't Misbehavin'* started to float across the room. Mesmerised, she moved closer and he beckoned her over, shifting up on the long piano seat to make room for her.

She swallowed hard. The music invited her. The way he made the song sound as if it had been written just for her. His sensitive fingers stroked the keys. Charlotte wanted nothing more at that moment than to sit next to him, be a part of this world. *His* world.

He raised one eyebrow at her hesitation, and the music swelled in reproach. She gave in and slid onto the edge of the stool, angling her body away from his.

'You'll fall off...'

The music dropped to a few notes, played with his left hand, while his right arm curled around her waist, pulling her further onto the stool. She was not quite touching him, and the seat was plenty long enough for two, but that didn't seem to make any difference. She could practically feel his body moving against hers.

There were a few chords that seemed to be his own addition to the mix, and then he segued into *As Time Goes By*.

'Mmm. Love this one.' She closed her eyes and let the music wash over her.

'Yeah. Kind of sad... Haunting.' He added an extra verse and chorus onto the end and then smoothly moved on into another melody that she couldn't name, but which she recognised from an old film.

'You like this?'

'I feel I should be in a cocktail dress and expensive jewellery. Leaning against the piano and sipping... I wonder what they were drinking in *Casablanca*?'

He chuckled. 'Champagne?'

'You remember?'

'No. Just a guess. I've got a bottle somewhere, if you'd like some.'

Charlotte laughed. 'No. I don't have the cocktail dress.' Or the jewellery. Her mother's ruby necklace, the one that she thought she'd never part with, had been sold and the money spent on the bricks and mortar of her house. The one that she'd been driven out of just a few days ago.

He seemed about to say something, then stopped himself. Moved on to play another song. The soft, melancholy chords filled the air around them.

Suddenly the music stopped. 'Hey... Hey, what's the matter?'

She felt him turn, but didn't raise her head. She didn't want Edward to see the tears.

Too late.

His fingers touched her arm, hesitantly at first, and then more resolute. She felt his arm around her and, try as she might, couldn't bring herself to break away from him.

'It's nothing. Just the music.'

'Much as I'd like to think that it was my playing that moved you to tears, I doubt it.'

She wanted to hold on to him. It felt so natural to do so. But she shouldn't. She'd always been a sucker for the quiet type, and the last one she'd got involved with had almost destroyed her life.

'I...I'm just afraid that I'm going to lose everything. And you've been so kind...'

'You're not going to lose anything.'

He hugged her tight and she gave in and buried her face against the protective arc of his chest.

'Did you ring my father this afternoon?'

'Yeah. I've arranged to leave work early tomorrow and go and see him.'

'Good. You can stop worrying, then. He'll sort this out for you.'

'I know. Thank you. I'm just being silly.'

She felt his fingers stroking her hair. Just for a moment, before he snatched his hand away again. This must be torture for someone like Edward. So self-contained, so controlled. He didn't really *do* tears. She tried to move away from him, but his arm kept her firmly in place.

'You're not being silly. You lost everything once. It's natural to fear that it'll happen again.' He drew back, holding her shoulders tightly. Bending to capture her gaze in his. 'It's not going to. You're going to fight it.'

'I haven't got anything to fight with. All my savings are gone, and…' She couldn't even say it. The money was just a number. It was the loss of little things that she'd hoped she'd always keep that hurt the most. Memories… presents that people had given her over the years. The cot which, at one time, she'd hoped might see some more use. All Isaac's baby stuff. It hadn't fetched much, but every penny had counted when she'd been trying to put the deposit on the house together.

He shook his head. 'I wish you'd told someone. The clinic might have arranged an employee loan, or if not…' He pressed his lips together, apparently not wanting to finish the 'or if not'.

'I'd only been there for a couple of months. I was just glad to have the job. The extra income meant I could make the mortgage. Anyway…it would just have been another debt that I couldn't pay back.'

'So you sold everything you had?' His grip on her shoulders relaxed and his hands slid down to her elbows.

'Pretty much.' Charlotte put it to the back of her mind. 'But that's okay. Things are easier now. I've had a pay rise, and the first year's always the worst with a mortgage.'

'And I guess the extra shifts come in handy?'

He'd noticed, then. The way that she grabbed every bit of overtime that came her way, even though it meant that she had less time to spend with Isaac. 'Yes, they do.'

'You've worked hard. No one's going to take that from you. Just explain everything to my father and let him sort it out. And in the meantime you can stay here. Isaac seems… well, he doesn't seem to mind the arrangement.'

'You've made us both very welcome. Being here has been so good for Isaac.' It was Edward who had been good for Isaac, not the house. Providing a broad pair of shoulders that her son felt he could rely on. For that matter, he'd been good for Charlotte, as well.

'You can stay as long as you like.'

'Thank you. But we won't outstay our welcome.'

Like always, his smile was reticent, hard won, but all the better for it.

'Then I think we'll be okay. I can outlast you.'

No doubt he could. At the moment Charlotte reckoned that she had about ten minutes before she made a fool of herself and threw herself into his arms if she didn't find something to distract him.

'Will you play something else?'

Edward couldn't get the image out of his head. Charlotte in a dark figure-hugging dress. Something sparkly at her wrist and around her neck and a glass of champagne in her hand. Leaning against the piano, the gold flecks in her eyes reflecting the light better than any jewel could.

He played for a while on autopilot, while he added the

fine detail to his vision. Then the real Charlotte broke in, her body warm and moving to the rhythm next to his.

'You'll have plenty of offers if you ever decide to give up the day job.'

Her smile made him stop thinking and start feeling as he ran his hands across the keyboard in a short, improvised cascade of notes.

'I used to play in a bar. When I was at medical school.'

'Yeah?'

'It paid better than stacking shelves. And I got to keep the tips as well.'

'Tips are always good.'

'Yeah. Made a big difference.'

'I bet you spent them on books.'

'Um… Yeah. Okay, you're making me feel predictable again.'

With Charlotte he could begin to fathom what people saw in small talk. It was easy. Delightful. Maybe they were getting a little too close to flirting, but that would be okay as long as he kept playing. Somehow the music made pretty much anything permissible.

She laughed. 'I think you're one of the most unpredictable people I've ever met.'

'Dancing to the beat of a different drum, you mean?' People had said that to him, and *about* him, all his life. That he was gifted. Different. That he didn't need the company of his peers as much as he needed to fulfil his potential.

'*Is* it a different drum? I rather thought that it was the same drum, but you just hear it a little more clearly.'

Edward let the thought percolate. 'That might be one of the nicest things anyone's ever said to me.'

The unexpected idea that words might not be enough to express his feelings on the matter occurred to him. He wanted to hold her again.

She smiled and his theory morphed into a tried and tested fact. Charlotte's smile held so much more meaning than words, and he allowed himself to bathe in it, feeling its warmth lap against his skin.

He didn't know how long he played for, and didn't much care. However long she sat here next to him, her body melting into the rhythm of the music, it wouldn't be enough.

When finally she drew away, another of those gorgeous smiles on her lips, the world felt suddenly cold.

'You play wonderfully.'

He nodded in acknowledgement. 'You listen wonderfully.' It was more as if she'd been a part of the music, shaping the emotion and cadence with him, although her fingers had never touched the keys.

She laughed, getting to her feet. 'I should go and get some sleep, though. Thank you for a lovely evening.'

'My pleasure. We should do this again.' The words escaped his heart before his head could issue the caution against asking for trouble.

She flushed a little and nodded quickly. 'Goodnight, Edward.'

He played a short, quiet goodnight, listening to the sound of her footsteps on the stairs. Then he closed the lid over the keys.

Charlotte was everything that he held himself aloof from. The instinct and emotion that he saved only for his music seemed to bleed into her whole life. It was captivating—tantalising, even—but it was a language that he didn't know how to speak. However much she tried not to disrupt his life, however well-behaved Isaac was, the two of them had the power to turn his well-ordered existence upside down.

Archie roused himself, stretched, and joined him on a restless errand to the kitchen, which had no particular purpose other than his need to go somewhere. Edward poured himself a glass of wine from the bottle they'd opened at dinner, leaving Archie to pounce on his food bowl as if he hadn't eaten in years, and wandered back into the sitting room. The book that he'd abandoned in favour of going to talk to Charlotte still lay on the sofa, and he picked it up, flipping it open. This, at least, he knew how to handle.

CHAPTER SEVEN

CHARLOTTE KNEW THAT Edward would be here somewhere. She hated that she needed to see him so badly, but she had nowhere else to go. She slipped through the reception area, avoiding the last stragglers on their way out of the clinic at 200 Harley Street, and ran up the stairs.

Edward's office door was closed and locked, but she could see his jacket, slung over the back of his chair. There was only one other place that he could be.

She left her coat and bag on one of the chairs in the closed-up nurses' station and took the stairs down to the basement. The gym was in darkness, but she could see lights shining through the glass doors which led to the pool.

Suddenly her courage failed her. She'd already accepted too much from Edward. Already allowed herself to get too involved with his life. He was quiet and kind, creative and a little quirky. But then her husband had been quiet and kind, too. She'd thought that she could see hidden depths in him, where actually there had just been an angry void that he'd sought to fill with the thrill he got from risking everything on the cards.

Charlotte turned. She knew that Edward was here, and that at this time in the evening he was probably alone. Walking away was the best thing to do. The only thing to do.

She'd go upstairs to fetch her coat. Then come back down again, using the back stairs, so that no one would see her.

'What are you doing here?'

She'd been so lost in her own emotions she hadn't even seen that there was anyone on the stairs below her. Instinctively she turned to run upstairs, but it was too late. Edward had seen her.

It *had* been him in the swimming pool. His dark hair was still wet, slicked back from his face, and his white shirt was open at the neck. Not sure what to say or do, Charlotte focussed on the logo splashed across the gym bag that was slung over his shoulder.

'Charlotte...?' He was standing two steps below her now, and they were face to face. 'What's the matter?'

'Nothing.' *Everything.* 'I just forgot something and popped back...'

The whole difficulty of dealing with Edward was that excuses were practically impossible to get away with—unless, of course, you had the time to construct a well-thought-out, fully featured alibi.

He raised one eyebrow in disbelief and shooed her up the stairs.

'Come to my office.' His keys were in his hand already, and he strode past the deserted nurses' station and unlocked the door, motioning her in. He slung his bag on the floor, in the corner, and sat down in his high-backed leather chair.

'I feel as if I'm being hauled up in front of the beak.' Small talk was the one thing that she was better at than Edward. Her only chance.

His brow clouded, but then he refused to take the bait. 'Why don't you sit down, then?'

'Do I need to?'

'You don't need to do anything. It's an invitation.'

He leaned back in his chair, propping one foot on the desk, and Charlotte slumped down into one of the visitors' chairs.

'So…what is it, then?' One last try at putting the ball in his court. Making Edward talk first.

'I…um…'

He seemed suddenly hesitant. Maybe she was going to get her way after all. They could go home, she'd make dinner, and then on the excuse of an early night she could go and cry into her pillow. That was the thing she should have done in the first place—not come running to Edward every time something went wrong.

He tried again. 'There seems to be something wrong. I was wondering how the meeting with my father went…' He backtracked slightly. 'Not in detail. I wouldn't presume to interfere with a confidential exchange between lawyer and client…'

There was no such thing as a simple question in Edward's vocabulary; there was always some accompanying detail. The way his mind worked made Charlotte smile, however bad things were. 'No. I'm sure you wouldn't.'

'It's just a broad brush enquiry. About whether you're happy as a result of…whatever it was that was said.'

'Your father was very kind.'

Straight spikes of hair had begun to fall across his forehead, and when he smiled it looked almost rakish.

'Good. And apart from being kind…?'

'He's offered to represent me, and I've accepted. I gave him some details on the phone yesterday, and he's already got an investigator to follow up on them. He's thought of everything.'

Edward nodded. 'I imagine he has. There's no need to worry.'

Her heart was almost tearing itself apart with panic. 'No. I'm sure there isn't.'

He got to his feet, unhooking his jacket from the back of his chair. 'I guess I should call your bluff and just take you home, then.'

'Peter applied for a loan in Isaac's name. One of those quickie ones you can get on the internet.' Charlotte couldn't help it. She'd blurted out what she'd come to say—what she knew that Edward couldn't mend, but somehow wanted him to know.

He slumped back down into his chair, shock on his face. 'Did he get it?'

'No, thank goodness. And your father's going to do all he can to protect Isaac from that happening again.' Charlotte could feel her shoulders beginning to droop, but the effort of keeping her spine straight was finally too much to do anything about it.

'And what about the phone bill that you were being chased for?'

'He's putting pressure on the phone company to leave me alone. It seems that there's a bit of a mix-up with names and I might be facing a few more where that one came from.'

His eyes narrowed. 'A mix-up? How could that have involved *you*?'

She'd faced a pair of blue eyes and a sharp legal mind once already this afternoon. Edward's were as kind as his father's, but somehow much more challenging. The truth had been easier the first time around.

'When Peter and I were living together…'

Tears again. What must Edward think of her?

'Hey…' He rounded his desk, dragged one of the heavy armchairs over towards hers and sat down opposite her, leaning forward until his hands almost touched hers. 'It's okay, Charlotte. I just want to help.'

All she wanted right now was to feel his arms around her. If Edward was on her side she could do anything, be all kinds of strong. She met those blue eyes again. They gave her courage for the thing that damned her the most.

'The phone bill dates back to when Peter and I were living together. He must have taken the contract out in my name and...' She shrugged. 'I didn't know about that phone—it was his second one. He had someone else.'

His face became cold, as if she'd just slapped him. 'You mean he's expecting you to pay for the calls he made to his mistress? While you were living with him?' Edward shook his head angrily. 'Oh, no...you're not doing that.'

She reached for him, but he wasn't there. He was too angry now even to see her, and he sprang to his feet and started to pace the office like a caged tiger.

'Edward. Please, don't... Peter probably didn't think of it like that. He doesn't think anything through. The phone was registered at my old address and it's up to me to prove it isn't mine...'

'Don't make excuses for him, Charlotte.'

Her own anger flared in response to his. 'I'm not. I'm just trying to work out what happened...'

'And if you keep on taking his side you'll always be a victim.'

'Oh, so *that's* what you think, is it?' She was on her feet, catching his arm, forcing him to face her. 'I am *not* a victim. I've stood on my own two feet since Peter left me, provided for Isaac...' She took a deep breath. Shouting wasn't going to do any good, and if there was anyone still in the building they'd be sure to hear them.

'I know.' Edward's rage turned abruptly cold. 'But this is not your responsibility.'

'No, it isn't. But there's another child, too—a little girl. She's not my responsibility either, but I still can't help thinking that somewhere out there that child's mother is going to be facing the same thing that I did. I might not like her very much, but I can feel for her.'

'There's a baby?'

'Not a baby—a child. She'll be three years old now.'

He didn't need to be a genius to be able to do that particular calculation. Peter hadn't just had someone else while he was living with her, he'd had a child as well.

'You've told my father this?'

'Yes. I said that he could do whatever it took as far as Peter was concerned, but that I wouldn't go out of my way to implicate his partner if there's been any fraud. That's my decision, Edward, whether you like it or not.'

Warmth bloomed in his face. 'Most people wouldn't be so forgiving.'

'I'm not either. I don't forgive her, but I won't hurt her daughter. She's no more responsible for any of this than Isaac is.'

'Maybe the best thing you can do for this woman is to show her exactly what she's got herself into…'

'That's what your father said.'

'Must be right, then.' A ghost of a grin shimmered on his mouth.

'I suppose so. But all I really want to do is to be free of Peter. Your father's agreed to review my divorce papers, to see if there's anything I've missed, and to do all he can to push it through without any hitches. That's a big weight off my mind.'

He nodded. 'My dad's not going to let you down. Once he gets his teeth into something he's like a dog with a bone, and he won't let up until he's got everything sorted out.'

She could smile now. His impassioned rage had shown that Edward didn't just pity her. He hadn't shrunk from demanding answers from her, asking the really hard questions.

'That's something you both have in common. I appreciate it more than I can say.'

He gave the customary small nod, which said he'd heard. A smile which said he'd understood.

'I should go now. I need to pick Isaac up soon.'

He shook his head. 'One more minute.' His back was against the door and he was leaning on it, his arms folded. 'I'm afraid it's no more Mr Nice Guy, Charlotte.'

She swallowed. Edward was getting darker and more dangerous again. She had to admit that she rather liked it.

'Really?' She took a step forward, tilting her head up to meet his gaze. If he wanted another confrontation he could have it.

'Yeah. You can put up a fight if you like, but you and Isaac are staying on with me until this is all sorted out. However long it takes.'

'We've had this conversation before…'

'And we can have it again if you want. You'll tell me that you don't want to impose, I'll say that you and Isaac are no trouble and that I like having you both around, and then you'll give me that look…' He grinned. 'The one that you're giving me right now…'

'And…?'

'And you'll say that you and Isaac have managed on your own up till now, that you don't need anyone.'

'That's not quite true…'

'No, it's not. You'll say it anyway, though, just to put me in my place.'

That smile of his didn't have a place. Neither did Edward.

'You're reading my mind now, are you?' Just as long as he couldn't access the part of her imagination that was engaged in stripping his shirt from his shoulders. Running its hungry fingers over his skin and allowing him to back her against the desk…

He narrowed his eyes and she shivered. There was something tender about the curve of his lips, something raw about the look in his eyes. 'I should warn you that I have a Joker up my sleeve.'

She nodded. 'Isaac. You'll say he's happy where he is and it would be wrong to put him through any more upset. That I might be able to see the debt collectors off, but I can't protect him from the stress.'

John North had said as much, advising her that if she had somewhere else to stay she should do so.

Edward nodded. His gaze flipped quickly to the sofa, which was relegated to the one corner of his office that wasn't lined with bookshelves, and then back again to her face. Maybe he really was reading her mind. The sofa would be admittedly more comfortable than the desk.

'And I'd be right?'

'Yes. You'd be right.'

The smile that made his eyes seem impossibly blue, the one that he had no trouble in sharing with Isaac, was all for her this time. 'Are we done, then?'

Not by any stretch of the imagination. 'I suppose so.'

'And your answer…?'

'Thank you. Isaac and I would like to stay.'

At least he had the grace to nod, as if the outcome of this particular skirmish hadn't been a foregone conclusion.

He stepped away from the door, hooking up his jacket and slinging his sports bag over his shoulder. 'Let's get out of here. What's for dinner?'

She'd tried to palm him off with peppered steak, but Edward had rather liked the idea of eating early and sharing pizza with Charlotte and Isaac. He liked the execution even better.

Isaac stood on a chair, a folded-down apron tied around him, dipping into bowls of sliced tomatoes and mushrooms to decorate his pizza. This was the kind of fun he hadn't had in a long time, and the feeling that the woman and child he so wanted to protect were here, safe with him…

Edward paused for a moment to consider whether *safe* and *with him* weren't in fact a contradiction of terms and then gave up the unequal struggle. For tonight it was more than enough to know that they were having fun, and that he was there to turn back anyone who came knocking on the door.

'So who's this meant to be, then?'

A grave face stared out at him from Isaac's pizza.

'It's…' Isaac had a showman's mastery of the expectant pause '…*you*!'

'Me?' Edward ignored the stifled giggle behind him. 'I don't look very happy.'

'That's your thinking face.'

'Ah. Well, I suppose that's all right, then.'

'What's yours?' Isaac peered across at Edward's pizza, and would have toppled off the chair if Edward hadn't shot a hand out to steady him.

'It's…just a pattern.' He was beginning to learn that details could get him into trouble.

Isaac twisted his head from one side to the other. Edward wondered whether the complex symmetry was really so beyond him, and came to the conclusion that somewhere, on a chiefly instinctive level, he understood.

'It's different from Mum's.'

Charlotte had decorated her pizza with swirls and curlicues of tomato, mushrooms and olives.

'Well, your mum and I are different. We like different things.'

'Hmm…'

Isaac returned to his pizza, adding another mushroom to Edward's brow to indicate a stray lock of hair, leaving Edward to contemplate the essential differences between himself and Charlotte and thank his lucky stars that Isaac hadn't asked him to enumerate them.

The evening was warm, and while the pizzas baked in the oven Edward opened the French doors onto the patio, spreading a cloth on the table and unstacking the chairs. They ate together in the evening sunshine, and as the shadows lengthened Isaac was allowed to get down from the table. Edward fetched a ball for him to play football in the garden.

'Mind the flowers, sweetie.'

Charlotte was down on her knees, her arms around her son, talking quietly to him the way she did when she had anything serious to say.

'You can play there, on the lawn, but don't kick the ball too hard.'

It didn't matter. Isaac could have flattened every last one of the flowers in his garden and Edward wouldn't have cared. But Charlotte was his mother, and she wanted to teach him respect for the things around him, so Edward said nothing.

'How are you doing?' As the daylight failed the light in her eyes seemed to fail as well. The effort of getting through today was beginning to tell on her.

She smiled at him. 'I'm fine, thank you.' Her gaze shot back towards Isaac as the ball veered close to the flowerbeds and he ran to pick it up. 'You've been such a star, Edward.'

Warmth suffused the whole of his body. Edward made a difference every day. The complex surgery he performed had the power to change people's lives, and it would be false modesty to claim that he didn't do it well. He wouldn't do it if he didn't believe that he excelled at it. But that was different. Somehow making just the slightest difference in Charlotte's life had the power to move him more than the considerable satisfaction he got from his job.

'I might see if Isaac wants a hand with the football in a moment.'

Her laugh was sweet and clear. Closer to the laugh that had filtered into his consciousness more than once at work, jolting him suddenly out of whatever he was doing.

'If he thinks he's got someone to play football with he won't give you a moment's peace. I don't want to keep you from anything else…'

The books would still be there tomorrow. So would the paper he was writing. This moment would be gone.

Edward stood, rolled up his shirtsleeves and prepared to take on the simple intricacies of the Beautiful Game.

She had put Isaac to bed and only returned downstairs for long enough to bid him goodnight. Edward knew why, and he hated it. She'd faced the day, but now she needed to fall apart—and she was determined to do that alone.

He spent a miserable hour trying to review the notes of a young surgeon he was mentoring, and then climbed the stairs. He could hear a quiet, muffled sound coming from Charlotte's room. She was crying.

Should he tap on her door?

No. Late in the evening, her bedroom, offering solace… Things didn't get much more hazardous than that. He'd have to comfort her, take her into his arms, perhaps. Feel the softness of her body against his own taut, screaming frame. It wasn't a good idea. On the other hand just carrying on along the hallway and going to bed was impossible.

Edward sank to the floor at the top of the stairs. Waited. If he couldn't console her, the least he could do was watch over her—even if she'd never know he'd been there.

CHAPTER EIGHT

CHARLOTTE GREETED HIM the next morning with hot coffee, toast and a smile. Her capacity to smile never ceased to impress Edward, as did her ability to bounce back from whatever life threw at her.

'So it's the Lighthouse this morning.' She seemed to be looking forward to it.

'Yes. Sure you're up to it?'

She'd already had a hell of a week, and it was only Wednesday.

'Of course.' She settled into the front seat of his car. 'Why? Do you have any concerns?'

'No. I think it's a great idea for you to come and talk to Mercy before she's transferred over into the clinic's care. I wish I'd thought of it myself.'

He had, actually. He just hadn't been quite sure how to broach the subject. When Leo Hunter had suggested it, Edward's concerns that he might be seen to be favouring Charlotte above any of the other nurses had been put to rest.

'Lizzie didn't tell me much about Mercy. Just that she was very frightened about being in the hospital, and it took the nurses there a long time to calm her.'

'Yes, it did. That's why you'll be with her for all the procedures that we're going to do at the clinic. So that she's always got a familiar face to reassure her.'

She smiled. Mercy was going to love that smile.

'I'll do my best for her.'

Charlotte snapped into work mode as soon as they entered the doors of the hospital, following quietly behind him, listening carefully to everything that was said. Edward stopped at the nurses' station and caught the attention of a trainee nurse who seemed to have nothing to do.

'Will you get me Mercy's notes, please?'

The nurse jumped to attention, handing him the file. 'She had a good night last night. Woke up a few times, but she wasn't crying the way she did before.'

'Good. This is Charlotte King. She's going to be looking after Mercy when she comes to the Hunter Clinic.' He squinted at the nurse's name badge, because he couldn't for the life of him remember her name. 'Charlotte, this is Kendra.'

Charlotte ignored Kendra's dismissive look and stepped forward. 'Hi, Kendra. It's good to hear that Mercy's been so well looked after here.'

Kendra sniffed, obviously feeling that her role as a very junior nurse at one of the best children's hospitals in the country made her in some way superior to Charlotte. She had a lot to learn.

'You're a qualified nurse?'

'Yes, I'm an RN. Working towards being a Nurse Practitioner,' Charlotte replied quietly. She didn't seem to mind Kendra's attitude, however much it rankled with Edward.

'Charlotte!' A voice behind them made her turn. 'How good to see you—how are you?'

The senior nurse who greeted Charlotte obviously knew her well. Kendra realised her mistake and disappeared out of range as quickly as she could, followed by a small smirk of satisfaction from Edward.

'So how's Isaac?' Sandra Morton gave Edward a brief nod and then turned back to Charlotte.

'Oh, growing up. He's going to school now.'

'Really? Yes, I suppose he must be. He was such a cute baby. And how's Peter?'

A small pause.

Edward wasn't sure whether he should intervene or not, and decided that Charlotte was perfectly capable of handling the situation herself. Much better than he could, probably. He started to leaf through Mercy's notes.

'Actually, I haven't seen him for a while. He left.'

'No! But he was such a nice guy—' Sandra stopped herself. 'Obviously not.'

'It just didn't work out. But everything's good now.'

'Great. I hear you're working at the Hunter Clinic?'

'That's right. I'm here with Mr North to see one of your patients.'

'Ah, Mercy. Well, I'm glad to see that you'll be looking after her. The kid's had a bad time, and she deserves the best.'

Charlotte grinned. 'She'll get it. Just as she has here.'

Sandra nodded. There was clearly a great deal of mutual esteem between the two women and it warmed Edward to see Charlotte being treated with the respect she deserved.

'Well, I'd better get going. Call me some time—or I'll call you. Maybe we can go out one evening?'

'Yes. It's good to see you, Sandra.'

Charlotte turned back to Edward, and he flipped a page in the notes in front of him.

'You can stop pretending to read now…' She leaned towards him, whispering.

'What makes you say that?'

'Your eyes aren't moving.'

Fair enough. Edward hadn't thought that anyone would

notice that he was staring at the same word on the page in front of him, listening to what the women were saying.

'I know what it says, anyway.' He snapped the notes shut.

'Can you fill me in on Mercy's history? Before we go to see her?'

'Yes, sure.' Edward looked at the sign above the door of the conference room and saw that it was empty. 'Let's go in here.'

He sat down, and Charlotte took a seat opposite him. He'd seen her at the clinic, and he knew that she was great at her job, but she always made it seem so natural. This change in context let him see just how professional she was.

'We don't know much about Mercy's background. She's thirteen years old, an orphan, and was clearly fending for herself for a while before being picked up by one of the charities working in the area. They've found a new adoptive family for her, back in Africa, and by all accounts she's very happy with them. She's been going to school and doing well.'

'Sounds good so far. Have they accompanied her to the UK?'

'No, she's staying with a foster family. I've spoken with the mother and she seems to be doing an excellent job. The problem is that Mercy doesn't want to talk about what happened to her before she was taken in by the charity.'

'So you've not been able to take a detailed medical history?'

'Yes and no. We know what's the matter with her, but I'd like to know what caused some of her problems as well. For instance, she has a perforated eardrum.'

'Hmm… Not usually a result of trauma. Although it sounds like a good probability in this case.'

Charlotte pressed her lips together in thought, and Edward ignored the little thrill of pleasure that seemed to accompany all his dealings with her.

'Your first objective is just to let her get to know you, though. See if you can reassure her so that she feels she's got a friend at the Hunter Clinic. Any information you can get is a bonus.'

'Okay. What else do I need to know?'

'She's here for surgery on a healed Buruli Ulcer.'

'That's a bacterial infection, isn't it?'

Edward nodded, pleased that Charlotte wasn't slow in asking for more information when she needed it. 'Yes, that's right. A Buruli Ulcer is relatively easy to treat when it's caught early, but if it's not—as was the case here—patients can develop large ulcers which result in disabilities and restricted joint movement as the scars heal. In Mercy's case there was a contracture which had multiple joint involvements—hand, wrist and elbow.'

He scrunched his own arm up to demonstrate the way that Mercy's arm and hand had been folded tightly in on themselves and Charlotte winced.

'Poor kid. It must have hurt like nothing I can imagine.'

'She's been through a lot. But the operation to straighten the limb, grafting in new material where necessary, was a success.'

'You did it?'

'Yes.'

That warmth again, as if her smile were caressing him. Pride because she cared that it had been Edward who had carried out the precise skin and muscle grafts which would restore some of the movement in Mercy's arm and hand.

'How much mobility will she recover?'

He shook his head. 'Difficult to say at this stage. But the prognosis is good, and if she keeps her physiotherapy up she should do well. That's another thing I want you to look at. She needs to be committed to this, and to understand how important it is for her to continue the things that she's being taught when she goes home.'

'Right. Okay, then. So I'm working on her heart, not her medical condition.'

'Primarily. Although she's going to need nurse-led care at the Hunter Clinic and you'll be providing that.'

If anyone could do it, Charlotte could.

When Edward ushered Charlotte into Mercy's room she wasn't quite sure what to expect. She found that Edward hadn't been quite honest with her.

The girl's face lit up when Edward smiled at her. 'Hello, Mercy. How are you today?'

'I am well, Dr Edward.'

'I'm pleased to hear that. I've brought someone to see you.'

Mercy's dark eyes never left Edward's face. If he reckoned that his quiet kindness hadn't got through to her, then he was fooling himself. Charlotte began to wonder what she was doing here. Edward had clearly underestimated his own capacity to reassure the girl.

There was tenderness in his eyes as he spoke again. 'Nurse Charlotte is going to look after you when you come to see me at the clinic. She's come to meet you.'

Mercy gave Charlotte a small nod.

'I'll…um…leave you, then.' Edward seemed suddenly at a loss as to what to do next.

'No. Please stay. Just for a few minutes.'

Charlotte didn't share Edward's conviction that she could gain Mercy's confidence instantly, through some magical process that he knew nothing about.

She pulled up a chair and sat down next to Mercy's bed. 'It's nice to meet you, Mercy. I hope that I can be your friend.'

Mercy nodded again, clearly deciding to adopt a wait-

and-see policy. Charlotte was going to have to prove herself, but that was okay.

'I've brought you some pictures of my family.' She had photographs in her bag—of herself with Isaac when he was a baby, together with some more recent ones, and some precious images of her parents. 'Would you like to see them?'

'Yes.'

That was a start. Charlotte began with the picture of Isaac. 'This is my son. His name is Isaac, and he was born on a Saturday.'

Mercy studied the picture carefully. 'Then in my country he would be called Kwame.'

Edward's curiosity got the better of him and he leaned forward. 'For Saturday?'

'Yes.'

'I was born on a Friday.'

Mercy smiled. 'Nurse Efie.'

Charlotte grinned. 'That's a lovely name. Thank you for telling me. What's yours?'

'Abena. My English name is Mercy.'

'You have a lovely smile, Mercy Abena.'

Charlotte had been alone with Mercy for almost an hour when Edward's phone beeped. He checked the text which had just arrived and made for Mercy's room. Charlotte was waiting for him outside the door.

'Thanks for coming so quickly.' She looked nervous, moving her weight slightly from one foot to the other.

'You said "asap".'

Charlotte wasn't one of those people who peppered all of her communications with either 'asap' or 'urgent'. When she said it, she meant it.

'I've noticed something…about Mercy.' She seemed almost reticent to tell him.

'Right. What have you seen?'

'It may be nothing…'

'What have you seen, Charlotte?'

She took a breath and seemed to loosen up slightly. 'We were talking together, getting on fine, and then all of a sudden she seemed to zone out. It only lasted for a little over ten seconds.'

He nodded, turning the various possibilities over in his mind. 'The nurses have said that she seems very withdrawn sometimes. Do you think it could just be her mental state?'

'Maybe.' She clasped her hands together—a small, nervous gesture. 'It doesn't feel like that to me.'

'Okay. What *does* it feel like?' This wasn't his normal method of diagnosis, but he was willing to give Charlotte the space to prove him wrong.

'I think she may be having Absence Seizures.'

'Epilepsy?'

Charlotte nodded. 'Her eyes rolled back, very briefly, and her eyelids fluttered a little. I leant forward and put my hand on her arm and she didn't react. Afterwards she didn't seem to have any recollection of what had happened.'

'That was quick thinking. Well done.' Most people would have attributed a short period of absence to being the daydream of a teenager, far from home and trying to block out what was happening around her.

'I could be wrong. I looked on her notes and no one else has reported anything like this.'

Edward shrugged. 'Which just means you're a bit more observant than the rest of us.'

It wasn't only that. Charlotte had a habit of looking at people when she talked to them, giving them her full attention. Until he'd met her he hadn't realised just how few people really did that.

She flushed pink with pleasure. 'So you'll take a look at her? Ask her about it?'

'Nope.' He turned towards Mercy's door, twisting the handle. 'You're going to do that. I'll watch and learn.'

She was cheerful and relaxed with Mercy, as if nothing had happened, sitting down by her bed and motioning Edward to do the same. Charlotte worked her way round to the subject of the seizure quickly, but deftly, as if it was just another routine set of questions which had to be asked.

'When we were talking together just now you seemed to lose me for a moment. Dr Edward and I would like to ask you about that, if it's all right with you?'

'There is…nothing.' The sudden look of hostility in Mercy's eyes spoke far louder than her words.

'I'm sure there isn't. But can we ask, all the same?'

Charlotte leaned towards Mercy, a look of gentle encouragement on her face, and Mercy shrugged.

'Okay, then. Well, you seemed not to hear or see me for a little while. Has that happened to you before?'

Mercy's gaze flipped sullenly from Charlotte to Edward, then back again.

'It doesn't make you a bad person, Mercy. A little boy in my son's class at school has the same thing.'

'He does?'

'Mmm-hmm. The doctors can stop it, though. Dr Edward could stop it.'

'Can you?' Mercy's gaze fixed on Edward.

'Yes.' He wondered whether he should say more and decided not to. Charlotte would fill in any of the details that she thought were necessary.

'We'll have to do some tests.'

Apparently a quick wrinkle of the nose was enough to help describe a blood test to rule anything else out, and an EEG which would pick up any unusual electrical activity in Mercy's brain.

'They're okay. They don't hurt.'

'And you can cure it?'

'Of course. If it's what we think it might be, then it might well just stop all of its own accord when you get a bit older. In the meantime we can stop it.' Charlotte reached forward, taking Mercy's hand. 'But Dr Edward needs to know all about this first, so he can do the right thing.'

Mercy hesitated. 'Some people say that this is a bad spirit…'

'No. It's nothing like that, Mercy. Trust me. Sometimes we just…skip a beat for a few moments.' Mercy looked unconvinced, and Charlotte tried again. 'Dr Edward told you that he could make your arm better, didn't he?'

'Yes.'

'And he did, right?' She waited for Mercy's nod. 'Then ask *him* if this has anything to do with bad spirits.'

Mercy seemed disinclined to ask a second time, but Edward answered anyway. 'It's nothing to do with anything like that, I promise you. It's an illness, and we can make you well with medicine.'

Mercy nodded. 'I do skip a beat sometimes.'

'How often? How many times every day?' Edward leaned forward.

'Three or four. Sometimes more.'

Charlotte nodded, as if that was just the right number of times to 'skip a beat' every day. 'And how long has this been happening?'

Mercy shrugged. 'Always.'

'Mmm…' Charlotte seemed to approve of that, too, although Edward couldn't see its significance. 'So is it all right if we do the tests, then? Like I said, they won't hurt.'

'Yes, Nurse Efie.'

A quick nod of her head and she turned to Edward. 'Blood test?'

'It's what I'd do.' He couldn't resist teasing her, just a little. 'Want me to go and fetch a kit for you?'

She rolled her eyes at him to conceal her smile. 'No. I'll go.'

'Nurse Efie, eh?' Edward leaned against the railings of the hospital's roof garden, the breeze rearranging his hair into the maverick version of his usual clean-cut style. 'So come on, then. What's mine?'

'I didn't ask. You can find out for yourself. Mercy will tell you.' Charlotte took a sip of her coffee. 'She really likes you. Says that you're kind.'

'Does she?' The idea seemed to surprise him.

'So what's wrong with being kind?' She grinned up at him.

'Nothing. I try to be kind. I'm not as good with people as you are, though.'

'I think you underestimate yourself. Didn't you see her face when you walked into her room this morning?'

Either Edward didn't have an answer to that, or he wasn't sharing. 'So what made you cotton on to the name thing?'

'The mother of one of my patients told me, years ago. Apparently it's quite important which day you were born on in some parts of Africa. I just gave her the information about when Isaac was born to see if she'd pick up on it.'

Edward nodded. 'I'll have to find out a bit more about that…'

'Poor old Archie. He's not going to have his name changed, is he?'

'I don't think so. It would probably confuse him. Cats are all instinct and not much brain.' He took another sip of coffee. 'So I've put a call in to the Head of Neurology. Is there anything else I should know? I'm wondering whether there's any connection between the seizures that Mercy's been having and the burst eardrum?'

'I don't think so. We mainly just talked, but Mercy said that after her parents died she lived with an uncle. I think that was when she was beaten, because she said that her aunt made her deaf.'

Edward shook his head, staring at his coffee. 'Someone would have had to hit her pretty hard.'

'Yes. But she was having the seizures before then. So hopefully the two things are unconnected and the seizures aren't a result of brain damage.'

She looked up at Edward and he blinked quickly. Took a swig of his coffee, and then wiped his eye.

'Something in your eye?'

'No. Yes, probably.' Whatever it was it seemed to be a source of embarrassment.

'Want me to take a look?'

'I think I'll manage.' He took another mouthful of coffee. 'These kids… We have to do something…'

Charlotte laid her hand on his arm. Tried not to think about the way the hard muscle flexed at her touch and to convince herself that this was simple reassurance. 'You *are* doing something. You've given her back the use of her arm. She knows that, and she says that she's going to exercise every day.'

'It's not enough.'

'It's what we can do.'

If the other nurses at the clinic could see them now. Edward, impassioned and almost weeping over a patient. Charlotte, resorting to reason and logic. It was so unexpected as to be almost bizarre.

'I know.' He drained his cup and dropped it into hers, scrunching the two together to make a ball, which he lobbed into the nearest recycling bin. 'I want you there when Mercy has the EEG, to reassure her that no bad spirits are out to get her. I'll clear it with Leo.'

'Thanks. And thanks for listening.'

'You were right. You've done a really good job here today.'

His praise meant a lot. More than a lot. Everyone at the clinic knew that Edward's praise had to be earned. Charlotte felt her cheeks flush with pleasure. 'Thanks. I'd like to just pop in and say goodbye to her before we go. Tell her that I'll be back soon.'

He grinned. 'Do that. Then I'd better be getting you back to the clinic, or Lizzie will have my hide for kidnapping you.'

CHAPTER NINE

It WAS CLEAR when Leo Hunter telephoned to check whether Edward had anything he'd like to raise at this afternoon's review meeting that he was not expecting him to attend. Leo knew him well enough to understand that Edward's pledge to support the new charity arm of the Hunter Clinic was on the level of research, operating procedures and maintaining clinical excellence. It didn't involve attending meetings which didn't deal with those goals.

The usual procedure was that Leo informed him that a meeting was taking place, more as a gesture of courtesy than anything else, and Edward tendered his apologies and read the minutes when they were circulated. That had always worked perfectly.

'You mean you're considering some research?' Leo's voice sounded perplexed.

'No, not really. Well, maybe if something presents itself. I'm just interested in how we can help these kids outside of simply giving them the medical treatment they need.'

There was a pause and Edward shook the handset of his phone, wondering if the line had suddenly gone dead, before realising that Leo was just taking his time in getting his head around the proposition. Edward's forte had always been in the operating theatre, making clinical decisions and implementing them. That was his skillset. He usually left community issues to someone else.

'I'll see you later, then.' Leo still sounded a bit suspicious. *'We've had to move the time from four o'clock to six, in order to fit in with the operating schedules.'*

Edward's heart sank. Six o'clock. He'd been to his share of these meetings, and they were renowned for going on until late into the night. Usually he'd be the last to object, but tonight... Actually, he wasn't doing anything tonight. But he'd been rather looking forward to doing nothing with Charlotte and Isaac.

All the same, he'd just asked for this and it seemed grudging to turn it down now. 'I'm free at six. I'll see you then.'

Edward got home at ten o' clock. Isaac was already in bed, and he hadn't expected to have a meal waiting for him, but within moments of him depositing the armful of papers that he'd brought home onto the hall table Charlotte was calling him into the kitchen

'Is that enough?' She surveyed the full plate, with three different kinds of salad and a large slice of home-made quiche.

'Are you mad? You obviously don't have any idea what I usually manage to feed myself when I get home late.'

His diet was relatively balanced, and usually healthy, but when Edward was busy cooking didn't figure much in the equation.

She dismissed his customary eating habits with a small sniff and walked over to the fridge. 'Would you like some juice? Or there's some of that sparkling fruit cordial left over.'

'I'll have a glass of wine, if you'll join me.' Edward put his knife and fork down and got to his feet.

'Stay there. I'll get it.' She walked to the wine cooler and opened the glass door, her hand hovering over the rows of bottles.

'That one…' Edward indicated a light, fruity white, and nodded when she pulled it out, holding it up so he could see the label.

He was beginning to see what his father saw in marriage. Not the meal on the table, or the fact that the lights were on in the house, but just that there was someone *there*. Someone to share the little things with—eating and drinking. Someone to talk to. Somehow the fact that Isaac was asleep upstairs and Charlotte was relaxing here downstairs gave Edward an immense feeling of well-being.

'I've got some treacle tart for afters.' She took a dish out of the fridge and put it into the oven to warm, then carried the bottle over to the table.

'Mmm. I love treacle tart. I haven't had it in years. And this quiche is really good, thank you.'

Edward opened the wine, and poured a glass for her. She took a sip and smiled.

'This is nice.'

The bottle probably cost more than the whole of the rest of the meal, but Edward wasn't about to tell her that. You couldn't buy what made the food so special and the wine so incidental. It was all about the cooking and the care that had gone into the preparation. About the knife and fork set precisely on the table, with a napkin and a glass. The flowers from the garden—just a couple of blooms—in a jug that usually lived under the sink.

'I've been stuck in a meeting for hours. It's good to get home.'

She raised one eyebrow. 'Which meeting was that?'

'Oh, one of Leo's. Reviewing the progress of the charity arm of the clinic.' Edward wondered whether she'd pick up on the unlikeliness of the whole thing.

'Really?'

If she had, it looked as if she'd decided not to ask.

'Yes. Leo seemed really pleased. There's a lot of progress being made.'

She nodded. 'So Leo and Ethan are getting on a little better?' It was an open secret that while the brothers remained professional in their dealings with the staff, they had what was euphemistically termed 'issues' with each other.

'Looks like it. Leo was praising Ethan's work, and Ethan looked genuinely pleased. A little bit surprised, as well.'

'I imagine Ethan felt he had to prove himself when he came back.' Charlotte was staring speculatively at her wine glass.

'I don't see why. Ethan's a superb surgeon.'

'Oh, Edward!' She narrowed her eyes at him. 'It's not all about how good you are at something. Ethan could be the best surgeon in the world, but he's still recovering from his injuries. He had to feel that there was an element of pity involved when Leo brought him back into the practice.'

'Yeah, I suppose anyone would. I think Ethan's realised that was never the case, though, and that Leo wanted him back for his medical skills. He was talking about the work that Leo had put into regaining the Hunter Clinic's reputation as well.'

'Really? That's good. Sounds as if they've got a bit more respect for each other now. So how's everything else going?'

'There are a lot of possibilities for expanding the charity side of the operation. Community issues to be taken into consideration—' He broke off as Charlotte hid a smile behind her hand. 'What?'

'*You've* been engaging in chit-chat about community issues, have you?'

He didn't blame her for her amused disbelief—he'd been both disbelieving and slightly amused himself. 'Well, someone's got to think about it.'

'And that's you, all of a sudden?' She couldn't disguise the warmth in her eyes.

'Maybe. We'll see. Anyway, I have some really interesting opportunities in the pipeline, both at the clinic and at the Lighthouse Hospital. And there's an opportunity for me to join one of the teams visiting Africa for a few weeks. I'd like to hear what you think.'

He paused, aware that he didn't usually do this either. Edward made his own decisions about the way his career was going to go, without any reference to anyone else. But suddenly he not only wanted to tell Charlotte, he wanted to hear what she had to say.

'That sounds fantastic. I want to hear everything.'

She pointed at the food in front of him, which had all but completely slipped his mind in his enthusiasm.

'Finish your meal first, though…'

'Yeah. Then I'll tell you all about it.'

They talked for an hour, and then Charlotte's rapt attention was overtaken by fatigue. Edward turned to a book, and when he lifted his eyes after only a page she was asleep. He lifted her feet gently up onto the sofa, put a cushion beneath her head, and went back to his reading.

Calmed by the low sound of her breathing, he let the words on the page fly through his mind, forming pictures and patterns as they went. It was as if her very presence made him more receptive—somehow more creative. The raw excitement of new thoughts, new challenges, reared up and dragged him headlong into the heady world of new possibilities that he so loved.

A sound penetrated his consciousness. Something outside in the hallway. The kind of thing that he would normally never heed, but which now somehow managed to jar all his instincts and set his nerves onto red alert.

He rose quietly and went to investigate.

'Hey, buddy. What's the matter?'

Isaac was at the front door, clutching Stinky with one hand and trying to pull the door open with the other. He ignored Edward, redoubling his efforts.

He should probably go and wake Charlotte. But she was sleeping so soundly, so peacefully. He could at least give this a go before he did so. Walking over to Isaac, he went down on one knee beside him.

'You want to go out?'

Isaac shook his head, giving the door one last tug.

'Ah, I see. You're just checking that we're locked up safely for the night. That no one can get in.'

Isaac nodded, staring at the floor as if he was being hauled up in front of the headmaster in disgrace.

'Right, then. That's a good idea. Let's do it together.' Edward imagined that Isaac probably wanted Charlotte to accompany him, and when the boy curled his arms around his neck he almost jumped back in surprise.

'Okay.'

'Well, let's fetch your dressing gown, then, so you don't get cold. And we can have a story afterwards if you'd like.'

Isaac nodded, and Edward hoisted him up in his arms. Lifting that small weight made him feel stronger than normal. As if he was some kind of superhero who could make things right and conquer all manner of monsters—even the ones in Isaac's head.

Surgeon and Dragon-Slayer General. Edward quite liked the sound of that. And if one involved precision instruments, the other involved a large sword which could be brandished flamboyantly when the opportunity arose. There was even a fair maiden, who was currently fast asleep on the sofa, and an apprentice who was also asleep, worn out by a brief but thorough inspection of the locks on all the doors and windows and the first few pages of his favourite bedtime story.

The last half-hour hadn't involved scaling any high walls, or actually rescuing anyone, but that was okay. Another time, perhaps, when the fair maiden wasn't in such immediate need of her beauty sleep.

Isaac stirred against him, snuggling up tight.

'Let's get you back to bed, little man.' Edward whispered the words so as not to disturb the sleeping child, and rose, carrying the boy up to his bed.

And then, before he had the chance to think about any such thing with Charlotte, he gently shook her awake, turning back to his book as soon as she had bidden him a sleepy goodnight.

CHAPTER TEN

IT HAD BEEN one hell of a tough week. The meeting with Edward's father, when the past had reached out, snatching her back into the nightmare that she thought she'd survived. Being afraid all the time, and trying not to show it to anyone.

One glass of wine with Edward on Friday, after Isaac had gone to bed, and she had fallen asleep on the sofa, waking with a start when she felt his hand on her shoulder, gently shaking her.

Today she woke to silence. A slow, sleepy climb into wakefulness, cocooned in comfortable forgetfulness. Something was missing, and she groped around in her mind for what it might be. No alarm. No… She sat up straight, propelled by panic. No Isaac, bouncing on her bed, telling her to wake up and get on with the day.

Hitting the floor at a run, Charlotte sped into his bedroom. The curtains were drawn back, the room was bathed in sunshine, and the bed was neatly made. Then she heard a noise from downstairs: Isaac's laughter, threaded through with Edward's quiet, rich chuckle.

Stupid. There was nothing wrong, no need to be this jumpy. All the same, she crept downstairs, just to check on them.

They were so involved with what they were doing that they didn't see her. Isaac was sitting on the edge of the sofa, next to Edward, with the coffee table pulled up in front of him so he could reach the keyboard of Edward's laptop. Edward, leaning back on the sofa, was concentrating hard on the screen.

'Way to go, partner!' Edward's face lit up and Isaac threw his arms up above his head, bouncing up and down on the cushions. Edward leaned forward, hitting a key. 'Do you want to try the next one?'

'That's all my teacher told me to do…' Isaac turned to him.

'Well, we don't need to do exactly what she says.' Edward shot him a look that mirrored the mischief on Isaac's face. 'You don't have to stop unless you want to. You're pretty good at this.'

'Okay…' Isaac giggled '…partner.'

Edward chuckled and pressed another key. It looked as if the two of them were fine without her for a while, and Charlotte could take her time in the shower.

When she got back downstairs, showered, dressed and feeling better than she had for weeks after a good night's sleep, she smelled coffee. The patio doors were open, and Isaac's voice drifted in from the garden.

'Is that a fresh pot of coffee I smell…?' She followed the aroma into the kitchen and found Edward there.

'Yep. Want some toast?'

'You are a wonderful man.'

He looked over his shoulder, shooting her a rakish half-smile. 'If I'd known that it just took a pot of coffee and some toast…'

'And a good night's sleep. Where's my alarm clock?'

He nodded at the clock, sitting innocently on the kitchen table. 'I happened to wake up early. I heard Isaac rambling around, and I sent him into your room to get it. I reckoned you could do with a bit of a lie-in.'

'Oh, so you've been enlisting my son in your machinations, have you?'

'Yep. He seemed to think it was a good idea, too. And I reckoned that if you did wake up, then you'd probably be a little happier to find Isaac creeping into your room.'

A good deal more relaxed, maybe. Happier...? That would depend on what Edward was there for. Charlotte dismissed the thought, and with it her fantasies of waking up to find Edward there.

'Has he had breakfast?'

'Yep. I told him that I'd be in trouble with you if we didn't keep to the straight and narrow, and he took me through the procedure step by step. Cleaned his teeth, had a wash, showed me where his clean clothes were. Do you *always* let him have chocolate biscuits for breakfast?'

'No!' Charlotte supposed it couldn't hurt just for today.

Edward chuckled. 'Gotcha. We had toast with peanut butter, and banana smoothies. Then we did some number games on the internet.'

So that's what they'd been up to. 'Isaac's homework?'

'Yes. He showed me the sheet that his teacher had given him. I found a game on the internet that made it a little bit more fun.'

'Thanks.' That feeling of dread she had when Edward did anything either for her or Isaac had almost completely disappeared now. Maybe because Edward so clearly enjoyed playing with Isaac.

'No trouble.' He buttered the toast and set it down in front of her, adding a jar of marmalade and one of apricot jam. Then coffee, hot and aromatic, with a dash of milk. Just one cup.

'I've got to go out...'

He was searching for his car keys and Charlotte pointed to the hook under the kitchen cabinet, where they were supposed to be.

'Right. Thanks. I'll be back shortly.'

'Shortly' could mean practically anything with Edward, and generally did. Charlotte opened her mouth to ask whether he'd be home for lunch, but he was already gone.

He returned an hour later, and appeared in the doorway between the hall and the living room carrying a long, thin parcel. He dumped it on the coffee table and sat down next to Charlotte on the sofa with an air of anticipation.

'What's that you're reading?' He craned over her shoulder, and Charlotte hugged the library book to her chest.

'Nothing… What's that you've got there?'

'Hmm…nothing.'

Another moment of quiet, and Charlotte returned to her book.

'Looks interesting. I haven't been there for ages.'

He was reading over her shoulder again, and Charlotte snapped the book shut.

'It's the summer holidays soon, and I thought I'd take Isaac out on a few daytrips. This book's got some really great ideas.' It seemed that—for the moment anyway—the plan that they should just get on with their lives without disturbing each other too much had gone by the board.

He grinned. 'The Natural History Museum's great for kids.'

'And for adults.' Charlotte had been looking for places which would interest her and Isaac—something that they could share—as well as a few fun places where he could work off his energy.

'And the Science Museum's just down the road, of course. There are some wonderful things there.'

'Yes.' He was going to be volunteering to come along any minute now, and the thought of Edward and Isaac together in the Science Museum sounded far too much like hard work. 'So what's in the parcel, then?'

'Ah! Thought you'd never ask.'

'So did I. Looks as if you've worn me down.' She grinned at him and he was suddenly seized with motion, grasping the parcel and tearing the wrappings from it.

'What do you think?'

'It's a...' Isaac had run in from the garden and nosed his way in between them. 'What is it?'

'Here—see?' Edward pointed to the picture on the label. 'It's a kite.'

It wasn't just any old kite, but then Charlotte doubted that Edward would be much interested in anything that didn't have a complex structure of cords and an unlikely shape. He began to unwrap the collection of disassembled struts and sails, fishing out a small booklet.

Isaac watched open-mouthed and confused, looking to his mother for an explanation. 'Edward has to put all of those pieces together, sweetie, before it'll fly.'

'Yeah, shouldn't take long.' Edward was already laying the pieces out on the coffee table. 'Then we can go and fly it, eh, buddy?'

Charlotte left them to it and went to make drinks for them both. When she returned, Edward had already snapped into the fearsome concentration with which he approached almost any task, leaving Isaac shifting restlessly from one foot to the other. Charlotte placed his coffee on the table and he nodded absently.

'Thanks... Don't touch those, Isaac, I've put them all out in order.'

Isaac's hand shot away from the metal strut as if it had suddenly become red hot, and he hid it behind his back.

'Come here, sweetie.' Charlotte motioned her son towards her and put her arms around him. 'We'll just watch, shall we?'

Isaac nodded, obviously wishing that he could be a part of the construction project, craning to see what was happening. Edward seemed almost oblivious to the two of them, quickly selecting the pieces he wanted and deftly fitting them together.

They watched in silence. 'Look, sweetie, it's almost ready...' The structure was recognisable as a kite now, and Edward was attaching twine to the steering loops at each side.

Isaac nodded. But as Edward had worked she'd felt the excitement ebb out of her son's body, and now he was leaning against her legs with an air of boredom, his eyes on the television.

'Is it time for my programme, Mum?'

'Which programme, Isaac?'

'You know. *Eddie and the Magic Fish*.'

'Don't you want to wait until the kite's finished?'

'I want to see my programme.'

She saw the hurt in Edward's eyes. 'Okay. Come upstairs. You can see it there.'

There was a television in the guest bedroom, and perhaps it was best to let Isaac watch TV while Edward finished the kite. When they got to the point of flying it—and she was sure that Edward wouldn't be able to wait to try out the magnificent creation—Isaac's interest would be rekindled and everyone would be happy.

She left Isaac sprawled on her bed, clutching Stinky, captivated for the moment by the adventures of the Magic Fish. When she went back downstairs, the sitting room was empty. Charlotte could see Edward in the garden, ranging restlessly along the far end of the lawn, kicking at the inconsistencies in the smooth line between grass and flowerbeds.

Perhaps he needed to be left alone for a while, with his thoughts. He'd work it out; the mathematics weren't all that difficult. Isaac was five, and there were times when Edward's focussed ardour for the task in hand simply left him behind.

But there were elements to this equation that intellect, even one as all-consuming as Edward's, couldn't grasp. Twisting her mouth, and in defiance of all that was logical, Charlotte slipped through the open French windows and walked across the grass towards him.

He was lost in his thoughts, seeming not to notice her. 'Given up, then?' She might as well start with a challenge, if that was the way she meant to go on.

'The kite's finished.'

'Yes, I saw that.'

He turned to her, giving her a speculative look, as if he was trying to weigh the situation up. 'He didn't like the kite. That's okay. Isaac's free to have his own likes and dislikes...'

'Edward, did you ever go to school?'

He blinked at her, struggling to make the connection. 'As it happens, no. By the time I was five I'd already got a handle on calculus and my parents had me tutored at home.'

There was a note of sadness in his voice.

'That must have been lonely.'

He shrugged. 'I don't have anything to compare it with.'

'When everything's fine, you don't need anything to compare it with.'

There was something dull in his eyes as he focussed on her. 'You're saying I don't play well with others.' One hand clenched into a fist. 'That's not exactly an original thought.'

He just wasn't listening to her. It was as if it had been drilled into Edward that being clever meant that you didn't have a heart. 'Maybe it's just a self-fulfilling prophecy. If you believe it's true, then ultimately it is.'

He glared at her. 'And you have a better idea?'

He turned, as if the conversation was now at an end. He was used to having the last word. Used to being right.

'Don't be so arrogant…' Even before he turned back she knew that she'd missed the mark by about a mile. Edward might look and sound arrogant, but somewhere beneath that there was a lonely child.

'I am what I am, Charlotte. If you want to think that's arrogant, then go right ahead.'

All of his defences were up now. The aloof, unsmiling man, whom no one seemed to be able to get close to, was turning away from her again.

She did the unthinkable. Marched straight up to him and grabbed his arm, pulling him around to face her. 'You don't fool me, Edward. I've seen you with Isaac. I saw you with Mercy the other day.'

Something behind his eyes ignited. Dark blue ice turning to sparkling heat. There was more than enough emotion here. It was just a matter of whether she could deal with it. Whether *Edward* could deal with it, without ducking back into the comfort of his books.

'Mercy opened up to you, not me.'

'Edward! Sometimes I want to shake some sense into you…!'

The provocative twitch of his lips told her that she could go right ahead, if that was her inclination, and she resisted the urge.

'What on earth happened to you when you were a child?'

'You think I was a poor little bright boy, with his nose in a book and no friends? It wasn't like that.' He pursed his lips. 'Not quite like that, anyway.'

'What *was* it like, then?'

'I was different. By the time I was ten I could keep up with a university undergraduate on an intellectual level. On a social level, I wasn't quite ready for women, all-night parties and beer-drinking contests. It was difficult to find my own space.'

'You felt out of step, you mean? Your emotions and theirs?'

He looked at her gravely. Then suddenly he smiled. 'Most people assume I don't have any emotions.'

His look taunted her. Dared her to tell him different.

'That's not true, though, is it?' She dared him back.

'I don't think so.'

The dare turned dangerous all of a sudden. He was waiting for her to kiss him. Charlotte baulked at that one.

'Look, Edward, I know that you're used to being better and faster at everything than everyone else, and that it's a lot easier to do things by yourself. But if you want Isaac to be interested in what you're doing then you have to slow down a bit and do things at his pace.'

He hesitated. 'I'm…not very good at that. As you can see.'

'No one's born good at things like that—you have to learn. You're supposed to be a genius. Can't you learn? Or don't you want to learn?'

'I want to.' The admission was a little stiff, and left Edward nonplussed for a moment. 'Why don't you go and tell Isaac…?'

She glared at him and he grinned.

'Why don't I go and tell him myself?'

'Good idea.'

'Right.' He clapped his hands together, as if he was about to embark on one of the most complex experiments of his life. 'Do you think he'd like his own kite? One that's more his size, perhaps?'

Charlotte almost told him no, that Isaac didn't need a kite. But she knew he'd want one, and Edward needed this.

'I think he'd love that. Go and ask him.'

Edward didn't deal in half-measures. The shop he took them to sold nothing but kites, and on a bright late summer's morning, was full of people. He led Isaac straight to a selection of different coloured children's kites, and the two of them became immediately absorbed in sorting through them. Charlotte decided to leave them to it.

'I'm just going to pop to the chemist, to buy some soap. I won't be long. Stay here with Edward, won't you, Isaac?' She nudged his shoulder with her hand.

Isaac ignored her in favour of the kites, and Edward looked up at her. He seemed to know how hard it always was for her to leave Isaac, even for a few minutes, and he took hold of the boy's hand as a gesture of intent.

'I won't let him out of my sight. Go and do your shopping.'

She decided to take her time, to give Edward and Isaac a chance to buy the kite by themselves. There were some nice apples on display outside the greengrocer's and she stopped to buy three, to go with the packed lunch in the boot of the car.

In the chemist's she ran her finger along the lines of jars and bottles which were beyond her purchasing power, now.

Her old soap, the one she'd used to buy before she'd begun to make all her decisions on the basis of price, was there. Something from her old life, when she hadn't needed to question every word, every action, every penny that she spent. She so wanted that back.

Charlotte picked it up, hesitated, put it back on the shelf, then picked it up again.

It wouldn't matter if she had something that she wanted for once. The soap smelled nice and felt creamy on her skin, and it wasn't so very much more expensive than the more economical brands. As luxuries went, this wasn't so very ostentatious.

'Come on, Mum…' Isaac broke into the debate, tugging at her arm.

She looked round to see Edward, with a firm hold on Isaac's other hand to prevent any possible escape.

'Okay, just a minute. Did you get your kite?' It was clear that he had, Edward was holding a large plastic bag.

'Yes, do you want to see?'

'Mmm. Yes, please.'

Isaac grinned up at Edward, who delivered the bag into his grasp. Inside was a small blue kite with a blue and silver tail.

'Oh, that's so pretty!' She drew the kite out to examine its tail. 'Those sparkly bits are going to shine in the sun when you fly it.'

Isaac nodded, carefully showing her everything. There was a ball of twine, mounted on a reel, to protect Isaac's hands from any friction. 'You tie it on there—see?' Isaac indicated the reinforced eyelets on the kite. 'With a special knot.'

Charlotte nodded, impressed. 'A special knot, eh?'

'Yes. Edward's going to show me how,' Isaac responded proudly.

Her little boy was growing up. It was almost a surprise to find that she didn't mind that Isaac wanted Edward to help him tie the knots on his precious kite, when it felt only a blink of time since her son had looked to her for everything.

'That's great. Make sure you watch what he does carefully.'

'Can we go, Mum?' Isaac was impatient again, jigging up and down on the spot.

'Yes, let me get my soap and we'll be off.' Charlotte looked up to see Edward, in a world of his own, working his way along the shelf and inspecting the ingredients lists printed on all the soap wrappers. 'Edward?'

He jolted back into the here and now. 'Ah. Yes.' He focussed on the soap in her hand and took a matching bar from the shelf. 'That one smells nice.'

She didn't really need it. The thought that Edward liked the smell of it made her want it, though. 'They're all much the same. I'll get this one.' She put the bar back onto the shelf and reached for the cheaper brand.

'I imagine they're all pretty easy to make...' He still had one foot in that world of possibilities that seemed to know no bounds. He inspected the bar in his hand. 'Pretty standard ingredients.'

'*You* might be able to make it. *I'd* probably blow the kitchen up. It's just soap, Edward.' Nothing was just anything to Edward. Everything fascinated him, from pizza-making to nuclear physics. When she was with him the world seemed bigger, far more interesting.

'Hmm. You like this one, though?' He still had the bar that he'd taken from the shelf in his hand.

'This will do. It's cheaper.'

Before she could reach into her bag for her purse Edward had given her preferred choice to Isaac, along with a note from his pocket. 'You want to get it for your mum?'

She met his gaze. This wasn't anything to do with kites, or soap. It was about whether she had the right to a treat, however small. Whether Edward had the right to give it to her, to claim a place in their little family.

'Okay. Thank you.'

He nodded, grinning.

'At last!' Isaac conferred his displeasure on both of them and ran to the counter.

Charlotte watched as the woman at the cash desk smiled down at Isaac, took his money and put the soap into a bag, counting his change into his hand.

'Hey! Hey, give Edward his change back.' Isaac had pocketed the coins.

'That's okay.' Edward winked at her. 'He might be need-ing it later for ice-cream.'

Isaac looked from Charlotte to Edward, then back again, waiting to obtain a final decision. 'All right, then. Here—let me zip your pocket up, so you don't lose it.'

She bent and fastened Isaac's pocket, then gave way to the pressure from both Edward and Isaac and hurried with them to the car. The afternoon was bright and blustery, just right for kite-flying, and the three of them seemed in complete accord. No one wanted to miss a moment of it.

CHAPTER ELEVEN

THEY DROVE FOR an hour, right out of London, making a beeline for high ground. The last five hundred yards had to be walked—or rather climbed—until finally they reached the exact location that Edward wanted.

'It's windy enough here.' The words were almost dragged away on the breeze as soon as they left her mouth.

'Yes. I think this will do.' Edward looked around with an air of satisfaction. 'Which kite shall we try first?'

'The big one!' Isaac was jumping up and down with excitement. 'I want to see the big one…'

'Okay.' Edward grinned, laying the large kite onto the ground, clipping together the last pieces of the framework so that it was ready to fly. 'You see, I think that the wind will catch it here…' he indicated the breadth of the kite '…and funnel through this way…' A sweep of the hand to show the anticipated wind direction. 'That should give it extra lift, and the weight of the tail makes it steadier.' He grinned. 'That's the theory, anyway.'

'Will it work?' Isaac stamped his foot impatiently.

'That's what we're here to find out. It's all very well to have a theory, but you always have to test it out… Here, you hang on there.'

Edward gave the kite to Isaac and winked at Charlotte, walking away from them as he unravelled the twin reels of lightweight cord.

He paced out the distance and called back to Isaac, 'Okay, hold it up...'

Charlotte kept a discreet hold on the top of the kite, in case Isaac decided to let go of it before he was supposed to.

'Now, on my count... One...two...three...let her go!'

The kite rose in a straight line, up into the clear blue sky. Isaac shouted at the top of his voice in excitement, and suddenly the only thing to do was to shout with him.

'Nooooo!' The kite dipped erratically and Isaac screamed in horror.

Edward fought for control for long moments and then the kite soared upwards again. Charlotte cheered, and Isaac followed suit, running towards Edward.

'That didn't quite work...' Edward was grinning at her. 'Perhaps I'll just concentrate on keeping it up there at this stage.'

'I want to hold it... Pleeeease...' Isaac was pulling at Charlotte's windcheater in excitement.

'I don't think so, sweetie. It's very hard to control. We don't want you flying away with the kite.'

'Owww.' Isaac seemed to think that flying away was an added bonus.

'What about yours?' Edward reeled his kite in and turned his attention to Isaac's blue and silver kite.

Isaac's face was a picture. Happiness that he was a part of their great enterprise and not just relegated to watching. Pride when the kite soared up into the sky, with Edward kneeling at his side, showing him how to control it.

'Thank you.' Charlotte caught at his sleeve as he stepped back, letting Isaac go solo. 'Thank you so much.'

Edward nodded in satisfaction. 'Every boy needs a kite. I'm just going to make a few adjustments to mine and perhaps you'll help me launch it again.'

A few knots, a little staring into the middle distance as Edward estimated airflow and wind speed, and the kite was up in the air again, this time flying more steadily. Charlotte ran back to Edward's side and he looped his arms over her head.

'Here, you try. Take hold of the reels.'

She pressed her hands over his, trying to stop her fingers from trembling. The wind around them buffeted her, but she was safe in his arms, her back against his strong body, his scent surrounding her and then blown away by the wind.

'That's right.'

His lips were almost touching her ear.

'Pull it a bit to the right.' He guided her arm and the kite dipped to the right, shooting back upwards as the breeze caught it again. 'Ooops. Hang on tight.'

Suddenly he had left her, and was loping across to Isaac, who was struggling to keep his kite in the air.

Charlotte concentrated hard on controlling her own little bit of airspace while Edward restored Isaac's kite safely back above their heads. He made sure that Isaac was happily in control again and then he was back.

'What do you think?' He was surveying the flight path of the kite.

'It's pulling really hard...' Her arms were already beginning to ache.

Edward chuckled, looping his arms around her again. 'Let me give you a hand with it.'

He wasn't helping at all. All that happened was that she melted into his arms, turning to jelly and losing whatever strength she had left. He was controlling not only the kite but her as well. She let go of the kite strings and he strengthened his grip, catching them just in time. Turning in his arms, she faced him.

His rakish half-smile told her that this was just what he wanted. 'Giving up already?'

'You're so much better at it than I am.'

'Think so? You dip beautifully.' He leaned towards her.

She couldn't do this. Not with Isaac just yards away—even if he was paying them no attention.

She ducked out of the circle of his arms, feeling the wind suddenly chill her. 'Are you hungry?'

Edward chuckled. 'Ravenous.'

She fixed him with a glare. Even the thought of Peter's quiet charm, and the way that had worked out, wasn't enough to calm the insistent thunder in her veins. Peter was like a faded shadow of a man next to Edward. Edward was different. Different from pretty much everyone she'd ever met.

'Would you like an apple?' She gritted her teeth and doggedly refused to take any notice of the alternative interpretation of hungry that the curve of his eyebrow suggested.

'In a minute. I've got my hands full at the moment.' His gaze left her, flipping over towards Isaac. 'Steady on, there, chief...'

Charlotte ran to her son, helping him to pull on the string so that the kite fluttered upwards again. 'Enjoying yourself, sweetie?' She whispered the words tremulously in his ear.

'Yes, Mum.' Isaac's attention was on the kite, its tail shimmering and sparkling in the sunshine. He submitted to a hug for a moment and then wriggled free.

'Good. I'm glad.'

She could have cried. The scared little boy who had clung to her when the debt collectors knocked on the door was gone. In his place a child who was enjoying himself so much that he had no time for his mother's cuddles.

'All right over there?' Edward nodded over to Isaac.

'Just fine. He loves this.'

'Yeah. Me, too.'

* * *

Edward sat at the piano, his fingers wandering across the keys, playing a soft melody of his own composition. He'd had a great time. The kite had flown better than he'd expected once he'd made a few adjustments to the lines which had altered its angle of flight slightly. Isaac had liked his kite, too, and had insisted on taking it to bed with him. And Charlotte...

He'd planned to give her a great day—help her forget about the troubles of the past week. And she'd shone in the sunshine like a beautiful jewel, full of life and light. But however hard he tried to please her he seemed to end up only pleasing himself, as the echoes of her *joie de vivre* washed over him.

Charlotte. The chords seemed to sing out her name. A sudden slip into a minor key lent an element of yearning to the music that hadn't been there before.

'Why so sad?'

He hadn't noticed her behind him, standing in the doorway which led from the kitchen. He stopped playing abruptly, aware that the music had given away much more than he had ever intended. 'It's a slow piece of music.'

A slight frown of disbelief. It seemed that he could lie to the rest of the world, but Charlotte caught him out every time.

'I recognise it. You've played it before.'

When he'd played it before it had been just a dalliance with the keys. Now it was a full-blown, passionate love affair, full of all the conflicting emotions in his heart. 'It's a work in progress. It changes every time.'

She nodded. Walked over to him. 'Will you play it again?'

'No.' She couldn't lure him in like that. If the music insisted on betraying him, then he'd stick to other people's compositions. 'I mean...I need to think about it a bit more.'

She nodded and he beckoned her over. This time she sat down next to him on the piano stool as if it was the most natural thing in the world.

'Would you like something else?'

'If you want.' She smiled. 'Whatever you want.'

'Your turn to choose.'

She grinned. 'What was it you were playing the other night?' She hummed a few chords, her voice clear and tuneful.

'You've got a good ear. Most people don't get that bit right.' He reproduced the chords she'd sung and she smiled, singing along with the music.

He'd played this song thousands of times before. Kathy had liked this one, too, but it had never felt like this. Never as if he was caressing someone with the music. Never so head-swimmingly erotic.

He hadn't thought about Kathy in years. If asked, he would have said that he'd forgotten her, but it seemed that she'd just lain dormant in his memory, waiting to emerge and reprimand him for having ignored the lesson she'd taught him.

'What's the matter?'

Charlotte was closer now, and Edward realised that he'd stopped playing.

He shrugged. 'This song reminds me of...someone I used to know.'

'Should I be sorry?'

He shook his head. 'I don't think so. It was a long time ago. When I was at university.'

'Which time?'

'The second. Kathy was a medical student.'

She nodded. 'First love?'

He shrugged. 'I suppose so.'

It had been more like a first friendship, really. Kathy had been quiet, studious, so like him that everyone had reckoned they were made for each other and it was just a matter of time before they got married.

When she'd left him, citing a lack of emotional commitment on Edward's part as her reason, it had been proof positive to all their friends that Edward was the cold fish they'd always marked him down as being.

She nodded. 'My first love was Isaac's father. That didn't work out too well.'

'But you loved him once...' The words almost choked Edward.

'You know they say that love is blind?' She looked up at him and he nodded. 'Well, I don't think so. I think that real love sees everything.'

'Do you think you can really ever see everything about someone?'

'I don't know. In the absence of any substantive evidence either way, I'll have to say that it's just a theory. But they say that true love lasts, and I don't love him now.' Her mouth twisted, as if the joke was really on her.

Something inside him raged in bitter triumph. The impulse to tear Charlotte's ex limb from limb de-escalated to wanting to give him a more minor, if acutely painful, set of injuries. If she didn't care about him any more then Edward could live with that.

'You can't regret all of it. Isaac...'

'Isaac's the best thing that ever happened to me.' She laid a finger on his shoulder, as if alerting him to something. 'Good things do come from bad.'

'If you make them.'

Charlotte had that ability. As for himself... Nothing good or bad had come from his time with Kathy. Just a lingering doubt about whether he really could ever commit to anyone. After everything that had happened today that doubt suddenly seemed to matter a great deal.

She was looking steadily at him. That silent interrogation which he found so difficult to withstand. Why didn't she just *ask*?

'How long were you and Kathy together?'

'Three years.'

She nodded. Seemed to be about to ask more, and then didn't. That was as well, really. The nagging feeling of failure whenever Kathy's name was mentioned made him uncomfortable.

'So we're two of a kind, then.' She gave a little sigh.

'What makes you say that?' Charlotte was warm, bubbly—everyone knew without even thinking about it that there was nothing she didn't know about emotional commitment.

'Both still waiting for the right one to come along.'

It felt as if the right one was sitting next to him. But that must be another mistake, because Charlotte clearly didn't think so.

'No. I'm not waiting.' Edward told himself, with less conviction than normal, that he had everything he needed. His work, his books. The textured, multicoloured, harmonic flow of the world around him, perfect in all its intricacies.

'Better watch out, then.'

He was aware that her gaze was on him.

'Why?'

'That's when things sneak up on you from behind. When you least expect them.'

He turned to tell her that she was wrong—one smooth movement which began with a shake of his head, and ended with her lips. She gave a little start of surprise and then... Then she kissed him back.

Soft...slow.

Edward was taking it gently, giving her every opportunity to draw back from him, but that was the very last thing that Charlotte wanted to do. When he brushed his fingers against her neck, his thumb caressing her jaw, she felt her breath quicken.

He was all for the moment. Each touch was special and not to be rushed. Every breath was one they wouldn't take again, unique and remarkable. His fingertips found hers, touching, sensing, and then wrapping around her hand, drawing it upwards. Holding her gaze, he brushed his lips against the back of her fingers.

There was more. Simmering beneath the surface. Waiting. He took the pace up a notch, just one, his hand on the nape of her neck, pulling her in for another kiss. This time there was an edge to it, a promise of so much more if she could only stand this long, slow preamble.

He didn't call out her name. Made no profession of desire, or love, or even friendship. He didn't need to. It was all there in his kiss, the heat banking and flaring until she felt herself begin to tremble.

They broke apart. Charlotte's heart was thudding in her chest, her lungs pulling in air.

'Does that make any difference?' he asked.

'What do you mean?' Of course it made a difference. Edward's kiss made all the difference in the world. Fear clutched at her.

'I mean does that make you or me into different people? Change any of our views on life?'

She wished it did, but all of the old doubts were still there, the dread that she might fall back into disaster again. 'No.'

'Then I guess we'll say that there's someone out there for you, and someone for me. Leave it at that.'

So this was the way he wanted to play it. Just a kiss between friends. *Like hell it was.* That had been the first step on a path which led straight to two naked bodies and mind-blowing sex. They needed no words to know that.

He was right, though. Sex with Edward, if she ever

managed to survive the intensity of the foreplay, would be like jumping from the frying pan into a searing fire. She couldn't afford to be fooled again by quiet charm and hidden depths. She wanted—needed—everything to be in plain sight.

'Yes. That would probably be sensible.' It seemed almost wrong to stand up now. Like the biggest lie of all to deny what had just happened. But she did it. 'I'm going to…'

Saying that she was going to bed would sound like a come-on. And his gaze was still so very enticing. Charlotte was under no illusions about whether she would be able to say no to him if he reached out for her now.

His slow smile was laced with all of the intentions that neither of them seemed able to follow through on. 'I'll leave you to it.'

'Thank you.'

What was that for? Starting things? Stopping things?

She leaned forward and planted a kiss on his cheek, drawing back again. 'Goodnight. I'll see you in the morning.'

CHAPTER TWELVE

IT HAD OCCURRED to Edward to burst into her room, carry her off to his, and make love to her until the raging in his blood let up. That might well have been a long and exhausting process, but that wasn't what had stopped him. It was what came afterwards—the falling in love and realising that he couldn't give her what she needed.

He was older now, and perhaps a bit wiser. He'd seen more of the world. Met Charlotte. Maybe things could be different. But *maybe* wasn't a good enough word for someone like Charlotte.

No emotional commitment. The words on Kathy's lips had puzzled and upset him. If he dared to make love to Charlotte, then those words on her lips might just kill him.

So he wouldn't. Instead he'd carry on as normal.

More or less normal, anyway.

It was with a pang of unusual regret that he rose from the kitchen table at seven the following morning and began to scribble a note for her, saying that he was going to catch up on some work he had to do at the Hunter Clinic and wouldn't be in for lunch.

'You're up early.'

Her bright morning smile interrupted him, almost choking him with desire.

'You, too.' The house was still quiet, and Edward wondered whether he'd made a mistake in not following his instincts last night. If Isaac was asleep, there was still time…

'Oh, I've just taken the opportunity to come down and make some sandwiches. Isaac's playing in his room. He'll be racing around wanting to get dressed soon.'

'Ah. I'll leave you to it, then…' It looked as if the Hunter Clinic was his best bet after all.

'We're going to the park this morning. Some of Isaac's friends go boating on the lake on Sundays. I'll leave you a salad for lunch…'

'There's no need…'

'Or you could come with us if you'd like?'

Charlotte, Isaac and Edward. Almost as if they were a family.

Edward picked up the note he'd been writing, screwed it into a ball and dropped it into the kitchen wastebin. 'Yes, I'm at a loose end today. That would be nice.'

The summer sunshine sparkled on the water like diamonds swept up from the bed of the lake in the wake of the small boats which bobbed on its surface.

'Mum… Mum, they're already here. Quick!'

Isaac was running back and forth, trying to hasten the easy pace which she and Edward had fallen into.

'There's plenty of time. Don't you want to go and find Sam first?' Sam was Isaac's best friend from school. 'Look, there he is.' Charlotte waved to Sam's mother and Isaac ran off across the grass, leaving her and Edward to follow in their own time.

'It's a nice day for it.' Edward was surveying the water.

'Yes. It gets a bit crowded sometimes on Sunday afternoons, but if you come before lunch and bring a picnic—' Charlotte broke off, shading her eyes against the glare. 'What are those two boys up to?'

A small boat was rocking precariously as two boys in

their early teens took it into their heads to start a mock-fight in the deepest part of the lake. One caught the other with a flailing fist and they both crashed into the water, the boat rocking wildly and threatening to capsize.

'Edward…' She caught his arm and then started to breathe again as two heads bobbed to the surface of the lake and the boys started to doggy paddle towards shallower water. 'Those kids—they could have hurt themselves… Where's the attendant?'

Heads turned as the park attendant jumped into a boat, quickly pushing off towards the boys. Then a shrill wail floated across the still air.

'What's that…?' Charlotte scanned the water and located the source of the scream. She'd thought that the boys were alone in the boat, but there was also a shock of blonde curls just visible inside of the boat. 'Sit down!' she screamed at the child, even though it was unlikely that her voice would carry that far, much less be heeded.

The child managed to get to her feet and the boat bucked wildly.

'Edward, she's going to fall in…'

Her words met thin air. The bag he'd been carrying lay where he'd dropped it, and Edward was already powering down the steep slope which led to the lake, throwing off his jacket and shoes. By the time the other adults gathered around the lake started to notice the little girl he was already wading into the water, then swimming towards the child with long, easy strokes.

The little girl had calmed down now, and it seemed as if he would soon reach her. Charlotte glanced quickly in Isaac's direction and saw that Sam's mother had both him and Sam firmly in her grasp, stopping them both from running down to the lake's edge.

Edward was nearly there. Only another fifty yards.

It was fifty yards too much.

The wake from another boat made the craft wobble and the child screamed again, panicking, throwing herself from one side to the other. The boat capsized, taking her with it.

No time for the curse of disbelief which sprang to her lips. Charlotte ran to the waterside, one eye still on Isaac. Sam's mother shouted a reassurance that she'd look after him and Charlotte hitched up her skirt and began to wade into the water.

Edward had reached the spot where the upturned boat lay in the water and was looking around for the child.

'Edward… She's under the water.'

He didn't turn his head, but he must have heard. His body seemed to rise in the water, and then disappeared as he dived beneath the surface.

Long moments.

The water was almost opaque here at the edge of the lake, and Charlotte could only hope that it was a bit clearer further out. He had to find her.

How long was it now? Thirty seconds? A minute? Charlotte knew that Edward wouldn't come back up until he'd found the child, and prayed that it would be soon.

The surface of the lake erupted in a frenzy of bubbles and water as Edward broke the surface. He struck out immediately for the shore, not stopping to take a breath although his lungs must have been screaming for air. As soon as the water was shallow enough he gained a footing and waded, the little girl clinging tightly to his neck.

For a moment all Charlotte could feel was relief. Water was sluicing from Edward's chest and legs and the child moved in his arms, leaving a watery red stain on the shoulder of his white shirt.

'Edward…' She waded further into the water, meeting him as he strode towards the bank. 'You're bleeding…'

'It's not my blood.' He nodded quickly towards the little girl, who was whimpering now, holding on tight to his shirt collar. 'Clear a space for me, will you?'

Charlotte stumbled, splashing up onto the bank. 'Some space, please, guys. My friend's a doctor—give him some space.'

Two women assumed the responsibility of moving everyone back, and someone threw a waterproof sheet down onto the ground. Edward dropped to his knees, ready to examine the child, but she wouldn't let go of him.

'All right, honey. You're such a brave girl, and you're safe now. Let me look at your arm…'

He gently tried to move the child and she hung on even tighter. Charlotte could see a gash on her forearm, which was gushing blood.

'Okay. That's okay.'

Charlotte expected him to use his vastly superior strength to free himself, but instead he held the child closer, motioning to Charlotte.

'Looks as if you're going to have to look at her arm *in situ*…'

Charlotte dropped to her knees next to him, gently lifting the little girl's arm. 'She's got a nasty cut, and it's bleeding badly. She'll definitely need to go to hospital.' She looked up, and almost simultaneously half a dozen mobile phones appeared.

'We'll just need the one ambulance.' She grinned at the knot of people around them. 'Are her parents here?'

Sam's mother's voice sounded above the general hubbub. 'Dave, call an ambulance. Everyone else—see if you can find her mother. Who are those boys she was with…?'

Charlotte left Maggie to it, with only the briefest glance in her direction to check that she was still holding firmly onto Isaac's hand.

'I'm going to have to wrap something around her arm to stop the bleeding.'

'All right.'

The little girl screamed as Charlotte gently wrapped her own scarf around the wound, pressing firmly and extending the arm upwards.

'It's okay, honey. I know it hurts, but you're all right.' Edward's voice was almost painfully gentle, and the screams subsided to a whimper. 'You're doing really well.'

She couldn't tell whether the child understood his words, or his manner. Whichever it was, she was beginning to calm.

'What's your name, sweetie?' Edward managed to disentangle himself sufficiently to ask the question face to face, rather than direct it at the top of the child's head.

'Laura.'

'Well, Laura, you're safe now. I expect your arm hurts, but we'll put a bandage around it and it'll be better in no time.'

Laura nodded up at him. It occurred to Charlotte that she might like to remind Edward of his own words on the subject of his ability to communicate with patients, and she promised herself she'd do it later. He might not want to admit to being so very wrong in front of all these people.

'What happened? She was under the water for a very long time...' Charlotte had half expected to see Edward bring Laura up unconscious.

He grinned at her. 'She instinctively did just the right thing. When the boat capsized she ended up in an air pocket underneath it, and she held on to one of the seats. The biggest problem was getting her to let go of it and hang on to me instead.' His free hand patted Laura's back. 'You've got a great grip, there, young lady.'

Laura looked up at him, favouring him with a tremulous smile. At that moment the knot of people around them parted as a woman came stumbling through.

'Laura…' The woman fell to her knees in front of Edward. 'Laura, I'm so sorry… Is she all right? They said you're a doctor…'

'She's okay.' Edward delivered Laura into her mother's arms while Charlotte kept a tight hold on her arm. 'She has a cut on her arm, and needs to keep it elevated until the ambulance arrives. She'll need a few stitches, but the main thing is that she didn't stop breathing.'

'Laura…' The mother held her daughter tight, her eyes squeezed closed.

Charlotte knew just what scenes were playing in her head. She'd had her own share of them with Isaac recently.

'It's fine. You have a very resourceful young lady for a daughter, there.'

The woman's eyes opened and tears spilled from them. 'I only left her for a minute… The kids wanted ice-cream and I told Trevor to look after her.' One of the boys who had been fighting in the boat stood beside her, soaking wet, bedraggled, and not a little shamefaced.

'She's fine. That's the main thing. Her head was only under the water for a few moments—'

He broke off as tears coursed down the woman's cheeks. Someone proffered a handkerchief, but she wouldn't let go of her daughter for long enough to wipe her eyes.

Edward turned to Charlotte. 'How's that cut doing?'

'I think it's stopped bleeding.' She loosened her grip on Laura's arm and blood began to seep between her fingers. 'Ah. Not quite.'

'Okay. Can the ambulance get to us here?'

'Yes, the park gates are wide enough for them to get through, and they can use the service road that runs through the park, right there.'

He nodded. 'Good. We'll just sit tight here, then.'

* * *

The paramedic from the ambulance returned Charlotte's scarf to her with a wry smile. 'Try washing it in cold water...'

'Thanks.' Charlotte took the scarf. Hot water would only fix the bloodstain and it would never come out. Cold water might do the trick.

'I should have offered to rip my shirt up for a bandage.' Edward's voice sounded behind her. 'It's already ruined.'

Ruined it might be, and bloodstained and dirty from the lake, clinging to his shoulders and chest in the places where the sun hadn't dried it, but it was still better on than off. Marginally. When he'd emerged from the water the white lawn fabric had left very little to the imagination.

'Probably best you keep it.' She grinned up at him. 'We don't want to get all the mothers talking. I have to face them at the school gates, remember.'

He gave her a hurt look. 'I'm allowed to rip up my shirt for bandages, aren't I? I thought it was practically par for the course when a doctor has to improvise.'

'Only when there's nothing else to use. I'm a nurse, re-member, and I had a scarf handy.'

'Hmm. Shame to spoil it, though.' He caught the end of the fine material through his fingers. 'It's pretty.'

It was her favourite. It went with her blouse, and she'd chosen both from her wardrobe this morning because they were a little smarter than the T-shirts she usually wore at the weekend. If she had allowed herself to examine her motives for that choice she would have had to admit that Edward had played a major part in it.

'It'll wash out.'

'Hmm. You've got a spot of blood on your cuff, as well.'

'That'll wash out, too.' Charlotte rolled the sleeves of her blouse up a little, to hide the stain.

'Yeah. Look, I'll take it home with me and put it in a bowl of cold water. Sam's father...'

'Dave?'

'Yeah, Dave. He's offered to run me home to get a change of clothes. We'll only be half an hour.'

'You'll be coming back?'

'Of course. We haven't eaten our picnic yet.' Edward watched as Laura's mother climbed into the ambulance, shepherding her son with her. 'His ears are going to be ringing tonight.'

'I imagine so.' It was so easy. You only had to take your eye off them for one minute... Charlotte shook her head.

'Isaac's okay.' He pointed towards Sam and Isaac, playing together in the grass under Maggie's watchful eye.

'Yeah, I know.' Still she couldn't help the terrible feeling of foreboding.

'I can understand your fears. With everything that's happened. But no one's going to let anything happen to him.'

'No.' She had to be content with that. With Edward's promises, his father's reassurances. 'Look, you're shivering. You must be freezing.' His hair and shirt were beginning to dry, but Edward's jeans were still soaking wet.

He shrugged. 'I could do with getting those dry clothes. Will you be okay here with Isaac?'

'Yes, fine. See you later.'

He grinned. 'I wouldn't miss this afternoon for the world.'

Charlotte sat with Maggie on the grass, hugging her knees in front of her.

'So, Edward's...a friend of yours...?'

'Yes, I work with him.'

'Ah. A colleague. Well, it was lucky he was here today. He was a real hero.' Maggie laughed. 'I told Isaac and Sam that I thought he was a hero, and Isaac asked if that made him a hero, too. Since Edward was his friend.'

Charlotte grinned at the thought. 'What did you say?'

'I said that it did. Then Sam wanted to know if he was a hero, too, as he was Isaac's friend…'

'I reckon it's catching, this hero business.'

'Definitely.' Maggie leaned towards Charlotte confidingly. 'Mind you, even my heart skipped a beat when he walked out of the water carrying that little girl.'

'Yeah?'

Charlotte's heart had almost stopped. Edward's jeans, moulded tight around his strong thighs… His shirt clinging to a broad, muscled chest which had been heaving from the effort of getting to Laura in time and pulling her from the lake… The droplets of spinning silver that had scattered as he shook his head… It was an image that she wasn't going to forget in a hurry.

'Guess mine did, too.'

'It's instinct. Man saves child. Guaranteed to pull at the heartstrings.'

Head, heart and all points south. If Laura hadn't been the most pressing priority she would have had little choice but to fling herself into his arms.

'Yeah.' She turned to Maggie with a bright smile. 'And it all ended well.'

'Yep. Thanks to you two.' Maggie lay back in the grass. 'I think it's going to be a great afternoon.'

'So, if you ever tell me again that you're no good at reassuring patients…'

Charlotte was grinning at him, as if she knew that Edward was expecting something of the sort from her. At least she'd left it until Isaac was safely tucked up in bed.

'Okay.' He looked up from his book, holding his hands up in mock surrender. 'You just had to say it, didn't you?'

But it had felt good to be the one who gave comfort for a change. He could see the extra dimension that it added to Charlotte's job.

She laughed. 'Do you mind?'

'No. I'd mind if you hadn't noticed.'

Charlotte's approval was becoming more important to him than he was strictly comfortable with. It was one thing to gain satisfaction from trying out a new approach and finding that it worked, but that didn't mean that he'd changed. He might be older, and a bit wiser, but were Kathy's words so very wide of the mark?

She jutted her chin at him. 'So you admit that you've underestimated yourself?'

The phone interrupted any possible answer to that, and Edward reached for the handset. He heard his father's voice, with a quick enquiry about how he was doing and a request to speak to Charlotte.

'Here.' He spun the handset across the coffee table and she caught it adroitly. 'It's my father. He wants to speak to you.'

He couldn't have asked for a better illustration of Kathy's point. Even his father seemed to be captivated with her, and somehow found far more to chat about with Charlotte than he did with Edward.

He retreated into a book, hardly hearing what Charlotte was saying on the phone. After half an hour she replaced the handset into its cradle.

'Everything okay?'

'He wanted to set up a meeting for this week. I'm going to see him on Wednesday, after work. He's got some things for me to sign.'

'Good. Anything else?' That would have accounted for about two minutes' worth of their conversation.

'He asked me if I knew anything about the different cuts you can get on precious stones.'

'Really? Do you?'

She nodded. 'My father was a jeweller. The old-fashioned kind, who knew how to make pieces as well as sell them. So I know a little.'

'I imagine he's got their fortieth wedding anniversary in mind—that's only a few months away now.' Edward wondered whether he should follow his father's lead and enlist Charlotte's help in choosing a gift for his parents.

'Mmm. He wants to get something really special. I'm going to give him the name of an associate of my father's who deals in rubies when I see him. He does very fine work. I used to have a necklace that he made for my mother.'

Her voice was matter-of-fact. Just the smallest hint of regret.

'Used to have?' Edward hoped against all reason that the necklace was somewhere tucked away safely—the one thing that Charlotte hadn't sold.

'I sold it. It gave me a few thousand to put towards the deposit on my house.'

'I'm sorry you had to do that.'

She shrugged. 'They're only pretty sparkly things. I remember my parents, and that's the thing that really matters.' She pulled her shoulders back, as if telling herself for the hundredth time that it really didn't matter. 'Anyway, I know a good ruby when I see one. I'll make sure that your father gets a really nice stone.'

'Thank you.' She was quite unselfish in her generosity. Even though she'd lost everything herself, she wanted to make sure that another woman had the perfect gift. 'So, do you need someone to look after Isaac on Wednesday evening?'

'I can have the childminder pick him up from school. That's what I usually do.'

'I've got a free afternoon. I can pick him up and bring him back here if you like.'

She nodded. 'If it's not too much trouble. I don't want to...'

'If you were going to say that you don't want to impose, you can save your breath.' He kept the stern glare up for about two seconds, until she flushed and it melted. 'You're not imposing. It's been a pleasure having him around.'

She grinned, a hint of mischief in her eyes. He could get lost in that mischief, let it bend and break him...

'You two are getting to be quite a gang...'

'Yeah?' Edward had never been in a gang before, even if this was an exceptionally small one. He quite liked the possibilities that it opened up. Going fishing for tadpoles. Wearing their ties like bandanas around their heads.

'I just... Well, I hope that he's not been too demanding. Of your time.'

For someone who seemed to know pretty much what he was thinking for a good proportion of the time, Charlotte could be shockingly unperceptive sometimes. 'No. I think I've been demanding of *his* time, haven't I? It'll be my pleasure to pick him up from school on Wednesday.'

CHAPTER THIRTEEN

EDWARD WAS PLEASED to see that the school made him sub-
mit to a thorough check, to make sure he was who he said
he was, before they would let him take Isaac. He'd been
worried that Charlotte's husband might try something, and
it seemed that his father had, too, because when Edward
had broached the matter quietly with him he'd told him
that was all seen to.

'So. What shall we do, then?'

The feeling that he was playing hookey was almost
overwhelming. He wasn't, of course. The clinic knew exactly where he was, and he was just taking a few hours
from the hundreds he was owed. But Edward didn't let
that spoil the fantasy.

'What would *you* like to do?'

He dumped his keys and phone onto the hall table, and
extricated Isaac from his backpack and coat.

'We could play a game on the internet. Or play football.
Or perhaps you'd like to go to the park?'

Isaac nodded. He, too, had an air of being about to embark on an adventure. 'The park.'

'Okay. Do you think we should take some supplies with
us? In case we get lost? You never know what might happen.'

Isaac smiled. 'Stay with me. I know my way around.'

'Okay. But perhaps we'll take some juice. And one of those fruit and nut bars your mum bought.'

'Mmm. Good idea.'

They rambled together through a small wooded area, picking up fallen branches to swish on the path in front of them. Edward turned over stones with his foot, and they both inspected the creatures which lived in the damp darkness below them.

'Look. A piece of flint.' He held out the broken pebble for Isaac to see.

'What's that?'

'Flint's a type of stone. A long time ago cavemen used to make axes and arrowheads out of flint. It's very hard.'

Isaac inspected the stone carefully. 'Can we make an axe out of this?'

'Maybe. It's a little small. Let's find a bigger piece and perhaps we can take it home and give it a try.'

They searched together and found a bigger piece of flint. Edward put it into his pocket, and then saw a couple of flat, circular stones on the ground. 'Hey, look at these. Do you know how to skim stones?'

'No.'

Edward grinned. 'We'll collect some of these up, then, and I'll show you.'

The house was quiet when Charlotte got back home. The meeting with Edward's father had been longer than she'd thought it would be, and she was tired. She didn't much feel like cooking straight away, but she was going to have to.

'Hey? Guys...?' She called into the silence and only silence answered her. Perhaps they were out in the garden, playing football. She walked through to the kitchen and opened the back door.

No one there. Edward's car was parked in front of the

house, and his suit jacket was slung over the bannisters. He must have walked down to the school.

Even if he had they should be back by now. He'd been due to collect Isaac more than two hours ago. Charlotte pulled out her phone and checked it. No calls or texts from the school. That meant that everything had gone to plan. Flipping through her address book, she found the entry for Edward's mobile and called it. Tapping her foot while the call connected, she then let out a huff of exasperation when the tones of his mobile chimed out from the hall table.

'Edward. Where *are* you?'

She wasn't sure whether to be cross or worried. She dropped her bag onto the hall table, slung her jacket over the bannister, and wandered into the sitting room, sinking down onto the sofa.

'Where are *you*, Isaac?'

'Yeaaah!' Isaac jumped up and down, cheering. 'Six!'

Edward straightened, smiling with satisfaction. 'I think the smooth ones do better, don't you?'

Isaac nodded. 'Those big flat ones are the best, though.'

'Hmm. Less air resistance. Larger surface area.'

Isaac nodded sagely, although it was doubtful that he understood the finer points of it. Actually, for once, Edward wasn't much interested in the finer points. Just in counting the number of times their stones skipped across the water out loud with Isaac.

'I'm hungry.'

'Are you? We've had our drinks and...' Edward looked at his watch, his heart sinking when he saw the time. He felt in his pocket for his mobile and realised that he must have left it at home when he changed his jacket. 'Isaac, we've got to get going, mate. Your mum will be waiting for us.'

* * *

The list of possibilities was endless. A car accident. The lake. Surely Edward couldn't be so irresponsible as to take Isaac out on the lake—not after what had happened at the weekend. She couldn't think about that any more; it was making her feel sick. Peter's face flipped up into the void that not thinking about a freak accident had left. Could *he* have taken Isaac? Perhaps Edward was out looking for him?

She was being alarmist. They were probably out somewhere together. But Edward was normally so responsible. Charlotte couldn't imagine that he'd possibly become as involved with a game of football as he did on a day to day basis with his piles of papers and the intricate problems that his patients posed.

One of them had been taken ill. Perhaps she should call the local hospital. But wouldn't Edward have called? Left a message for her on his own home phone if he couldn't remember her mobile number? She checked the answering machine again. Nothing.

Where were they?

Edward had hoisted Isaac up on to his shoulders, was striding out as fast as he could without dislodging the boy from his perch. He should have left a note for Charlotte, telling her where they were. Or remembered to bring his mobile with him. That would have solved the problem. It was too late now. All he could do was hope that she wasn't worrying about Isaac.

He loped up the drive, gravel scrunching beneath his feet. There was no opportunity to pull his keys out of his pocket because the front door flew open. He could see from the way she rubbed her hand across her face that Charlotte was upset, but by the time he reached her she seemed to have regained some of her composure.

'Isaac! How was your day, sweetie?' Her eyes were red, but she was smiling, trying to pretend to Isaac that nothing was the matter. He let Isaac down and the boy ran to her to give her a hug.

'We had a brilliant time, Mum. We've been skimming stones. We've got a special method.'

Her gaze flipped up towards Edward at the mention of the special method and her lips pursed. Before he had a chance to apologise she was smiling at Isaac again.

'That's great. You're going to have to show me how you do that.'

'We've got a piece of flint, too.' Isaac twisted his face up towards Edward. 'Edward's going to make it into an axe.'

Right now, putting an axe anywhere within Charlotte's reach might not be such a good idea. She shot him another glare, and Edward put his hands into his pockets. He didn't particularly want to go into the house, or to be anywhere near her at the moment. Generally speaking, keeping out of the way until it all blew over was his preferred modus operandi in these situations.

'What's for tea, Mum?'

'Wait and see. Go inside, now, and take your coat off.' She stood aside as Isaac ran past her and into the house, then directed her gaze at Edward.

He already had his car keys in his hand, and had pressed the remote to unlock the doors. She stood, arms folded, in the doorway. 'And where do you think you're going?'

Nowhere. Anywhere. 'I've…um…got to pick something up from the hospital.'

'Something important, no doubt?'

'I guess it must be.' He turned towards the car and heard the safety catch on the front door flip. Felt her hand catch in the crook of his arm, spinning him round.

'Afraid?'

'Yep. Terrified.'

He faced her at last. She was trembling with an emotion that he found hard to identify. A cocktail, maybe, of all the feelings that he didn't much want to think about at the moment.

'And running's the best option, is it?'

'I'd prefer to call it a tactical retreat.'

'Call it whatever you like.'

Her chin jutted provocatively. Eyes golden in the early evening sunshine. Her hair was slightly mussed, as if she had dragged it out of the neat knot that she usually wore it in for work and not bothered to comb it.

'Look. You're angry...' It was a very old cliché, but she was one of those people who became even more beautiful when angry. 'I'll let you go and see to Isaac...' He wanted to kiss her.

'Unless you hadn't noticed, Isaac's perfectly capable of switching the TV on by himself and sitting in front of it for ten minutes.' Perfectly on cue, the sound of a children's song washed through from the living room and Isaac's voice joined in with the melody.

'All the same...'

'Don't you dare...'

He felt her hand brush against his and the hairs on his arm stood on end. She pulled the car keys out of his hand and flipped the locking mechanism. Two beeps and a flash of the headlights told Edward that his car had just changed sides and was firmly in her camp now.

He didn't much blame it. She was difficult to resist. Throwing a backwards glance at the treacherous machine, he stalked into the house.

Isaac's head popped up over the back of the sofa. 'Edward. Come and see...'

All his resistance melted. That cornered feeling, which he usually dealt with stony-faced and emotionless, didn't matter any more. 'Hey, buddy.' He strode into the sitting room and plumped himself down next to the boy. 'Have you washed your hands?'

Isaac inspected his grubby fingers. 'No.'

'Well, you'd better do that. Mine could do with a wash as well.' He led Isaac into the kitchen, kicking the plastic box that he stood on to reach the counter-tops in front of the sink. He squirted a dollop of soap into Isaac's palm and then soaped his own fingers.

'Is Mum angry with us?' the boy whispered conspiratorially.

'Nah. Not with you.'

'You?'

'Don't you worry about that. I'll handle it.' Edward didn't bother with any details of exactly how, on the basis that he hadn't formulated them yet.

'Do you want to borrow my ray gun?' Isaac twisted round to face him, splashing water onto his shirt.

'Thanks. But I think I'll manage.' He bent down, keeping his voice low. 'We don't want to hurt her, do we?'

Isaac shook his head, taking the other end of the towel that Edward was drying his own hands with.

'I'll tell you what...' There were no signs of food preparation in the kitchen. Charlotte had clearly been spending her time glued to the front window, waiting for him to bring Isaac home. 'Do you like Chinese food?'

Isaac nodded.

'Okay, then. I'll go out and get some.' Isaac shot him a questioning look. Clearly takeaways didn't figure much in his experience. 'I'll bring it home and we can eat it here.'

'You don't need to do that. I can have something ready in half an hour.'

Charlotte's voice sounded from the doorway. If she'd heard the bit about the ray gun she was clearly undaunted by it.

If she was so keen on him staying in, then she was going to have to put up with the consequences.

Edward reached for the takeaway menu, taped to the door of the fridge, and handed it to her. 'There's a nice place just around the corner. I'll phone in our order and go and pick it up. We can be eating in fifteen minutes.'

She gave a little huff and unfolded the card. The strains of another children's tune floated in from the sitting room and Isaac dropped his end of the towel and ran in to see what was happening on the television.

'Okay.' Edward closed the door into the sitting room behind the boy. 'You want to talk.'

She didn't really. But when Edward had started to retreat back into himself, his face losing all the animation that she saw whenever he talked with Isaac, she'd panicked. It had been as if she was losing him back into the realms of considered thought and few words.

She twisted her lips together, pretending to read the menu. He came closer.

'Afraid?' He plucked the menu from her hands and held it behind his back.

'Terrified.'

'Good.' That tantalising half-smile. 'I won't be needing the ray gun, then.'

'If you want to get a takeaway you'd better do it. Otherwise it'll be no quicker than if I cook.'

'If it's an apology you want…'

'No.' She'd overreacted. She was the one who ought to be apologising.

'I'm sorry. I should have let you know where we were. I lost track of time and you understandably got worried. It won't happen again.'

'It's okay. It doesn't matter.'

His blue eyes. You could always tell what was going

on in Edward's head by those eyes. Now they were dark, as if an old anger had seized him.

'It does. I know that I can't really understand because I'm not a parent....'

'What?' Where had *that* come from?

'I'm not stupid. I know what people think of me.' He turned away from her, one hand slicking his hair back across his head. 'That I'm too bound up with my books to even notice what's going on under my nose.'

Not that again. 'Face me, Edward.'

'Is that better?' When he turned, his face was brooding, angry from the hurt that seemed to have steeped in his soul for a long time now.

'A little bit.'

This was like a crazy game. Each trying to drive the other away, protect themselves, and yet fascinated by each other.

Unable to resist the temptation to dig deeper. Charlotte stepped forward. 'Touch me.'

He looked at her as if she'd gone stark, staring mad. If she'd taken a moment to think about what she'd just said then she would have agreed with him completely.

'Like this?' His fingers trailed the line of her jaw. 'Or this?'

His other arm snaked around her waist in a strong, domineering motion and suddenly she was pressed against him. She should have known better than to taunt Edward.

Charlotte reached up, cradling his jaw in her hands. Not even the fact that Isaac was in the next room could stop her now. 'Now. Listen to me.'

'I'm listening.'

He was listening all right. She had every piece of his attention, from the strong curl of his body to the ever-fascinating eddies of his mind. It was all-encompassing, irresistible.

Charlotte took a deep breath. 'You should have let me know where you were, but I should have trusted that Isaac would be safe with you.'

'And...?'

His anger had subsided and she could feel the tautness of his frame relax against hers. Melting, almost...

'I just...'

'Find it hard to trust?'

Was she that transparent? 'Yes. I suppose I do. It's a big world out there, and Isaac's starting to be interested in it. My job is to keep him safe, make sure that he's got what he needs, and...'

'Let him go. Just a bit, maybe.'

'Yeah. Just a bit.' She reached up and touched the side of his face with her fingertips. 'Who says that you don't understand?'

He let her go abruptly. Probably just as well. Their bodies seemed to have taken on a life of their own. Moving against each other with an almost imperceptible but blissful friction.

He shook his head as if to clear it. 'It's not rocket science. You've had to fend for yourself and Isaac for a long time, now. Isaac's father, the one person who should be helping you, is only making things worse. You've had to struggle to make ends meet, and been chased out of your home by debt collectors. I would think that trust issues go hand in hand with that.'

'Hmm. Life's a bit more complicated than rocket science sometimes.'

Edward leaned back against the kitchen counter, his hungry eyes still on her. 'Rocket science isn't really that complicated. One of those illustrations that doesn't stand up to too much scrutiny.'

For a moment Charlotte could see the lure of his books. Something that was constant in an ever-changing world.

If she could have seen the same beauty in numbers and science that Edward did…

Damn the books. They couldn't give him this.

She stepped forward and found him there, ready. His body seemed to mould to hers—a close fit that left no room for anything else to come between them.

She kissed him. She couldn't help it. And once she'd brushed her lips against his she couldn't help but go back for more. His response was thrilling, strong and tender all at the same time.

One hand travelled lightly down her back. Across the rise of her hips and to the top of her leg. This was too much. She'd bitten off far more than she could chew.

'Isaac…' She just managed to get the word out.

'Yeah…'

His grip on her loosened, but Charlotte couldn't bring herself to pull away.

'He's just in the next room.'

She wasn't telling him, she was telling herself. Giving herself the one and only reason that could stop her from keeping going until all the pent-up frustration came screaming from her lungs.

'We should stop.'

Edward seemed as disinclined to bring this to a close as she was, but he was the stronger. He gave her one last, head-spinning kiss before he gripped her shoulders, carefully propelling her backwards, away from him.

'That's…sensible.' Her cheeks were burning, and she still couldn't quite catch her breath.

'Yes. I'd better go and get us something to eat. Before…'

'Before we get too hungry…'

'Yes.' He pulled the takeaway menu out of his back pocket. 'What would you like?'

'Anything. Surprise me.'

His lips twitched into a half-grin before he straightened his face. 'All right. I'll be fifteen minutes.'

Enough time to splash cold water on her face and take a breath. 'Have you got chopsticks here?'

'No, I'll get some.'

He opened the kitchen door and disappeared into the living room. Charlotte heard him exchange a few words with Isaac, and as the front door slammed she shook her head. It was going to take a lot longer than fifteen minutes to get Edward out of her system.

CHAPTER FOURTEEN

'Is IT SO very wrong to feel like celebrating?' Charlotte wondered if she sounded cold-hearted.

'No.' Paula swirled her herbal tea thoughtfully in her cup. 'It's exactly the right thing to do. You've got to look forward, not back.'

Paula clearly thought that Charlotte was being brave about this. It was nothing of the sort. Ever since she'd received the Decree Absolute this morning Charlotte had wanted to do nothing but dance. And, finding herself alone with Paula in the employees' lounge, she'd been unable to contain her news.

'Actually, it's quite a relief. I was afraid my husband...' Charlotte couldn't help smiling '...my *ex*-husband would make some kind of objection somewhere along the line.'

'From what you've said in the past...' Paula looked at Charlotte thoughtfully. 'Okay, so you've asked for no maintenance. Your ex didn't ask for any rights to visit Isaac. Am I right in thinking that this guy was bad news?'

'Between you and me...?'

Paula nodded. 'Of course.' Paula might gossip, along with the rest of them, but she knew how to keep a confidence.

'Yeah. Very bad news. He hasn't seen Isaac for months, even though I've asked him time and time again if he'd come.'

Paula snorted in disgust. 'What kind of slug doesn't want to see a cute little guy like Isaac? No wonder you want to celebrate. You want to come down to Drake's tonight? We could crack open a bottle of champagne.'

'I'd love to. But I've got to go and pick that cute little guy up.'

Paula nodded. 'And the cute big one?'

'There's only one guy in my life who's even remotely cute. And he's three feet tall...' Charlotte told herself that you couldn't really call Edward cute.

'Yeah, right. You're either blind, or crazy, or...' Paula grinned, her words taking on a sing-song intonation '...you're telling porkies.'

'I'm just out of one bad relationship. I think I'll take some time to pause for a breath.' Charlotte shrugged. 'Twenty years or so.'

Paula leaned towards her. 'I wouldn't leave it twenty seconds if I could get my hands on Edward North.'

'Who says I can?'

Only about half the clinic. And the other half reckoned she already had. Keeping secrets about what you did out of hours was easy enough. Keeping secrets about how you felt about the people you worked with was nigh on impossible in such a small community.

Paula had the grace not to remind her of the gossip. 'Whatever. But in another four hours' time it's going to be the weekend. Tell me you'll find *something* to do to celebrate, eh?'

'Yes, I will.'

Paula nodded. 'Life's too short to worry about what other people say. Even me.'

'Thanks, Paula.' Charlotte looked at her watch. 'I've got to go. I've a clinic in twenty minutes.'

'Edward North?'

'Yes, Edward North—if you must know.'

* * *

'Two more to go?' They were in one of the Hunter Clinic's plush consulting rooms.

'Yes.' Charlotte flipped through the notes. 'April Ashe is next. She's just coming in for a follow-up visit.'

'Ah, yes, April. Have you seen her yet?'

'Yes, she's in the waiting area.'

'How is she?'

Charlotte laughed. 'Isn't that what she's here for? For *you* to say how she is?'

'You know what I mean.'

Yes, she did. And it was a question that Edward wouldn't have asked just a couple of weeks ago. 'She looks great. She's got a new dress on.'

Edward searched her face for some clue. 'How would you know that? Or am I intruding into a knowledge base that's for you to know and the male of the species to wonder about.'

'You'll have to wonder.' Charlotte grinned at him. It was simple, really. When Charlotte had admired April's yellow and white summer dress her mother had said it was new. But it was good to keep Edward wondering from time to time.

This time April walked into the consulting room alone. 'Hi, April.' Edward got to his feet. 'You look very nice today.'

April nodded. 'Thanks.'

Charlotte wondered whether he would ask, but he didn't. Instead he set to, examining the skin on the side of April's face. 'That's healing very nicely, April. What do you think of it?'

'It's…different. Good… It itches a bit still.'

'Yes, that's natural. It itches as it heals.' Edward smiled. 'You've been massaging the oil that Charlotte gave you into it? And I can see you've been keeping out of the sun.'

'Yes.'

'Good.' Edward returned to his chair. 'Well, I don't think that I need to see you again.' He smiled at April and she grinned back.

Experience had taught Charlotte that this was the point where she stepped in.

'You will, of course, be seeing Charlotte again, and she'll monitor your progress. But I was wondering whether you had any questions for me.'

Okay. This was new. Usually he left the questions part to the nurses.

'Um... Not really...'

'Hmm. So what's this question you don't *really* need to ask, then?'

April smiled self-consciously at him. 'Well, I'm going to my end-of-year party at school in a couple of weeks' time.'

'Ah. That might be a little out of my area of expertise.'

He looked at Charlotte and she raised her eyebrows at him. So he was going to leave her something to do, at least.

'I think that April would be interested in knowing whether another couple of weeks is going to make an appreciable difference to the look of the scar. And whether she can use a little make-up. Is that right?'

April nodded. 'Yeah. There's someone I...'

'Yes. Of course. Well, the wound's been dry for a while now, and there's no reason why you shouldn't start to use light cosmetics occasionally, as long as they don't irritate your skin. Charlotte can advise on which types to use and so on. As to the look of it...' He paused, thinking for a while. 'Generally speaking, I'd expect that area to look better in two or three weeks' time than it does now. May I ask you a question, April?'

'Sure. What is it?'

'Well, it's a long time since I was your age...' He paused, as if waiting for a contradiction.

'Mmm,' April agreed.

'But I can certainly remember it.' He shot a stern look at Charlotte, who was barely repressing her laughter. 'And I have to say that any young man who disregards your smile and your personality, and who only sees a scar, isn't worth your time.'

'That's what my mother says...' April gave him a wry look.

'Well, it must be right, then.' Edward snapped his notepad shut with an air of finality.

'But...' April looked at him thoughtfully. 'But when I said I wanted my scar done she was all for it. So was my dad.'

Some of Isaac's questions prompted that very same baffled look from Edward, but he regrouped almost instantly. 'I look at it like this. What I do can't change who you are, because you're already special. My aim is to give you what you deserve.'

A slow smile spread across April's face. 'Nice one. Thanks.'

'You're very welcome, April.' Edward rose from his seat. 'Well, I can see that you ladies have some...um... things to talk about. Is your mother outside? I'd just like to have a quick word with her.'

April nodded and watched him go, before turning to Charlotte. 'You know, I thought that Dr North was a bit stand-offish. But he's really nice, isn't he?'

Charlotte laughed. 'Yes, he is. Really nice.'

Charlotte wished Paula a good weekend and watched her go through the doors to the outside lobby. She waited for a few minutes and then made for Edward's office. She'd been saving her good news until they could talk uninterrupted.

'You got it, then?' He looked up when she tapped on the door, pushing the papers in front of him aside.

'How did you know?'

'I saw the courier delivery for you on the reception desk this morning.'

'Okay.' Charlotte sat down. 'So I had a delivery. It could have been anything.'

'That's just the first of my observations. The second was that the envelope was my father's stationery.'

'So you went to the Sherlock Holmes School of Medicine, did you? You'll have to do better than that. It could have been a letter from him telling me that there was some kind of problem.'

'Ah. Yes, it could.' Edward leaned back in his chair, the tips of his fingers touching to form an inverted V. 'But then you wouldn't have been looking like a cat that's just got the cream all afternoon.'

'I haven't!' That Edward had noticed the letter and known where it was from was hardly surprising. That he'd noticed *her* was still a new enough experience to make her shiver with pleasure.

'Yes, you have.' Edward gathered up some papers and stuffed them into his briefcase. 'Let's go.'

He picked up the heaviest of her shopping bags and ushered her out of his office.

He nodded a goodnight to Ethan Hunter, who had appeared from the lobby, and kept walking when Ethan spoke.

'Do you have a moment, Charlotte?'

'Yes, of course.'

It was all very well for Edward to walk on ahead, as if they both just happened to be leaving work at the same time, rather than together. But the canvas shopping bag with 'Smart Girls Recycle' emblazoned across it was hardly going to be his.

'Mrs Ashe asked to speak with me before she left.'

'Is there a problem?' Charlotte had thought that the session with April had gone well, but generally clients stopped to complain, rather than praise.

'She was very pleased with the way that April's procedure has been handled, and she especially mentioned how well you'd looked after her. I hear you even gave her some make-up advice. Well done.'

'Oh! Thank you, Ethan.' Perhaps it was relief, but she thought she saw a flicker of warmth in Ethan's normally impassive face. 'It was very nice of Mrs Ashe to take the time to speak with you.'

'She mentioned that Edward was very kind, as well...' Ethan was clearly a little perplexed by the concept.

'He always does his best for every patient.' Now probably wasn't the time to go into any apparent change in Edward's demeanour.

Ethan nodded. 'Yes, of course. And it's always good to hear that our clients value our people as much as we do. Passing their praise on is one of the more pleasant duties which falls to me when Leo's not around.'

'I appreciate it that you did. It means a lot.' Charlotte smiled up at Ethan and made a move towards the exit.

Ethan walked with her. 'You have a son?'

He'd clearly decided that this was one of those getting-to-know-you moments that a good employer should take with his employees. Charlotte wished he'd chosen a time when Edward hadn't been waiting for her outside.

'Yes. Isaac's five.'

'Must be quite a handful, then. Was he the boy I saw Edward playing with in his office a couple of weeks ago?'

'Um... Yes.'

'I've never seen Edward look so animated.' Ethan was smiling now. A little distant, as if he was thinking about something else at the same time, but definitely a smile. 'You and Edward make a good team.'

Charlotte swallowed hard and decided to interpret *good*

team in a purely professional context. 'Isaac has a way of involving people. I suppose all children do...'

'Yeah. I guess they do. But Edward's a pretty tough nut to crack.' The smile faded and was replaced by Ethan's usual thoughtful look. The one that implied his thoughts on the matter were not particularly happy ones.

'No one's that tough.'

Ethan raised one eyebrow. 'I wouldn't go as far as to say that.' He stepped forward, opening the door to the lobby for her, and Charlotte walked through.

Edward was waiting there, her shopping bag nestled against his own briefcase at his feet. He nodded briskly at Ethan, who returned the nod and disappeared along the hallway.

'Everything okay?' Edward waited until Ethan was out of earshot.

'Yeah, fine. Mrs Ashe told Ethan that you and I had done a good job with April, and he stopped to say thank you.'

'That's nice.'

'He said we made a good team.'

'Well, we do, don't we?'

That slight quirk of Edward's lips told her that he, at least, didn't have his mind completely on the professional. 'Why are you looking so glum? You've just had a vote of thanks from the boss. Ethan doesn't say these things unless he means them.'

What Ethan had really meant was beyond Charlotte. He'd seemed genuinely pleased for the little family unit which was forming before his eyes, but somehow... Charlotte sighed. If Ethan thought that it was beyond his own reach, then Charlotte was inclined to think it was beyond hers, too.

'What? What's the matter?'

'Nothing. Let's go home.'

* * *

She'd pushed the boat out and bought steak for dinner, cooking it in a peppered sauce with home-made chips. Edward and Isaac had tucked in with an almost identical glee, and been unanimous in their praise.

'I've been thinking.' Edward was helping her stack the dishwasher while Isaac played in the garden.

'Oh-oh. That generally means trouble...' She smiled at him.

He shot her a look of amused reproach. 'Would you like to go out tomorrow evening? To celebrate...or perhaps to commiserate. Whatever you feel like doing, I'll keep you company.'

'I feel like... No. Let's not do anything, eh? My marriage is over now, and I don't want to look back. I want to look forward.'

'Fair enough. So why don't you just let me treat you, then? My mother's coming over tomorrow afternoon, and she can look after Isaac for the evening if you'd like. We can go somewhere nice.'

Going out. On a Saturday night. It was years since she'd had the money to go anywhere, nice or otherwise, let alone pay for babysitters and... 'I don't really have anything to wear...'

He shrugged. 'You have clothes. We'll go somewhere where clothes are *de rigueur.*'

She couldn't help but laugh. 'Okay. Thank you. I'd love to.'

His smirk looked far too much as if this had been a plan and not an off-the-cuff invitation. 'Good. Mum'll be here about three tomorrow.'

It all seemed to go like clockwork. Edward's mother arrived on the doorstep at five to three the following day, and burst into the house like a friendly tornado. She kissed

Edward, hugged Charlotte as if she'd know her for years, and made a beeline for Isaac, who was sitting on the floor playing with a construction set.

'That looks interesting.' Penny North had sat down on the sofa and was now looking hard at Isaac's handiwork.

'It's a spaceship.' Isaac looked up at her.

'Well, of course it is. Silly me.'

Isaac made his decision and opted to trust this stranger with some more information. 'Look, this is the engine.'

'Oh, I see. How clever.'

Edward nudged Charlotte. 'You want to leave them to it?'

His breath caressed her neck and she shivered. Suddenly it all seemed real. She had a date for tonight. Not just any old date, but a darkly handsome, sophisticated, talk-all-night date. And it looked as if Isaac was making his own arrangements for the evening.

'Yes. Let's go and make a cup of tea.'

After Kathy, his mother had seemed to give up all hope of seeing a woman, let alone a child, in Edward's house. Charlotte had gone upstairs to change and he sat with his mother on the patio, watching while Isaac ran around the garden. He liked this more than he was prepared to admit. His mother was clearly overjoyed, and had exceeded all expectations in her enthusiasm for both Charlotte and Isaac.

'Can't you take her somewhere nicer than that, Edward?'

'I like it there.'

'Yes, but a girl wants to be taken somewhere glamorous.' His mother waved her hand, encompassing all the glitzy nightspots that London had to offer. 'Somewhere she can kick her heels up and forget about everything.'

'Like Dad did with you?'

'Yes, now you mention it. Your father wined and dined

me until I was far too giddy to say no when he asked me to marry him.'

'Don't jump the gun, Mother. We're just friends.'

'Yes, and that's all you'll ever be if you carry on like this. Just call upstairs, tell her to put her best dress on, and get on the phone and book somewhere nice....'

'She doesn't have a best dress. She's been living hand to mouth for the last few years...'

His mother let out a tut of disapproval. 'Well, couldn't you have taken her out and bought her something?'

'I could have tried, but she wouldn't have let me. She's... proud.' *Proud* wasn't really the word for it. Charlotte didn't have a lot of trust. But Edward didn't want to go there with his mother. 'And she looks great anyway, with or without a new dress.'

His mother nodded in satisfaction at the assertion. 'Well...yes, all right, then. I can see the difficulty. But for goodness' sakes tell her how nice she looks, won't you? You can't expect women to just know what you're thinking.'

That was the thing. He'd thought that Kathy had known what he was thinking—if anyone should have done it would have been her. And she'd said he had no emotional commitment. Those words had been seared into his brain and had stayed there, like the ultimate condemnation.

'I don't expect anyone to know what I'm thinking.'

His mother quirked a smile. 'Well, that's just as well, dear. You'd already lost me by the time you were about ten. But this is different. We're not talking about advanced mathematics. We're talking about...' His mother groped for the right word.

'Emotions?'

'Yes, exactly. We all have the same emotions, irrespective of whether we can do complex equations in our heads.'

That was a matter of opinion. But Edward was saved

from the rigours of that particular debate by Isaac, who tripped over his own feet and suddenly toppled, flat on his face, onto the grass. In a movement that was rapidly becoming instinctive Edward rose and hurried towards the boy.

'Hey, there.' Edward inspected him rapidly for any damage. 'Okay, mate. You're all right.'

Isaac didn't seem to think so, and clung to him, crying. Edward gave him a hug and his sobs subsided. 'There you are. Just a bit of a shock, eh? Have you hurt yourself?'

'No.' Isaac seemed ready to start careening around the lawn again, but then his attention was drawn to the patio.

Charlotte was wearing a simple white dress, with a lacy bodice that showed the curve of her shoulders and upper arms. Her light brown hair tumbled around her shoulders, shining in the sun. He wasn't close enough to see her eyes, but Edward knew that they would be shining, too.

'What do you think, mate? Doesn't your mother look gorgeous?'

Isaac nodded and Edward let him go. The boy rushed towards her, shouting at the top of his voice.

'Muuuum! Edward says you look gorgeous.'

Well, that was one way of doing it. His mother obviously approved, and Charlotte went pink with pleasure. He almost didn't dare go any closer, in case she captured him in some kind of spell.

'Well, thank you.' She was holding both of Isaac's hands, trying to keep them away from her dress. 'I'll just go and clean him up...'

'That's fine.' Edward hoisted the boy upwards, tucking him under his arm, and Isaac squealed with delight. 'We don't want to get your mother all dirty, do we?'

Finally they were alone. Instructions had been given, telephone numbers written down, and Charlotte had elicited a promise from Isaac to be extra good for the whole of the evening. The taxi had arrived, and she had allowed Edward to help her into it.

'This is nice.'

She seemed excited, even though she didn't yet know where they were going. Edward wondered whether it would be appropriate to put his arm along the back of the seat, and decided that he should probably wait until the way home.

'I didn't want to worry about parking. Or having a glass of wine if I felt like it.'

She nodded and smiled at him. That warm, bubbly smile of hers which so lifted his spirits when he saw it at work. Here, combined with the fact that she smelled absolutely wonderful, and with her skin just inches away from his touch…Edward was lost

CHAPTER FIFTEEN

THE TAXI LET them off in Soho. Bubbling with life, on a warm summer's evening, the atmosphere was going to Charlotte's head. Edward took her hand, easing them through the crowded pavements.

'Where are we going?'

'Here.' He stopped suddenly, then descended a set of steps which seemed to run down to a basement. Opening the door at the bottom, he gave his name to a woman, handed his jacket over, and they were waved through.

She already knew what this place was. Soft jazz was floating towards them, beckoning them into a small auditorium. They were shown to a table and the waiter gave them each a menu, and left.

The place wasn't posh, or glitzy, nor was it sleazy. It was the kind of place that no one other than a real jazz enthusiast would know about, and its clientele didn't come here to be seen, but to listen.

'Is this okay?' He leaned across the table, his mouth almost touching her cheek. 'We can go somewhere else if you don't like it.'

'It's wonderful. Can we stay?'

He nodded in satisfaction. 'Of course. What would you like to drink?'

The long cushioned seats were comfortable, and the wine that the waiter brought to the table was excellent, but it was really all about the music. A three-piece band played smooth, moody melodies, which made everything seem so very easy. She slid along the seat, closer to Edward, so that they could exchange a few words without distracting anyone.

The band finished their set to enthusiastic applause and a great deal of crashing about as they left the small stage.

'Would you like something to eat? We've got about half an hour before they bring the next band on.'

The waiters suddenly seemed to leap into action as they were beckoned by one table or another.

'There's going to be another one?'

'More than one. Until about four in the morning, usually.' Edward grinned at her.

'And how many times have you stayed until then?'

'Once or twice. I used to come here a lot, but not so much lately.'

'Can't do the late nights, eh?'

He shrugged. 'Not really. But you can come in here, have a glass of wine, go home early and be tucked up in bed by ten. It's more a state of mind.'

He did seem younger here. As if his quiet manner was more a result of relaxation than introspection. 'Are we going to stay for the next set?'

He nodded. 'As long as you like. The plan doesn't go any further than this.'

'What plan's that?'

'The plan for the evening. It ends here. We're on our own now.'

They weren't, of course. Charlotte knew that they had to get back at a respectable time so that Penny could get on home. But for a few sweet hours it seemed as if there was nothing else in the world. At some point Edward's arm seemed to have snaked along the cushions behind her. She appeared to have moved a little closer to him, and now she was in the circle of his warmth, talking to him, listening to the music with him.

The spell hardly broke when they left the club. The streets were dark now, lit by the glittering lights of Chinatown, and they strolled together through the crowds until they reached Oxford Street, where Edward flagged down a taxi.

The roads were clear of the daytime traffic, and it was starting to rain. Yellow light streaked the windows of the cab as they reached the leafy suburb of Hampstead. A sudden left turn, which would have thrown her against Edward if she hadn't already been leaning against him, and they were home.

'He's fast asleep.' Penny was smiling and seemed in a hurry to be off. 'I gave him some tea and he ran around in the garden until he dropped. Then we watched some TV together and he was out like a light when I put him to bed.'

Charlotte could hardly get a thank-you out before Edward had kissed his mother and was walking her to her car. He watched her out of the drive and then turned back to the house.

It was suddenly very quiet. And Edward was abruptly the only focus of her attention.

'Would you…um…like a cup of tea?'

'No.' He moved a little closer. 'Would you?'

'No. Not really.'

She knew what was coming next. It was drawing her in, like the dark, unknown depths of his eyes, with a force that she couldn't resist. Didn't want to resist. However unsure she was, however hard it was to trust Edward, tonight she didn't seem to recognise any of that. All she saw was him.

'I'll…I'll just go and check on Isaac.' Maybe he was awake. Maybe that would solve the debate that was going on in the back of her mind about what to do next.

'Okay.' He backed off, and flopped down onto the sofa.

Isaac was sleeping soundly, Stinky clutched in his arms, and Charlotte walked slowly back downstairs. That was it, then. It was just her and Edward.

'Is he okay?'

His voice was low, like honey on her senses.

'Yes, he's fast asleep.'

'Just you and me, then.' He motioned her to come and sit down next to him.

'Yes. Just the two of us.' She perched herself on the edge of the sofa, her legs tucked under her. For a moment it seemed that they would simply sit like this for a few minutes and then say goodnight.

Then he reached forward, curling his arms around her waist, almost lifting her onto his lap. His movements were so slow, so deliberate, that they might be mistaken for hesitancy, but there was no uncertainty about him. It was just Edward, doing what he did best, squeezing every last drop from each moment that passed.

'I had a great evening.' She leaned towards him, speaking quietly into his ear.

'Had?'

'Am having. Are you being pedantic?'

'No. Just working out where I stand.'

'This is where you stand.' She kissed his jaw.

He said nothing. For a moment she thought that she'd done the wrong thing, that this wasn't what he wanted. Then he turned and kissed her. Long and deep, leaving her breathless and melting in his arms.

'I've been wanting to do that all evening.' One hand rested lightly on her leg, travelling upwards towards her thigh.

'I've been wanting you to...' He didn't let her finish, before he kissed her again. That was okay. She'd said all she needed to, and now all she wanted was to be part of the strong, flowing tide of his passion.

'Come upstairs.'

'We'll have to be quiet. Isaac...'

'That's okay. We won't disturb him.' He kissed her again, his lips so soft on hers. So demanding. 'I'll stop if you get too *fortissimo*.'

'Funny man. What happens if *you* get too loud?'

'You'll just have to crack me over the head with a table lamp. Or suffocate me with a pillow. Plenty of options...'

A whole world of options, if those still waters ran as deep as she thought they might. More options than Charlotte really know how to deal with right now. But even that couldn't stop her.

'I'll bear it in mind.'

He smiled, that quiet half-smile which seemed touched with every possibility that she could think of, along with a few that she didn't know how to imagine. Then he gathered her close in his arms, lifting her effortlessly and making for the stairs.

Even though she'd been living here for two weeks now, Charlotte had never been inside his bedroom. She'd glimpsed pale, creamy walls bathed in sunlight when she passed by in the mornings, but had never dared to even put her head around the door. The first thing she noticed when he flipped on the lights was that, unlike pretty much every other room in the house, there were no books. Built-in wardrobes ran the full length of one wall, and a wide bed stood opposite the window, ready to catch the morning sun. It was like a soothing blank canvas for the rich pattern of Edward's thoughts.

He set her down onto her feet and closed the door quietly. Then he kissed her, backing her slowly towards the bed. 'Do you have...?'

'Yes.' He moved away for a moment, flipping open a

drawer and taking out a box of condoms, putting it onto the small table by the bed.

'Thank you.' He made everything easy. Thought of the things she needed as well as the ones she wanted.

He reached around her, undoing the buttons which ran down the back of her dress. He slipped it from her shoulders, kissing each inch of flesh as he uncovered it. The fabric fell to her feet and she stepped out of it, kicking her sandals off.

'Say something, Edward.' She suddenly felt small and fearful in the shadow of his bulk.

'What can I say? You're beautiful beyond words.' He ran his fingertips down her arms. 'I want you more than I know how to express.'

'That's…' she gulped '…that's just fine.'

'Good.' His fingers again, tender on the side of her face. 'Because you put me at a loss, Charlotte.'

'That's just where we're supposed to be. If we weren't, then we wouldn't need each other to find the way.' She reached up to unbutton his shirt, pulling it open and off his shoulders.

She guessed she had his swimming to thank for the hard, muscular physique that was so good to look at, so warm and enticing when she ran her fingers across his chest. Each time he kissed her it was hotter. Deeper. Each time he laid his hand on her it was a little more demanding.

Before they even got to the bed they were both naked, trembling. He sat down on it, pulling her down onto his lap, astride him.

'Here.' He reached for the condoms, handing her one.

Slowly she rolled it down, loving the way that he gasped when her fingers touched him. Loving the warm feel of his skin when he pulled her close, lifting her. And then it went past loving, or adoring, or any of the other words that had seemed like something to aim for. Pure feeling washed over her when he lowered her slowly down, sliding inside her as he did so.

'Edward…' His name was the only thing on her mind.

'Charlotte…' He choked her name out, his hands twisting her hips so that they both gasped.

His hands, his mouth, caressed her. It was beyond bearing. Her body knew what to do, but he was holding her firmly in his lap, not letting her move the way she wanted to.

'Edward…please.'

One hand slipped between her legs and she almost cried out. He was intent on wringing every drop of pleasure from each moment, and the only doubt in Charlotte's mind was whether she was going to be able to bear it.

'I…can't…take much more of this.'

'Really?' His hand moved to her breast.

'Really. Edward…'

He didn't reply. He rolled his body round, until he was pinning her down on the bed, and with a look of unutterable tenderness slid inside her again. She felt her body mould to his, her hands grabbing at the sheets. Was that a moan? She put her hand to her mouth, biting hard on her knuckle.

He twisted his hips and her head spun. He caressed her, capturing her gasps in a kiss, and she was his. No thought, no fear, just feeling flowing through her, washing her clean of everything other than him. She gazed into his eyes, because they were the only things that made sense any more, and saw them darken. Felt his body stiffen and knew that he, too, had finally reached the point where he was as lost as she was.

Suddenly he was all fire. Coaxing her on, raising the temperature to boiling point. Stronger, sweeter, until her body arched of its own accord and waves of pure feeling washed through her.

* * *

Edward couldn't trust himself to speak. If he did he would say he loved her, that he would do anything for her if she'd just stay with him. And that was surely just the heat of the moment.

He felt a cool trickle of sweat trace its way down his spine, pooling in the small of his back. She was so beautiful. So giving. Her body was still quivering, little jolts still shaking her after the one great explosion of feeling. Then, as he watched her face, seeming to find endless fascination in the ever-changing detail, she broke him completely. A single tear trickled from her eye.

'Okay, sweetheart?' Perhaps he had been too demanding. He hadn't been able to help himself.

She gave him a slow, lazy smile which said that everything was better than okay. 'Yeah. Just fine. Happy tears.'

Charlotte wound her arms around his neck, pulling him close, and he rolled over onto his side, curling his body around hers. Perfectly happy. Perfectly... Just perfect, really.

They woke in the night and made love again, but when he opened his eyes in the morning she wasn't there. He hadn't really expected her to be. Isaac couldn't know about this just yet. Maybe one day—if they lasted that long.

He showered alone, and dressed, drawn downstairs by the sound of her voice and Isaac's. She looked up as he stood in the doorway of the kitchen and smiled.

'Good morning.'

'Yes, it *is* a good morning.' His whole body felt as if it had been bathed in sunshine.

She flushed a little. 'Did we wake you?'

He shook his head. Isaac raced out of the kitchen, ready to attack the day, and Edward took his place at the table.

'I was going to bring you breakfast in bed as soon as

I'd finished with Isaac.' Her mouth twisted in an expression of regret.

'Just as well you didn't.' He pulled her onto his lap and kissed her on the cheek. 'If I'd woken up and found you there I wouldn't have let you go.'

'No? Even if I'd had fresh coffee?'

He weighed the question up. 'Maybe if you'd had coffee... Is there any?'

'Right here.' She went to stand up, but he pulled her back down again.

'Charlotte, I know we have to keep this away from Isaac...'

'Yeah. I'm sorry. I just don't want to confuse him...'

'Don't be. I understand.' It didn't mean that he liked it, but he wouldn't hurt Isaac for anything. 'But that doesn't mean I won't be waiting for you. Tonight.'

She gave him a smile. 'Tonight it is, then. In the meantime, do you want some coffee?'

CHAPTER SIXTEEN

EDWARD WAS SMILING to himself. He could see Charlotte from his office, passing and re-passing the nurses' station. Something about the way she moved sent memories of last night and the night before pulsing down his spine.

He shouldn't be doing this. There were things to do—cases to review, patients to see. Admittedly there wasn't actually anything to do at this moment, but he was slipping. He hadn't touched the paper he was writing for a week, nor had he been swimming. He badly needed some thinking time.

The phone rang and Edward glared at it. He was far too busy interrupting himself at the moment to encourage anyone else to do so. He snatched up the receiver.

'North.'

'Edward, it's Ethan. I've a case here that I think you might be interested in.'

Something tingled at the back of his neck. The excitement of a challenge. He could do with that at the moment—before the tilt in the balance of his life became a catastrophic slide.

'I'll be right there.'

Edward was, indeed, interested. The surgery was slated for a couple of months hence, and it would be complicated, demanding, and require painstaking preparation. It was just the thing.

Their review of the notes was interrupted by the phone. Ethan's brow darkened. His habitual cool courtesy when dealing with the clinic staff was clearly being tested.

'Can you take a message please? I've asked for all of my calls to be put on hold for the next half-hour....' Someone spoke urgently at the other end of the line. 'Ah, Helen, it's you...' He listened again, and then nodded briskly. 'Okay. Yes, thanks, Helen. You were right to let me know. Put her through, please.'

Edward made to leave, but Ethan waved him back into his seat. 'I have to take this, but I won't be long.' He turned back to the phone. 'Olivia...?'

A pulse was beating at the side of Ethan's brow, but his face was fixed, impassive. The look of a soldier about to go into battle. He listened, concentrating on the phone and the notes that he was scribbling. 'Repeat that, please... Okay, got it. All right, consider it done. We'll courier all the paperwork out to you.'

He placed the phone back gently into its cradle. Ethan seemed deep in thought and Edward didn't ask.

'Can you do something for me?' Finally Ethan spoke.

'Of course.'

'That was Olivia Fairchild. Leo's away, and there are some problems with a visa for one of the kids she's sending to the clinic. I'm not sure quite what's involved, but I think there's just a declaration of some sort to be made from our end. Olivia will be travelling with the girl and her mother, so we can send any necessary paperwork straight through to her.'

Edward nodded. 'Leave it with me.' Was that relief he saw on Ethan's face? It probably wasn't anything to do with the legal complexities involved, because there weren't any. 'Give me your notes.'

'Thanks.' Ethan made a few more jottings on the pad in front of him and handed the paper over to Edward. 'Appreciate it.'

It was like leading a double life. A triple life, actually. There was the persona that she adopted at work—the one that hardly noticed Edward was even there unless he was giving instructions of a medical nature. The one that she had fallen into at home, being a part of the unlikely family that she, Edward and Isaac seemed to have made for themselves. And there was the one which lasted from the time that Isaac went to bed through to the early hours of the morning.

Evenings spent by the piano, talking together or just keeping each other company. Or reading together, their limbs entwined, Charlotte with her book and Edward with his. Early nights, when they had the opportunity to do all the things that they dared not talk about during the day, and which were increasingly bleeding into her thoughts at the most inappropriate times.

'Where's Edward?'

She and Isaac were having tea in the kitchen together. Edward had made it back home only just in time to say goodnight to Isaac for the last three evenings, and Isaac had missed playing with him after tea.

'He's at the hospital, sweetie. He's got to stay and make sure that the people he's looking after are okay.'

Isaac frowned. 'What people?'

Good question. But her own uncertainties weren't the issue here. It had been less than two weeks since she and Edward had first spent the night together, and it had taken only a week before the slow, subtle sense that he was withdrawing from her became apparent. When he was there he was still as committed, still as quietly loving. He just wasn't there as much as he used to be.

'People who are sick, sweetie.' She leaned across the table towards Isaac. 'There's a little boy, about your age, who's had an accident and lost his thumb. Edward's going to give him a new one.'

Isaac regarded his own thumb thoughtfully. 'A bionic thumb…?'

'No, a real one.' Charlotte decided to skip the bit about how the child had lost two other fingers as well, and that the reconstruction of one side of his hand was ground-breaking in its complexity.

'Is that what Edward's doing now?'

Difficult to say. She'd heard about this particular case from one of the other doctors, not Edward. 'The opera-tion's tomorrow. I expect he's preparing for it.'

'And Edward will make the boy better?'

'Yes, he will, sweetie.' Charlotte could give that assur-ance, at least, with a clear conscience.

'Good.'

Isaac seemed satisfied, even if Charlotte didn't share his confidence. Isaac was too young to remember the ex-cuses that his father had made for being out every evening. Things to do at work. Client entertaining. She reminded herself that Edward was doing something worthwhile, and not running up debts that he couldn't pay.

She heard a noise at the front door and Isaac slipped down from his seat, running into the hallway. So differ-ent from the child who, just four weeks ago, had nearly jumped out of his skin when someone knocked on the door.

'Hey, buddy.'

She heard Edward's voice and suddenly all of her fears and uncertainties seemed unreasonable. Not that they stopped pinching at her heart, but for the time being they receded to mere what-ifs instead of painful certainty.

'Is he better?' Isaac was perched against Edward's side, tugging at his shoulder to gain his attention.

'Is who better?'

'That boy…?'

Edward's querying gaze lit on Charlotte's face.

'Isaac was asking where you were.' Charlotte hadn't dared ask, thinking that it was assuming a bit too much. 'I told him that you were making another little boy well. The one you're operating on tomorrow.'

'Ah.' He turned to Isaac. 'The boy's not better yet, but he will be. We're taking good care of him, and he's going to be just fine.' He set Isaac back onto his feet and sat down.

'Would you like something to eat?'

He looked up at her. That dark blue gaze made everything else seem beside the point. The smile overrode every other sensation apart from pleasure.

'No, that's fine, thank you. I've already eaten. I've still got some more to do tonight, but I came home to see Isaac before his bedtime.'

Charlotte turned quickly. She wasn't being fair. He had things to do. He didn't take her for granted, as Peter had done, expecting his dinner to be on the table whatever time he came home.

'Coffee, then.' She smiled brightly at him. 'You'll have some coffee? And I made cheesecake.'

'That sounds fantastic.' He caught Isaac's eye. 'Hey, are you having cheesecake, too? Or are you just going to run around the kitchen while I eat?'

Isaac swooped towards the table, flapping his arms like a pair of wings, and sat down next to Edward. For the moment, at least, before Edward retreated again into his study, the world was as it should be.

The operation must have finished hours ago. It was ten o'clock, and Edward still wasn't home. Charlotte had tried his mobile and it went straight to voicemail. She didn't dare try again, because a list of missed calls from her would look as if she was crowding him. There was only one thing to do, and that was call the hospital.

It took a while to pluck up the courage to do it, and then another five minutes of waiting on hold before she got to speak to the right person. Then she wished she hadn't. It was only a twenty-minute drive from the hospital at this time of night, and Edward had left at nine.

'Not to worry. Thanks.' She smiled into the phone, as if that might give some believability to her words. Of course she was going to worry.

'He said he was going to check back in again when he got home... If there's any message?'

Charlotte pursed her lips and then went for it. 'Can you tell me whether he's done that yet? Checked back in?'

'Yes, hold on...' A keyboard clicked into the silence on the line. *'Here it is. Yes, he called in about twenty minutes ago. Said we could reach him on his mobile if there was any problem.'*

'Thanks. I'll try that, then.'

Charlotte hung up. So what was she going to do now? Edward obviously hadn't been in an accident on his way home because he'd called in. And he obviously didn't want anyone to know where he was.

She knew exactly what she *wasn't* going to do. She'd been here before and refused to believe what was staring her right in the face. The cold, hard proof of the credit card statements that her husband had kept hidden for so long. The affair that he had denied for so long. It had almost broken her.

Not again. Edward was a man with secrets, and she wasn't going to sit around, waiting for them to shatter her life. This time she'd protect Isaac—and she'd protect herself.

The following day was a Friday, and he was home early for the first time that week. Last night Charlotte had been unable to sleep until she'd heard the front door close quietly at two a.m. and Edward's footsteps on the stairs, disappearing along the hallway and into his room. She hadn't slept much after that, either, and in the morning Edward had left for the Lighthouse Children's Hospital before she was out of bed.

'I've been thinking.' She'd waited until Isaac was in bed before she spoke with him.

'Yeah?' He looked up from the papers that he was reading.

'I think it's time for Isaac and me to go home.'

He set the papers to one side, blank shock on his face. 'Is there something the matter, Charlotte?'

Everything that she could imagine. Edward was tired of her and didn't know how to tell her. He had another woman somewhere. He was too self-absorbed to really care about her or Isaac. One or more of those, in any combination. Or something else, perhaps, that she hadn't thought about.

'We were only going to stay for a few days. It's been nearly a month and…' She took a deep breath. 'I'm so grateful for everything you've done for us, Edward. But we can't stay on here indefinitely.'

This would be the time for him to say that they weren't overstaying their welcome. That he wanted her and Isaac to stay. They'd have to talk a bit—about how he seemed to have drawn back recently—but perhaps there was an explanation for that.

He stared at her. 'You want to go?'

Disappointment curled around her heart. 'I think that we should.'

She could see him changing before her eyes. The lover who had turned her world into something that was closely akin to magic was turning into a man. One who accepted her leaving as if it had been inevitable all along and wouldn't say one word to persuade her to stay. Cold grief began to trickle into her heart.

'And us?'

She was almost ready to beg him. She would have done almost anything to keep him just for one more day. One more day when anything might happen, when she might find a way to penetrate the icy shell that seemed to be forming around him. Then she thought of the way she'd worried about him last night. The way Isaac had fought to stay awake so that he could say goodnight to Edward.

'Edward, I have no hold on you. Whatever you were doing last night is none of my business...' He opened his mouth and she held up her hand to stop him from speaking. 'No. Really, I don't want to know. It can't work between us, and I think it would be better if we just accepted that.'

He could rage against this. Tell her that she was crazy—that he'd been called away to some medical emergency and hadn't been able to call her. At this moment she would have believed lies, excuses—anything. But tomorrow she'd wake up and hate herself for allowing a man to betray her again.

He ran his hand through his hair and a few dark spikes fell back across his forehead. 'Okay. If that's what you want... I'll help you move back over the weekend.'

'That's all right. You must have things to do...'

He shook his head. 'No. I brought you here and I'll take you home.'

She didn't have to say it. He'd heard it before, and Kathy had just been proved right. *Emotionally unavailable.*

Edward couldn't argue with her. She needed more than he could give and so did Isaac. Scratch that. They both *deserved* more than he could give. If breaking his heart was the only way they were going to get it, then so be it.

He hadn't slept much last night, and more than once he'd

gone to the door of his bedroom, ready to march along the hallway, gather her up and bring her back. Plead with her— beg her, even—or make love to her until she changed her mind. But each time the futility of such a course of action had stopped him. She didn't want him.

She clearly didn't believe him when he went out early on Saturday morning, with the excuse of having to go to work. Unable to set his mind to anything, he wandered the busy streets, fed the ducks in Hyde Park and dropped in to one of his favourite restaurants for a solitary meal. By the time he got back, late in the afternoon, she had packed hers and Isaac's things and explained to the boy that they were going back home.

Then it was time for them to leave. They somehow managed to stay civil with each other, for Isaac's sake, but they were like actors in a soap opera. As soon as the cameras stopped rolling the smiles fell from their faces and there was no emotion, no more to say. Nothing.

He loaded up his car with their bags and they made the short drive to Charlotte's house in silence. She opened the front door and Isaac ran inside, but it seemed from the way that she blocked the doorway that Edward wasn't welcome. He put her bags down on the doorstep and went back to the car to fetch the rest of them.

She called for Isaac and turned towards Edward. 'Thank you. I'm so grateful for everything that you've done for us.'

Yeah, right. And she was showing him just how grateful she was by leaving. Blocking her own doorway as if he was one of the people that he'd protected her from. The words were on the tip of his tongue when he saw a tear, perched in the corner of her eye and ready to fall.

'If there's anything else you need…'

There was no point in even saying it. They'd lost their opportunity of being friends. He'd blown it—hadn't paid enough attention to the woman he'd thought might be the saving of him—and now they had to part. Better now than some time down the line.

She nodded. 'Say thank you to Edward, Isaac.'

He almost couldn't bear this. Charlotte's cold determination was one thing, but Isaac seemed genuinely sad at their parting. He dropped to one knee and the boy flung his arms around his neck.

'Thank you, Edward. I've had a good time.'

'Me, too.'

'Can we come back to see you again?' Isaac turned his questioning gaze up to Edward.

'Yes, of course. Any time you like. But I'm going to be working hard for the next few weeks. We might not see each other for a little while.' Isaac would probably forget all about him in the space of those weeks. He wouldn't make this more difficult for Charlotte than he had to.

Isaac nodded. 'Okay.'

His trusting acceptance of the lie almost made Edward choke, and he hung for dear life onto the thought that at all costs the child should be protected from the mistakes of his elders.

'Thank you.' Charlotte's face was flushed and she was a moment away from tears.

He should go. Her tears didn't make any difference, and the tearing pain in his chest didn't either. Whatever he felt, whatever he did, it wasn't enough. He didn't have it in him to give any more, and more was exactly what she deserved.

'Take care, Charlotte.' He turned on his heel and walked down the front path without looking back.

CHAPTER SEVENTEEN

CHARLOTTE HAD BEEN dreading returning to work, but it seemed that Edward had dropped out of the life of the Hunter Clinic almost as effectively as he'd dropped out of her own. Even when he was there she wasn't part of his patient care team, and she wondered whether he'd had a quiet word with someone to make that happen.

Perhaps it would be a good idea to look for another job. It was going to be awkward, being faced with the possibility of seeing Edward day in and day out. Particularly since this feeling didn't show any signs of going away. If she had to grieve the loss of the man she'd hoped might be everything to her, then she'd rather do it in private.

She made a few calls and managed to get Friday off. She presented herself at an employment agency at nine o'clock that morning, and by ten she'd been interviewed, the consultant had reviewed her CV, and had promised that she'd be able to find her another job easily.

It was the first step. The next step was to go and see Edward's father, explain the situation to him and ask whether he'd take payment for all that he'd done. It might take a while, but she'd pay that debt off even if she couldn't pay the one she owed to Edward.

When she called his office, his secretary said that he was out all day and took a message. On to step three. She hurried home, changed into an old pair of jeans and T-shirt, and went up to Isaac's room. He'd been so good this week, obviously missing the extra space to play and Edward's large, widescreen TV, but he hadn't complained. Isaac was playing with a friend this evening and she wouldn't be picking him up until eight. She had plenty of time to finish off the little treat she had planned for him.

She surveyed the blank wall opposite Isaac's bed. It wasn't Edward's garden or his TV that Isaac missed. Her son was feeling the same way that she was. He missed Edward. The way he played with him, the way they laughed at the same jokes, how he'd been there for him when things got tough.

'Stop it.' She admonished herself as harshly as she could. Every spare moment she'd had for the last week, whenever she'd been alone, she'd spent the time crying. It was time for her to face facts and get on with it. She'd gone into this with her eyes open, knowing full well that a quiet guy with things to hide was going to cause her pain. Now she'd just got what she had asked for.

She looked at her watch. Eight hours before she had to go and pick Isaac up this evening. She'd better get moving. She hurried to her bedroom and pulled the box of paints and the carefully cut stencils out from under the bed. Time to get to work.

Edward didn't need to think too hard about what he was about to do. He'd already thought it to death, and the one thing he needed to do now was to act. His diary was clear for the day, and he'd hoped that he could make some progress on the research paper that he was writing, but when he'd heard that Charlotte had taken the day off he'd grasped his opportunity.

When he drew up outside her house he noticed that the front window was open. She must be home. He knew that she wouldn't go out without locking the place up securely.

He pressed the doorbell. Flipped the letterbox open and heard the sound of music coming from somewhere. Looking upwards, he thought he saw some movement behind the thick muslin curtains that shaded what must be her bedroom.

'Charlotte…' He called through the letterbox and waited.

Nothing. The music seemed to have stopped and the house was quiet. He slipped the package he'd brought through the letterbox. That was hers, and if she wouldn't let him in he could at least make sure she got it.

The first part of his plan was achieved. The second would be a little more difficult. He straightened up, wondering whether he should go and wait in his car. She had to come out sooner or later.

His gaze lit on a small arched alleyway which ran between Charlotte's house and next door's, giving access to the back gardens. At the far end were two gates, the one on Charlotte's side slightly ajar.

The gate opened into a small, neat garden. There was washing on the line, and when Edward twisted the handle of the back door it opened.

'Charlotte?' He poked his head inside and called to her, not wanting to frighten her. 'Charlotte, it's Edward.'

'Go away. Please.' Her voice sounded strained and insistent.

Maybe she was upstairs with someone. Another man, perhaps. Edward shook his head. He knew her better than that.

'Charlotte, I want to speak to you.'

Silence.

'I'm coming upstairs, Charlotte.' He called up the stairs and in the absence of an answer kept walking. He could hear the muffled sounds of movement now, coming from the bedroom at the back of the house.

The door was closed and he knocked, left it a moment and then twisted the handle. The first thing he saw was the plastic taped onto the carpet along one wall. There were pots of paint on the floor, and the start of what looked like a mural on the wall—a giraffe which grinned towards the bed. Then his heart lurched. Charlotte was sitting cross-legged on the floor, in the corner of the room, crying.

'Charlotte. Please don't cry. I only want to talk to you.' He knelt in front of her, afraid to touch her.

She raised her face towards him. Stained with tears and flushed with defiance. 'So much that you broke into my house to do it?'

'Well, technically I didn't break in. The back door was open.'

'Edward!' Her cheeks bloomed a shade redder and she jumped to her feet, almost knocking him backwards. 'It doesn't matter. I want you to go.'

He stood slowly. He needed a moment to debate what to do next, but she wasn't going to give it to him.

'Just go!' Her outstretched arm pointed the way for him.

'No.'

'I could call the police. You told me that.'

'Fair enough. It's your right to do that. But I'm asking you not to.'

'Why should I listen? You're not listening to what I'm saying.'

'Because I love you, Charlotte.' He'd blurted the words out without thinking. He stepped forward until he was almost touching her, but his head was cool now. 'I love you.'

'Don't!' She dissolved into tears, sobs racking her body. 'Stop it…'

'Can't do that.' He had to go through with it now, because after this he sure as hell wasn't going to get another chance. 'Won't do it.'

'I can't trust you, Edward.'

'You mean you can't trust anyone. You just can't let go, can you? You might just as well still be married to that husband of yours.'

One sharp intake of breath and she raised her hand and slapped him. Edward had never been slapped by a woman before, and he'd underestimated how much it would sting.

'That might be construed as assault.'

Her hand had flown to her mouth in horror at what she'd done, but she still wouldn't back down. 'You're in my space. I'm just defending myself...'

'I know. You don't need to, Charlotte.'

'What do you know about it?' She pushed him away. 'He did nothing but lie to me—all the time. He told me that he was working when he was out spending every last penny, putting us in debt. He had a mistress and I never even knew about it until their child was three years old...' Tears were beginning to streak her face.

'And you gave him the benefit of the doubt and believed him.'

'Yes. And I'm never going to do that again...'

'Then we're done, Charlotte.'

Edward had never seen himself as a gambler. He weighed up the chances, took the safest route. He'd never before staked everything on one precarious throw of the dice.

Her nerve broke first. 'All right, then. So where were you that night when you didn't come home until two in the morning? Don't tell me you were at the hospital, because I know you weren't.'

'How do you know that?' The old guilt pushed back into his heart. Why did no one ever seem to understand that he needed to be alone sometimes?

'Because I phoned there. You left at nine and said you were going home.'

'I had some work to do at the clinic and I popped in

there…' Edward shook his head. This was never going to work on lies. However much he was ashamed of the truth, it was that or nothing now.

He'd had a taste of nothing, and he didn't want to go back to it.

'I went to the clinic and took a swim. Then I went out for something to eat and…just walked for a while. Sometimes I need to regroup.'

She stared at him. 'What's so bad about that? That you couldn't just tell me?'

Suddenly the room seemed too small. Even with the windows open the pressure of their emotions was intolerable. But he couldn't leave. Mustn't leave. If he did that then he would only prove that he couldn't fight for her.

He took a deep breath. He'd start from the beginning and he'd get it right this time. 'When Kathy left me she said I was emotionally unavailable. That's stayed with me, and I let you go because I didn't believe that I had any right to ask you to stay. I was never sure that I could give you and Isaac the commitment that you both need.'

She opened her mouth to protest and he brushed his finger across her lips.

'Please. I have to say this. I'm older now, and a bit wiser. I know that I can change, and it's time for me to do just that if I've got any hope of you taking me back.'

She shook her head in disbelief. 'No. Oh, no. You don't need to change. Edward, I see right through you. You have feelings and emotions just like the rest of us. You just need to say what they are—not hide them away in case someone doesn't understand you.'

'I think…that's one of the nicest things you've said to me.' She'd said a lot of nice things, and he couldn't be sure.

'What? That you have feelings…?'

'No, that you see right through me. If you do, then

you'll know how much I love you. How happy you make me. That I'll never let you down.'

She stared at him. This was everything she'd ever wanted. All she had to do was take it.

'You have to trust me, Charlotte. You told me once that I could learn. So can you.'

'I…I'm not such a quick study as you… I'm going to be rubbish at this.'

'Fair enough. We can both be rubbish together. Do you believe that I can give you my heart? And that it'll be enough for you and Isaac?'

It felt as if she was making a solemn vow. 'Yes, I do.'

'Well, then it follows that you must trust me.'

She took hold of the end of his tie. Tugged a little. He moved closer. 'We're two sides of a coin, aren't we? Very different.'

'Yeah, but it's the same coin.'

'Back to back?'

That smile that Charlotte loved so much. Sexy, thoughtful, provocative.

'I prefer face to face.' His hands moved to her waist, and she melted into his warmth. 'Although…'

She stopped him with a look. There was time to talk sex later. This was more important and she couldn't wait any longer to say it. 'I love you.'

'I love you, too, Charlotte.' He glanced around, as if looking for some way to prove it. 'I love you so much that I'll help you finish that mural for Isaac. Even though I'm wearing an Italian silk suit.

'You could go home and change.' But suddenly she didn't want him to go anywhere.

'I won't get that twenty minutes back again.'

She was going to have to get used to feeling this happy.

At the moment it was too heady, and she could hardly breathe. 'I could come with you.'

He nodded. 'That's a great start.'

CHAPTER EIGHTEEN

'WHEN DO YOU need to pick Isaac up?' He was carefully putting the finishing touches to his part of the mural.

'Not for another couple of hours. He's gone to play at a friend's house. I have to pick him up at eight.'

'I'll take you, if that's okay. I've missed the little guy.'

'Of course it's okay.' A thought occurred to Charlotte. 'I always wondered...'

'Yeah?'

'Why do you have a child's seat in your car?'

He chuckled. 'I got it for when my sister and her little girl came to stay with my parents. She only used it once. I was going to take it out of the car that weekend, but then it came in handy for Isaac.' He paused, his hand hovering over the last delicate part of a lion's eye. 'What? You thought that I had a child tucked away somewhere?'

'No, not really. I just didn't know. Was it okay for me to ask?'

He chuckled. 'Yep. And, in the interests of complete transparency, there's something I need to know too.'

'Fire away.'

'Why does Isaac call that blue rabbit of his Stinky?'

'Ah. The blue rabbit. I seem to remember he was the one that started everything...'

'That's why I feel such an attachment to him.'

'Well, he was originally called Rabbit.' She grinned at

him. 'For obvious reasons. Then Isaac threw him into the
pond at the park, and when I'd fished him out again I told
Isaac he'd need a good wash because he was really stinky.'

'Ah. Makes me feel so much better to know that there's
a logic behind it.'

She laughed. 'Anything else you need to know?'

'Not at the moment. You've got paint on your nose.' He
closed the distance between them and swiped at her nose
with his finger.

'Better?'

'Not really. I just seem to have smudged it.' He grinned,
looping his arms around her waist. In the last few hours all
the barriers between them seemed to have disappeared. At
some point, while they were painting the bright, colourful
mural, all the promises they'd made, the honesty and the
trust, had turned from just words into reality.

'Do you think he'll like it?'

'Well, *I* like it.' Edward grinned. 'I think he'll love it.
The monkey's great.'

'And your lion. He looks a bit like you.' She pulled at
one of the dark spikes of hair that had fallen across Edward's forehead, which mirrored the slightly rakish look
of his lion's mane.

He laughed, sweeping his hair back off his forehead
with one hand. 'He's more like you.' Edward kissed her
eyelids. 'Golden eyes…' he loosed her hair from its bonds
at the back of her head, smoothing it over her shoulders
'…golden hair…'

'A nasty roar…?'

'That's one of the things I love about you.'

'What else?'

'Let's get cleaned up. Then I'll tell you.' He backed out
of Isaac's room, pulling her along the hallway. 'You'll have
to hurry. There's a lot to get through.'

They showered together, his strong, gentle hands soaping her clean as if they were washing away what had gone before, starting again. Then they made love. As if it were possible to actually create and mould love into the shape and texture that fitted both their hearts, feeling it grow and flourish between them.

Charlotte had wondered whether there could be anything better than the slow, almost silent build of heat that Edward gently nurtured until the fire in him broke loose and roared through them both. Now she knew. When he told her everything that he was feeling her heart spoke back, sharing the warmth, sharing the longing. Body and soul. He made love to her body and her soul.

They lay together, perfect and still, a fine sheen of sweat covering their bodies. Even that seemed to be something shared…his scent covering her skin. She knew that she was never going to be able to wash it off.

'It'll be time to go soon.' He smoothed a strand of hair back from her face. 'However much I want to see whether next time can be as good as the last.'

'Hmm… Me, too. Will you stay for something to eat tonight? Isaac would love to have you read a bedtime story for him.'

'I'd love that, too.' A thought seemed to occur to him. 'What did you do with the packet that I put through your letterbox?'

'The one with your father's practice logo on it? I thought that came in the post?'

'No, I left it there.' He grinned at her. 'Go and get it.'

Edward knew that she'd torn the wrappings from the parcel as she walked back up the stairs because he heard her gasp of surprise. She walked back into the bedroom, tears streaming down her face and her mother's ruby necklace in her hand.

'Edward. Where did you get this?'

'Put it on and I'll tell you.'

Her hand flew to the neck of her silky dressing gown. 'I'm not really dressed for it.'

'Then take that off.'

She laughed, jumping onto the bed and handing him the necklace to fasten around her neck. 'So tell me where you got this.'

'I had help. You put my father in touch with the guy you sold it to. Luckily he keeps good records, so he was able to forward our letter on to the woman he'd sold it to.'

'And...she sold it back to you?'

'Well, I didn't break into her house and steal it, if that's what you're worried about. I told her how much I wanted it, and why, and she sold it to me. And now it's back where it belongs.'

'Edward... It must have cost you...'

He silenced her. 'I wanted to undo what's been done. Give you some reason to trust.'

Her eyes filled with tears. 'You're the only reason I need.' She clasped her hand to her neck. 'I love that you've done this for me, but I don't need anything other than you.'

'You have me.' He held her close, revelling in the sound of her heart beating beneath the thin fabric of her dressing gown. 'There's nothing to stop me from giving you more, is there?'

'But I have nothing to give you in return.'

'You and Isaac have already given me everything I'd ever want. More than I ever thought I could have. But there is something you can do for me.'

He wondered whether he should really ask this of her. Charlotte had said she trusted him, and he believed her, but perhaps this wasn't the time to be testing that out.

'What is it?'

'There's something I have to do tomorrow and I can't tell you about it. That'll be the last time you don't know where I am.' He watched her intently, looking for any signs of suspicion in her eyes.

She took his hand and laid it over her heart. Then kissed him. The taste of happiness, right there on his lips. 'I'll see you on Sunday, then.'

'You can rely on it. Eleven o'clock.'

At five to eleven on Sunday morning Isaac jumped down from his perch at the sitting room window and thundered into the hallway. 'He's here...'

'Open the door, then.' One last look in the mirror at her hair and make-up, and the pretty white top that she'd splashed out on yesterday, and Charlotte hurried downstairs to find Isaac and Edward deep in conversation in the hallway.

His smile, when he caught sight of her, told her everything she needed to know.

'You look gorgeous.'

'Thank you. You look pretty gorgeous yourself.'

Edward grinned, pressing on with what was clearly a well-planned preliminary to their afternoon. 'I've just been asking Isaac, as the man of the house...' he glanced conspiratorially at Isaac '...whether it's all right to kiss you.'

Charlotte could feel the happiness radiating from her. 'And what did he say?'

'I said yes. That will be quite all right.' Isaac seemed to be taking his duties seriously.

'Good.' She grinned at Edward and he took a step forward, kissing her lightly on the lips.

'Is that all?' Isaac sounded disappointed.

'You think I should kiss her a bit more?'

'Yes.'

Edward took the hint. Taking her in his arms, he bent her backwards until she would have slipped over if he hadn't had her safe in his embrace. He kissed her on the lips until she was dizzy.

'Better?' He set her back on her feet.

'Much,' Charlotte whispered into his ear.

'Yes.' Isaac gave his blessing to the proceedings. 'Can we go now? I want to fly my kite.'

Edward laughed. 'That's all part of the plan.'

They drove to the same spot where they'd flown their kites the last time, carrying their bags up the steep slope to the summit. Laying a rug out on the grass, Edward opened the picnic basket she'd prepared, inspecting its contents.

'Strawberries?' He grinned up at her.

'Yes. And I've saved some more for later. When Isaac's in bed.' She grinned back at him.

'That I like the sound of. Come here.'

They sat together in the sun, watching Isaac, who was running around in circles, emulating one of the gliders they'd seen in the sky.

'I still can't believe it.'

'What can't you believe?'

'That you're here. That I love you so much.' She shifted into the circle of his arms. 'You and Isaac. I don't think I could ask for anything more than the both of you.'

'Shame. You won't be wanting any of this, then.' He reached for the cool bag he'd brought and drew a bottle of chilled champagne out of it.

She chuckled. 'Well, maybe just a glass. But won't it be a waste? You won't be able to finish the rest; you're driving.'

He shrugged. 'We can finish it when we get home.'

The cork popped out of the neck of the bottle and flew spectacularly through the air. Isaac's head followed its trajectory and he ran to pick it up, stowing it in his pocket before resuming his imaginary flight up and down on the grass.

Edward turned towards her, handing her a glass, his own only half full. She tipped hers against his, smiling. 'To today.'

'And all the others to come.'

'Yes.'

She took a sip, aware that he was watching her intently. 'This is nice.'

He nodded. Took a sip from his own glass, never taking his eyes off her.

'What?'

'You're so beautiful.'

He made her feel beautiful. She leaned forward and kissed him.

'I love you, Charlotte. You and Isaac.' His gaze was still on her, dark and intent. 'You've shown me how to live my life, and I won't let you down.'

He seemed to have something on his mind. 'What's the matter, Edward?'

'Drink your champagne.'

She lifted the glass, and as she tipped it something solid slid against her lips. Jumping, she emptied the glass onto the grass beside her. 'What was that?'

Edward started to chuckle, flopping onto his back on the blanket, as she searched in the grass.

'Don't laugh—there was something in my drink…' She searched in the grass to find whatever it was, and then she saw it. Sparkling in the sunlight.

'That didn't go quite the way I planned.' He was still lying on his back, laughing.

'Did you put this in my glass?' She leaned over him, holding the ring in front of his nose.

'Yep. I thought it might be romantic. You know—finding a ring in your glass. But you weren't looking at what you were drinking.'

'That's because I only have eyes for you.'

He chuckled. 'Clearly.' He wrapped his arms around her and she leaned in for a kiss. 'So now that I've messed that up completely...'

'No, you haven't. You couldn't have done anything nicer.'

'Well, will you? Marry me? I meant everything I said, Charlotte. About loving you and looking after you and Isaac...'

'I know. I love you, too, Edward. And, yes, I'll marry you.' She handed him the ring, wanting more than anything for him to slip it onto her finger. 'Was this what you were doing yesterday?'

'Mmm-hmm. Do you like it?'

'It's perfect.'

She looked at the ring in his hand. Three large diamonds. One for each of them—the family that she'd so wanted. Her heart was going to burst if things got any better.

Isaac skidded to a halt next to Edward and flung himself across his stomach.

'*Ooof.* Steady on, mate, I was just having a conversation with your mother.'

'What about?'

Edward laughed, giving in to the inevitable. Heaving himself upright, taking both her and Isaac with him, he held the ring up for Isaac to see. 'I've asked her to marry me.'

'Do you love her, then?'

Charlotte smiled. Isaac seemed instinctively to know the only thing that mattered.

'Yes, I do.'

'Does she love you back?'

'Yep. I think she's crazy, but she loves me.'

Isaac looked from Edward to Charlotte and then back again. 'Will we come to live with you?'

'What do you think about that?'

'Can I have animals on my wall? At your house?'

Edward chuckled. 'Well, it'll be *our* house if you come to live there. And you can definitely have animals on your wall. I'll paint them for you myself.'

'Okay.'

Isaac watched as Edward slipped the ring onto her finger. It fitted perfectly.

'Well, that's a relief.'

His smile said it all. Charlotte wanted to see that smile for the rest of her life.

'Are you going to kiss her again?' Isaac was clearly interested in doing things properly.

'You know what, mate? I think I just might.'

* * * * *

A sneaky peek at next month…

MEDICAL ROMANCE

THE ULTIMATE IN ROMANTIC MEDICAL DRAMA

My wish list for next month's titles…

In stores from 4th July 2014:

❏ 200 Harley Street: The Shameless Maverick
   – Louisa George

& 200 Harley Street: The Tortured Hero – Amy Andrews

❏ A Home for the Hot-Shot Doc

& A Doctor's Confession – Dianne Drake

❏ The Accidental Daddy – Meredith Webber

& Pregnant with the Soldier's Son – Amy Ruttan

Available at WHSmith, Tesco, Asda, Eason, Amazon and Apple

Just can't wait?

Hot reads!

These 3-in-1s will certainly get you feeling hot under the collar with their desert locations, billionaire tycoons and playboy princes.

**Now available at
www.millsandboon.co.uk/offers**

Discover more romance at

www.millsandboon.co.uk

- ♥ WIN great prizes in our exclusive competitions

- ♥ BUY new titles before they hit the shops

- ♥ BROWSE new books and REVIEW your favourites

- ♥ SAVE on new books with the Mills & Boon® Bookclub™

- ♥ DISCOVER new authors

PLUS, to chat about your favourite reads, get the latest news and find special offers:

- 🔲 Find us on facebook.com/millsandboon

- 🐦 Follow us on twitter.com/millsandboonuk

- ♥ Sign up to our newsletter at millsandboon.co.uk

Join the Mills & Boon Book Club

Want to read more **Medical** books?
We're offering you **2 more** absolutely **FREE!**

We'll also treat you to these fabulous extras:

- Exclusive offers and much more!

- FREE home delivery

- FREE books and gifts with our special rewards scheme

Get your free books now!

visit www.millsandboon.co.uk/bookclub
or call Customer Relations on 020 8288 2888

SUBS/ONLINE/M1